# THE HOURS BEFORE DAWN

# THE HOURS BEFORE DAWN

ROGER A. OTT II

RO2 Solutions

Cover design, logos, and text by Roger A. Ott II.
Cover background artwork by VladGans, purchased via istockphoto.com
ISBN: 979-8-218-11492-3

First Printing, 2023

for mom
who gave me that very first typewriter and let me off the chain

It's always darkest before the dawn.
-Thomas Fuller

# CONTENTS

# FOREWORD

I'm going to keep this short, because I'm reasonably sure you didn't come here for me to talk *about* writing. You came here to read, and to be entertained by what you read.

I love writing. Like most authors, that came from a love of reading. As a kid I devoured books as soon as the skill became available to me, and I fell in love with countless alternate worlds, ranging from one where a boy buys two hunting dogs in *Where the Red Fern Grows* by Wilson Rawls, to another where Martians attack Earth in H.G. Wells' *War of the Worlds*, to every type in between. The earliest fiction I remember reading (outside of Dr. Seuss) was the *Alfred Hitchcock and the Three Investigators* series of mystery books when I was in the 3rd grade. At some point, I sat down in the basement of my grandfather's house writing longhand in a wide-rule notebook, making up my own *Three Investigators* stories. I don't recall what happened to those first works, but I presumably lost them over the years in a handful of home relocations.

The good news is, I never stopped writing. And I never stopped reading. I graduated from the Three Investigators to the Hardy Boys, and a few years later, to my first full-on horror novel, Stephen King's *IT*. That was when I knew I wanted to write my own fiction.

The oldest story within these pages, The Cornfield Blues, came to life via the keys of a manual typewriter my mother had gotten for me in the mid 1980s. Most of the story's first line is still identical to the original, with only the town name added in. I didn't have a direction for that story back in those days, and only wrote two single-spaced pages. Honestly, I rarely have a plan when I sit down to write. I just start stories and see where they take me. That's the magic of it.

I ejected the rest of these tales from my subconscious in the decades following, where I graduated to an electric typewriter, then to a portable Brother word processor, and finally to the personal computer by the late 1990s. The stories I've written matured over that expanse of time, and several of the really old ones I've more recently revised to fall more in line with my middle-age sensibilities. Over-the-top gore was my teenage thing, and there's still a bit of that in here from time to time where it benefits the story, but I've backpedaled on some of the more visceral stuff. Your imagination can likely picture something far worse than I could ever describe in words.

One last bit before we start: I always enjoy author notes and behind-the-scenes stuff writers share with their readers. After each story in this volume, I'm going to take a little space to explain where each of these stories came from, as best I can recall. Skip this if it isn't your thing. The stories won't care a bit if you don't know the bloody womb from which they sprang.

If nothing more, I hope these stories take you on a journey. Maybe you'll forget the horrors of the real world for just a short time while you enter the world of *my* horrors, where the night seems just a little darker, and the monster in the closet might just be real enough to snatch you from your bed in the hours before dawn.

--Rog

# THE THIEF OF YEARS

Saturday, May 2nd. 8:30am

The morning *Black Rapids Press* headline read:

## COUPLE FOUND DEAD IN BIRCHWOOD

Ralph Mayhew sighed and folded the paper without even reading the article. He already knew the details, and even more that wasn't published. As the lead detective assigned to the investigation, it had been a long night. It would now be a busy day.

Sunlight streamed through the curtains of the open window, casting a bright patch on the small table in the breakfast nook where Ralph sat, drinking coffee and enjoying his morning cigarette. The smoke spun and twirled in the sunlight, along with the steam rising from his coffee mug, before being broken apart by a light breeze.

He had promised Helen he would stop smoking and had cut back. Once a pack-a-day smoker, he was now down to just five cigarettes a day, and his favorites were the one with hot black coffee in the morning and the one just after dinner at night. The others were mostly to help him think when he was on the job. He believed there was no better focus-assist than a good smoke. Maybe a shot of bourbon was close, but the department frowned at drinking on the job.

Helen was still asleep upstairs. She'd been sleeping in later the past few weeks, and that concerned him. Since the cancer diagnosis, it felt like she was declining far too fast. He'd considered taking a leave, but after getting caught up in this serial murder investigation, he needed to see it finished. That dogged determination had earned him the nickname "Bulldog Mayhew." He didn't mind it much, though he considered dedication to one's job nothing worthy of extra attention.

Helen insisted, of course, that he not take leave. She didn't want him fawning over her. But he still called her at least twice during the day to check on her, which she noted was also unnecessary. If something happened, she'd call him. He kept it up, anyway. That's what you do when you love someone: annoy the shit out of them.

Ralph stubbed out his cigarette in the ashtray and downed the last cooling swallow of coffee. The warmer than normal breeze for mid-May felt nice coming in the open window, but when you lived in the Midwest, you understood it could be seventy degrees one day and twenty the next. May was a spiteful bitch sometimes, but today, she was feeling generous to those who'd managed through a harsh winter.

He picked up his cell and dialed Ethan Stolliday, his partner of five years. Ethan was young, energetic, and put the word 'detect' in detective. He spotted clues nobody else could, and Ralph, as a joke, had himself nicknamed his partner "Eagle-Eye Ethan." Joking aside, Ethan was focused and dedicated, the finest partner Ralph had ever worked with in his twenty-seven years as a lawman.

"Morning," Ethan said when he picked up.

"Morning. I'm heading over to the Brinkworth house soon. You want to join me?"

"Absolutely. I love hobnobbing with the rich and famous."

"Alright. Say, nine-thirty?"

"Make it ten, and I'll stop and get those custard-filled donuts you like on the way."

"Deal. Ten it is." Ralph ended the call and put his coffee cup in the sink. He trudged upstairs and looked in on Helen before heading to the shower. She was still sleeping peacefully. He could see the steady rise and fall of her chest. That was good. Sooner than later, that simple act was going to become difficult, and he dreaded those days ahead.

He hoped he could get this damned investigation over before things got bad, but the doctor's prognosis wasn't good, or long.

Ralph showered, shaved off two days of gray beard growth, then dressed in slacks and a buttoned shirt. He hated wearing a tie, but thought it might help a bit since they were going to be, as Ethan put it, hobnobbing with the rich and famous, so he grabbed a burgundy tie off the tie rack in the closet and knotted it with practiced ease. *The rabbit hops over the log. The rabbit crawls under the log.* He'd recited that mnemonic in his head since his father had taught him when he was seven.

"Off to work?" Helen's voice came from behind him.

"Hey," Ralph said, turning as he snugged up the tie. "Did I wake you?"

"No. It's time to get up."

"How you feeling?"

"Better today. I should have gotten up earlier and enjoyed the sunrise."

"It's nice out. Supposed to be sunny all day. You should catch some rays on the deck."

"I think I might," she said, shuffling past him to the bathroom. When she'd finished and brushed her teeth, he hooked her arm in his and he walked with her down the stairs. He noted she felt stable this time, but other days, he worried she would take a fall and he'd find her at the bottom landing with a broken hip, or worse.

"Coffee?" Ralph asked.

"Please," she replied, and sat down in the breakfast nook. She wrinkled her nose at the ashtray he'd left there. "Can you take care of this?"

"Sorry, meant to empty it before I came up." Ralph grabbed the ashtray and dumped it into the trash. He poured her a fresh cup of coffee, added cream and sugar, and set it down in front of her.

"Thank you," she said, and traced her finger around the edge of the mug to pick up stray sugar that had fallen there. She put it to her lips and stared out the window. The lawn was greening up fast, and soon there'd be that smell of fresh cut grass she always looked forward to.

"Need anything else before I go?"

"No, I don't think so. I can take care of myself, you know?"

"I don't mean any disrespect, hon."

"I know you don't, Ralph. But we have to face facts, that soon I won't be able to do anything for myself, but while I can..." she trailed off and kept looking out the window. The breeze tossed the curtains, and she closed her eyes and breathed it in.

"I just have to do an interview across town," Ralph said. He had his hands in his pockets and was looking at the floor like a scolded little boy. "Then I'll come back and we can go get lunch. How's that sound?"

"That sounds good." She turned and smiled, and he fell in love with her all over again. Her face had gained some wrinkles, but she was still as beautiful to him as the day he'd asked her on their first date thirty years prior.

He leaned over and kissed her on the lips, lingering for just a second longer. "Love you."

"Love you, too," she said, and smiled up at him.

As Ralph walked down the steps toward his car, a single tear welled in his eye and slid down his cheek.

* * *

Behind the wheel of his car, Ralph ran the events of last night over in his head.

The butler discovered Kendall and Gena Wiltshire dead in the foyer at their townhouse just before midnight the evening before. No signs of forced entry, no signs of struggle, no items missing from the house. Their lives were the only thing lost. According to the medical examiner on the scene, time of death occurred between nine and eleven pm. The Butler had just returned from the airport after picking up the Wiltshire's daughter, Kylie, from a delayed flight. That alibi checked, so, "The Butler did it" was out, since he was off premises from eight until just before midnight.

The responding officer had secured the scene, then woke Ralph up out of a good sleep. Ralph let Ethan off the hook on that one; he'd need him clear and alert now, during the day. The crime scene unit arrived, did their due diligence in processing the scene, while uniformed officers canvassed the area surrounding the Wiltshire's townhouse. However, there were no immediate witnesses to be found.

Nothing out of the ordinary. Standard double homicide. Until you dug in a little deeper. On the back of both the Wiltshires' necks, just below the base of the skull, there were a trio of unexplainable puncture marks, approximately 1/16th of an inch in diameter, spaced half an inch apart in a triangle formation.

Odd, but not the first time Ralph had seen this. Four homicides in the preceding months had the same pattern on the victims' necks, and the ME deemed them not the cause of death. Her off-the-record opinion was that someone had drained the life out of them, as preposterous as that sounded.

This case, however, had two victims, while previous cases only had one. The killer was upping his game.

* * *

Birchwood, suburb of Black Rapids. 10:05am

"How's Helen?" Ethan asked.

Ralph scooped up a glob of custard that had squeezed out of his donut and sucked it off his finger. "She's having a good day. Not sure how many of those we'll have left."

"What was the doctor's latest prognosis?"

"Six months, but he's confident that if she'd just accept chemo, they could get years."

"But she won't."

"But she won't," Ralph echoed, leaning back against his car. "And I can't say I blame her on that one. Chemo's a nasty mess on a good day. Chief Bell was before your time, but he had it in the stomach, and the chemo was almost as bad as the cancer. The cancer just ate at him and the chemo just wore him down. By the end, he was hoping to die. I don't want that for Helen."

"Oh, hell no," Ethan said, and polished off his raspberry jelly donut. "Personally, I'd eat a bullet before I'd let cancer take me down."

"Yeah, same."

They tossed their trash into the can next to the lamppost. Ralph pulled his pack of cigarettes from his pocket, considered lighting one, then put the pack back.

"Ready to do this?" Ethan asked.

"Let's get it over with."

The imposing two-story brick facade loomed over them, spanning the length of two standard brownstones, specifically built for its current occupant.

Zola Brinkworth had been an internationally renowned fashion designer in her younger years. Now, at eighty-two, she was just a wealthy old woman who split her time between London, England, and Black Rapids, Michigan. The tabloids once asked her why not New York City, or LA, and she responded that the American Midwest offered the most genuine people in the country. If you were from the City of Angels or the Big Apple, you might challenge that statement's veracity, but Ms. Brinkworth purchased a home in neither.

Decade earlier, when Ralph Mayhew aged in single digits and Ethan Stolliday was but a twinkle in his father's eye, the fashion world considered Zola Brinkworth a big deal. Never married, the public often saw her with both males and females on her arm at events across the globe, stirring the tabloids into a frenzy, questioning her sexual orientation. The consensus, unconfirmed, surmised she went both ways.

One verifiable statistic noted Zola was a confirmed workaholic. She began building her empire in the late 1960s, when businesswomen were still a fairly unknown quantity, and presided over her company well into the new Millenium. Firm but fair, she garnered respect and loyalty, a rarity in an enterprise as large as Zola International became.

Well into her 70s, Zola retired from the day-to-day operations of her worldwide fashion empire, passing the reigns to Millicent Stevens, her right hand for most of thirty years.

Ralph had done a little homework on Zola, and though a bit of a Black Rapids celebrity, she kept her private life tight. No juicy scandals unearthed in his early morning research, which meant she might actually be human. Or just very good at hiding things.

Ralph knocked on the heavy oak entrance door. It opened a second later, at the hand of an elderly but impeccably dressed gentleman. Most likely the butler.

"May I help you?" the man said.

"I'm police detective Ralph Mayhew," he said, holding up his badge. "This is my partner, Ethan Stolliday. We're investigating last night's murder from next door, and would like to speak with anyone who was here between nine and midnight."

"Ah, yes," the man said. "Quite an unfortunate event, I understand. Please come in and wait while I fetch Mr. Brinkworth for you." He pivoted on his heel and walked away.

Ethan looked at Ralph. "Mr. Brinkworth? I thought she never married?"

"She has a younger brother, Emmet. Rode her coattails to success, of course."

"Ah, that's why she never married, I'd bet. Her brother probably cock-blocked anybody who got within five feet of her."

Ralph laughed just as the butler returned with a tall, thin man behind him. "Misters Mayhew and Stolliday, I present Mr. Emmet Brinkworth."

"Thank you, Dryden," Brinkworth said, and dismissed the butler with a haughty wave. His air of superiority bordered on smugness, and Ralph already didn't like him.

"Mr. Brinkworth," Ralph said. "We're investigating the murder—"

"Oh, such dreadful business," Brinkworth interrupted. "I can't believe that sort of thing would happen so close to me and my dear sister."

"Yes, well, we'd like to talk with anyone who was here between 10pm and 12am."

"Only Dryden, my sister, and myself were in residence during that time. All the other staff had left hours before."

"We'll need to speak to each of you," Ethan said.

"My sister is not well, if you must know. Alzheimer's disease. She would be of no help to you."

"Sorry to hear that," Ralph said. "My partner would like to speak with Dryden while you and I talk?"

"I suppose there's no harm in that."

"Thank you."

"Dryden will be with the kitchen staff, making lunch preparations." He motioned to a large archway, and Ethan disappeared through it.

"Did you notice anything out of the ordinary last night around 10pm?"

"I pay little attention to things beyond these walls, Mr. Mayhew. Dryden had drawn me a bath before retiring for the night, and I was having my evening soak before bed."

Of course you were, Ralph thought, then said: "Even if you saw nothing, did you maybe hear anything?"

"I listen to Bach while in the bath. Last night, specifically, It was the Toccata and Fugue in D minor."

"And you're sure your sister wouldn't have seen or heard anything?"

"Absolutely not. She stays in the south bedchamber, and in her current state, is practically immobile."

"Again, I'm sorry to hear that."

A heavyset black woman rounded the corner then, dressed in white slacks and a flowered pullover top.

"Ah, Marcy," Brinkworth said. "How is my sister?"

"She's having a good morning, sir. Seems quite lucid."

"That is good news!" Brinkworth exclaimed. "I'm sorry to cut this short, Mr. Mayhew, but I'd like to go see my sister now."

"Of course. If you think of anything that might be of interest, please reach out to me." He handed Brinkworth a business card.

"Good day, Mr. Mayhew. Best of luck with your investigations."

"Thanks," Ralph said as Emmet Brinkworth walked away. Once he was gone, Ralph turned to the woman, who was near the door.

"Marcy? I'm Ralph Mayhew, investigating the homicide next door."

"Oh yes, I read the paper this morning. So horrible."

"Marcy, what do you do here?"

"I'm Ms. Brinkworth's home health nurse."

"And you say she's doing well today? I assume that means she's been sick?"

"She has advanced Alzheimer's. Most days, she cannot remember anyone or anything. The past few months, she's had many difficulties. Today seems to be a good day."

"When do you normally work?"

"I come in every other day, at seven in the morning, and stay with her through the day. I'm usually out by five or six in the evening."

"That's a long time for a home health nurse, isn't it?"

"Yes. But Mr. Brinkworth hired me exclusively. I came back today because she'd had such a bad day yesterday."

"What time did you leave yesterday?"

"Five-thirty."

"Did you notice anything odd while you were here? Not necessarily here in particular, but outside or even next door?"

"No. I was with Ms. Brinkworth most of the day, and she's in the south bedroom overlooking the garden. It was quiet there."

"Thank you, Marcy. Sorry to keep you."

"No bother. I hope you catch whoever murdered those people."

"Me, too."

* * *

"Anything useful?" Ralph asked Ethan when they were back on the street.

"Not much. Dryden Underhill retired to his quarters at nine-thirty, read a book until eleven. Heard nothing, saw nothing. How'd you fare?"

"Mister stick-up-his-ass was listening to Bach while playing with his rubber ducky in the bath, so nothing there, either."

"Now what?"

"I told Helen we'd go for food. You're welcome to come along. We can discuss the case and call it a work lunch."

"I'm in. Where at?"

"Thought maybe we'd try that new cafe downtown. They have outdoor seating, and it's going to be a nice, sunny afternoon."

"Sounds positively divine. See you there."

Ralph watched Ethan's Camaro speed away, then he leaned up against his own car, a 4-door Bonneville, and fished a cigarette out of his jacket pocket. He lit it, dragged deep, and leaned his head back, exhaling into the cloudless sky.

* * *

Ralph picked up Helen, who had been sitting out back in her reclining deck chair, where the sun was just peeking over the tops of the trees and basking her in its glow. They drove downtown to Nellie's Cafe, and Ethan was there waiting. He'd gotten a good table outside in the sun.

"Hello there, gorgeous," Ethan said, standing to give Helen a hug.

"Oh, you're ridiculous," Helen replied, and squeezed him tight. Even though Ethan was only ten years younger than Ralph, Helen treated him like the son they'd never had.

A waiter dropped by with menus and brought a complimentary carafe of iced tea. Helen ordered a chef salad, Ralph a club sandwich, and Ethan a bacon double cheeseburger. With fries. Always with fries.

"I hear your arteries clogging with every bite," Ralph told Ethan as they ate.

"Grease makes everything slide right on through," he replied.

"How is the case coming?" Helen asked.

"Deadlocked right now," Ralph said. "Even stumped old 'Eagle-Eye' here."

"Last night's murder relates to four others, spread out over the past six months," Ethan said. "The first was last December, then not another until February, then one in late March, another in mid-April, and now one so far in May. All using the same murder weapon."

"They're escalating," Helen added.

"Yes. And that's concerning," Ethan said. "But that means the killer's likely getting overconfident, which will make him slip up and leave something behind to lead us to him. I'd rather another person doesn't die to get there, though."

"Right," Ralph said. "We've interviewed the neighbors—oh, Helen, you'd get a kick out of this. Remember Zola Brinkworth?"

"The fashion lady?"

"Yeah, that's her. She's the neighbor."

"Did you meet her?"

"No. Sadly, she has advanced Alzheimer's. Got to speak to her gem of a brother, though."

"Oh, that's so sad. She always seemed like a charming lady."

"She definitely got the charm," Ethan added. "Her brother was quite the douchebag."

"Ethan!" Helen scolded.

"He's not wrong," Ralph said, and popped the last bite of his club sandwich into his mouth.

"Both of you are terrible," Helen scoffed. "You deserve each other."

They finished their meals and the carafe of iced tea. Ralph got the check, and they said their goodbyes on the street, where Ethan gave Helen another hug.

"I'm going to drop Helen off at home," Ralph said. "Then I'll meet you back at townhouse alley. Got a text saying uniforms might have uncovered a witness."

"Be there or be square," Ethan said, saluted, then headed for his car.

As Ralph's Bonneville merged onto the freeway toward home, Helen's hand rested on his thigh.

"Ethan needs a good woman," she said.

"What makes you say that?"

"He's got too big a heart to keep all to himself."

"He'll get there in his own time."

Ralph put his hand on hers, and they both smiled.

* * *

Ralph and Ethan walked across the street and two doors down from the Wiltshires, hoping for some good news.

"Who's this, again?" Ethan asked.

"Gordon and Theodora Kemp." Ralph stepped up to the door and knocked. They heard voices behind the door, a female said "Get the damned door!" and a male said, "I am!" The door sprang open then to reveal Gordon Kemp, five-feet-four, two-hundred and twelve pounds, his wiry gray hair writhing in all directions on his head. He peered at them over heavy-rimmed bifocals, and his face wrinkled.

"We're not interested," he grumbled, and began to close the door.

"Sir, we're not here to sell something. I'm Detective Stolliday and this is my partner, Detective Mayhew." Ethan held up his badge.

"Oh. More cops, eh? I talked to one earlier this morning. What you want?"

"We'd just like to ask you some more questions, sir, if you have a few moments." Ralph said. "The officer you spoke with this morning said you might have seen something last night, correct?"

Gordon's eyes widened. "Yeah. Let's talk out here," he said, and led them to the front patio. They sat down in cushioned deck chairs. Ralph noticed that from here they could see between the street foliage, directly to the street, and the front door of the Wiltshire townhouse. "Mind if I smoke?"

"Go right ahead," Ralph said. He wanted one himself, but refrained.

Gordon produced a polished silver cigarette case from his shirt pocket, fished out a cigarette, and lit it. He puffed three times, inhaled, and blew the smoke out above their heads. "I come out here at night to sit and smoke, because she doesn't allow me to in the house." He jerked a thumb toward the inside. "One of the first things you should realize when you get married: you give her your balls at the alter and she keeps them with her for the rest of your life. If you're lucky, she might let you look at them once in a while."

"Noted," Ethan said with a wry smile.

"Anyway, I don't fight her about it. The house smells better that way, and I get a little peace at night. I smoke two or three cigarettes, then get ready for bed. It's traffic-free at ten o'clock. We get a few late-night joggers since that new fancy condo went in at the end of the street and it's getting nice enough to be outside again. I watch them go by with their reflecting vests and armbands. Sometimes they wave, but most times they're listening to whatever passes for music these days in their headphones, and they just go right on past. Either is fine with me, long as they don't stop to talk."

"Getting back to last night..." Ralph said. He wanted a cigarette more by the second.

"Oh, yeah. Sorry. I tend to ramble." He laughed and smoke puffed out his nose and mouth, making him look like a strange comedic dragon. "Anyway, so last night, I'm sitting out here around ten-thirty. It's quiet, a little cool, no joggers. Theodora had gone to bed half an hour before, so it was just me and the street, y'know? Some people would play with their cell phones or some shit, but me, I just sit here and enjoy the silence. When you have a wife like mine who never shuts her gob, you learn to appreciate the quiet moments, am I right?"

"Sure," Ralph said with a sideways glance at Ethan, who seemed riveted to the conversation.

"Anyways, I can see across the street, between the trees there. I don't normally pay it much mind. The Wiltshires are good people, and quiet, just how I like 'em. I've only talked to them maybe two or three times since they moved in a few years back, but they seemed like good eggs, y'know?"

"That's what most everyone has been saying," Ethan said.

"Right? So, I just light my last smoke and as I look up, I see someone coming down the street. The lights are dim down in this area— gives it kinda an old gaslight glow, or some shit—so I can't see details, just dark shapes but it's definitely a man, and he goes up the steps to the Wiltshires and knocks on the door. I'm far enough away I can't hear anything, but I see the door open. I'm guessing they talk for a few seconds, then whoever it is goes inside and the door shuts. I didn't really think much of it then."

"Did you see anyone leave?" Ralph asked.

"Nope. I was only outside for another few minutes to finish my smoke, then I went back inside and washed up for bed. Got up this morning and saw a headline about murder. Didn't cross my mind that the late night visitor might have done it until your guys showed up bright and early this morning. You think it might be him?"

"We're still investigating, Mr. Kemp," Ralph said. "Did you see where this person came from?"

"No," Kemp said, and blew out another plume of smoke. "First I saw anything was when he appeared between the trees right before their stoop."

Ralph uttered an internal expletive, then said: "Anything else you can think of that might help us?"

"Nada. Like I said, I was in bed shortly after that, and I have a CPAP machine, so I don't hear shit once that starts up."

"Thanks for your time, Mr. Kemp," Ethan said. "Here's my card, in case you think of something else."

Gordon took the card and stood up with them. "I hope you catch the scumbag. If a friendly couple like them can get aced, what's that mean for the rest of us?"

"We're doing our best. Thanks again." Ralph and Ethan left the patio and took the steps back to the sidewalk. They heard the door open, and Gordon Kemp disappeared back inside.

"Holy shit, that guy was the polar opposite of Brinkworth," Ethan remarked.

"Just goes to show that money affects everybody differently."

"Wonder what I'd be like if I had money."

"You'd still be an asshole," Ralph said, and they both laughed.

"Most likely," Ethan said as they walked to their cars. "That's the most we've gotten yet."

"Sounds like whoever did the Wiltshires was someone they knew. I can't imagine them letting a complete stranger into their house at ten-thirty at night."

"Agreed. Now what?"

"I'm headed home to check on Helen. Gonna process this and see where it might lead." Ralph fired off a finger gun and slipped behind the wheel of his car.

* * *

Three nights later, Ralph woke to the sounds of vomiting. It was 2:43am by the alarm clock's neon numbers, and Helen wasn't in bed. He threw back the sheets and crossed the room in three steps.

"Helen, you okay?" he said through the door.

There were more retching sounds, followed by "I'm fine, just got a touch of nausea."

"Can I come in?"

"Go back to bed, Ralph," she said. "I'm fine."

The vomiting recommenced, and Ralph stood there for a few moments more, then opened the door.

"Go away, Ralph!" she yelled. She was on the floor, kneeling in front of the toilet of pink-stained water, her hair sweaty and falling around her face in strings. Ralph got down on the floor and pulled her to him. She buried her face in his shoulder and sobbed.

"I'm sorry," she said later, both of them sitting on the bed.

"Hon, you have nothing to be sorry about."

"I'm getting worse, Ralph. I've tried to deny it—like if I don't talk about it, it doesn't happen—but I think we have to face it now."

"We'll face it together."

And they did. An appointment with Helen's oncologist the next day confirmed the cancer was spreading rapidly, more than previously thought. They left the specialist's office with a feeling of helplessness. There was nothing an oncologist could do to make it feel different, not when you've just been told you're in the last stages of an aggressive and ravenous cancer. There was no going back now. It had gotten to where remission was simply impossible. And it would go fast. "Only a few weeks at most," were the doctor's words.

Ralph took a couple of days off to help get things set up at home. He had contacted the home healthcare operation that Marcy Crawford worked for, and requested her specifically. When they'd briefly met at the Brinkworth house, Ralph liked her from the onset. He had a good sense of people, and she seemed like a kind soul. Thankfully, they worked out a deal.

Marcy would come in on the mornings when she wasn't tending to Zola Brinkworth, and Ralph was glad for her to be there. Within a few days, Helen lost almost fifteen pounds and was having difficulty getting to the bathroom on time. Having Marcy there spared Helen the indignity of calling her husband to help her to the toilet, though he would have done it in an instant. She just hated the idea that she would have to rely on anyone else after holding her own head high for so long. Her strength of will had attracted Ralph in the early days, she knew, so the thought of not having that strength anymore weighed heavily.

Helen and Marcy established an immediate rapport, and Marcy would even stop by in the evenings on the days she administered to Zola Brinkworth. With this newfound support, Helen ordered Ralph to go back to work.

"I'm tired of looking at your face," she'd said with a smile, but he knew she just didn't want him to see her decline in real time. For him, that was actually worse, because he would leave for work and come home afterward and visibly see how different she looked from when he'd left in the morning.

But, he conceded to her wishes and went back to work, only on the days Marcy was there, when he felt a little better knowing she was being cared for. The case was still gnawing at his brain. Ethan had kept working on the investigation, but there was little progress over the next week.

Then there was another murder.

* * *

Bryce Walker's car broke down on the interstate near Black Rapids on May 15th, while the twenty-year-old was on his way home from college for the summer. State troopers found his body in the front seat of his car in the early hours of May 16th, leaned over his steering wheel. The hood of the car was up. Initial investigation of the scene showed

Walker's neck had the same three-point punctures which had by now become notorious. Ralph and Ethan were called right away.

"He's changing his MO," Ethan said. "Maybe getting desperate."

"You think so?" Ralph asked.

"Before this, the murders happened in or near homes," Ethan said. "Likely premeditated. Even more likely, the killer knew the victim. This one, though, seems random. Like the killer happened upon this kid with his broken-down car and took advantage of the opportunity."

* * *

Sunday, May 17th.

Marcy arrived at eight-thirty and talked to Ralph for a few moments before heading upstairs to tend to Helen. He was working at the dining room table and had papers spread across the entire expanse.

"I just checked on her a few minutes ago," Ralph said. "She's awake, but not feeling much up to moving right now."

"Hopefully, we can get her up and around some today. Supposed to be a delightful afternoon. Maybe some sun will do her good."

"I hope so."

Marcy took the stairs and disappeared off the landing to the bedroom. Helen was indeed awake, but was looking like she had slept little, if at all. She had wanted to move into the spare bedroom, to spare Ralph having to deal with her increasing restlessness, but he refused. Inside, she was glad. His presence next to her at night soothed her as much as anything.

They played a rousing game of Scrabble, which Helen won. Her body may have been failing, but her mind remained sharp. She was getting weaker, though. Marcy noticed her eyes getting droopy at the end of the game. Once they finished, Marcy said she would take a break and let her rest.

She came downstairs and walked through the dining room toward the front door. On her way by, she noticed Ralph's work on the table as she passed. Curious, she glanced over. Her eyes widened, she stopped, and looked again.

Marcy found Ralph in the living room, watching TV.

"Mr. Mayhew," Marcy said. "I hope I'm not overstepping, but I've seen these markings before."

"What markings?"

"These," she said, and held up one picture from the table. "I didn't mean to look, and I'm sorry."

"Marcy, you're telling me you've seen those puncture marks?"

"Yes, sir."

"Where?"

"On Zola Brinkworth's neck."

After a moment of shocked silence, Ralph called Ethan.

Half an hour later, the three of them were standing around Ralph's kitchen table, where he'd spread out pictures taken from all the crime scenes. Marcy pointed to several photos that showed the three tiny marks on the victims' necks.

"Those are identical to the markings I saw on Ms. Brinkworth."

"You're absolutely sure?" Ethan asked.

"Yes, sir. I examined them closely myself."

"When?"

"Last Monday, I believe. I was giving Zola her bath and found them on the back of her neck. They appeared to be small punctures, in a triangle pattern."

"Jesus," Ralph said, and let out a rush of air.

"What does this mean, Mr. Mayhew?"

"It means your employer may have been involved in the murders of half a dozen people."

"Oh, my goodness," Marcy said, and cupped her hands over her mouth. "That can't be true. Mr. Brinkworth would never—"

"That's what we've got to find out."

"How long have you worked for the Brinkworths, Marcy?" Ethan asked.

"I came on in early April. Their previous in-home nurse quit because —well, because Mr. Brinkworth can be difficult."

"And you only noticed the markings this past week?"

"Yes. Mr. Brinkworth insists on giving Zola her baths. But he was out of the house last Monday, and Zola was having a good day and begged me for a bath. I remember Mr. Brinkworth being rather upset when he returned."

"Because he was afraid you discovered the markings."

"That makes sense, looking at it now," Marcy said. "I feel so terrible for Ms. Brinkworth. What is he doing to her?"

"That's really the million dollar question, isn't it?" Ethan observed. "Other than Zola, everyone with these puncture marks is dead. So, why is she alive?"

"You ask all the fun questions," Ralph said.

*  *  *

Monday, May 18th. 9:47am

"So, I did a little armchair research on the Internet last night, and guess what I found?" Ethan patted the laptop sitting next to him while waiting for his coffee to cool. They were in the breakfast nook at Ralph's house the next morning.

"Enlighten me, o surfer of the web," Ralph said.

"Tabloid journalism has its uses now and then. The Brinkworths came to the States from merry old England about six months ago."

"So, roughly around the time the murders started?"

"Exactly. The first was just over a month after they arrived."

"Unfortunately, that's nothing but circumstantial evidence. Nothing concrete to nail him with. Did you, by chance, check to see if there have been any unsolved murders back in the hometown?"

"I did, indeed. I contacted the police department in London, and get this, there were a half dozen murders there with the same MO we're seeing here."

"Including the three puncture wounds?"

"Sure as shit. And, just like here, the time between murders gets shorter with each subsequent one. The first two were a year apart. Then ten months later, then eight months after that, and six months. The last one was in August of this past year."

"Three months before the first murder here in Black Rapids."

"Yep."

"God damn, that's one helluva pattern."

"Yeah, so then I went a step further down the rabbit hole and looked up Zola Brinkworth, specifically for any big news before the first murder happened."

"And?"

"In May 2014, doctors diagnosed her with Alzheimer's disease. Shortly after, she publicly announced her retirement, turning Zola International over to her protégé, Millie Stevens, and within a few months, Zola dropped out of the spotlight entirely."

"We'll assume she was getting medical advice from the best doctors you could throw enormous stacks of cash at, and the prognosis wasn't good."

"No doubt. Then, just a little over a year later, in March 2016, the murders started. And if you look at a timeline since they started—not just the six here, but all twelve of them—you'll see the time between each one gets shorter. So, the big thousand dollar question is: what's the connection between the murders and Zola's Alzheimer's diagnosis?" Ethan looked at Ralph, who had parked a cigarette between his lips.

"That's the toughest nut to crack, but we're putting things together. With no hard evidence, though, we can't go after Emmet Brinkworth. Yet."

"Then let's get him to confess."

"We can try that, but I'd really like to talk to Zola," Ralph said. "Marcy probably violated several HIPAA laws in telling me, but said Zola's been fairly lucid the past couple of days. Maybe she'd be willing to shed some light on what we're up against."

"Should we loop the department in on this?"

"Not yet. We're already treading the edge of legality as it is. I want to confirm some things before we go for an official arrest warrant."

"You're the boss." Ethan gave him a thumbs-up.

"It makes me moist when you say that." Ralph smiled. With all that was happening with Helen, the kid gave him a reason to smile a little, difficult as it was.

"I doubt Emmet's just going to let you march into the house and talk to Zola, though."

"That's why you're coming along: to distract him. Maybe you can work on that confession angle."

"Shit. Maybe I was a little hasty on the 'you're the boss' comment."

"Too late now, kid. You said it, and I heard it."

* * *

"So, what did Emmet have to say when you asked if we could come back?" Ethan asked.

Ralph cleared his throat and gave his best impression of a self-important Englishman. "I say this is most inconvenient. I cannot imagine what more help I could give than I already have."

"But he agreed to see us again?"

"Yeah."

"Then let's do it."

They rode together in Ethan's Camaro to Birchwood. When he pulled into the wide drive next to the Brinkworth townhouse, Ralph looked up at the rows of windows across the second floor. He swore he saw someone looking out from behind one of them. It brought up his hackles and he snuffed.

"What?" Ethan gave him a look.

"Nothing. Just saw someone looking out an upstairs window at us. My brain immediately recalled the investigator approaching every creepy house in the movies, and there's always somebody looking out the window."

"You're just a bastion of joy today, aren't you?"

"I'm doing my best," Ralph said. "Let's get our Brinkworth on."

Dryden opened the door before Ralph could knock. Inside the foyer, Emmet Brinkworth stood in all his dry, stuck up glory.

"Good afternoon," Ethan said. "Thanks for letting us come back."

"Of course," Emmet said, with contempt. "I cannot think of any-thing I'd rather spend my afternoon doing than entertaining the local constabulary."

"Duly noted," Ralph muttered. "Hey, you got a bathroom? Too much coffee on the way over, y'know?"

"Dryden, show Mr. Mayhew to the lavatory," Emmet said, and turned his attention to Ethan. "Now then, Mr. Stolliday, however may I be of assistance?"

* * *

"This is quite the castle," Ralph noted as Dryden led him down the hall, past the stairs to the second floor. The interior architecture was a mixture of traditional and modern—ornate moldings offset by sharp angles—affording it a unique flair Ralph felt served perfectly for some-one of Zola Brinkworth's eclectic tastes.

"Ms. Brinkworth had it specifically commissioned when she chose her estate location here in the States," Dryden said. "And here we are." Dryden motioned to a door that opened into an area larger than Ralph's dining room.

"No need to wait," Ralph said, and half-smiled. "I can find my way back."

"As you wish, sir," Dryden said, then did a sharp about face and retreated down the hall. Ralph closed the bathroom door and waited a full minute before reopening it. He poked his head out into the hall and saw nothing and no one.

Ralph crept past the bathroom and at the end of the long hall, he found the back stairs, likely used by workers. He took them one at a time, dreading a telltale creak as he ascended to the second floor. His luck held, and he reached the landing in silence.

Ralph recalled Marcy stating Zola's room was at the back of the townhouse, facing the garden, and he found her with no difficulty. The room was dim, lit by a single soft lamp on the dresser next to the adjustable bed. She lay there, thin and withering, skeletal, her face tight and wrinkled with advanced age. But her eyes, Ralph noticed, seemed sharp and focused as they met his.

"Ms. Brinkworth," Ralph said. "My name is Ralph Mayhew. Can you hear me?"

"I told him to stop," she whispered.

"What?" He leaned in close and could detect the sour sickness of her shallow breath. It reminded him of how Helen had smelled more recently, and a lump caught in his throat.

"I ordered Emmet to stop this madness." Zola coughed, and deep in her throat, something broke loose. She leaned over and spat something red and greenish into a bowl on her serving tray. "But he's obsessed."

"Obsessed with what?"

"Keeping me alive."

"I don't understand."

"Nor do I, Mr. Mayhew. I should have been dead long ago."

Ralph's face tightened. "What's he done, Ms. Brinkworth?"

"Get away from her!" Emmet shouted from the doorway. Ethan was behind him, out of breath. "I want you out of this house! How dare you distract me to get to Zola?"

"Emmet," Zola said, her voice stronger this time. "This has gone on long enough."

"I agree with that," Ralph said. He stood and turned to Emmet. "We need to talk."

* * *

"Where did you get that?" Ralph asked. The strange device Ethan had found in a drawer in Zola's room lay on the table between them. It looked like an extra large syringe, with a draw tube eight inches long and the head protruding with three inch long titanium needles in a triangular pattern.

"When you are wealthy, Mr. Mayhew, few things are beyond your reach."

"That doesn't answer the question." Ralph was becoming impatient.

"I obtained the device in the back room of a pub in Glasgow. Filthy establishment."

"From who?"

"I do not know precisely. These sorts of transactions insist upon absolute discretion, which was carried out on both sides. Eccentrics such as myself have a small circle of like-minded individuals with whom we associate. I made an inquiry with one, which was passed on to another. Someone brokered the deal, and for a godly sum of money, I came into possession of the device you see here."

"What exactly is it? What does it do?"

"According to legend, the design originated with a man of medicine long disbarred for his outlandish theories and pursuits in the name of medical science. An order of 16th century druids enchanted the resultant creation and made it able to drain an individual's life force. It is, frankly, the perfect symbiosis of ancient science and sorcerous magic."

"Um, okay," Ethan said. "That's not possible." He was watching Emmet, studying his body language, looking for the liar's tell. Skeptical didn't cover how he felt.

"There is such a fine line between possible and impossible, Mr. Stolliday. One has only to search deep enough into history to find a time when the impossible was all there was to believe in. And centuries later, those impossibilities are now a common occurrence."

"So, this 'life force extractor', it kills whoever it's used on?"

"Unfortunately, yes. There is no way to alter the amount it takes; it is literally everything or nothing. Then the process is reversed, and it can inject the captured life essence into someone else. Here and now, that would be Zola."

"And what does that do?" Ralph was leaning forward across the table, his hands clasped together.

"By account of legend, it would stop aging, even reverse it over time, making the recipient essentially immortal. In someone like my sister, however, who suffers from an advanced disease, the injected life essence attacks the disease and suppresses it. Much like an aspirin eases a headache."

"And I'm guessing, like any medication, if you stop administering it, it stops working."

"Yes, unfortunately. And similarly, over time the patient builds up a tolerance to them, requiring more, and more often, in order to maintain."

"And that's what happened to Zola?"

"Yes. When we first began her treatments, she only needed an injection once a year, then it was every ten months, then every 8 months, so on and so forth. Now, it's once a week, or she slips again."

"So, you're playing God," Ralph said.

"God?" Emmet scoffed. "God, if He ever existed, stopped caring for those of us who crawl across this wretched planet ages ago. We are, I'm quite certain, beneath His notice."

"Nice sentiment." But Ralph could understand, just a little.

"Mr. Mayhew, I would do anything, cross any line, to save my sister. She is the world to me, and this debilitating disease should not be her fate. What benevolent entity allows that to happen?"

"You've killed thirteen people that we know of, Mr. Brinkworth. Murder is a very serious business, both here and abroad. At best, you're looking at life in prison. At worst, a straight ticket to lethal injection."

"Do you think I take any of this lightly?" Emmet said, and his tone seemed genuine. "I gained no joy in taking those lives, any of them. Some of those people were close associates of mine or my sister's. But I am not a man of physical means. I could not attack someone outright, so it had to be people unsuspecting of me. It was the only way to ensure I succeed. The only way to save Zola."

"What about the college kid downtown?" Ralph pondered.

"An unfortunate act of desperation, and one I have no desire to repeat."

"Ralph," Ethan broke in. "Can I see you alone for a minute?"

"Sure," Ralph said, and got up from the table. They walked across the room. "What's up?"

"You don't believe this horsehit, do you?"

"I'm not sure what to believe." Ralph ran his hand through his hair. "It sounds impossible. But what if—what if it is true? You heard what he said."

"I know what you're thinking, Ralph. Don't—"

"If it is true, what worked for Zola might work for Helen."

"Okay, let's just say it really does what he says. But remember the part where he explained it's taking more and more to keep her going. If all of what he said is true, what then?"

"I'd do anything to have an extra year, even six months with her. Hell, if it got me an extra week, I'd give my soul. You saw her. She only has days left, if that."

"Ralph, this is a bad idea."

"Listen, Ethan, have you ever been truly in love with someone?"

"Probably not—"

"Then don't presume to tell me how I should react when the person I love more than anything is dying."

"You're sounding like Brinkworth. You realize that, right?"

"Maybe he's not wrong."

"Ralph, I'm just saying, don't do anything rash."

"I appreciate the concern, kid." Ralph turned and walked back to the table. Emmet still sat with his hands folded and back straight, ever the stoic Englishman.

"Alright, Brinkworth," Ralph said. His face was solid. "This is how it's going to go."

* * *

Back out on the street, Ethan asked the hard question: "Do you believe Helen would want this?"

"Helen can't answer that. She's unconscious twenty hours a day, and barely alive the other four."

"I'm just saying, man. Doesn't this go against nature? Against God?"

"I'm not the one to say, Ethan. Maybe Brinkworth is right about God. Maybe he just doesn't give a shit about us anymore."

"That's a slippery slope, Ralph. You sure making a deal with Brinkworth is a good idea? He's letting you take the syringe and use it as long as you also help Zola. That's a deal with the devil."

"Better the devil you know, Ethan. I'm out of options. Brinkworth's desperate, and so am I. If we turn him in, the device goes away. If I help him, he doesn't turn me in. All I know for certain is if I don't try, Helen'll be dead."

"It's murder, Ralph. No other way to say that."

"Yeah, it is. I won't even try to candy-coat that. But I'll just take out drug dealers and other scumbags. Nobody's going to miss them when they're gone."

"Jesus. You can't mean that, man."

"I do," Ralph said. His eyes coldly met Ethan's. "The real question is, are you going to stop me?"

* * *

One year later. Saturday, June 5th. 8:40am

The morning *Black Rapids Press* headline read:

## ANOTHER DRUG DEALER FOUND DEAD

Ethan Stolliday sighed and folded the paper without even reading the article. He already knew the details, and even more that wasn't published. As the lead detective assigned to the investigation, it had been a long night. It would now be a busy day.

First, though, he was stopping over at the Mayhew household for breakfast. Helen's cancer was in full remission, and she felt better than she had in well over a year. She even looked younger. Ralph, too.

Though not a religious woman, Helen's oncologist had said, given how advanced the cancer had been, Helen's recovery was an absolute miracle of biblical proportions.

*Yes,* Ethan thought. *A God damned miracle.*

## AUTHOR NOTES - THE THIEF OF YEARS

This story began as a spark on the 20th of June in 2012, just a scrawled note in my computer's "story ideas" document: "Story about a man who drains the life forces of people to retain his youth."

I have tons of ideas that are just one short blurb, something that comes to me when I'm already in the middle of something else, so I take a quick note and tuck it away for another day.

Obviously, this story went other directions, and it all fell out of the creation of Ralph and Helen Mayhew. I really enjoyed writing those two characters, and fell in love with their love for each other right away, and the desperate gamble Ralph made to save his wife's life. The story's very first scene was like I'd opened a faucet and let it pour onto the page. Those really are the best characters, the ones who tell you who they are and where they need to go. Ralph and Helen did just that, and they surprised me.

# I TOLD YOU COMIC BOOKS WERE BAD FOR YOU

Jason raced across the deserted construction site, listening to what sounded like his own heart pounding heavy in his chest, but wasn't his heartbeat at all. It was the thundering footsteps of the thing chasing him, the thing not human, the thing that wanted to kill him.

Jason hurdled over a chunk of broken cement, sweat streaming off his face in rivers, his breath coming in quick, stealing gasps. How long had he been running? Minutes? Hours? It didn't matter. He glanced behind him and saw his pursuer closing in. Jason was done for. No one could outrun the Crusher.

The Crusher stood seven feet tall, his entire muscled body composed of some strange flexible stone hide, his eyes like emotionless, blood-colored marbles poking out from under the thick expanse of his brow. He had no protruding nose, just two small oblong holes underneath those blood pools of eyes. His mouth, a long narrow slit in his feature-less face, opened in a snarl that showed several rows of symmetrical razor-sharp teeth.

Jason struggled to gain distance between him and the rock-like mass following, but one look too many over his shoulder brought him crashing into a wheelbarrow. He did a half-cartwheel in the air and landed face down in a pile of dirt, his legs throbbing in pain. Crusher was on him, and Jason never stood a chance. The creature, unbelievably fast for its bulk, bolted across the construction yard and snatched Jason by the arm, twisting him up in the air like a carnival gymnast, then down to hang like a child's old rag doll in front of the Crusher's face. Jason watched through watery eyes as those shining rows of needle-like teeth opened and closed in a satisfied smile.

With an easy flip of Crusher's huge wrist, Jason sailed across the construction yard, his body skidding into the dirt several yards from an old building scheduled for demolition. Jason scrambled to his feet, most of his muscles straining to work as the Crusher approached again. Jason moved toward and into the building, tearing past the plastic yellow strips warning against unauthorized entrance.

Crusher stopped at the doorway, peered up at the height of the twelve story brick building, another razor-smile appearing on his thin lipless mouth. Crusher pulled back one gargantuan arm, then punched hard into the side of the building. Bricks turned to fine powder and fragments against his blow. The building swayed, an almost human groan coming from deep within as the structure strained to hold its ground.

Inside, Jason choked back a scream as chunks of plaster and wood cascaded down around him. Dust flew, filling his lungs with thick, chalky air. He heard Crusher outside, punching hard at the building's block exterior again and again, every strike jarring more of the structure loose. As he zigzagged his way through the architecture, dodging falling beams and chunks of concrete and plaster, he knew it was over if he couldn't find another open exit before Crusher brought the house down.

Then, the building rocked on its foundation, the receiver of Crusher's mightiest blow, administered by a hand that registered no pain. Inside, the structure fell in on itself. A large beam swung down from the second floor, glancing off Jason's head and knocking him to the floor. Blood ran down his forehead into his left eye. He had to keep moving, but his vision blurred, and he screamed out to his executioner: "I'm sorry, Crusher! I didn't mean it! I didn't mean to kill you! I'll bring you ba—"

Then the world spiraled away in a twisting river of black.

* * *

Jason Carmichael sat straight up in his bed, gasping in huge, laboring breaths. He pulled his rumpled sweaty sheet off and crawled to the edge of his bed. He grabbed his phone and hit the wake button. 2:43 AM, Jason saw, and rubbed his eyes to clear his vision.

*My God, what a nightmare,* he thought, getting off the bed and shuffling into the adjacent bathroom. Fourth night in a row of the same dream. Jason splashed cold water on his face, toweled off, and then returned to his bedroom. He pulled on his pants, leaving the belt unbuckled, and headed downstairs.

He stopped first in the kitchen and fished a cold beer from the refrigerator. He popped the tab and took a long drink, the cold bubbly malt momentarily numbing his throat. He stood there until half the can was gone, and then walked from the kitchen, through the living room, and down the hall to his office, the place where he did his daily work. He opened the door and stepped inside.

There was a large desk just inside the door, where his computer sat, along with several note pads filled with his distinctive scrawl. On the opposite side of the room was a large industrial drawing table with a drafting machine and desk lamp clamped to its surface. Next to the table was a shelf littered with his drawing tools, as well as stacks of art board. The walls were covered with artwork. Comic book pages he had purchased from his favorite artists, and some of his own work - alien landscapes, strangely garbed figures, muscle-bound men, strong empowered women. It had been a hard market to get into, but Jason Carmichael had believed in his dream.

His comic book, a team book called THE RENEGADES, had been a lifelong labor of love. He had created it when he was thirteen, an awkward teenage boy in a small Michigan town, with little to do to escape the confines of his harbored existence but use his imagination. Jason spent the intervening years taking any art related classes his small school offered, as well as any composition classes to hone his writing skills. He graduated and attended the local community college, which offered a course on comic book art. Jason was nineteen when he wrote and drew the first issue of THE RENEGADES as part of an art project. His instructor thought it had potential. So did Jason.

Derek Milford was a scientist in the employ of a company called Breakstone Laboratories, who discovered an alien energy source he dubbed The Shade. Something accidentally exposed Derek and four other Breakstone employees to The Shade, and they gained fantastic powers. Security Head and former Marine Sergeant William Trader became Carbon, able to tap into The Shade and manipulate it. Verna Carlyle, Milford's project lead, became Thunderhead, super strong and able to create solid sound constructs. Calvin Rennie, the custodian, became the super fast speedster Racerback. Anastasia Blanchard, a research intern, became Blindside, gaining telepathic and precognitive abilities, while Milford himself became the energy manipulator known as Fission.

Shortly after gaining their powers, Blindside saw a flash of the future, where aliens invaded the Earth and destroyed humanity. To prevent this, the group commandeered an experimental Breakstone Labs spacecraft and took off into space to prevent the invasion. Captured by the violent alien race known as the Krill, they thought all lost until a sympathetic alien named D'kerr freed them and helped them stop the invasion. Nicknamed Crusher by Racerback, D'kerr came back to Earth with the others, and a grateful planet christened them The Renegades.

And thus had begun the rise of THE RENEGADES, and subsequently, of Jason Carmichael.

Jason attended that year's Motor City ComiCon, the largest convention in the state of Michigan. He had studied up on who would be there, and while big publishers like Marvel and DC were not accepting unsolicited work, there was a new player in the game that had gotten his attention. Empire Comics was a fairly small press publisher, who opened shop two years prior with their debut series, THE GAUNT-LET PROTOCOLS, a sci-fi series about an armored man traveling back in time to stop an alien invasion. Their initial effort was well-reviewed, and subsequent books also gained critical acclaim. Empire was on the rise. Jason wanted to rise with them.

Jason got a one-on-one with an editor from Empire, and impressed him with his work on the self-produced first issue of THE RENE-GADES. A week later, a phone call from Empire ended with him signing on as an exclusive writer/artist for Empire Comics. They flew him to New York to meet the entire staff of Empire at their offices, and introduced him to Carl Williams, a twenty-plus year veteran of the comic book industry. Williams would be editor of Jason's creative works.

Being the rare combination of writer and artist, Jason never failed to produce a well-written, character-driven story with enticing and realistic artwork. Fan polls across the country hailed his comic as one of the best works of the decade, destined to become one of the all-time greats. Copies of first issues of THE RENEGADES flew off the shelves at comic shops everywhere, digital sales were strong, and current price guides proudly announced the first issue of the hit series, which had a fairly low print run, was currently selling for close to fifty dollars, and the book had been out less than a year.

Jason couldn't believe the news that his was the number-one selling comic book in America. The book also had strong sales in Europe, and it was even doing moderately well in the hard-to-penetrate Japanese market, where Anime was king. Out of nowhere, offers arrived from other comic book producers, wanting to team up his characters with theirs, or to offer him lucrative assignments, writing and drawing stories with their characters. Carl Williams had made the statement that Jason could very well be the next John Byrne or Walt Simonson. High praise indeed for the young writer/artist.

Royalties from the second and third printings of THE RENE-GADES #1 bought Jason his first brand new car, and he signed a lease on a decent apartment. Yes, things were coming up aces for Jason Carmichael.

Until four months ago.

* * *

Jason had arrived in New York early on a Friday morning, for a long weekend convention appearance, and headed over to the Empire Comics offices to talk to Carl about plots for the next several issues. They spent a lot of time on the phone, and sending e-mails, even Zoomed a couple times, but Jason liked Carl for his wisdom, and he thought Carl liked him fine as well. And there was nothing like a face-to-face meeting to hash out plot details.

In Carl's office, Jason laid out his diabolical plan: he wanted to kill off one of the main characters in his book, but hadn't decided which one. Carl thought that was a brilliant idea, so the two spent the next hour and change going over the order of characters in THE RENEGADES.

"We can't kill Carbon," Carl said, leaning back and propping his feet on his desk. "As team leader, he's too important. Let's not pull a Byrne here. We'll just seem repetitive."

"Alpha Flight was like almost forty years ago, but that's okay," Jason said. "I like Carbon anyway, and have a long-term plotline for him. My dad was a military vet, so Carbon is my favorite character to write. What about Thunderhead?"

"Nope," Carl countered. "She's one of two women on the team. We need to maintain that balance. Besides, the way you present the women in the book is one of the main things we feedback on. It seems every teenage girl in the country loves your strong female leads. So, that means Thunderhead's on the 'live' list. And so is Blindside."

"That leaves Racerback, Crusher, and Fission. I've got some big plans for Fission, so he's got to stay."

"What about Crusher? He's not much more to the team than a strongman. And my grandson Eldon loves Racerback. I'd hate to tell him I was partly responsible for killing off his favorite character."

"Well," Jason said, jotting down a few notes on the pad he'd brought along. "Killing Crusher would have the dramatic effect I'm looking for, without upsetting that balance you mentioned. Thunderhead's pretty tough, too, so she could take over in the brute strength department. That would also give her an expanded role in a couple of my other up-coming plots."

"Good," Carl said. "Crusher it is then. What issue did you have this planned this for?"

"Well, issue seven just hit the stands yesterday. I've got the next two issues drawn and layouts wrapped up through issue eleven. It would fit perfectly in for the double-size issue twelve, allowing room for me to deal with Crusher's death and its impact on the team."

"That would have been my suggestion. Issue twelve comes out smack in mid-summer, and that's when all the publishers are going for the next big event to draw sales during the summer. Killing off a character should pull a vast audience for us. I want you to draw up some myste-rious teaser shots ASAP that we can unveil this weekend and run in the next couple of issues of our entire line. That'll get some buzz started, and then marketing can take it from there."

The weekend was Jason's first real convention as a serious comic book creator, so he was both excited and overwhelmed by the experi-ence. He spent most of his time at the Empire Comics booth, signing autographs and doing sketches. It was beyond surreal. Jason felt strange having gone from fan to pro so quickly. Creators he had stood in line for hours to meet were now coming by the booth to talk to him. Empire hosted a panel that Saturday afternoon, showcasing Jason and his work, capped by the announcement that the double-size issue twelve of THE RENEGADES would feature "a heart-wrenching tale of family and loss." The crowds cheered, and for just a moment, Jason wasn't sure he could live up to fan expectations.

So, they had decided Crusher was to die in issue twelve. Jason wrote up the plot at breakneck speed, which Carl thought was one of the most tragic stories he had ever read. Two months ago, Jason sent in the finished art for digital lettering and coloring, and four days ago, THE RENEGADES #12 arrived at comic book specialty shops across the nation, and fans ate them up. The fall of the Crusher was a poignant, heart-wrenching story, and early reviews across the web called it a masterpiece of art and story.

* * *

Four nights ago, the same day RENEGADES #12 went on sale, Jason Carmichael started having his recurring dream. Crusher, it seemed, didn't like death. Didn't like it at all. It seemed he wanted revenge on whoever had killed him, and it wasn't the alien creature that stabbed a hole through his chest in issue twelve; it was the man who had created him.

That thought gave Jason a shiver as he sat in the chair at his desk, though the idea was ridiculous. Comic characters are just pencil and paper. Ink and color. Crusher couldn't any more hurt him than he himself could grab hold of a handful of wind.

There was a feeling of nervousness nagging at the back of his head that would not allow him to sleep. He turned on his computer and began working on the plot points of his latest issue. It was after seven o'clock in the morning when he finally stopped, printed out the plot, and reread it. Then he picked up the telephone on the far side of the desk and called Carl Williams' home in New York City.

"Hullo," Carl said, his voice swimming in the last stages of sleep.

"Hey, it's Jason. I've got an idea to run by you for the latest issue of THE RENEGADES."

"Jason, it's only a little after seven in the morning. Can't this wait until I'm at the office?"

"Sorry, Carl, but I've been up all night working on this. I just couldn't wait to tell you about it."

"What is it then?" Carl said, finally sounding like he was awake.

"I want to bring Crusher back to life in issue sixteen. I've got it all worked out. The alien that killed him in issue twelve got away. Well, he comes back in issue sixteen to kill the rest of the Renegades. It turns out the alien tainted its talons with some kind of poison and it only put Crusher in a death-like coma. So, Crusher digs himself up out of the ground just in time to help his teammates defeat the alien. How's that sound?"

"Sounds like you've lost your mind," Carl said. "There's no way I can let you bring him back, kid. Did you see the sales figures for last week? Issue twelve went through the roof, all because you killed off that big muscle-head. It's already going to second printing and none other than Ron Frenz is going to do the variant cover. If you bring Crusher back now, it could have just the opposite effect. Believe me, I've seen it. We're on a roll here, Jason. You're on a roll. Let's not screw it up."

"But I don't think it's a good idea to leave him dead, Carl. He doesn't want to be dead."

"What?" Carl's words came both surprised and confused. Apparently, he wasn't fully awake yet, after all.

"Look, you're going to think I'm nuts, but ever since issue twelve hit the stands, I've been having this dream. In it, Crusher is chasing me, and he's pissed off because I killed him."

"You're right, kid. I do think you're nuts," Carl said.

"But I—"

"Leave it alone, Jason," Carl said, then after a pause, "Listen, we'll talk later today after we've both had some coffee." Then he hung up.

Jason sat motionless in his office for several minutes, his cell phone clutched in his hand, and stared at the plotted pages before him.

*I can't leave it alone, Carl, because I'm afraid if I do, I might never sleep again.* He reread the plot one more time, then brushed the pages off onto the floor.

"Great. Now what do I do?" he said to no one.

* * *

At 10:40 that morning, under a beautiful, cloudless sky, a hairline crack appeared on the sidewalk in front of the Empire Comics offices in New York City. No one even noticed. Cracks appear on the sidewalk every day.

* * *

Carl Williams sat at the desk in his office on the sixth floor of that building, going over his morning agenda. A hot cup of coffee lofted tendrils of steam into the air next to him, and an unlit cigar was perched between his lips. He wouldn't light the cigar, not within the confines of the building, at least. But he needed it to think. Later, he would light it and close his eyes, and the world would just float away on a smoke trail. For now, he was still running Jason Carmichael's words through his head and trying to process it all.

His door opened and Jim Garrison, Executive Editor of the entire Empire Comics line, walked in. He looked happy, and happy Jim Garrison was a good thing.

"Morning, Carl," he said. "Just got off the phone with Malice Toys. They wanted to talk about action figures. Renegade action figures. This could be the big time here, Carl. This kind of stuff could put us up there in competition with the Big Two. That Carmichael kid could be our golden goose."

"That's great," Carl said, fiddling with his cigar. "You know what? Jason called me at home this morning. He wants to bring Crusher back to life."

"So what? You let that kid do whatever he wants. He's a damn genius!"

"I told him it was a bad idea. It could kill the book, bringing back a dead character so soon."

"Well, Carl, I'm overriding your authority here. I say let him do what he wants. You call him back and tell him to turn the bunch of his characters into super-powered frogs if he wants to."

Jim Garrison walked out, closing the door behind him. Carl sat behind his desk and chewed his cigar.

* * *

At 11:00 that morning, the crack in the sidewalk suddenly turned into a two-inch fissure in front of the doors of Empire Comics. Shards of concrete sprayed out of the hole into the air, followed by four fingers, large and craggy, colored a dark stone-brown.

* * *

Carl Williams sat, pondering his situation. He kept looking at the telephone sitting on his desk. He'd been told to call Jason back and tell him to go ahead with this ignorant Crusher resurrection plot. But Carl Williams had been in the comic book business for over two decades, and he knew what the repercussions of such a thing could be. He'd watched many a successful comic book series go right down the tubes into Comic Book Limbo because of hotheaded decisions like the one he was being told to support.

He was the editor. He was the one whose job was to keep the talent in check. Now, it seemed everyone around him had lost their damn minds. And nobody would listen to him. It was as if he'd woken up this morning in the Twilight Zone.

He decided he would have another talk with Garrison, try to get him to understand what he was saying. If he couldn't do that, he'd have to call Jason back and try to reason with him, at least.

Carl got up from his desk, downed the last of his coffee, and opened his door. He walked down to Garrison's office and peered in. No one was there.

"He's down on the first floor," the voice came from behind him. It was Mary Wilson, Garrison's administrative assistant. "He's talking to the letterers and colorists about some new software, I guess."

Carl headed toward the elevators, still chewing on his unlit cigar. The ride to the ground floor seemed to take forever, but finally the car came to a padded halt and the doors hissed open. Carl stepped off and headed for the offices where the production staff worked. He took three steps when he heard the loud crashing sound of breaking glass and twisting metal coming from the opposite way, accompanied by screams. Carl turned and ran down the hall toward the commotion. When he entered the reception area, his cigar fell from his open mouth to the floor.

The entire front wall of the building was caved in, concrete, glass and twisted metal from the huge windowed facade covering the floor. At the center of it all, Carl Williams instantly recognized the cause.

It was Crusher, the dead Renegade.

But that couldn't be. Crusher was only a comic book character. So, logic dictated it must have been someone in a very well done Crusher costume.

But Carl knew it wasn't. He could see those rows of unbelievable, even razor-sharp teeth gnashing together, saliva dripping from the corners of its slit-like mouth,

(Carl, he doesn't want to be dead)

those ruby-red eyes piercing out from his overextended brow.

*Oh my God,* was all Carl could think. *It's really him.* He wanted to run, but fear rooted him to the spot.

Crusher knew who Carl was, too: One of those involved in his execution. Rage bellowed from deep within his massive chest in a grotesque howl, and he started toward Carl, his enormous feet making craters in the floor with each step.

Carl Williams' last thoughts exploded out of his mouth at the frightened receptionist, cringing in fear behind her desk. "Call Jason Carmichael! He created this goddamn thing; he'll know what to do!" The receptionist did not move. "Go, you stupid bitch! Go!"

But it was too late for Carl Williams. Crusher's gigantic hand grasped Carl by the head and turned his skull into a mass of splintered bone and greasy brain matter.

** * **

Six hours later, someone finally made enough sense of the entire tragic escapade, and Dale McReed, staff letterer at Empire, who had worked on THE RENEGADES, called Jason Carmichael.

Jason sat in his office, an expression of pale fear filling his features as he listened to the surreal story. Carl Williams was dead. The Empire Comics offices were in shambles, but most everyone had gotten out alive. When Jason finally ended the call, he looked haggard.

*No, Dale. It wasn't some maniac in a costume, pissed off because his favorite Renegade got offed. It was the real thing. Somehow, some way, Crusher is really alive, and I'll give you three guesses who he'll come after next.* Jason headed into the kitchen for another beer. *I can picture him stomping across the country between New York and Michigan, probably not even going around the Great Lakes between. He doesn't have to breathe. I should know; I made him that way. And when he gets here, I'm going to pay for killing him.*

*Because he didn't want to be dead.*

## AUTHOR NOTES - I TOLD YOU COMIC BOOKS WERE BAD FOR YOU

I've loved comic books since before I could read, and I've been fortunate enough to even get a bit of writing work from Marvel Comics over the past decade, which is truly a dream come true. This little story was originally written in 1994, on my newly purchased Brother portable word processor, during a period when the comic book industry was going through some rough patches. I've always had that wondering notion what would happen if a comic book character came to life. I realize this isn't a new idea, fictional characters coming alive, but it's one I've always wanted to write, and it was a hoot and a half! One criticism I've gotten from a few people who've read my stuff is that sometimes the story really doesn't end when I stop writing. Such would be the case here, and we're left wondering if Jason Carmichael found a way to keep from being ground to paste beneath the Crusher's stony hand.

I recently pulled this one back out and did a minor rewrite on it, adding some more backstory to THE RENEGADES comic book characters, and modernizing things just a little.

# REACTION

Thad Matthews skipped down the steps in front of his home with a childlike vigor known only to nine-year-old boys. His sandy brown hair tossed lightly in the morning breeze, and his green eyes twinkled with childish innocence. He wore a down-filled jacket with brightly colored splotches of red, yellow, blue, and green covering its entirety. He carried his Spider-Man lunch box firmly in his right hand, swinging it wildly as he walked down the sidewalk toward the bus stop.

It was a cool October morning, and Thad's breath puffed out in front of him in a visible cloud. He stopped to observe as it faded away and wondered why that happened only when it was cold out, not during the summer. It was strange. It was different. Thad inhaled really deep and felt the bite of the cool morning air, then exhaled heavily, watching as the cloud of his breath spewed out. He smiled and continued walking.

Thad arrived at the crowded bus stop, and saw Cory Roberts—his best friend—there. When the young boy saw Thad approaching, his eyes lit up.

"Hey," Cory said, stepping out from the group and rushing up to Thad. "Did ya bring it?"

"Yep," Thad replied, patting his right coat pocket. "Right here. Sheila's gonna flip."

Before they could continue, the school bus neared, red lights flashing back and forth as it droned to a stop in front of them. The door folded open, Thad and Cory bounced up the steps and down the aisle before taking a seat together close to the back.

"How'd you get it?" Cory asked, his eyes widened in anticipation of the story that would follow.

"I had to wait 'til mom and dad went to bed, then I snuck into the basement and grabbed it. Nobody even knew it was there."

"Cool. Let me see it."

"No way."

"Aww, c'mon. No one's gonna see."

"Nope." Thad folded his arms across his chest and snickered. "Not yet."

The school bus rolled down the highway, stopping periodically to pick up several more children. At the last stop before the school, Thad looked out the window and saw Jeremy Cochran walking across the street to board the bus. Thad moved nervously in his seat. He didn't like Jeremy. Jeremy was a year older than him, the biggest bully in the third grade, and he didn't seem to care for Thad at all. They had held Jeremy back the year previous, so he was repeating the third grade, and seemed determined to vent his frustrations on anyone who got within kicking distance. He was just mean.

"Don't let Jerkface Jeremy get to ya," Cory said. "My dad says he's a putz just like his old man. Guess they went to school together, too."

"Well, he's always bugging me, and he won't leave me alone. Just once, I'd like to show him."

Jeremy Cochran moved down the aisleway, past Thad and Cory, and sat down directly behind them. The hairs on Thad's neck stood out. He wanted to turn around, but he knew Jeremy was back there, looming over him. He sunk down in his seat instead.

"Morning, pusbags," Jeremy said, snapping at the back of Thad's head with a finger. "What's in the ol' Spidey lunch box today?" He lurched over the seat for Thad's box, but Thad yanked it out of his reach.

"Nothing," Thad said, sinking further into his seat. "Leave me alone." Thad felt his ears turning red hot, and his heart pounded in them. He could feel Jeremy's breath brushing against the back of his head. All he wanted was for the bully to go away.

Before Jeremy could make another attempt to take Thad's lunch, the school bus rolled to a stop in front of Lakewood Elementary. Kids began lining up in the aisle immediately, and Thad and Cory slipped in far ahead of Jeremy. Thad's heartbeat calmed. A little.

* * *

The two boys hopped down the steps of the bus and walked through the large glass doors into the school. Cory looked over his shoulder, but didn't see Jeremy behind them. He leaned closer to Thad as they walked down the hallway toward their classroom.

"Why don't you give Jerkface what you got in your pocket?" Cory said, and a small, devilish smile creased his face.

"No way," Thad responded. "If he found out it was me, he'd kill me. Like dead."

"Chicken," Cory said, playfully pushing Thad away from him.

"I am not. I just don't wanna die."

"Then you're chicken."

"Am not."

"Are too."

"I am not," Thad said. He was getting disgusted, and his ears burned again. "Fine. I'll do it. I'm not chicken."

He pushed Cory back, and they continued down the hall with smiles on their faces.

* * *

Thad's opportunity to administer some payback came an hour and a half later. Jeremy asked to go to the bathroom, and after Mrs. Wormeister dismissed him, she turned back to the blackboard and continued with the math lesson. Thad was three seats ahead of Jeremy's in the next row over. Thad reached into his coat pocket and slowly withdrew his cellophane wrapped prize and held it in front of him, out of sight under the desk. His hands turned sweaty, and his ears burned hot as fire for the third time that day.

"Do it," He heard Cory whisper from the row next to him. Thad turned to his friend and gave him a disparaging scowl, but he knew he was honor bound to do the deed. He'd promised, and that was a big deal. His initial plan had been to place the item now tightly gripped in his hand inside Sheila Brigman's desk to scare the wits out of her, but there had been no danger in that other than getting caught by the teacher. But doing this to Jeremy Cochran was a probable death wish, plain and simple.

His fingers trembled as he unwrapped the package underneath his desk so as not to alert anyone else to what he was doing just yet. He looked around and saw Jeremy wasn't back from the bathroom yet. The teacher was still writing on the board, so he slid out of his seat, catching curious glances from the other kids as he moved—ninja-like, Cory would say later—over to Jeremy's desk. He lifted the lid a couple inches and stuffed the contents of his right hand underneath it, then let the lid back down quietly and scooted back to his seat. The empty cellophane wadded into a ball and he tucked it into his pants. No one made a sound.

Thad felt feverish. As soon as he settled back into his chair, he heard the door in the back of the room open and he knew Jeremy had returned. Thad's hands continued to sweat. He cast a slight glance over to Cory, and his friend gave him a thumbs up and a big smile. It didn't make Thad feel any better. He was terrified. And the ghostly look on his face would surely give him away when Jeremy opened his desk and saw what was inside it. He was dead.

Mrs. Wormeister finished writing on the board and turned back to her students. Everyone kept looking forward. No one said so much as a word. The teacher smiled and laid her piece of chalk down on the tray at the bottom of the board.

"Now," she said. "If everyone will take a sheet of paper from their desk, we'll begin going over these problems one at a time."

Thad knew this was the moment, and he wanted to get up and run out of the room, but couldn't feel his legs anymore. He wanted to say something to stop everyone from opening their desks, but his mouth dried up and he couldn't find his voice. He was sure he was going to vomit. Good God, what had he done?

The screech came from behind Thad loud and clear. He heard a desk lid slamming, then a tumbling and a thud, but he didn't want to look. Everyone else did. Mrs. Wormeister was moving down the aisle before Jeremy hit the floor. Thad turned his head as she frantically passed by, and he could see Jeremy Cochran lying on the floor, his chair overturned, and he was still screaming, his face as white as Thad's. It was then Thad knew for sure he was not long for this world.

"What's wrong?" Mrs. Wormeister said, leaning over Jeremy as he scrambled away from her. "What is it?"

"In my desk!" Jeremy croaked. "It's freaking huge!"

Thad turned to look at Cory, who was smiling at him like a clown. Thad felt a sudden lump in his throat, and his stomach clenched in a knot. Oh, he was dead for sure.

Mrs. Wormeister calmed Jeremy down, and then she reached out for the desk lid and slowly lifted it up. She, too, jumped back as she flung open the lid.

Lying on top of a sheaf of wrinkled papers was a large dead mouse. Beady black eyes stared up in a lifeless, haunting stare. Mrs. Wormeister closed the lid and spun her head around the room.

"Who did this?" She asked, her voice stern. Thad wanted to sink into the floor and never be seen again. He just knew someone was going to speak up and say they saw him at Jeremy's desk while he had been in the bathroom. Now he was not only dead, but likely to be expelled, too. Oh, why had he done it? What a stupid idea. If Jeremy didn't kill him, his parents would.

But no one said anything. Everyone remained silent, not one childlike voice rising to uncover Thad's secret. Jeremy's bullying behavior toward the other kids in the class had apparently earned Thad some respect from them. Inside, he breathed a silent sigh of relief, but had a feeling it wasn't over.

* * *

The noonday air was only slightly warmer than the morning, with scattered clouds blotting out the sun occasionally. Children played across the schoolyard; swing sets creaked, baseball bats cracked, the voices of the young traveled long on the breeze. Thad and Cory stood together at the edge of the large brick school building, facing out onto the playground.

"Did ya see the look on his face?" Cory asked.

"Yeah," Thad responded. "And he's gonna kill me if he finds out it was me that did it."

"Don't worry, nobody's gonna squeal. Nobody likes Jerkface Jeremy, so they're not gonna tell."

"I hope you're right." Then there was a hand on Thad's shoulder, and his blood turned to ice. He knew without looking who it was.

"Hey, pusbag," Jeremy said, turning Thad around. "It was you, wasn't it?"

"I—I don't know what you're talking about," Thad came back, trying to twist out of Jeremy's grip. "Let me go!" Thad broke free and tried to run, but Jeremy gave him a hard shove, and Thad sprawled face first into the hard packed dirt. When he turned over, a small trickle of blood ran from his nose. His eyes filled with tears, and he didn't see so much as feel Jeremy pounce on him and pound him with his fists.

Cory tried to pull Jeremy off, but the brutish ten-year-old pushed him away, and Cory landed hard on his back. Jeremy struck Thad in the chest and face several times, and Thad could feel the blood running from his nose and lips. His heart banged in his chest.

"Get off me!" Thad screamed, but the fists kept pummeling him. "Get off!"

Then suddenly, the beating stopped, and Thad could hear Jeremy shouting. Thad opened his tear-filled eyes and wiped them with his hands. Then, those same eyes grew wide and scared.

Jeremy Cochran was floating in the air ten feet above Thad, flailing helplessly and wailing in fright. Thad, Cory, and the crowd of other gathered children all stared up in amazement. The schoolyard guard that had come rushing when the fight had started now stood frozen, his mouth gaping open in disbelief.

Thad scrambled to his feet, turned away, and ran. When he did, Jeremy's body fell back to the earth, landing with a crunch on the ground, knocking his wind from him. As the guard moved in to see to Jeremy, another that had arrived from across the yard went after Thad, who was making fast time across the playground, tears still streaming down his small, round face, mixing with the runners of blood which had turned cold in the fall breeze. The guard quickly caught up to him and snatched a hold of his jacket, stopping him.

"Hold on, boy," the guard said, pulling Thad to him and looking down into his frightened face. "Where you think you're going?"

"Get away from me!" Thad screamed, and the guard flew back away from Thad twenty feet across the playground, landing beneath one of the swing sets. As he slowly got back to his feet, Thad turned and ran again.

He was afraid and confused. Something was wrong. Very, very wrong. He didn't know how he made Jeremy stop hitting him, or how he had made the guard let him go, but he knew he wanted to be gone from this place. He bolted across the playground, but he knew there was no way he could escape the school. Ahead of him, a large, ten foot high chain-link fence surrounded the playground, keeping others out and the children from leaving the schoolyard. There was no way he could climb that before the guard caught up to him again. Beyond that fence, though, he saw a thick wooded forest, and knew if he could somehow reach it, he could hide there. All he needed to do was get beyond that fence. That was all.

As if in answer to his thoughts, the fence suddenly twisted in front of him, stretching away in opposite directions, securely cemented posts pulled up from the ground and away from each other, tearing the fence in two. The chain link came apart with a staccato of metallic pops before Thad's astonished eyes, but he took no time to be amazed; he rushed between the separated steel and down the embankment into the woods. Behind him, the uprooted fencing collapsed.

Thad's heart beat heavy in his chest as he hopped over fallen trees and wound his way through the thick pines. Looking back over his shoulder, he couldn't see anyone behind him, but knew they would come, and when they found him, he was certainly going to be in trouble. He had probably hurt Jeremy, and he had definitely hurt the guard; he had seen him limping when he got up and started after him again. Thad knew for sure he was going to get the principal's paddle, or worse, when they caught him.

So he decided he would not be caught.

*  *  *

It was late in the afternoon. The sun was low in the trees, and the light filtering through was becoming dimmer. Thad was cold. He could see his breath again, like he'd remembered this morning. His fingers were getting cold, and he stuffed his hands into his jacket pockets. He knew they were still after him. He was supposed to have been in school, learning with his classmates, but he was out here, in the woods behind the school, and he knew they couldn't be too far behind. Every once in a while, he could hear faint voices in the distance, several of them. Probably the school guards, maybe some teachers. His parents by now, for sure. He was certain he could hear them calling his name, but he just kept running, their cries drowned out by his own labored breathing and the sound of his heartbeat hammering in his chest.

He didn't know what to do. He could stop, go back to them. But he was afraid, not only of what they would do, but of what he had already done. He read comic books and watched sci-fi action movies. What he'd done to Jeremy and the guard to stop them, and how he had thought about the fence parting and it had, that was called telekinesis. He could move stuff by thinking about it. That was both an exciting and frightening concept.

After all, comics and movies were made up stuff. What he'd done was real. And how could that be? And if he had powers, who else had them? He couldn't be the only one, right? Then who else? Anybody he knew? Were there teams of people with powers out there, like the X-Men?

And what about Cory? What would his best friend think of him now? Would he accept him as a cool friend with superpowers, or call him a freak and turn him away? Too many things could happen, and more than anything, he wanted his friend there to help him understand it all. But he saw the frightened and bewildered look on Cory's face and the faces of the other kids on the playground. He knew little about the world yet, but he did know that people rarely liked other people who were too different.

Deeper into the woods, the trees grew thicker, and the sun was almost at the horizon, so what light got through cast heavy shadows. Soon it would be dark, and he wasn't sure what to do then. Keep going forward, he guessed, but he wasn't even sure of his direction now.

He could have gone home. He certainly could use some provisions. Home had a camping survival kit he'd put together during the summer, and it had a compass, matches, a small first aid kit, and other helpful items. Going home wasn't an option, though. He wasn't even sure how to get there, and by the time he could, the school would likely have alerted his parents, and someone would be there waiting for him. So that was out.

Without warning, he stepped out onto a path. A man made path winding through the trees. Thad decided he could move much faster on that, and followed it for several hundred yards, stopping just before it ended.

Beyond the edge of the trees was a small cabin, old and dilapidated, the windows too dirty to see in. Thad couldn't spot anyone around it. No smoke from the chimney along its side. Abandoned, maybe? He stepped out of the protective covering of the trees and strolled toward the small shed next to the house. Maybe he could hide in there for a while, he thought. He was exhausted, hungry, thirsty, and cold. And becoming more scared as the sun continued to set.

Thad moved along the edge of the shed until he found the door. He just wanted to rest for a few minutes. Then he'd leave and go some-where. He wasn't sure where after this. But what could he do? He was alone and being pursued. Options were slim.

The door wouldn't give when he pushed on it. Locked. He shoved harder, but still it refused to yield. He could make it open, though, couldn't he? Yes.

Thad concentrated on the door, thinking of it opening, swinging in on its hinges, and he saw the door shake.

"What the hell ya doing?" The voice came cold and gruff from behind him. Thad whirled around, startled, and the shed door stopped shaking. The old man stood ten feet away with a pump-action shotgun pointed at Thad. His hair was long and disheveled, a frizzy white beard hung down his chest. He spat a stream of Copenhagen chewing tobacco onto the ground. "What ya want? Ain't got no business in there."

"I was—" Thad started, but the old man pumped the shotgun and Thad felt his voice retreat.

"You were gonna break into my shed an' try to steal something, weren't ya?"

"No, I wasn't," Thad croaked. "Honest!"

"Well, ya ain't the first one, kid. I've scared off lots of you punks before. Someone dare ya to break into old man Garney's shed? Huh? Are they out there in the woods waitin' for ya?" He waved the gun around carelessly. Thad froze, certain he was going to pee himself.

"Hey, mister," Thad stammered. "I don't want to take nothing. I was just—"

"Don't gimme none of that bullshit. I know what yer here for, an' I ought to take you over my knee for it." The old man moved toward Thad. "I'll teach ya not to trespass on my property."

"No! Please!" Thad pleaded, terrified. The old man had a gun pointed at him, and Thad didn't know if Garney meant to shoot him or not.

"Had enough of you punk kids trying to steal from me. I'm gonna teach you good. Beat the devil out of ya, if that's what it takes."

"No!" Thad screamed. Behind the old man, a long length of broken fence post twitched in the grass and shakily rose into the air. The old man held his shotgun in one arm and grabbed hold of Thad with the other. His grip was firm for his age, and his bony fingers dug into Thad's upper arm. In his mind, Thad pictured Jeremy Cochran beating him earlier that day with his fists, and he remembered the pain and the salty taste of his own blood in his mouth.

"I'm gonna beat ya so bad ya won't try this ever again." He shook Thad violently. The broken fence post quivered in the air and inched closer. Closer.

"No," Thad said, staring into the old man's eyes. His voice suddenly calm, Thad shook his head. "Nobody's gonna hit me again. Ever."

## AUTHOR NOTES - REACTION

This story is one of my personal favorites. Originally planned as part of an epilogue to an unpublished novel I wrote in high school, I pulled this story out (along with two others) and refashioned them as standalone tales (see I CAN'T DIE DEAD ENOUGH and VOICES in this volume). Kids always fascinate me in their innocence, and at the beginning of this story, Thad Matthews is innocent, but mischievous. By story's end, he's forced to protect himself against people who might hurt him, and at that point, innocence is gone. It's a hard world we live in, and what would you do if you were nine years old and found yourself suddenly possessed of the power to move things with your mind? People would come after you, some to help, some to harm. What would you do when they did? Who could you trust? I think I got into the mindset of a child pretty well regarding that.

# THE CORNFIELD
# BLUES

Had you been there, you would have called it just another shooting star streaking across the night sky above Lansford, Michigan, in the small hours of a mid-August morning, but it wasn't. If you had been sitting out on your porch at 2:43 AM watching the Perseid meteor shower with your girl or a pack of your friends, it would have appeared harmless at first, just another of many fireballs burning out in the atmosphere, not even worth talking about over coffee at Charlotte's Restaurant when you went in for breakfast.

Except it wasn't a normal meteorite disintegrating tens of miles above earth. It was much closer than that, and if you had been out sitting on your porch just before the three o'clock hour, you would have seen the fireball draw closer as the meteorite angled deeper into the atmosphere, then watched as the incandescence fizzled out with deceleration some ten miles above. The meteorite's final descent occurred in unspectacular near-total darkness, ending as it plowed at a low angle into one of Sam Tanner's vast cornfields, creating a twenty-foot wide crater in the earth, shredding cornstalks in its juggernaut path where it came to rest, a four-foot diameter ball of space debris, nestled in the center of Tanner's livelihood.

Though hardly above ambient temperature, the meteorite produced an uneasy fire-like glow which pulsed and faded like an alien heart beating in the cool breast of Mother Earth. Haunting shadows ebbed and flowed amid the endless acres of corn.

* * *

Sam Tanner sat bolt upright in his bed just as the meteorite buzzed past his house to its resting place in the field. It wasn't the sound that woke him, but the energy, an almost static-like charge that made the hairs on his body stand up, and left a soft rhythmic humming in his ears.

He threw back the covers and stumbled out on the cool hardwood floor, grabbed his overalls from the heap of clothing on the rocker next to the bed, and opened the curtains while he dressed. The night was full black as he scanned from the second-floor window until his eyes stopped on the eerie pulsing glow in the middle of the eastern field.

"Damn kids," Sam mumbled to himself as he buckled the straps of his overalls. He fumbled along the bureau for his glasses so he could get a better look. *Fourth of July's over a month gone,* he thought, sliding the wire-frames onto his nose. *Little bastards are still out lighting off firecrackers or up to some fuckery or another.*

Sam sat back on the bed, switched on the antique lamp on the nightstand, and worked his boots onto his feet. Arthritis knotted up his fingers as he tied the laces, and he mumbled a curse. The wind-up clock next to the lamp told him he wasn't set to take his morning cocktail of meds for another three and a half hours, but he supposed a couple Motrin would at least take the edge off. His doctors had told him that his body was just getting old from years of hard work, and that the best they could do at this point was try to maintain. Sam shuffled into the bathroom and grabbed the small, square pillbox from the medicine cabinet. Those god-damned child-proof caps were a bitch for someone whose hands knotted up for the first few minutes after waking, so he'd transferred the Motrin capsules into something his fingers could operate at 3am. He popped three pills into his mouth and took a shot of water. He'd probably be back home and in bed again before the drugs finally kicked in, but at least he'd likely sleep better.

Sam flipped the switch at the top of the stairs to light up his descent to the first floor. His knees popped as he stepped downward, but he paid them no heed; just standard operating procedure for an eighty-two-year-old. He'd considered moving his sleeping quarters to the first floor spare bedroom, but he'd be damned if he was going to let a little rheumatoid take him from the place he and his late wife Agnes had shared their intimacy for the better part of sixty years. If the stroke hadn't taken Agnes away, it would be near sixty-five years now.

After setting foot on the first floor's hardwood, Sam walked through the kitchen, opened the door leading out to the covered porch, then stopped. After a moment's pause, he reached behind the door to grab the twelve-gauge resting against the jamb. He gave a weak smile when he noticed his fingers had already limbered up some. *Thank you, Motrin.*

"I'll show 'em firecrackers," Sam grumbled as he stepped off the porch and headed for his old Ford pickup.

* * *

Deep in the cornfield, the meteorite pulsed, casting its eerie, seething glow into the night sky. The only witness to the destructive arrival of the space rock had been a farmer's scarecrow some fifty feet away. Each summer, Sam Tanner would hang several of them throughout his fields, more out of habit and nostalgia than any practical use.

This scarecrow stood, held upright by a long 2x4, while its coal black button eyes watched the rise and fall of ghoulish haze surrounding the object that fell from the sky. Its mouth, a crude slit punctured in the gunnysack of its head by Sam's old pocket knife, hung open almost in amazement, stems of straw poking out like tiny disfigured teeth. An old flannel shirt and a patched pair of blue jeans stuffed with straw completed the body, and Sam tied a pair of his old work boots to the pant cuffs with bailing twine. A set of hole-ridden jersey gloves dangled from the ends of the shirt cuffs. Sam had found a straw hat in the ditch after the snow thawed, and that now sat atop the scarecrow's head, to shield its buttoned eyes from the late summer sun that would rise before long.

Perhaps it was just the shadows thrown from the meteorite's glow, but it almost appeared as if the scarecrow was leaning toward the small extraterrestrial boulder, bathing in its soft radioactive light.

* * *

Sam Tanner's 1987 Ford F-150 rumbled and belched down the beaten paths running along his eastern field, shocks squealing in agony as it bounced over large rocks and into deep ruts left behind by his tractor tires. Several scarecrows watched from their perches.

Some days when the sun got to boiling, Sam would fire up the old John Deere tractor, grab a six-pack of Blatz and just putt around the fields, stopping now and then to sit and drink a beer and talk to the scarecrows. Some people in town had the notion old Sam was perhaps gathering a little dust in the attic, but Sam couldn't have cared less. He paid his taxes just like everybody else, and if he wanted to sit in his own bought-and-paid-for fields and drink cheap beer with a bunch of straw-stuffed burlap bags, he'd do just that, God be damned. The scarecrows weren't good for much else anyway. The blasted crows seemed more attracted to than scared by them.

Sam piloted the pickup as it careened through the field toward the faint pulsing light still several hundred yards away. Perhaps they'd set fire to something out there and were already gone. Lord knows one of those damned firecrackers could have caught something alight. It'd been nearly a month since the last rain. The DNR had issued a burning ban two weeks ago after George Grendel had started a brush fire at his farm on the other side of town. He and George were good friends, but that crazy old bastard had the worst luck. Sam laughed a little at that. But at least George didn't have punk kids messing in his fields.

He brought the truck to a halt a hundred yards from the meteorite's impact point, but Sam still couldn't see what it was. The path curved around and headed back toward the farm, so this was the closest he could get with the pickup. He parked and turned the truck off, leaving the lights on despite the glow ahead. He opened the door and pulled the shotgun from the seat, double-checking to make sure there were a couple of rounds available, and then started into the thick foliage of the cornfield.

Leaves from the stalks rustled behind him as he walked. Once, he turned back when he thought his one good ear heard someone, and almost fell face first into the crater the meteorite had opened in the ground. He twisted his ankle trying to stay upright, and he felt a pop in his lower leg as he went down. The pain ribboned up his left leg all the way to his hip, and the world went white for a flash, but he didn't pass out. Sam laid there in the dirt for a few moments until the initial pain subsided, but there was still a low, dull throb in his leg. As his focus returned, he surveyed the area, the shotgun across his lap. What he saw would've turned his hair white if it hadn't already been silver.

He was sitting on the edge of the crater, the center of which was a glowing, pulsing amber. Sam blinked his eyes rapidly several times and adjusted his glasses on his face.

"What in the name of God—?" he whispered, the words hissing over his dry lips. He shifted himself onto his right leg and, using the shotgun as a crutch, he slowly shuffled down into the crater. It wasn't heat that radiated from it, but Sam felt something breeze against his face despite the air in the rest of the cornfield being suddenly still.

Sam stooped over, trying to get a better look at the object nestled snugly in the earth. In between the bright pulses, he could fairly well make out the meteorite's surface. It was a mixture of black and gray, deep pits, crags, and holes cutting into its hide like open sores. Sam seemed mesmerized by the throbbing light and stood there for a full minute. He was sure no punk kids from Lansford High had put this thing there. He'd heard of meteorites, even had seen one when he was a lot younger, in one of those historical museums. To him, it looked amazingly like the surface of the moon, which he first saw pictures of back in '69 right after the first man set foot on there. Yep, a little moon, sitting right smack in the middle of his property. What a moneymaker that could be, and he pictured people coming in droves from all over to see an actual meteorite. But, he also figured maybe those space people down at NASA might probably want to get hold of this, and they'd maybe pay him a pretty handsome price to get it.

Engrossed in his fantasy of wealth and fame, Sam didn't hear the movement behind him until it was almost too late, then he turned back a millisecond before something collided with the side of his face. He jolted sideways into the crater, the right half of his face split open in a wide fan of blood. There was more shock than pain at first as Sam rolled sideways, fumbling madly for the trigger of the shotgun. When he found it, his finger pressed into the cool metal and he swung around, blood running into his eyes. He couldn't see through the red haze, and the blow had knocked his glasses off into the dirt, but he could make out a vague human shape, and he pointed the shotgun in that direction. At this range, his accuracy didn't matter. That shotgun would blast anything apart in its immediate path. Before his trembling finger could squeeze down, he heard a harsh whooshing sound, and the shape knocked the shotgun out of his hands, and it thudded coldly into the earth, out of his reach.

Sam scrambled backwards, but the combination of pain in his left ankle and that now coursing through his rapidly swelling face nearly paralyzed him. In the next thirty seconds, his body took repeated blows from a hard, blunt object he could not see. He reached out with his hands to stop the onslaught, only to feel his fingers snap under the force of another crushing blow.

Sam howled at the pain now pulsing across his body. His eyes were useless; a combination of his own blood and the good farming soil of Lansford clogged what little unaided vision he had. So, he didn't see what happened next, not that it would have mattered. A hard, sharp point stabbed through the thick expanse of his torso and into the ground beneath him. His chest rose in a convulsive gasp, then settled back as a last rush of air and clotted blood escaped his lips.

Behind Sam Tanner's defeated body, the glow of the meteorite suddenly and finally faded, settling the expanse of the Tanner cornfields back into darkness.

* * *

"Christ on a crutch," Deputy John Larson said, leaning over Tanner's body. It was seven thirty in the morning, and he had just arrived on the already very busy scene. Several black and yellow sawhorses streamed with warning tape had cordoned off the area surrounding Sam Tanner and the meteorite. Along with four men from the county coroner's office and attendants from the ambulance crew, there were five Lansford police officers, including himself, and what John guessed were the State Police Forensics crew—the lab rats, as he referred to them—scanning the area, one of them asking questions of local farmhand Phil McDermitt, who had found the body on his way to work. John saw Sheriff Jake Stockton talking to Carl Shriefer, the head lab rat, and he walked toward them.

"What's the scoop?" he asked when the Sheriff turned to him.

"Still trying to figure that out, John," Jake said, running his hand over the increasing baldness of his head. "Looks like two major events came together here in the middle of this cornfield. We've got a strange chunk of space rock that fell outta the sky, and an old dead man. An old dead, murdered man, more precisely."

"Maybe there isn't a connection," John mused. "Maybe old man Tanner was just out checking on this meteorite and somebody was sneaking across the field, saw him, and did him in."

"Doesn't feel that simple," Jake said. "Whoever did this beat him and drove a tree branch through his chest. That requires a bit of strength."

"Maybe the scarecrow could answer a few questions." John said, looking a few rows into the cornfield where Sam Tanner's handiwork stood, a silent, stoic observer.

"Not even funny, John," Jake said, walking away.

John stayed behind, looking at the scarecrow a few moments longer. *Looks to me like he's got something to say,* he thought. The sun glinted out from behind a cloud, sparkling across the scarecrow's dark black button eyes. John could have sworn he saw them blink, but that was just the light playing tricks, he guessed, and walked up to where Jake and Undersheriff Kevin Slater were now talking to Phil McDermitt, the man who'd found Sam's body.

"I was heading out to George Grendel's farm to milk the cows this morning around 4:00am when I saw a light in Sam's field," Phil said, visibly shaken. "I found Sam's old pickup out there with the headlights still on. And then I found Sam laying a few feet away from that weird rock. Good God, Sheriff, he had a tree branch sticking out of his chest."

Slater was taking notes. "You disturbed nothing on the scene?"

"No, other than I walked up to Sam to see if there was any possibility he was still alive. When I got close enough, I knew there was no coming back from that. Then—and I know it sounds strange—I lost some time between then and 6:00 when I called you."

"Lost some time?" Slater asked.

"Yeah. I remember standing over Sam, and the air was kinda hazy, misty like fog, but thick. It actually hurt to breathe. Then, I felt real dizzy, and next thing I remember, I'm sitting up next to Sam's body in the dirt, and the sun is up."

"You didn't see anybody else?"

"Nope, not that I recall."

There had been boot tracks in the area surrounding the meteorite's landing path, but the prints didn't match either Tanner's or McDermitts. They had entered and left the cornfield from the nearby highway. That left them with an unidentified and unaccounted for person in the vicinity after the meteorite had come down. And this person was likely the killer of Sam Tanner.

"You worked for Sam, too, right?"

"Yeah. Sam didn't need a full-time farmhand, but he was getting up there where he couldn't do everything himself, so he worked something out with George Grendel to share me a couple of days a week. Been doing that for three years or so. Sam was a good man."

"I know he was," Jake said.

"Who would do something like this, Sheriff Stockton?"

"I don't know, Phil. Sam has had some run-ins with teenagers over the years, and a shotgun got discharged into the air once or twice to scare them off, but this seems to be beyond teenage rebellion."

"That's for sure," Phil said.

Jake changed the subject. "You'll have to go to the hospital to get some testing done. The lab boys won't have a real good idea of how radioactive that meteorite was until they can do some real inspection on it, and they've called in a special division of the FBI to assist. It seems to be inert now, but they said the meteorite could have been giving off some pretty potent rads this morning. Just as a precaution, they want you checked out."

"Sure thing," Phil said, sitting on the back bumper of an ambulance. "Don't wanna start losing my hair or anything." He brushed his hand through the thick blanket of curls on his head and half-laughed. It was a haunted laugh, and Jake Stockton didn't find Phil's humor any more amusing than John Larson's scarecrow quip a few minutes earlier.

"Also, keep in mind that since you were the only person on site for a couple of hours, we have to rule you out as a suspect."

"I understand, Sheriff. I'll cooperate however you need."

"Thank you, Phil."

"I just hope to God you find who did this."

"Me, too, Phil. Me, too."

Phil left in one ambulance, with Sam's body loaded in another, then about a third of the forensics crew also departed. The rest were going to be busy for a while. Jake gathered his men together. Deputies Paul Miller and Rex Jackson were to stay on guard duty. To the others, he said: "Let's wrap this up. Hopefully, the state lab can give us something to work with by this afternoon."

With that, Sheriff Stockton got into his cruiser and bounced across the worn roads of Sam Tanner's fields toward the highway. John Larson took one last look at the scarecrow before he got into his own patrol car, and he swore he saw it smile at him, but assured himself it must have been the sun again.

* * *

Jake Stockton arrived at the Lansford Police Station around 9:30, gave cursory greetings to everyone there, then went directly to his office. He sat down in his time-worn oak swivel chair, intending to read his mail and tackle paperwork. That's all he felt like accomplishing today, and he wasn't even sure he was up to that much.

Sheila Bonham, police dispatch, had tracked down Sam Tanner's only living sibling, Larry, a younger brother of seventy-one years, who lived in South Dakota. Jake called Larry and gave him the news of his brother's passing. They hadn't been close, Larry said, but he assured Jake that his granddaughter was a lawyer and would take care of anything that needed taking care of.

Jake shuffled paperwork for the next couple of hours, but he was restless. For lunch, he ordered a cheeseburger and fries to go from Charlotte's Restaurant, and while he was sure the burger was as good as always, he'd felt like he was eating cardboard and ended up throwing half of it in the trash.

Jake had known Sam Tanner since he'd taken the sheriff's position nearly a decade before. As with Sam's brother Larry, they hadn't been close, but Sam had been a kind man, sometimes overly gruff regarding younger generations, but still a kind man. Jake could remember every time he had to make a stop at Tanner's farm, the old man would try to give him a grocery bag full of fresh vegetables, and even if he refused, there would somehow be a sack in the cruiser's passenger seat. Jake laughed at this thought. That was all before Sam's Wife Edna had taken ill. The doctors diagnosed cancer, and it wasn't but a few months after that she passed on, leaving Sam Tanner alone. He'd stopped growing the little family garden then. He just stuck to the corn crop, because the vegetable garden had always been Edna's thing, and the old man said he couldn't bear the thought of doing it without her.

Jake's visits had almost always been on calls from Sam. Kids, it seemed, were fond of playing in the cornfields when they were younger, driving through them at night when older, both mowing down acres and acres of his crop, just for the hell of it. Jake would always come by personally instead of sending a deputy. Most of the officers cared little for Sam Tanner, but Jake Stockton liked him just fine and enjoyed listening to the old man talk. Jake guessed it was because maybe Sam reminded him of his own grandfather, who had raised him for a spell when his mother and father had gotten divorced, and who had passed on several years before. Jake would sit and listen to Sam jabber on with one of his 'back in my day' rants, and Jake could swear he heard a little of his grandfather's voice in Sam's, and by proxy, his grandfather was there, just a little. That had always made Jake smile.

And now the old man was gone. Not from cancer or old age, but beaten to death and impaled with a tree branch by a nameless assailant. Somehow, that didn't seem fair. And that made Jake Stockton furious.

To make matters worse, there were little in leads to go on. Phil McDermitt wasn't a killer. Jake knew that with certainty, and even with a supposed gap in Phil's memory, Jake knew enough about Phil Mc-Dermitt's character to not spend too much time on that as a possibility. The tracks they'd found in the soil around the crime scene that didn't belong to either Sam or Phil were the key, but they entered and left the corn field onto a paved road. No tracks once they hit the asphalt. Jake had sent a crew to check the fields on the other side of the road for more tracks soon after they'd left the primary crime scene, but corn fields for miles likened to more of a needle in a haystack scenario than he cared to admit.

Forensics was doing the CSI portion of the investigation, as well as preliminary quarantine of the exposed area, while waiting for the government to send somebody. He wasn't sure who that would be? The EPA, the Nuclear Regulatory Committee, NASA, Department of Energy? Hell if he knew. All he was certain of was that his little northern Michigan town was going to become a lot more popular soon.

So, all they could do was wait for the lab boys to give them something. In the meantime, he had to ponder if there was some kind of connection between Sam Tanner's murder and this mysterious rock from space? He wasn't ready to rule it out, but he felt helpless. Sam was dead, now awaiting autopsy in the morgue, while it left Jake guessing.

The intercom on his telephone buzzed and Sheila spoke through the speaker, "Jake, Carl Shriefer on line one. He sounded urgent."

"Thanks," Jake said, whirling his chair around and picking up the receiver on his desk. Shriefer and his high brows must have figured something out, he thought, and hoped to God the news was good. He stabbed his finger at the red flashing "1" on the phone base and spoke into the phone, "Sheriff Stockton here."

"Something's happened," Carl Shriefer's voice said, and Jake's face went pale.

"What's wrong?"

"The meteorite was inert by the time your boys showed up at the site, so I think they'll be okay, but a few hours before, the rad levels in about a 50-foot radius of that rock were off the charts."

"What about Phil McDermitt, then?"

"He's dead, Jake."

"Christ," Jake exhaled, and was silent a moment before adding: "Radiation poisoning?"

"That's the main reason I'm calling you. I don't think it was radiation sickness that did him in, Jake. At least not any radiation sickness I've ever seen."

"Then what?"

"I'm not entirely sure." It was Carl's turn to pause. "Phil arrived at the hospital about 8:30 this morning. They flew a special medical unit in from Detroit to check him out. They never got the chance."

"He died that fast?"

"No, not quite. He went berserk not ten minutes after they admitted him; trashed his room, injured several people at the nurse's station, and then just dropped over like a stone."

Jake was fidgeting nervously on the other end of the line. His mind was whirling. He had known Phil McDermitt, and while they weren't at best friend status, Jake knew him well enough to know violence was pretty out of character for him. Phil had got the shit kicked out of him two years prior in a bar fight because he didn't want to trade blows with an out-of-towner. He was a pretty mousy guy when it came right down to it. Jake finally said, "What the hell causes that?"

"I'm not sure yet. They're going to do an autopsy in a couple hours, but while it wasn't rad poisoning per se, my best guess is the radiation amped up his adrenaline output. He ripped the reception desk right off the floor at the nurse's station, Jake. That thing weighs a good seven-hundred pounds, at least."

"And then he just died?"

"Yeah. Like I said, he just dropped over. It was like whatever had juiced him up burned out his body until there wasn't anything left."

"Good God," Jake said. He wasn't sure what to think.

"All I can say now is it's probably a good thing Sam Tanner is dead, because the amount of radiation his body absorbed at ground zero was off the scale compared to what McDermitt got. If Tanner lived, it would have been like having the Incredible Hulk in town, at least for a few minutes."

"When are you autopsying Phil?" Jake asked.

"About an hour and a half."

"I want to be there. Can you swing that, Carl?"

"Sure, shouldn't be a problem."

"Good, I'm on my way," Jake said and hung up the phone before Carl could reply. Jake hurried from his office, told Shelia he would be out for the rest of the day, and stepped through the station doors into the scorching August afternoon. He crossed the parking lot, got into his Sheriff's cruiser, and headed south.

* * *

"In my office," Carl Shriefer said, and ushered Jake down a long, windowless hall. Once behind closed doors, Carl settled into an expensive leather high back and the Sheriff sat in an uncomfortable plastic steel post chair. Carl got little in the way of visitors, Jake imagined.

Carl took a cigarette from the pack on his desk and held it in his fingers. They prohibited smoking within the building, but he needed to feel it with him. "We've got a problem. Government agents—FBI, they say—just landed in Traverse City, along with a forensic specialist who will perform the autopsy. They're not allowing observers. They're not even letting me in on it."

"That's not normal, is it? I mean, the FBI showing up."

"No," Carl said, and rolled the cigarette between his fingers. "Not unless you're in an episode of the X-Files."

"Which, considering the circumstances, doesn't seem all that far-fetched, does it?" Jake's voice grew somber. He liked this situation less and less.

"No," Carl replied, and the cigarette rolled back and forth between his fingers. He leaned back in his chair and looked at Jake across the desk. "But I want to see that body for myself."

"Me, too," Jake added. "Though, Scully and Mulder aren't just gonna to let us drop in for a quick look."

"Maybe we can find a way around that. We've got about half an hour before the feds are supposed to get here." Carl picked up his phone and dialed an extension.

Things went quickly after that.

* * *

Ron Neely stood outside the autopsy room door, his eyes darting nervously back and forth down the dim hallway. His left hand was in his pants pocket, folding and refolding the hundred-dollar bill Carl Shriefer had given him. Behind him, he could hear muffled voices through the cold steel door. He was glad he couldn't tell what they were saying.

* * *

"Do you think that guard will keep quiet?" Jake asked. He felt nervous himself.

"Ron will do his part," Carl said. Ron's part had started out simply to keep watch at the door and let nobody near the room until the FBI arrived. One-hundred dollars had gotten him to overlook the two nobodies now standing around a corpse and alert them if anyone showed up.

Phil McDermitt's cadaver lay cold on the table. Carl had pulled the sheet down to the dead man's waist, and they huddled around the body. Phil's discolored skin made it almost appear as if he'd been burned.

"You sure this is safe?" Stockton asked. "He's not still radioactive, is he?"

"He's harmless now," Carl said, pulling McDermitt's head from side to side, examining his neck. "Radiations's long gone according to the tests they got to run before the federal lockdown." He pulled open one of Phil's eyelids. The orb underneath was milky white, the iris almost completely gone.

"Anything out of the ordinary?" Jake wondered aloud.

"The skin discoloration is from the radiation. That's normal. Since we can't open him up, I'm just looking for other surface signs that might tell me what earned our friend here the interest of the federal government."

As if in answer, something bulged upward from Phil McDermitt's stomach, distending the skin. The two men took a step back, their faces shocked mirrors of one another. The room suddenly felt tiny to both of them.

* * *

Outside the autopsy room, Ron Neely stood diligent watch at the door. That hundred bucks was going to buy a lot of beers at The Ruptured Duck tonight.

Five minutes away, in an unmarked Chevy Impala, by-the-book FBI agent Mark Thompson navigated the highway at 67 miles per hour. His less anal-retentive partner, Gavin Pierce, rode shotgun and looked out the window at miles of trees and fields, wishing he was anywhere but in the middle of nowhere. In the back seat, forensics specialist Doctor Gary Hopkins leafed through a dossier on the corpse he was soon to open. All four men would eventually know the exact moment this day went to hell.

* * *

"Oh my God," Jake Stockton hissed through his teeth. "What is that?" Carl did not answer. The bulge in Phil McDermitt's stomach had stopped moving, but the protrusion was still evident.

Then Phil McDermitt's corpse sat bolt upright on the table. Carl Shriefer screamed involuntarily, and Jake Stockton instinctively drew his sidearm. Phil McDermitt's body moved off the table in a lurch, landing in a simian posture, then crossed the distance between himself and Carl Shriefer with uncanny speed. Carl folded up in panic, and Phil merely shoved him aside as he headed for the autopsy room door. Jake Stockton leveled his weapon and fired two shots into the back of Phil's upper torso. McDermitt's body jerked as the bullets tore open the flesh of his right shoulder and upper back. Blood did not spray from the savage wounds; it oozed from them like sap. Phil's body did not fall, instead it turned to face the shooter. The Sheriff could see the lifeless face and the stony stare of dead white eyes looking out from their sockets at nothing. There was no rationalizing this, no explaining away the horror standing before him; it was an abomination needing to be stopped. Whether walking corpses made it into the policeman's 'to serve and protect' credo or not, stopping this thing fell squarely on Jake Stockton's shoulders at this very moment. He fired off two more shots, shattering Phil McDermitt's knees and bringing the animated cadaver down. Phil's body determinedly pulled itself along the floor toward the heavy metal door, dragging his now-useless legs behind.

Ron Neely burst in then, service weapon in hand, and saw the body scrambling toward him. A moment of astonishment gave him no time to react before Phil McDermitt's strong working-class left hand grabbed Ron by the ankle and dragged him down. Ron suddenly wished he hadn't taken that hundo from Shriefer.

The bulge in Phil McDermitt's stomach slid upward, disappearing under the dead man's ribcage for a moment, then reappearing in his throat as whatever was inside him made its way out through the path of least resistance.

Jake Stockton stood immobile as the thing within Phil McDermitt's body freed itself from Phil's mouth. It was vaguely humanoid, skin similar to a shark's, with two long thin legs and two long thin arms writhing madly as it slipped out of Phil's throat. It had a head the size of an orange; two large coal-black eyes cast a filmy sheen as they blinked. Ron

Neely got a good up close look at the thing as it worked its way toward his face. He opened his mouth to scream, and its tiny but strong hands grasped his teeth and yanked his jaw open. It squirmed into Ron's open maw as he flailed at it, and his service pistol flew across the room and clanged against a gurney. Jake Stockton had his own gun at the ready, but the thing was making its way into Ron and was therefore too close for him to fire. Later, in hindsight, Jake would wonder if he shouldn't have granted Ron some measure of mercy and ended him then.

Ron's body convulsed as the small creature forced its way deftly down his throat. He made choking sounds, his mind flashing ever briefly back to when he was six, and got a chunk of steak caught in his throat. His father had squeezed his belly hard until the stuck piece of meat had dislodged like a projectile. The Heimlich maneuver would not help today, however. What was in his throat had no intention of being dislodged.

Ron's fingers dug into the tiled floor and his nails scraped up curling stringers of wax. At that same moment, agents Thompson and Pierce appeared in the doorway to the autopsy room. They watched with what Jake Stockton thought was eerie familiarity as the creature's hind quarters slipped between Ron Neely's lips. Then Neely stopped moving.

The FBI agents calmly moved into the room, Pierce motioning for Jake to move back, which the Sheriff obligingly did. He noticed Carl Shriefer still cowering next to a cabinet, his hands over his head and his face buried. Jake could hear the man whimpering and didn't think less of him for it.

Then Ron Neely was on his feet and active, the speed and strength of his movement astonishing. Spider-like, he skittered backward into the room, trying to put distance between himself and the FBI agents. His eyes - something both human and alien in them - darted back and forth with nervous fervor.

"Get it out of my head!" He shouted, his hands clawing at the sides of his skull. Tears began streaking down his cheeks. "I can feel it in there…" he trailed off, his body dancing wildly around the room. The creature inside Ron Neely's body - now vying for control of his brain

- kept them at as much of a distance as it could manage. He tossed a gurney at them with a flick of his wrist; a wheeled cart tipped on its side and the various forensic tools scattered across the floor.

Jake observed the primary danger coming from the creature's frenzied and erratic behavior. He could see the well-dressed feds advancing cautiously. Ron Neely was still inside his head fighting the small alien thing for ultimate control of him, dividing the alien's concern between that task and keeping the agents away. It didn't even know Jake was there anymore. And it was backing towards him.

Jake crouched and swept his left foot wide and fast, taking Ron Neely's legs out from under him. Ron landed with a grunt, and Jake was on him, twisting his right arm and wrestling him onto his stomach. He pulled his handcuffs from his belt in one swift movement and latched the first onto the arm he held. Ron Neely's left arm had found the leg of a wheel cart and swung it wildly behind him. It missed Jake by inches and the Sheriff grabbed the swinging arm and latch the other handcuff around it.

Ron bucked up and knocked Jake off to the side. His foot landed squarely in Jake's chest and kicked him away. The police chief crashed into a cabinet and found himself next to the still-cowering Carl Shriefer, who yelped like a scolded pup. Ron Neely struggled into a sitting position, and Jake could see he was straining against the handcuffs. He heard the steel chains snap and in the space of a heartbeat Ron whirled around and crouched before him. Jake could see the madness in his eyes, the lack of humanity. The alien thing inside him had taken hold.

Before it could come at him, something struck it in the back and Jake watched as Ron Neely's body jerked in spasm and went down. Agent Thompson stepped up, a strange taser-like device in his hand.

"You should've stayed out of the way," Thompson said dryly as he stooped over to examine Ron Neely's prone body.

"You're welcome," Jake said with a bit of scorn as he got to his feet. His chest felt like a mule had kicked him in the chest, which he supposed was a pretty accurate comparison. He leaned against a marble-top table for a few moments to catch his breath. "Now, just what the hell was that?"

* * *

There were six FBI agents at the debriefing. Jake Stockton was sitting at the table in another of those uncomfortable plastic steel post chairs, Mark Thompson and Gavin Pierce sitting directly across from him. The other four agents stood in the background, flanking the door, looks of stoic indignation on their faces. They all wore matching suits.

"Coffee, Sheriff?" Pierce offered.

"No thanks," Jake responded with a thin smile. "I've already had my fill for the day." He had found sleep elusive the night before, dreams haunted by the vision of that creature—that alien thing—climbing through poor Ron Neely's mouth and down his throat. He had been up since 4:30 this morning, and had been through an entire pot of coffee all by himself, about half a pot more than on an ordinary day. But this was going to be no ordinary day, of that he was sure.

"Sheriff Stockton," Mark Thompson said. "What you encountered in the morgue was an extraterrestrial life form."

"That I do not doubt," Jake said. He had come to that clear conclusion all on his own, but having it confirmed by another person made it a reality. A week ago, he was just a small-town sheriff, going about his routine like he had for most of the past decade. Now, whether humanity was alone in the universe had become answered, and that was a revelation that changed a man. "I get the impression this isn't the first time you've dealt with something like this."

"Unfortunately, no," Thompson replied. "We have known this species for quite some time, though our last contact was several years ago. When the report came in of the meteorite landing in Lansford, we monitored closely. All the signs of alien arrival came in rapid succession after that. They travel in meteorites, you see.

"What do they do?" Jake asked.

"They're symbiotic, taking on a host body of some sort because, as you saw, they're not well designed for standard mobility. They're also telepathic and telekinetic, which is how they take control of and animate their hosts. The problem is, something in this process more often than not burns out the host body fast, so they have to jump to another one as soon as they can. As the case of Phil McDermitt shows, they can animate a corpse if they have to, but they optimally prefer the host body to be living, which is why it transferred itself to Ron Neely as soon as it could."

"How does this host/parasite scenario explain what happened to Sam Tanner? Phil McDermitt didn't find his body until after four in the morning. According to our autopsy, Sam had been dead for a couple of hours by then, bludgeoned to death."

Gavin Pierce broke in to respond. "We're suspecting there may have been more than one alien in that meteorite."

* * *

Ethan Colburn felt strange. His skin burned like it was on fire, and his head felt like it could burst at any moment, as if his forehead would just blow out and scatter his brains to the wind.

And deep within him, something unnatural was stirring.

He lay curled up under the oak tree, and his mind, hazy as it was, drifted back over the past day.

He remembered walking down a road in the dark, surrounded on both sides by acres of cornfield. It had been very early in the morning. Where was he going? He couldn't remember. Out of town, maybe. Why? He couldn't remember that either. Only that he had been angry. So furious. A woman? He remembered a woman, then. And a man, a man not him. He remembered being so angry. Angrier than he'd ever been.

Then the air had filled with a strange buzzing sound, not of cicadas or some other night bug, but the air itself seemed to become charged with an expanding electricity, right before he heard the heavy thump of something colliding with the earth in the field to his left.

Then, he remembered seeing a faint pulsating glow amid the end-less expanse of corn stalks a hundred yards off the road. He wandered into the field then, pushing his way through the stalks, hearing their wispy scraping sounds as they brushed against him. He emerged into a clearing that was not manmade. Something had fallen from the sky and created a long trench in the earth, tearing and spreading corn stalks in every direction.

He had approached the glow, mesmerized by it, and realized the light was coming from a large rock. A rock from space. The glow soothed him, made the anger he felt subside, momentarily. The rock's surface was rough, with small holes across its surface. He leaned in close to examine it and saw something move inside one hole. Unafraid, he reached out toward the rock.

Then it was on him. Something sprang from the hole, small and fast, and scrambled up his arm toward his face. He clutched at it frantically, but its speed was incredible. Ethan opened his mouth to scream and in that one instant, it forced itself inside him. Before he could do anything more, it was gone, down his throat. He coughed and breathed in heavy gasps for a few moments.

It moved inside him, but it was no longer an unpleasant sensation. He felt as if it was becoming part of him, entwining with him. His mind felt alien, foreign to even himself. His vision changed, fragmented, out of focus, then snapped back to crystal clarity. Ethan felt energized.

He heard the approaching vehicle, then. Can't be found, he thought, and scurried, primate-like, into the growth of corn stalks. His head darted back and forth, his ears picking up the sounds of someone exiting a pickup truck. He peered out through the corn and could see the old man coming into the clearing where the meteorite had landed. He watched him fall, lay still for moments, then continue on.

Somewhere, deep inside, Ethan had felt his anger rising again, and a blind fury overtook him. Beside him on the ground, he found an oak branch, sturdy, heavy enough to be used as a weapon. Ethan saw the man looking at the space rock, and then emerged, nearly soundlessly, from the corn, and attacked.

It was a rush of images, the old man's body falling under his onslaught, bones breaking, blood flowing. Ethan cried out in what seemed a mixture of pain and rage until the old man lay shattered at his feet. He remembered raising the branch, already covered in blood, and driving it through the man's chest, impaling him to the ground.

He remembered stumbling out of the cornfield, back onto the road, and being confused. The anger within him was strong, stronger than he'd ever felt. But he was also afraid and sad. So many emotions, so difficult to separate.

The old man had done nothing to him. But he'd killed him anyway, without a second thought. He had been so angry. More angry than he'd ever remembered being. Perhaps it was the thing within him that made his rage so strong. If so, he welcomed it. The exhilaration was indescribable.

Now, as he lay under the stars, the rage began consuming him again. The thing inside him stirred alive and reveled in the emotion. Now, his memory once again focused, he remembered the woman. The man, too. Why they had made him so angry, and that anger was rapidly building again.

Shannon had been his girlfriend. Adam had been his best friend. And he had found them together, and in that very moment, his life had changed forever. And it still continued to change, even now.

He had left after finding them in the bed he had shared with her. He had simply walked out, leaving the two of them with looks of surprise and horror on their faces, and bedsheets pooled around them. But now, with his rage at full power, he was heading back. He was dying—he knew that now—and he'd probably be gone in a few hours. But before then, they would not get away with hurting him.

He'd make them both pay. And they'd hurt no one ever again.

* * *

Deep in Sam Tanner's cornfield, the alien waited. Around it, human men in strange white suits combed the field where it and its two mates had arrived, expanding out in ever-widening circles, collecting samples of the earth. They had erected an extensive structure at the place where the meteorite had finally come to rest, and several men stood inside to examine the samples as they were procured. The alien had read this in their thoughts, though its own thoughts were becoming increasingly muddled and hostile. It wanted to kill, as it had felt its companion do to the aged human earlier. Something made it angry. Something in this planet's atmosphere, perhaps? Some chemical combination incompatible with its own composition? It had never experienced rage, and therefore wanted to explore it further.

The men in the white suits would come closer and closer, and then it could have a host. Then it could kill again, and take another host, and then another if it needed to. Then it would seek its companions. The telepathic rapport they shared had recently been severed, but the last empathic sensation it had received was one of terror and pain. The humans had done something to one of its mates, killed it perhaps. That fueled the alien creature's own rage even more.

As the men in the strange white suits came slowly closer, the scarecrow's head turned ever so slightly, its black button eyes seeming to follow their movement. Inside the burlap head, the alien sat nestled amongst the dried straw, waiting for the moment to strike.

## AUTHOR NOTES - THE CORNFIELD BLUES

This story started life in the mid-1980s on a single-spaced page written with an old manual typewriter given to me by my other. Most of the first line of that story remains, with only the town name added in. Somehow that sheet of paper stayed with me all these years, and one day I took it out and started thinking about what might have happened after Sam Tanner discovered that meteorite. I'd never done an ET story up to that point, and having become a fan of the X-Files during the latter years of the show's run in the late 1990s, I wanted to do something in that vein. So I did. If there was a plan for that story back in those years of adolescence, I do not recall it now. Having crossed the half-century mark of my life, the persistence of memory is sometimes lacking.

I finished this story some years back, but found the ending dissatisfying. I dusted it off and gave it another pass, adding some more characterization and revising the ending a lot. It's a better story now, in my opinion.

For those who like horror films, you'll undoubtedly notice a bit of a nod to "The Lonesome Death of Jordy Verrill" from George Romero and Stephen King's 1982 film *Creepshow*.

# LOOSE ENDS

I wanted her dead.

But there was no way I could do it. I'm not clever enough to get away with murder, and even more so, I simply don't have the balls for it. That's why I asked Jonas Killian to do it for me. And he did, with remarkable precision and an absolute lack of remorse that still makes me shudder. Unfortunately, Jonas doesn't like leaving behind evidence of his work, and as I am learning quickly here, evidence = me.

But I'm getting ahead of myself. This is the end, and for you to understand it all, I need to go back six months ago to a horrible event that set this all in motion. Before that, even, I should define relationships, both between Stephanie and me, and between me and Jonas. When I met each of them, I had no idea how entwined the three of us would become.

* * *

Stephanie was a good-looking woman. Not supermodel gorgeous, but pretty enough that she got noticed. Caring in a kind of way that warms you inside, like a fireplace takes the chill off an early spring morning. She worked hard, and she took care of what needed taking care of, especially me. I'm not sure what she saw in me, honestly. I'm certainly no catch. Average looks. Average build. Thinning hair. But I loved her. And I believe she loved me–and I mean really loved me–but there are some unforgivable things that happen in life, and that's the sad damn truth. Sometimes, once you cross a line, you can never go back.

I met Steph at a writer's retreat in Puerto Rico three years ago. She is–was–a gifted high school English instructor with aspirations of creating children's books. I was there trying to get the muse back after a disappointing sixth-month span of producing the literary equivalent of cow manure. That problem would have been mine, and mine alone, had I not signed a three-book deal, including a healthy advance, and only produced the first two. I was stuck. I'd recently lost my mother to a long and nasty cancer and I sank into months long depression. That's normally a good thing for a writer, as there's a bit of catharsis in pouring your emotions into your work. But this time I'd backed myself into a corner I couldn't find my way out of. I was pretty small time back then. It was a major alignment of the stars I'd gotten a three-book deal with a reputable publisher in the first place, and here I was about to blow it. I had started drinking, and while a guy like Hemingway can write up a storm while loaded to the gills, I was no Hemingway. My writing was headed nowhere, and I was going with it.

Steph changed all that. I'm a genuinely clumsy oaf around women, and as soon as I'd taken notice of her, I knew I would make a fool of myself. It was the daily social hour at the retreat, where all the guests convene to have cocktails, talk about their work, and breathe in the salty sea air. I had already downed a couple of martinis and was trying to catch a waiter for another when I caught my foot on the leg of some ornately designed deck chair and took down the waiter, tray and all. Little umbrellas flew everywhere. By fate's hand, I righted myself at Steph's table, and she laughed. But she wasn't laughing at me. She laughed at the circumstance, and that pulled me in. I fumbled to introduce myself and then sat with her for the next hour. We quickly came to enjoy each other's company and began spending an appreciable amount of our spare time together.

When we weren't writing. The muse had only to look into Stephanie's soulful green eyes to find the impetus to resume work. Two days after meeting Stephanie, I was dropping between four and six thousand words a day into my word processor, and they were good words, by damn. When the week-long retreat ended, I had the first draft of a fresh story in the can. My editor was thrilled. And so was I, for more than one reason.

Steph lived in Boston, and my home address was in Michigan, but we promised to keep in touch. After a few phone calls that rang up an inordinate bill, we planned for me to fly out to see her over the Thanksgiving holiday. We made love for the first time that weekend, and while I can't speak for her, I think that was the point I knew I wanted to be with her forever. It's sad, really, how things ultimately turned out, because at that moment, lying in bed next to her, hearing the light flutter of her breathing as she slept, I was never happier.

We saw each other several times over the ensuing months, and each was more magnificent than the last. But the seeming ages in between were lonely. Then one afternoon she called me, and her mood seemed solemn. I asked her what was wrong, and she explained how tired she was of a long distance relationship, and wanted to know what I thought about the two of us living together. I had been pondering that question myself for the prior few weeks, wondering if it would be too assertive to me to suggest such a thing.

So we moved in together. Steph came to Michigan right after the school year ended. Honestly, I think I would have preferred moving to Boston, but she claimed she needed a change of scenery and was rather insistent on it. Trading the frothy coast of Massachusetts for the splendor of the Great Lakes appealed to her, she said. And that was that.

My apartment was too small, so we found a new place together, and that felt good. It was the closest I'd been to a woman in my life, outside of my mother, and while letting my guard down in due course turned out to be a mistake, at the time I was the cliched happiest man on Earth. Steph found a job teaching an advanced writing course at a private school, and I cranked out two books in less than a year without a hitch. Life was perfect. So we got married.

It was grand for a little while, with all the things that came with being a newlywed: Spontaneous sex, romantic dinners, cuddling on the couch watching TV, more spontaneous sex, etc. Steph had summers off, so right after the wedding we vacationed on Mackinac Island for six weeks, renting a nice room at a quaint and quiet bed-and-breakfast a decent walk from the tourist attractions. In between spending time with my bride, I cranked out nearly two hundred pages in a month, a personal best for me. The words fell out of me at an almost unbelievable pace. We came back home a couple weeks before school started, and Steph got back to work. I put the final hundred and fifty pages of my latest novel to bed before the first frost.

It seemed like nothing could go wrong. And things stayed pretty much that way for the next year, though Steph was busy with school and I was gearing up for my next novel. I left for a two-week book tour in October and Steph wasn't able to come because of school obligations. Shortly after I came back, I started discovering there was a side to Stephanie I hadn't been aware of.

It happened by accident. It was mid-November. We had gotten no snow yet, and it was unseasonably warm for that time of year. Steph was gone for the day, and I had taken a short but restful nap out on the deck, followed by work on the new story. The sun was bright, temperatures in the low seventies, with just a hint of a breeze. I had my sunglasses on and a pitcher of iced tea on the small table next to me.

Sometimes, for a change of pace, I'll forgo the word processor and write longhand on a big yellow legal pad, because it works a unique set of creative muscles. One thing I believe got lost with the onrush of modern technology is the gift of pace. I can type between 85 and 100 words per minute, and often what I type during that rush is crap, because I put down everything that comes into my head. The slowed pace of writing longhand forces me to think about the words as I put them down, and later rewrites are often much quicker. So, I was writing by hand on the deck, and I needed to do a quick bit of research, just some medical terminology for a hospital scene. My laptop was in the den, across the house, but I spied Steph's on the coffee table just inside the patio doors. With pad in hand, I came in and flipped up the laptop lid, waking her computer from its self-imposed sleep.

Her e-mail was open, the reading pane displaying the last e-mail she'd read, something about a faculty meeting next Tuesday in the subject line. I ran my finger across the touchpad to move the cursor to the upper right so I could minimize the e-mail program, but I can't stand using those touchpads, and my dexterity with them is extremely lacking. The cursor stopped on the mail list, and when I moved my finger back to make another upward stroke, it performed a click instead. The selected e-mail popped up to the center of the screen. I never meant to read the e-mail, but it happened. One of the basic faults of humanity is we're curious. Nosy, even.

It was a message from one of the other teachers, a fellow English instructor named Ronald Davenport. The subject line read "Last Weekend" and before I'd read a word of the e-mail's body, I had hairs standing on the back of my neck. I don't remember the full text of the e-mail now, as I read it in a blur of emotion, but the gist of it was that this teacher had enjoyed a torrid weekend of sexual debauchery with my wife while I was doing a ten-store book signing across the country.

I'd met Davenport before, at one of Steph's school-related soirees. He seemed a likable enough fellow, good-natured, humorous. He was also nearly twenty years her senior. It's often never the people you'd suspect.

If you've ever been on the receiving end of an unfaithful relationship, you can imagine my reaction. My heart felt like it would burst from my chest. The palms of my hands were wet. I felt sick to my stomach as a rush of emotions waved across me. I was hurt, mad, sad, and scared all at the same time. Even for a writer, it's a nearly indescribable feeling.

What do I do? I asked myself a hundred times. Anger told me to confront her, but my insecurity made me frightened she'd leave, and she was everything in the world to me. She was my focus, my inspiration. She was my muse, the thing that drove me to do the grand things I was doing. Without her, I was afraid I'd go back to being nothing. I was afraid I'd never be whole again. So, I composed myself and acted as though nothing had happened. I went around with a lump in my throat and a knot in my stomach for days.

And that's when I contacted Jonas. I could always count on Jonas to help me out of a jam, and I felt he could do the things I couldn't. He always had. I was a mess, and Jonas Killian specialized in cleaning up the particular mess that is me.

* * *

I met Jonas Killian in college, about a third of the way through my first semester. His past was a mystery he never offered to reveal. He hailed from Chicago, he once told me, but that was the extent of it. The writer in me caught the notion that maybe Jonas had left home under less than ideal circumstances. Either way, that didn't matter. What I knew then was Jonas was straightforward, self-confident, unwavering in his convictions, and rock solid in a crisis. He didn't mince words; he simply told you how it was and you accepted it. Nobody wants to admit it, but that kind of brutal honesty is what most people need, really. Me, I was Jonas' almost polar opposite: a bundle of nerves, too scared to say shit if I'd had a mouthful, as socially awkward as they came. College frightened me. No. It terrified me. I'd never been away from the comfort and security of home before, so Jonas took me in and helped me get through it all. Whenever I was in a jam, Jonas Killian would be there to support me. If there was one constant in my life during college, it was Jonas.

The day I met him, I had confined myself to the library, trying to concentrate on an upcoming test. My roommate Patrick, about to flunk out of college altogether, apparently didn't care that I wanted to pass, because our dorm room that night contained a blend of 90s grunge rock and low-grade pot smoke. I couldn't focus at the library either, and was about to give up when, out of nowhere, this tall, well-dressed guy pulled up a chair across from me and introduced himself. He was energetic, and at first annoying, as I made it clear I needed to study. Then he snatched the notes out of my hands and started quizzing me.

We sat there for almost two hours, and he never once seemed interested in being anywhere else. After I felt confident I would do well on the test, Jonas suggested we relax and get some food. It was the first time I'd felt at ease in weeks.

I aced the test with no issues. We'd done good. After that, we started hanging together all the time, and Jonas became my best and only friend.

Not long after meeting the man who would years later kill my wife, I found myself tagged by a fraternity. Why teenagers are so goddamned cruel is beyond me, but these guys saw my weakness and pounced. I was used to being picked on, and most of it I would just shrug off, but they crossed a line when they stripped me naked and dropped me blind-folded and handcuffed at the front door of a faculty fundraiser. When I got back to my dorm, Jonas was there. He sat with me while I cried and said nothing at all, only listened. He made me get dressed, helped wipe the mix of snot and tears off my face, and told me jokes to make me laugh. Then he took me to the frat house. I didn't want to go. I was ready to run away, drop out of school altogether, but Jonas—rock solid Jonas—he just smiled at me, zipped up my windbreaker and pulled me along, anyway. It was raining, I remember, when Jonas knocked on the frat house door. After he finished, I never had an issue with the frat again, and for the rest of my college career, whenever I saw a Theta Delta Chi jacket, the wearer called me "Sir" with a look of absolute respect. And maybe just a hint of fear.

Jonas hooked me up with girls in college. He had a way with women—with all people, really—that I never would. I was just too timid while he was self-assured, forthright, and a smooth talker. All the things I could never, and would never, be. So, when I lost my virginity, it was because of Jonas. When that girl broke my heart, Jonas stood beside me, dusted me off, and sent me after another one. I can't imagine what he'd say to these girls to get them to go out with me, but as a teenager with a perpetually turgid penis and the self-esteem of an ostrich, I didn't really care. Jonas was the best wing man ever.

Jonas kept me away from alcohol. He said drinking took away self-control, and without self-control, everything unraveled. I didn't argue, and we didn't drink. At parties, we'd sip Perrier while Jonas worked his magic words on the ladies. He took no women for himself that I'm aware of, at least not when we were together. He set them all up for me.

After college, I only saw Jonas a handful of times. He'd be in the area for something or other, and he'd call me up and tell me he had a sense I was down, and I almost always was. It's like Jonas could sense when something was wrong, and he'd always be there just when I needed someone to chat with. I wasn't much of a socialite, and my friend list on Facebook had half a dozen people on it, three of whom were fans of my writing, so there really wasn't anyone I could talk to. But Jonas was different. When I got stuck in the middle of writing my first novel, I called him and read it aloud to him. He offered me advice; that brutal honesty is a godsend to a writer, though sometimes hard to take. He'd tell me if something was utter shit and provide a suggestion. I valued his opinions on almost everything, and he helped carry me through. I dedicated my first book to him.

* * *

So, I called on Jonas when I found out my wife of less than a year was fucking a 59-year-old English teacher. It was hard to do, but if anyone could help me, it was Jonas Killian. We met at a restaurant, sat in the back where we remained unbothered, and I laid it all out on the table. Speaking it aloud made every word stab another tiny needle into my heart. Jonas remained quiet the entire time.

"So, what do you want to do about it?" He asked me afterward.

I didn't know. I was still a basket case of emotion. Jonas just sat across from me, silent, in his stoic way, but I saw the wheels turning in his head. Exactly what I'd hoped for.

"Well, let me offer up this: you will go on pretending you know nothing. Don't change any of your habits; don't stray from your normal routine at all. While your suburban life continues its current course, I'll do a little digging."

And he did. Jonas hacked Steph's computer, her personal and work e-mails, and gathered a lot of background information on her. I don't know how he did that, and I don't particularly want to. My computer skills begin and end with Microsoft Word. What I do know is that by the time he finished, he'd piled up a substantial dossier on my wife's illicit activities. There was a lot more of it than I'd imagined.

Turned out the reason Steph was so eager to move away from Boston was because she'd been sleeping with a student at the school where she taught and had gotten caught. The administration offered her the opportunity to save face and avoid a publicity scandal, provided she left her position there and agreed never to teach in the state of Massachusetts again.

So, had she really wanted to be with me, or was she just using me to get out of a nasty situation on the east coast? These are the kinds of things that eat at you when you find out you can no longer trust the woman you pledged your life to.

There was more, of course. For whatever reason, Steph and Ron Davenport began e-mailing each other several months before. It started out as simple, innocent flirting (if there is such a thing), but quickly escalated to more. Jonas had accessed chat logs where the two of them talked explicitly about their desires. And she spoke of doing things she'd never done with me. Most of these chats occurred while she was working on grading papers in the evenings, while I read a book three feet away from her or researched on a story. Davenport e-mailed often, offering to take her to sex shops, buy her sexy clothing, and take her to sleazy night clubs to show her off. And eventually they did all that. The date stamps on the e-mails coincided with a trip I'd taken to New York to meet with my agent and editor.

She would also meet him on occasional quick trips to the grocery store, where they'd engage in quick and dirty sex, with her returning home just before too much time had elapsed that'd I'd worry. And based on their chats about these trysts, all of it excited her profoundly.

"She's been playing you, buddy," Jonas said. "Looks like her entire life revolves around some very dysfunctional sexuality. She's got some major issues, for sure."

Hearing that crushed me. I could tolerate a lot of things, but infidelity created a line that, once crossed, would never uncross. I had been oblivious to it all, struck dumb by my blind faith in our love. I broke down again; my insecurities took a stranglehold on me. Not the first time Jonas had seen that happen, and throughout this final nightmare, it wouldn't be the last. But, as ever, he helped me through it.

Looking back, I understand he fueled my anger, sowed the seeds that grew in my vengeful heart. Hindsight, as they say, is always 20-20. I realize now Jonas had his own agenda all along.

"How you want to handle this?" he asked, but I'm certain he already knew what my answer would be.

I held my face in my hands and looked down at the table. After a long pause I said, without lifting my head, "Kill them. I want them both dead." The sound of my voice saying it aloud chilled me to my core.

"Are you sure?"

"Yes. Kill them."

And so he did.

* * *

Ron Davenport walked his Pomeranian, Josie, every night at 11:30. Apparently, the little rat's bowel movements were on a particular sched-ule, at almost the same time each night. Jonas watched him for a week, taking notice of any deviations in timing, and charting the actions of other nearby residents to decide when it was best to move. The weather forecast called for rain on the coming Thursday, beginning at 9:00pm and lasting through the night until nearly dawn. Rain would keep casual walkers inside and reduce the possibility of being seen.

Thursday night, like clockwork, Davenport came out with Josie, and they took the sidewalk east. The rain had come around 9:30, but only as a slight drizzle. Jonas and I waited two blocks away, near a burned out street lamp that was the fruit of Jonas' efforts earlier that day. As luck would have it, the dog stopped to drop a deuce less than fifteen feet from the shroud of darkness. Jonas emerged from the groomed shrubbery and black-bagged Davenport from behind with almost in-human speed. The dog barked twice and ran off toward home as Jonas delivered a quick, stunning blow to Davenport before he could cry out or react. Jonas' car sat at the curb less than 10 feet away, and he stuffed Davenport in the opened trunk without breaking stride. As we drove off into the drizzling midnight, Josie the Pomeranian stood at the entrance to Davenport's house, waiting to be let back in.

Jonas pulled the car onto a deserted side street and killed the lights. He reached into the back seat for a small black bag and pulled out a syringe. He grabbed the keys from the ignition and walked to the back of the car, unlocked the trunk, and we stared down at Ron Davenport as he shrank to the back of the sizable trunk. Jonas popped the cap off the syringe, and I gave him a concerned look.

"Pentobarbital," Jonas said. "Veterinarians use it to euthanize pets. But don't worry. Ronny's just gonna be zonked out for the ride." With a quick snap, Jonas stabbed the needle into Ron's leg and jammed down on the plunger. Before the barbiturate could even take effect, Jonas slammed the trunk shut, and we drove away.

A week earlier, Jonas had paid a month's rent on a small one-room cabin a couple hours drive north, and that's where we headed. Arriving shortly after 1:00am through a low hanging fog, we unloaded Davenport's flaccid form and carried him inside. The rain had stopped, but the grass was slick and the mossy sod bloated with rainwater. I slipped once, and Ron Davenport's head landed in the mud with a wet splat. Unintentional though it was, it made me smile just a little.

Once inside, I realized Jonas had been here during the past week, preparing. He had covered the floor with plastic sheeting, the kind painters used to keep paint splatter off surfaces. A single heavy wooden chair sat lonely in the center of the room. Jonas had moved all the other furniture to the far side of the cabin. The room was silent, save for the low hum of a small refrigerator.

We folded Ron's limp body into the chair and secured his hands and feet to the chair's arms and legs with zip ties. Jonas pulled over a small folding card table and set it a few feet away from Ron, then went back out to the car and returned with the black bag and a plastic sack with the logo of a Winkleman's Hardware emblazoned on the side. The tagline under the store logo on the bag read, "Making all your home improvement projects easy", and that seemed appropriate. At that moment, I felt this was definitely improving my home. Jonas set both bags on the card table and pulled a hammer out of the hardware sack.

Jonas left the black bag over Davenport's head.

"For psychological purposes, of course," he said when I asked about removing it. "Sensory deprivation can be quite terrifying."

Of that, I had no doubt.

* * *

Ron Davenport's big toe exploded with a meaty pop and sprayed blood like sparks from a firecracker. His anguished howl didn't bring pause to Jonas at all. The hammer rose again, and Jonas brought it down on the second toe. I watched Ron's face twist beneath the black bag as the most incredible pain he'd probably ever experienced snaked up from his partially mangled right foot through the length of his leg. And Jonas was only getting started.

"Please. Please stop," Ron pleaded. Sweat and tears soaked through the black bag. "I'll give you whatever you want. Just please stop."

"No can do, friend," Jonas said. "We've got eight little piggies to go, and I don't see any of them crying 'wee-wee-wee' all the way home."

By the fourth toe, Ron Davenport had passed out from the pain. It surprised me he lasted that long, honestly. I looked down and realized I had been standing too close while Jonas worked, and stringers of various stages of congealing blood and grisly pink and white bits of Ron's exploded foot flesh covered my shoes. My gorge was at the top of my throat. I also felt concern because I'd spent a hundred and fifty dollars on those shoes.

We waited for Davenport to come to, and then Jonas started in again. His remorseless torture of my wife's lover lasted for another hour. After the toes, Jonas cut off three of Davenport's fingers with pruning shears and cauterized the wounds with a handheld propane torch. He removed the bag from Ron's head and pulled a few teeth. The cracking and grinding sound as he wrenched with a set of brand new pliers, coupled with the gurgling screams from Ron's throat as the rushing blood gagged him, left me chilled. There was a moment of recognition as the old boy looked at me in desperation, and I felt some small pangs of regret.

But he deserved it. He was having sex with my wife. His lack of regard for the sanctity of my marriage and his manipulation of my wife's emotions were now costing him everything. That part I never lost sight of. Just thinking of him in bed with Steph made me see red. And just like that, any pity I'd had for him disappeared, wisp-like into the ether. I stared back with contempt.

Jonas finally ended Ron Davenport's pain with a .38 caliber bullet to the forehead. I remember taking a long look into his terrified eyes just before Jonas pulled the trigger. He couldn't speak. I imagine the pain had pretty much clouded his mind. But he knew it was me.

"You brought this on yourself," I said. Those were my only words.

When Jonas fired, Ron's head snapped back, then sank to his chest. And that was the end of Ron Davenport.

* * *

I can't go into detail about what Jonas did to Steph; it's all jumbled in my mind, and it pains me to think about it, anyway. It wasn't pretty, but at least it was quicker. I do remember that. We brought her to the cabin the next day in much the same manner we'd taken Ron Davenport. His body now sat propped in a far corner, a lifeless marionette in the shadows of a single room cottage in the woods. All I recall vividly is this: As Jonas prepared to end her life, Steph just stared past him right at me, her eyes pleading for a mercy I could no longer extend.

And to her very last breath, she denied ever having cheated on me.

* * *

After it was over, I felt weak, tired, and sick to my stomach. Jonas told me to lie down and sleep while he took care of the cleanup. I don't think I had any choice in the matter. I fell down on the military cot in the back of the room and was instantly out.

I dreamed of Jonas, Ron Davenport, Steph, and me. A whirlwind version of the past six months, images swirling around each other, though sometimes the faces weren't right. Jonas would be me, I would be Ron Davenport, Ron would be Jonas. The tortures were as gruesome in memory as in reality. By the end of it all, Jonas was the only one left standing, a grinning Cheshire Cat leering over a litter of bodies. Dozens of them. I woke up with a gasp as realization dawned.

Jonas wasn't done yet. There was still one loose end left, and it came into sharp focus. He'd been playing with me all along. Far longer than I'd imagined.

"Yeah, that's right," he said, startling me. He stood in the doorway, the hammer he'd used to savage Ron Davenport's toes gripped in his left hand, blood now dried on it. "I've been the puppeteer for a long time."

I tried to say something, anything, but words wouldn't come.

"You probably realize now it was all faked," Jonas said. "The e-mails, the chat logs, all of it. Your wife was as saintly as they get. She would no more cheat on you than you would on her. But your sniveling insecurity made it easy to convince you she was a repressed sexual deviant."

"Why? Why would you do that?" I finally found my voice.

"Because I wanted to be needed again. It's me who takes care of you, not her. I've been watching out for you longer than either of us cares to admit. Picking you up, wiping the snot off your nose, pushing you to be better than you are. But you only have time for me when you need something. Well, I've had enough of that. Now I need something, too."

"I don't understand," I said. But I was beginning to.

"I knew it would take a lot for you to call on me after all this time, so I had to make it something big, something that would hit you so hard you'd come running with your tail between your legs. I faked the e-mails with no problem, and then just pushed you to discover them."

"And Davenport?"

"Just drew his name out of a hat. Nothing gets a guy's ire burning like being upstaged in bed by someone a couple years away from retirement. Davenport never touched your wife, by the way. He tried. He's a pretty fucked up individual in his own right, so maybe you can take some solace in knowing the world's a better place without him. But yeah, he tried, and her devotion to you kicked him to the curb every time."

"How could you—?"

"Let's cut to the chase. I've done some terrible things here, of which you have all the details. And you will not be quiet, will you? As a wise man once said, a secret between two people is only truly a secret if one of them is dead."

Again, I was speechless. Something wasn't right. One minute he talked about being needed by me, the next he's talking about killing me. But the last pieces were coming to me, and suddenly I understood. All of it. And so did Jonas.

His expression was one I'd never seen before. The always calm, self-assured Jonas Killian demeanor turned to a look of abject fear.

I honestly don't remember what happened after that. I guess I blacked out again, and when I woke up, I was at home and Jonas was gone. The first rays of daylight were coming through the bedroom window, but they didn't warm me at all. Why I was still alive is anyone's guess, but I was completely unhurt.

But now I know. Jonas wants to put an end to me, to protect himself. Understandable, I suppose. The real problem is what I realized at that very last second, that singular moment that put the terror in his eyes. I know what he is now.

* * *

I am Jonas Killian. Jonas Killian is me. Two people of the same mind. My failure to handle the stresses of college, being alone and afraid for the first actual time in my life, combined to give birth to Jonas. I released him on the world because he could do the things I couldn't. He didn't take shit from Theta Delta Chi frat boys. He didn't withdraw from women. He didn't have difficulty with anything. Prior to college, I had a structured existence, neat and organized. Controlled. College presented a chaos I couldn't get my mind around and reign in. I was lost. So, Jonas boiled to the surface and fixed the things that needed fixing, improved my life, and protected me without regard to cost or consequence. He was methodical and calculating, always seeing three steps ahead of where we were. Just what I always needed.

* * *

He's gone right now. I don't know for how long, but he's left me in charge and himself vulnerable. It's the alcohol, I think. I've been drinking since I woke up, trying to wrap my head around this. I suspect that's why Jonas would never let me drink in college, because it dulled his influence, pushed him down inside. Trapped him. That's why he wasn't around after my mother passed, because I'd started drinking. Then I was happy with Steph, so there was no reason to let Jonas out. Jonas Killian was the fixer, but there was nothing to fix, and with nothing to fix, he got put away. So, in desperation, he somehow exerted a subliminal influence over me to fabricate a need for him, to create a crisis only Jonas Killian could fix. And Jonas showed up just in time to do what he invariably did. Fix things. Fix me.

But he's tired of being the last resort. He's demanding center stage, to be in control all the time, not locked away in a cage in the back of my consciousness.

That can't happen.

I've got the syringe full of Pentobarbital, filled with a lethal dose this time. And I realize taking Jonas Killian out of the equation means taking me out, too. Somehow I'm dead either way. I know that with fearful certainty. I can't fathom how he plans to do it, but Jonas doesn't mince words, as I stated earlier. He just tells you how it is and you accept it.

He said he was going to kill me, and I believe him.

## AUTHOR NOTES - LOOSE ENDS

This was a story that had been percolating in the back of my head for years. What person hasn't had even the slightest fear of his or her significant other being unfaithful? It's one weakness of man, one insecurity that sometimes grips even the strongest of people. How would you handle it? Obviously, I took the story past a line that most people don't cross, but the unfortunate reality is some people do. I originally intended for Stephanie's infidelity to be real, not fabricated, but thought it would have more impact if it came to light that his wife died for false reasons. Upon reading the story, my wife said that the link between Jonas and the main character didn't really surprise her, but I think that was just because she knows me so well. Hopefully, it came as a bit of a shock to everyone else.

This story took 2nd Place in a short story contest put on by a Facebook Stephen King Discussion group in 2019, judged by the masterfully talented Richard Chizmar. I am humbly honored to have my work recognized.

# I CAN'T DIE DEAD ENOUGH

Jacob Raney was a dead man, trapped in a body that would not die. And of all the things in the world he wanted to do, dying was top on the list. Now, it seemed he couldn't even achieve that.

Misty air saturated his clothing as Jacob huddled beneath the overhanging branches of a tree. His eyes, bloodshot and full of anger, stared across the street at the apartment complex, to the third apartment on the ground floor, the one just three days earlier he had shared with the woman he loved. Now, she was in there with someone else—some other man—and the time for retribution would be soon.

* * *

Three days before, Jacob had left Angie asleep in their bed, with a soft kiss planted on her forehead. He had felt good that morning. Things were going to be better, he had thought. As he left the apartment, he wiggled the doorknob to assure he had locked it. The air outside was crisp, even for a mid-April morning, but the sun would soon come up. It was going to be a good day. He could feel it. He drove to work that morning, singing softly along with the radio, hopeful that whatever troubles Angie was having would soon pass.

They had met four months before when she had started at the assembly plant where Jacob worked, and while she was a few years older, she had immediately taken an interest in him. It started out as quick conversations during breaks, but quickly turned into spending entire breaks, then lunches together. Still, Jacob was shy, and Angie had to nudge him in the right direction just to get him to ask her out on a proper date.

Once he did, however, things went hot and heavy. Their first date was a nice dinner out, then back to his place for a movie. Jacob had a roommate, but Larry was out of town for the weekend. She stayed the night. After that, it was a night at his place, or at Angie's brother's home, where she had been staying. After two months, Angie got a place of her own and invited Jacob to move in with her. He accepted without hesitation.

Jacob thought they were in love. They had even briefly discussed marriage in the future, a word Jacob had never talked about with any woman before. But Angie was special, and he felt so sure it was right. He thought it had felt right to her as well. And at first, things went well, but the honeymoon, as people like to call that early relationship phase, seemed to be over soon after.

In the last two weeks, she had changed. She had grown distant without warning, as if she was having second thoughts, and Jacob had noticed the changes when her affections toward him receded.

He had tried to talk to her, but she simply responded that she didn't want to discuss it. Jacob kept pressing, attempting to get through to her, but she only became increasingly stubborn. Jacob unraveled. Thoughts he wouldn't have entertained weeks before clawed at the back of his mind like a starving animal tearing at raw meat. Was there someone else? And if so, why? Did she not love him anymore? As long as she kept it to herself, that animal continued to tear away at him.

Still, he attempted to keep a positive attitude. When she sorted out whatever was bothering her, she would be back to her old self, he had thought. She would again be the woman he had fallen in love with, the one who returned his love deeply and passionately.

Then, three days ago, the world came crashing down on Jacob. It came crashing down hard. And it broke him.

When Jacob unlocked the apartment door, he saw the notebook on the stand by the door. He instantly recognized her handwriting, and his name was at the top with several paragraphs underneath. He knew those words could not be good. His stomach clenched in a knot, and he wanted to throw up.

His hands were sweaty and trembling as he read the note the first time, then he not so much sat as dropped into the chair by the stand. He read the letter again, tears welling in the corners of his wide-open eyes as the words from the woman he loved came off the page and tore into his heart.

Jacob,

I know that I've been a total bitch lately, and I'm sorry. But there have been a lot of things on my mind that I've been trying to figure out. Well, I'm pretty sure that I've done that. I'm going to try to explain it all to you.

For the past year or more, I've been trying to get my life in order. I've been moving around, always to stay with friends and family, finding new jobs, starting over. Now that I finally have a place of my own to call home, I need some time to be alone, to get to know myself again. I still care about you, and none of this is because of anything you've said or done. It's me, totally. I just need the time and space alone to get my life back on track.

When we talked about getting married, I thought it was what I really wanted. Maybe I will want that someday, but not right now. I guess that I've still got a lot of doubts and insecurities that I need to work out yet. But I can't do that with you here. So, what I'm trying to tell you is that I want you to move out. I still want to see you, but I want to do other things, too. I'm backing this relationship off to a slow, very slow crawl. For now. I'm also telling you that if someone else should come along and ask me out, I want the opportunity to say yes or no. I want to see other people, and I want you to do the same. Please try to understand. I think you knew this was coming, eventually. I hope you believe that I in no way intended on hurting you. I never would do that intentionally. But, right now, I'm just not happy with my life and it's making both of us very miserable. So that misery stops now, today.

I'm sorry, Jacob. Please try to understand.
Angie

He didn't remember how long he had sat there before he picked himself up. He tore the page from the notebook, folded it, and tucked it into his coat pocket. As he gathered his things, he kept wondering where he'd gone wrong. How could she do this? He loved her with all his heart, and she was just throwing it all away without even trying. What had made her change like this?

Like a zombie, he shuffled around the apartment, gathering his things into a box he had gotten from the closet. As he did, his mind returned to all the things he had shared with Angie, all the things she no longer seemed to care for.

It didn't take him half an hour to gather all his things together. He hadn't brought everything of his out of storage when they had moved in, and after she had gotten distant, he had a feeling in the back of his mind he needn't bother with anything else until this mess had gotten straightened out. Now, her piece said—or rather written—he knew the answer. The fact alone that she couldn't tell him her feelings to his face was excruciating. She had to leave him a letter. Just words on paper. He couldn't believe them. Did she really still care? If he had seen her cry when telling him she wanted him to leave, he may have believed it. But this, a scrap of paper with its hollow words, that was cowardice. He sat his box down in the middle of the living room and read the letter again. The tears came again, too. Finally, he loaded the box into his truck and looked back one last time as he drove from the parking lot.

* * *

Now, he stood within a stand of trees, with the sky unleashing a sudden downpour of rain. He looked across to that same parking lot, this time the feeling in his heart not of love, but of betrayal. She had lied to him. All the words on the page had been lies. She didn't want to see him again; he was sure of that. He had come back the same night he had left, hoping to talk to her. After her training period at the assembly plant, they put her on second shift, which ended at midnight, and she would be home soon after that. He had waited until nearly one in the morning before leaving, with a nagging feeling of suspicion building in him. Several blocks away, the feeling came to him again. He parked the car and returned on foot, hiding in the trees where he was now standing. After 2:00am, a vehicle pulled into her parking space, idled for several long moments, then Angie had gotten out of the passenger side. It wasn't Jodi, her co-worker, who had brought her home, but someone else. The vehicle pulled out and its headlights swung into the trees where Jacob had crouched. He flattened to the ground until the vehicle had left. No, it hadn't been Jodi, and he hadn't the slightest clue who.

But it didn't matter. He would know soon enough, because now, that same vehicle was back, parked in her space, and the person who owned it was inside with the woman he loved. Or had loved. His emotions were such a tangled mess, he wasn't sure what he felt anymore.

The rain came down harder, soaking his shirt as he looked on. He noticed the shade drawn across the picture window in front of the apartment, as it always was, but he didn't need to see to know what was going on. He could feel it, someone else's hands on her, someone else's lips touching hers. All he wanted was for it to be over.

But that was impossible now. He'd tried. Barely three hours before, he'd tried to end the pain. But, in some cruel jest of fate, he had failed. The only recourse he could think of was to end her life.

He started across the street and into the parking lot. He knew what he was going to find, but it was too late for anything save ending that gnawing pain. His steps quickened into a run as he neared the apartment. Even through the rain, he could faintly hear the radio playing in her bedroom as he leapt.

The picture window shattered inward, the shade tearing as shards of glass and Jacob's body forced their way into the living room. He cleared the couch under the window, landed on the coffee table, and spilled off onto the floor. As he stood up, he could hear shouting from the bedroom. One voice belonged to a man.

She appeared first, wrapping her robe around her. The man appeared behind her, wearing only his jeans, the belt unbuckled. Jacob recognized him as Brian Stenson, Angie's shift leader from work.

"Jacob? What the hell?" Angie shouted. "What are you doing?"

"Angie, what's he doing here?" Brian asked, stepping in front of her. Jacob smiled at him, rainwater dripping from his face. Behind him, the wind blowing through the broken window frame twisted the remains of the shade and banged it against the wall.

Angie ignored Brian and stepped towards Jacob. "What do you want?"

"I want the pain to end," Jacob whispered. His eyes met hers and she saw a mixture of pain, sadness, and something sinister boiling in them. "I can't take it anymore."

"You need to leave," Angie said. Her voice was stern, angry. She planted her feet and pointed at the door. "Now!"

"I can't. Not until it's over." Jacob looked at Brian, who stepped up to Angie's side. "What is this, Angie? Did I mean that little to you?"

"Jacob, just go!" Angie was yelling now. Outside, thunder cracked, followed by a long, low rumble. "Just let it go!"

"Yeah," Brian said. He was in front of Angie again, hand out in front of him, just inches from Jacob. "You need to leave."

Jacob laughed. "Not until it's finished," he said, pulling the hunting knife from the sheath on his belt. A new flash of lightning reflected off the blade.

"Whoa, there..." Brian said, stepping back.

"I have to kill her, you know. It's the only way."

"No, Jacob," Angie said. She was crying now, her initial anger turned to rising fear. "Please."

"I've got no other choice, Ang," Jacob said. Tears and rain mixed on his face.

"I'll get you some help. Please, let me help you. I know this must be hard, but you've got to let it go. Please, Jacob." She was sobbing now.

"No," Jacob said calmly. Thunder boomed outside again. "There is no help. Only death. And even that's been taken from me." His grip on the knife tightened. His eyes were wild.

"W-what do you mean?" Angie asked. Tears continued to run down her face.

In answer, Jacob turned the knife blade around and thrust it into his own stomach. Angie and Brian stumbled backwards, their eyes wide with terror as Jacob pulled the knife upward to his ribcage, cutting a deep gash in his abdomen. He doubled over and dropped to the floor.

"Oh my God," Brian said, visibly scared.

Angie was in hysterics as she watched Jacob slump to the floor. Despite her fear of him, despite the urge to run from the room, she also wanted to run to him, help him if she could. Before her mind could decide, Jacob rose, tearing open the remains of his shirt. As he stood, both Angie and Brian noticed with horror the flesh of Jacob's stomach was sewing itself back together, as though the wound was running in reverse. Blood stopped pouring from the opening as the flesh knitted itself in criss-cross patterns. A section of Jacob's exposed intestine pinched off as the wound sealed closed.

"See?" Jacob sobbed. "I can't die. I can't even kill myself to stop the pain. I tried, Angie. Oh, Lord, I tried."

* * *

The shotgun had been his grandfather's single shot Remington, given to Jacob on his twelfth birthday. He kept the gun clean and in good working order, and had only fired it twice. Four hours before, Jacob went to the storage shed he rented for his things and found the weapon fitted into its case. He took it several miles away, to a desolate area he once called his playground, a forty-acre woodland his parents owned during his childhood. It was here Jacob planned to end his life and take the pain along with it.

He sat on the ground against a tree. Above him, in the thick bark of the tree's trunk, he had carved JACOB LOVES ANGIE in a corny, clichéd act of new passion when he brought her there several weeks ago.

This was his most beloved spot, and he wanted to share it with her. It seemed the best place to express his love to her, and now it was the most fitting for him to end it.

He loaded the shotgun—one twelve gauge slug into the pipe—and clacked the stock closed. He rerouted the gun and placed the barrel beneath his chin. His fingers shook as he reached for the trigger. There was no turning back. The pain had to end. He had to be done with her. This was the only way. The only way.

"I love you, Angie." his last words came, choked with tears, and the trigger fell. There was an instantaneous, blinding stab of agony as the slug obliterated his jaw and most of his face, then a shimmering flash of comforting light, then nothing. The blast echoed into the distance, but Jacob never heard it.

Forty-five minutes later, Jacob's eyes fluttered open. He felt a clouded buzzing sensation in his skull, like a hive of bees were loose in there. He thought he had missed his head, and the shock of the blast knocked him unconscious. He lifted himself up onto his elbows, and he knew that was not true. His shredded shirt was covered with partially dried blood. Behind him, parts of his own greasy brain matter and chunks of his face, flesh, and skull were embedded in the tree trunk and scattered for several yards beyond that.

His aim had been perfect. But somehow, he survived. Even more impossibly, he was fine. His blood-stained hands came up to his face, knowing only the end of his brain stem and bits of mangled flesh should have been sticking up from his shoulders, but finding his face, smooth and soft—eyes, ears, nose, mouth—intact. Everything there. Yet, all gone, too. The shotgun had done its job, but something was wrong.

He could not die. All he had left was death, and even she turned him away.

* * *

"I can't die," Jacob repeated. He was crying himself now. "I want to die, and I can't even do that right." He looked into Angie's eyes, saw the terror there, realizing nothing was bringing her back to him now. He was an abomination, teetering on madness. "But you, you can die. You can be cut and not heal."

Despite her fear, Angie still wanted to reach Jacob. "How did this happen to you?

"I—I don't know," Jacob said, his addled mind faltering for an explanation. That only increased his fury. "But I have to end this, Angie."

"You need to calm down," Brian said, tensing.

"Shut up!" Jacob drew back the blade. "Don't get near me!"

Brian brought his right arm in a sweeping motion, grabbed Jacob's arm at the wrist, and twisted the knife away. Jacob let the blade fall to the floor and used his free hand to grab Brian by the neck.

"This is not your problem, Brian," Jacob breathed through clenched teeth. He wrenched his other arm free and settled his fist on Brian's nose, sending Brian backward into a chair..

"You're crazy!" Brian scrambled back to his feet and grabbed the dropped knife. "I'll kill you myself if I have to!"

"Okay, take your best shot," Jacob responded, relaxing. His arms fell to his sides, and a smile crossed his features. He was becoming more insane by the moment. He tilted his head and stretched his neck out, motioning for Brian to advance.

Brian lunged forward, bringing the knife around with a wide swipe. The blade slashed across Jacob's exposed throat, penetrating deeply into the soft flesh there. Blood came out in an initial spray, then began running down his chest. His head fell forward, no longer supported, and he stumbled to his knees, issuing a gurgling laugh as blood poured into his throat.

Angie let out a hysterical cry, and Brian turned his attention away. Her hands were covering her face, and he could tell she was crying. He turned back to Jacob, who was still laughing, spraying blood from his mouth, then back to Angie.

"It's gonna be okay, babe," Brian said, his grip on the knife tightening. "I've got him." He moved across the room, bringing the knife above his head. As his arm descended, Jacob's head snapped up and his crazed eyes caught Brian's just before the knife blade sank between them, cleaving the bone and sinking deep into his forehead. Jacob uttered a low grunt and fell backward. His body convulsed for a few moments, then was still.

"Holy Christ," Brian breathed and stumbled backwards, almost falling over the broken coffee table. His heart was beating hard in his chest, and he felt cold as he turned back to Angie. She was gone.

Brian found her in the bathroom, huddled on the floor by the sink, her knees drawn to her chest, hair falling over her face. Brian moved next to her, and she flinched. He pulled her into his arms and she grabbed hold, sobbing into his chest.

"Is he gone?" She said weakly, her head still hidden.

"Yeah, baby. It's all over." He drew her tighter and kissed the top of her head. Then there was shuffling behind him.

"Lets—try that—again." Jacob's words came low, guttural, and full of breath as Brian whirled to see him filling up the doorway. Angie shrieked, pulled back from Brian, and cowered further away.

Still embedded in his face, the knife sat directly between Jacob's eyes, eyes now filled only with madness. Flesh and bone had healed around the blade, leaving the handle a misshapen horn protruding from his face.

Brian stood, leaving Angie curled up within herself again, and charged at Jacob. "What does it take to kill you?" he shouted. Jacob was faster, and using Brian's own momentum, he hurled Brians's body out into the hallway, slamming him headfirst into the wall. He was on Brian and hauled him to his feet before he could regain his footing.

"I think we need to reach an understanding, you and I," Jacob breathed, holding Brian against the wall by his neck. "You can't kill me. I'm beyond death now." Jacob brought his other hand up and stroked it through Brian's tousled hair. "Life used to be so innocent and precious? But I'm beyond that, too. And now, so are you."

Jacob's hands turned, followed by a sharp snapping of bone as Brian's neck twisted past its threshold. Jacob released Brian, and his body slid to the floor.

"I envy you," Jacob said.. "You die so easily."

Jacob heard a soft sob from behind him. Angie was still on the bathroom floor, holding her knees. He filled the doorway again, and his hand came to his face. He tugged at the blade between his eyes, finally wrenching it free with a grinding, sucking sound. Jacob's face wrinkled in pain, and fresh blood oozed out and down his face. By the time he took the three steps between them, the gaping hole was closing.

"I'm sorry, Angie," he said, leaning over to her, extending his hand. He pulled the hair away from her face and tilted her head up to his. Their eyes met, and he saw all the fear and pain and revulsion in hers.

"Go ahead," she said through more tears. "Do it if you have to."

He tore his gaze away, turning from her. "I can't," he whispered. "I wanted to kill you, to take the pain away. But I can't. I love you too much, Angie. Even now."

She didn't see him go, but felt his presence gone. When she dared lift her head, however later that was, she was alone.

* * *

The next day, an unidentified man ran in front of an oncoming eighteen-wheeler on northbound Interstate 75 near Gaylord, Michigan. The body was unrecognizable, and six hours later, came up missing from the morgue.

A day later, a man leapt from the center of the Mackinac Bridge and plummeted to the frigid waters of Lake Huron. Authorities never recovered a body. Several hours later, the man dragged himself to shore on Mackinac Island.

Sometimes, unfortunately, life goes on.

## AUTHOR NOTES - I CAN'T DIE DEAD ENOUGH

This story was originally one of the epilogue shorts for an unpublished novel. I started in 1993 and finished the first draft in 1994. The letter from Angie to Jacob was heavily based on a letter I received from a woman I had been dating during that period. Catharsis? Most certainly. All of that anger and frustration came out on the page. At the heart of this story is a cruel jest of fate: A man who wants so badly to die finds himself unable to do so. What would go through your mind? I think it would drive you batshit insane, and that's why I took this story to the extreme.

I don't remember the original story name, but heavy metal band Megadeth released a song called "Die Dead Enough" on their 2004 album *The System Has Failed*, and I liked it well enough to borrow and tweak the name because it seemed fitting for the subject of this story.

# GENERATION HYDE

My name is Willard Fredericks, and, God willing, I shall celebrate my hundredth year on this Earth in September. I am not in good health, though one might say nearing the century mark while still being functional is good health. However, death does not worry me, as I have lived a long and storied life. Born in England in 1920, I immigrated to the United States with my parents when I was but a child of seven.

New York City was a majestic marvel to behold back in the early decades of the 20th century. Buildings of intricate architecture reached forever into the sky, streets flowing with people of all shapes, sizes, colors, and creeds. It was a spectacle I cannot put in words and will probably never experience with that same awestruck wonder as I did that first time.

I love the city. It is a living thing, with so much good flowing within its corridor-like streets, despite what you often see on the evening news. Even today, as prevalent uncertainty for the future spreads like disease, I believe people will favor one another, given the choice.

However, we are all driven by our vices from time to time, aren't we? Sometimes we do terrible things simply because we covet something. Avarice is, in my opinion, the worst of the seven deadly sins. It turns us into monsters.

And I am no exception.

* * *

My father, Percival Fredericks, a lawyer of excellent reputation, continued his practice upon our arrival in New York in the latter months of 1927. Father was also an expert on the history of English law, and possessed numerous texts and documents from decades past. Once we had settled in the city, Dad bought a four-story building in Brooklyn, an entire floor becoming his law offices, where he prospered as an attorney. The second floor was our home, and Father took little time in setting up his private library. It was a sight to behold, those shelves of aging texts, spines worn by multiple readings, and framed parchments adorning the walls, preserved behind pressed glass. On occasion, when Father threw social gatherings, he was forever engaging guests in lengthy conversations about the library's artifacts.

Father rented out the other two floors of the building and the income from those, coupled with Father's proclivity for finding justice, left our family not necessarily wealthy, but considered upper class for the time.

My mother, Millicent Fredericks, nee Walters, was the glue that held our family together. In current times, the stay-at-home mother is an enigma, a relic of the past, but without my mother, I believe my father would have died young. As it was, he passed in 1955 at sixty-four from a heart attack. Father was a workaholic before a term existed for it. That's not to say he neglected his family. Father was good to us, and I have the fondest memories of my childhood. Mother, God rest her soul, would have said the same. She died two years after Father passed, likely of a broken heart.

* * *

I turned eighteen in 1938 and enlisted in the Army in 1940. When the United States entered World War II, I found myself in Europe, defending the planet from a tyrannical dictator. I saw many horrors there, and committed acts myself that I would not consider morally or ethically sound. But war makes or breaks you, molds you into the person it needs you to be in that moment. I survived, though the scars I still carry with me to this day are not on the outside.

When I came home in late 1945, Father tried to nudge me toward law, to study and become his apprentice. But my proclivities were not in the chambers of the court. I was good with my hands, had a knack for woodworking, and soon after coming back to the states, began working for a furniture maker. It was satisfying work, and both Mother and Father were proud. When Father passed in 1955, Mother encouraged me to use my father's office space to open my own furniture business, and so I did. Everything was handmade, and my craftsmanship garnered favorable review. Like my father before me, I had an excellent reputation in my profession.

After Mother passed in 1957, I suffered a long bout of depression. My work suffered, and I lost much of the foothold I had gained in the furniture industry. I drank, not too excessively, thank the maker, but it was enough to impede any forward progress in my life for a time.

It was 1960 when I spent time in my father's study, going through the various tomes he had collected. I was nearing forty years old, and I felt an aimlessness in my core. I wanted more. My parents should be alive. I wanted to regain my success. I wanted a family of my own. But I had spent the better part of my earlier years obsessing over work, to the detriment of my own social life. I had dated, but the prospects for marriage left me wanting. I suppose I desired someone like my mother, as most young men do, but Millicent Fredericks sat head and shoulders above anyone I had ever met.

I lusted, most certainly. Any man who chooses bachelorhood over marriage does, I suppose. And I coveted many a woman, but never acted on those desires. Despite my depression and my longing for a better life, I never gave into my base urges.

* * *

That's when I discovered the private notes and journals of Dr. Henry Jekyll, a noted London scientist in the late 19th century. Also among the papers my father had collected were case notes from a lawyer named Gabriel John Utterson, a close, loyal friend of Jekyll, and a name my father had spoken of with much respect. Utterson may well have been the influence my father took to become a lawyer himself.

I sat in my father's study for most of the entire night, behind his massive slab of a desk and under the reading lamp he had always used, and as I perused the stacks of papers, a surreal and horrifying tale unfolded through the interwoven notes of both men.

Dr. Jekyll struggled with his own duality, often suppressing urges that were unheard of from a man of his stature. After years of experimentation without success, Jekyll derived a solution that he hoped would separate this hidden evil from his personality, but Jekyll transformed into the cruel, remorseless Edward Hyde instead. His exceedingly violent nature brought Hyde to the attention of Utterson, and eventually Scotland Yard's Inspector Newcomen, after the murder of Sir Danvers Carew, a noted member of Parliament.

Jekyll's journals painted a portrait of a man who was under the supreme conflict of his own mind. And he lost.

At first, I thought nothing much of it all. But over time, I became enamored with the possibilities. So, despite knowing what the outcome had been for the poor soul of Dr. Henry Jekyll, despite reading of the barbaric exploits of Edward Hyde, I experimented.

It took several weeks, but eventually I was certain I had recreated the formula Jekyll had used. The ingredients had been difficult, but not impossible, to obtain. Decades before the Internet made finding anything easy, I had to track down the specific items I needed the old-fashioned way.

So it was, on the night of August 8th, 1960, that I first ingested the potion, standing naked in the secondary washroom I had converted into a makeshift laboratory. The taste was bitter on my lips, and its warmth spread like a fire inside me.

* * *

The details of what happened next are almost clear, but my memory sometimes appears to me as though viewing it through a thin sheet of gauze. However, I recall vividly that first transformation, the painful sensation deep within as my body twisted into something foul, something outwardly matching the intenseness of the altered mind within.

I felt like a passenger within my consciousness, unable to influence the person—the thing—now taking control.

But the first feeling was exhilarating. I won't deny that. The sudden freedom of remorse, the unrestrained lust of the heart and mind left me feeling more powerful than I had ever been. Even standing behind a heavy gun, raining fire upon the Germans in the great war, paled compared to this feeling that washed over me like a massive tide. I was slipping away as he grew more powerful, more intense.

He dressed then, this bestial man, putting on one of my best suits with twisted, long-fingered hands. His almost Neanderthal face stared back at me from the mirror with a gruesome smile while he buttoned the shirt. Then he lumbered out into the warm late summer night, where a breeze carried the myriad sounds and smells of the city to everyone.

* * *

I awoke the next morning to a heavy knocking at my door. I found myself in my bed, my clothes still on but disheveled, smelling of alcohol and something sweet, my mind fuzzy and throbbing, as though recovering from a drunken stupor.

I opened the door to a police officer, Officer Patterson, to be exact. I knew him from the neighborhood. Remember, this was a time when a police officer would walk the streets and stop to talk to most everyone he saw. Patterson was a surly looking man in his mid-thirties, face grizzled and hardened by what I could only assume were years of pounding the beat. But he was generally pleasant, nonetheless.

Today, however, he looked and sounded serious. Through the haze that was still working itself off my mind, I recall Officer Patterson asking if I was okay. I assured him I was, that I had drank a few too many cocktails the night before, and then he explained why he was there.

In the early hours of the morning, a woman had been assaulted, raped, and beaten, just blocks from my loft. Witnesses saw a thin, slightly hunched man, likely in his early forties, with scraggly hair and a pronounced limp, near the scene. He was wanted for questioning. The woman was in the hospital, and she had explained that this man had approached her on the street, and when she had resisted his advances, he dragged her into a nearby alleyway.

I told Officer Patterson that I had not seen this man of whom he spoke, and he asked that I alert the authorities if, by chance, I did in the future. I assured him I most definitely would.

After Patterson left, I sat down and put my face in my hands. The throbbing in my head was slowly going away, but my heart was now beating at an accelerated pace.

What had I done? Why had I unleashed this monster on the city I loved? I had to have known that a man, unfettered by conscience, devoid of remorse, would commit acts of unspeakable violence. But I had let him out, anyway.

The police never found the man who assaulted the woman, of course. Had there been comprehensive DNA testing as there is today, I believe he still would have remained unknown. He didn't exist, this Hyde to my Jekyll, unless I let him.

But I *had* let him.

That said more about me than it did the beast I had set loose on the world.

* * *

I had dreams after that, or perhaps memories, coming to me from the part of my brain where the beast lived. Where the beast waited.

In these dreams, I remember assaulting the woman, hitting her repeatedly, slapping her with the front and back of my twisted hand. I remember the feeling, the sheer joy of the act, and reveled in my superiority. I remember tearing at her clothes, feeling her soft flesh in my hands, and thrusting myself against her. I recall smiling at her screams. And I remember the final blow that left her unconscious.

I remember shambling down the streets, pausing once to look in the glass of a storefront. The face that stared back was a grotesquerie, a misshapen monster in fine dress. But a monster, nonetheless.

I would wake from these dreams soaked in sweat, my breath coming in ragged, stealing gasps. I would lie awake after those dreams, wondering what kind of man I was that would unleash such a creature on the world.

I have damned myself every day afterward.

* * *

I never got rid of the formula, for whatever reason. I should have torn the papers to shreds, burned them to ash, and been done with it. But, something this powerful, I dare to say, it wouldn't let me. Even decades later, Jekyll's work still held sway over me. That feeling of power, the freedom it gave me, made me understand the alcoholic. He may not drink, but he is forever an alcoholic. And all it takes is one drink to bring it all crashing down.

I have resisted that urge for the last sixty years, but sometimes, in the early hours of the morning, I can feel the beast inside, clawing for release. I believe that bestial personality exists in all of us, and for most, we can hold it in check. But Dr. Henry Jekyll devised a way to bring that beast to the fore, to give him control, and once having had that control, the beast never quite goes away. It is always there, always trying to find a way out again.

* * *

A week ago, three teenagers broke into the building my father bought for cash in 1927. They took many valuables, many things that had been with my family since we had come across the ocean to stake a claim in the United States. But most importantly, and most horribly, they found and took Dr. Jekyll's formula.

Ten years ago, I had security cameras installed in the building, partly to appease the tenants, but mostly to keep watch over my legacy. Those cameras were sharp, focused, and caught the faces of those three boys with crystal clarity as they rummaged through my father's old office.

With nearly one hundred years on this planet, I've cultivated many wonderful, and some very useful, relationships. One of those relationships that fits both wonderful and useful is with Alastair McCrae, a police detective, fifty-five years of age, and one of the smartest gentleman

I've ever had the pleasure of acquainting myself. Alastair took the camera images and applied some diligent detective work. A day later, he came back to me with three names: Connor Reeves, Davin Fisher, and Jason Stanley, all recent high school graduates. Following procedure, McCrae had officers attempt to bring the three young men in for questioning, but they were nowhere to be found. Their parents hadn't seen them since before the night of the robbery. That, I determined, did not bode well. While I had given a detailed listing of the things they had taken, I omitted the formula. That would draw more attention to myself than I'd care for, and I'm unsure how I would explain having it in my possession, anyway.

Four days ago, I saw the first newspaper article. Five gruesome deaths, mutilations according to the reporter, in a homeless district near to my building. I knew then what had happened, especially after the descriptions of the killers given by eyewitnesses. Three monstrous, brutish men attacked with no provocation. Those three boys had done the unthinkable, the unfathomable. Just as I had done those many years before.

I understood.

The lust for power, it is a terrible, vicious thing. Once unleashed, it cannot always be restrained, reeled in, and contained again. At least not fully. It leaves behind vestigial tendrils, deeply rooted into the psyche, corrupting, and influencing, even after decades pass. Only the strongest of wills can resist it. I have done my best, and it has become easier as I have aged, but it is never far from my mind.

Imagine then, this terrible id-driven thing, in possession of three teenagers, who themselves are id-driven things. And what if they were to share it with even more like themselves? What if there were hundreds just like them, roaming the streets, driven only by their baser instincts?

Imagine it.

Imagine it and beware.

God help us all.

## AUTHOR NOTES - GENERATION HYDE

*The Strange Case of Dr. Jekyll and Mr. Hyde* has always been one of my favorite stories, and in 2012, I started writing bits and pieces of what I thought would be an interesting modern day take on the classic. Then I molded those notes, asking: what would happen if someone recreated Dr. Jekyll's formula today? That idea stayed dormant for eight years, until I literally woke up on April 4th, 2020, with the elements necessary to tie everything together. It took me just a few hours over two days to write the first draft. It's one of my favorite stories in this volume.

# MONSTERS

I'm fairly certain I'm going to die today. And I suppose that's why I'm writing this down, not as a memoir about my life to publish someday and make big bank, or a juicy revealing tell-all for the tabloids, but because people need to know what's out there waiting for them. Their lives may well depend on it.

My name is Jeremy Cochran, and I'm a paranormal investigator. It's not a glamorous profession by any stretch of the imagination. You spend most of your time skulking in the shadows, staying out of the spotlight, trying to be as inconspicuous as possible. It's not like the stuff you see on the sensationalized TV shows. The pay's not really that steady; there's no vision or dental, and certainly no 401k plan. Making it to retirement age is unlikely.

Fortunately for me, my father was successful in the real estate game, and as his only living relative (mom died in a car accident when I was six, and I have no siblings), I came into a sizable trust fund when I turned eighteen. With some wise investments, I've milked the teat of that cash cow out for the last several years. It helps to have no immediate family of my own.

The investigator's life is lonely. I specialize in paranormal superhumans, people who have extraordinary powers. It's an obsession—it's safe to call it that at this point—dating back to when I was ten years old and to a third-grade classmate named Thad Matthews.

Thad was a telekinetic.

I know this, because I'm pretty sure the first time he ever used his power, it was on me.

* * *

I can admit it now: I was a bully. I had to repeat the 3rd grade, so I was the oldest kid in the class, and I carried a large chip on my shoulder since I knew the other kids thought I was stupid for being held back.

I remember paying particular attention to Thad. Maybe because I usually sat behind him on the school bus. Or maybe it was prophecy, if you believe in that fate and destiny stuff. Whatever the reason, I've certainly paid a lot more attention to Thad since the 3rd grade.

The incident that started me on this often self-destructive path happened almost twenty years ago, and I'll take only part of the blame for it. I'm not sure what gave Thad and his friend Cory Roberts the balls to do it, but they put a dead mouse in my desk at school, and I freaked out, plain and simple. Not a single kid in the class would rat out Thad for what he did, though. They all hated me. But I knew it was him. Sometimes you just know things.

My wounded pride wouldn't allow him to get away with it, so I cornered him on the playground at recess, in an area where the yard guards wouldn't see us right away. I was so angry and humiliated. I pushed him down, pounced on him, and started hitting him over and over.

Then I felt something like hands pushing me away from Thad. I was so tunnel-visioned about beating him, blinded by my hurt and rage, that I didn't realize it wasn't his hands pushing me away.

I was ten feet in the air above him, screaming, looking down at Thad as he wiped the tears and blood and snot off his face. I was just floating there, and it scared me witless. Then Thad started running away, and I dropped to the ground like a wet bale of hay. It knocked the wind out of me, but I remember watching Thad through watery eyes as he ran across the schoolyard with one of the guards right after him. The guard got hold of Thad by the coat, but then I heard Thad scream, and the guard just flew backward across the yard and landed by the swing sets. He had to have gone twenty feet or more.

Thad kept running, but the school surrounded the back half of the yard with a ten-foot high fence to keep kids from wandering off the school grounds into the woods beyond during recess times.

The fence didn't stop him. When Thad got close to it, I could hear the fence links snapping as the whole section pulled apart to let him through. I still couldn't believe what I was seeing. It was like something out of a sci-fi movie or a comic book.

Thad disappeared into the woods. The school sent some guards after him, and they also called his parents. Everyone spent the rest of the day looking for Thad, but they never found him. What they did find, though, was Ken Garney's dead body. The old duffer had lived in a run-down shack just off a trail a couple miles back in the woods. They found him with part of a broken fence post rammed through his chest, and a double-barreled 12-gauge at his side. Thad had killed the old man in his panic.

Nobody else would believe Thad Matthews could have killed old Ken Garney. It takes a pretty powerful man (superhuman, even) to stab a broken fence post through another man's chest, but I knew Thad had it in him. So did a few dozen first through six graders, and Larry Javits, the school guard Thad had flung across the way. They dismissed the eye-witness accounts of six to eleven-year-old kids (me included) because, well, we were kids. And they dismissed poor Larry because the psychiatric evaluation he had to take revealed a familial history of mental illness. My own thorough research years later showed that Larry's grandfather had gone mental shortly after coming home from the European theatre in World War Two. If anything was going to cause you to lose your mind, being a POW of the Nazis would do it. And in the case of his grandson, having a nine-year-old throw you across a schoolyard with his mind would do it, too. Last I knew, Larry had committed himself to a hospital in upstate New York and was probably going to die there. I visited him once, but he added nothing to my research I didn't already know.

So, Thad got away with murder because nobody could believe a nine-year-old boy could kill, and most of the eyewitness accounts were of kids not even close to puberty yet. Never mind the torn fence, which was never explained.

* * *

Maybe my obsession started because I couldn't let Thad get away with it. And I don't mean because a crazy old backwoods hick got murdered, but because he'd gotten one over on me. Two, if you wanted to include the mouse in the desk.

That's where it started. At ten years old, I became very interested in psychic phenomenon: telepathy, telekinesis, astral projection, etc. That eventually bled over to other superhuman attributes like regeneration and strength-enhancement. Using the school library's resources, I studied as much as I could, and Thad Matthews never left my mind for long.

My dad died when I was fourteen. He had a heart attack while out golfing one afternoon and dropped over like a stone on the 7th green. Dad and I were never close, so the loss didn't hit me awfully hard, and like I mentioned earlier, he left me a sizable trust fund, so I guess that was his attempt to make up for neglecting me as a kid. But I couldn't touch that trust fund until I was eighteen.

An aunt on my mother's side took custody of me until I emancipated myself when I was 17. I finished high school, though my grades weren't top-notch. By this time, I had become thoroughly entrenched in my pursuit of the superhuman, and that took precedence over high school geometry. Since the late 1990s, unnatural occurrences were steadily on the rise, as if some event in or around that time had served as a catalyst for all these people developing superhuman abilities. By the time my trust fund kicked in during the summer I turned eighteen, I had decided I was going to devote myself to searching out these paranormal human beings and to find out how they got that way. And the principal focus of that would be tracking down Thad Matthews.

That turned out to be a harder task than I first thought. Thad was nine years old when he disappeared. Where does a nine-year-old go? It's not as though he could be on his own without a job or a place to live. So, where had he gone? I started following news items of interest on the

Internet. There were a lot of red herrings in there, but the newspaper archives started putting together a pattern for me.

Eleven ATMs were broken into across the state of Michigan in the two weeks after Thad ran away, and the cases all went unsolved because the internal cameras were all broken. I'm pretty sure Thad was using his new talent to kill the cameras and pop open the cash boxes inside.

Thad's parents had filed a missing persons report, and I'm pretty sure Thad's face wound up on a milk carton somewhere, but they never found their son. I had once considered going to them with my information, but even at a young age, I realized I was in this one alone. Noone was going to believe me. And Thad, for reasons of his own, did not want to be found. Maybe he considered himself a freak, or maybe he was just scared of what would happen to him for killing Garney, or what would happen when they found out what he could do.

Thad had headed south after running the fencepost through Ken Garney; his pattern of ATM vandalism had shown that much. With the winter months approaching and no way he could go home to his family, he headed for a warmer climate. Smart for a kid who wasn't even double digits in age yet.

So, I started looking closer to the bottom half of the country for more unexplained thefts and strange occurrences. I was venturing into needle-in-a-haystack country, though, looking at information that was edging up on ten years old.

By this time, I'd gotten to be part of a rather extensive underground network of paranormal devotees. There were more than the average share of hacks, of course, delusional idiots that were more of a hindrance than help, but I learned quickly how to weed out the experts from the crackpot enthusiasts. I will not name any names here, because the real guys do honest good work, and I don't want to compromise that for them. They're the people you never see who are keeping you safe. Believe me when I say that.

I learned a lot from those guys over the years: tracking techniques, surveillance, fighting skills. I spent a couple of years apprenticing with a few of them. A lot of paranormal investigators turned out to be ex-military, and they had a lot of stories to tell. There are a lot more super freaks out there than you'd believe. On my ever-lengthening road to find Thad Matthews, I met a few.

Some of them were very close encounters. A pyrokinetic in Dayton, Ohio, burned down a grain mill trying to get away from me. It's eerie to watch a 15-year-old kid light fire with only a thought. It took a couple months for my eyebrows to grow back after that one.

A 30-year-old stressed out used car salesman in Portsmouth, New Hampshire snapped and started punching a psychic knife through his customer's heads. Not a good way to build up your sales reputation. It took me and two others to stop him, and I won't sugar-coat it and say it ended well for any of us. It was a bloodbath. Sometimes things don't go as smoothly as you expected.

* * *

Finally, a bunch of network leads and pulled strings put me in the general vicinity of Thad Matthews. He'd made a simple existence for himself in the small town of Rockdale, Texas. Then I came along to mess things up.

Sometimes people are just born evil; sometimes it's something they learn. I didn't believe Thad was the former or the latter, really, but he'd hurt me, hurt that school guard, killed Ken Garney, and I couldn't get that out of my head. It drove me, maybe to lengths I didn't believe I was capable of.

I would kill him the coward's way: from a distance, through a sniper scope. Even after all I'd faced up to that point, I was still more than terrified of Thad. I had the rifle sighted in on him, had the crosshair dead center on the back of his head. I took a deep breath, but when the moment came, I couldn't pull the trigger. Despite my trepidation, I wanted him to see my face. I wanted him to know what he'd driven me to.

So I followed him. He was staying in a run-down motel just outside of the town limits. Confronting Thad after so many years was going to be a strange feeling, and my heart was hammering in my chest when I closed in on him. It all seemed so surreal, the two of us, each still in direct opposition to the other after so many years.

When he opened the door and saw me, he knew immediately who I was. He pushed me back across the motel parking lot like the bullet I wanted to put in his head. When he came out after me, it was like a tornado had blown into town. Everything not nailed down came at me, all directed by his fury. In the years I'd spent preparing myself for that encounter, it appeared Thad had learned a few things himself, and he was showing them all to me in short order. A Pepsi machine crashed into the car I had dove behind with enough force to rock the vehicle onto two wheels, scattering cans of Pepsi and Mountain Dew all around me. I had definitely bitten off more than I could chew. I circled around the parking lot, dodging unrecognizable flying projectiles. At the center of it all stood Thad, his eyes burning into me. I felt his fury.

A Cadillac hood ornament spiraled after me and stabbed into the back of my right leg. The force of the impact alone drove me to the ground, and the pain paralyzed my leg. Before I could even pull myself up, Thad had "grabbed" me and tossed me against the side of the motel with enough force to knock the wind out of me. My twelve gauge skidded across the wooden threshold and out of my reach.

Then something terrible happened. I relive this part in slow motion over and over, like a horrifying movie reel on a never-ending loop. My vision clouded with pain, I tried to pull the hood ornament out of the back of my leg, while also focusing on where Thad was and what he was doing. I saw the movement to my left and wildly pulled out my sidearm, triggered three shots, and they all found their mark.

But it wasn't Thad I killed. When Thad had opened the door of his motel room, things happened so fast that I didn't realize he hadn't been alone. His sister Vicki had just stepped out of the room and I'd put three 9mm rounds into her chest.

With Thad's concentration broken, everything in the air, including me, dropped to the ground as he rushed over to Vicki. I froze with shock and fear as I saw the spreading pool of deep red spreading across Vicki's chest. I'd killed an innocent person.

Thad spun to look at me for half a second, and I saw the anguish on his face at the same time I felt those familiar, unseen hands from years ago push me up and away from him. I landed hard 50 feet away at the edge of the motel parking lot. With a Cadillac hood ornament still buried halfway in my calf, I got to my feet and fled, adrenaline fueling my escape. His distraction could have been my advantage; I could have killed him right then, but I filled with a combination of abject fear and utter horror at what I'd just done instead. I needed to get away, to process everything before I made another move. My car was through a stand of trees fifty yards behind the motel, and it wasn't easy for me to get there. My leg was on fire and I didn't want to stop to remove the cause of it.

I made it to the car and yanked open the door about the same time Thad decided focused his attention on me. I turned the key in the ignition and watched the trees explode to my left. Some tore loose from the ground and parted, others twisted and splintered into pieces to let him through. It was like some warped version of Moses parting the Red Sea.

Thad's mental reach was only about twenty yards by the look of it, so I gunned the engine and sped away. In my rear-view mirror, I saw Thad emerge from the woods behind me, but by then I was a couple hundred yards away.

Safe.

For the moment.

* * *

Now, here I sit in my motel room, sober with reality. I killed an innocent. There's no coming back from that. I wanted Thad for obsessive reasons, and now a person was dead because of my blind, unreasoning hatred.

I'm tempted to put my pistol in my mouth and end myself, but I don't deserve to get off that easily. Thad will want his revenge.

He's going to come for me.

And I'm going to let him.

I may not be the bully anymore, but now I'm something worse. I don't know what made Thad the way he is, what catalyst pushed the button inside the heads of untold scores of people across the world and made them different from the rest of us, but Thad and I aren't so different anymore. He took a life to defend himself, and now I've inadvertently taken one for the same reason. I guess that puts things in a different perspective.

I'm not that far ahead of Thad, really. And I have no intention of trying to hide from him. When he comes, I won't raise a hand to stop him. He's had time to come to terms with what he'd done when he was nine years old. I can only imagine what that does to a person, eating away at them over time like a personal cancer.

So, I write this to let people know that there *are* monsters out there. Some of them have powers like you read in comic books, or see in special effect blockbusters, and they want to do bad things. Others are just obsessive people disguising themselves as saviors who think they're helping the helpless.

You might do well to watch out for both.

## AUTHOR NOTES - MONSTERS

This story is a sequel to the short story REACTION (also in this volume), but it didn't start that way. I wrote the initial opening portion with no idea it would star a grown up Jeremy Cochran, and can't recall how it eventually evolved to what it became, but I'm glad it did. I always wondered what happened to Thad Matthews, and this satisfied me pretty well. Hopefully it did you, too. You have the advantage of reading both stories in a brief span. There were nearly 20 years between the two tales for me.

This story also gives a brief glimpse of the timeline between REACTION and MONSTERS. There might be some stories to tell around that, so don't act surprised if you see these guys again.

# KILL

"Kill!" Frank Sanborn shouted, swinging the large, bloody axe above his head. Sweat streamed down his maddened face, despite the forty degree temperature. "Kill you!"

The axe swiped forward through the air, sinking deep into Henry Kellum's chest with the wet thumping sound of a prize-fighter hitting a punching bag. Henry uttered a single strangled cry as blood sprayed from the gaping wound and his right lung collapsed. Searing pain erupted a second time as the axe hit him again, and Henry's last strings of consciousness frayed away. Warm blood soaked his shredded flannel shirt, and coated his jeans mixed with good, rich farm soil. Henry looked up through tear-strung eyes to see that twisted, unreasonable face staring down at him. And he saw the axe, wet with his own blood, again arcing high above that face, coming to strike at him a final time. His vision blurred, and then he mercifully died, spared the agony of feeling his skull splitting wide apart.

Henry Kellum had had the misfortune to wake up to a crashing sound outside his barn at ten o'clock that night. Investigating, the madman overtook him, and now his life, though long and fulfilling, came to an abrupt end.

"Kill," Frank said again, more passive this time, spent and satisfied with his work. He stood there, the bloody axe down at his side, still tightly clenched in one fist, staring at Henry Kellum's grossly disfigured head.

Then Frank Sanborn laughed, turning his head to the sky and laughing a hoarse, wheezing laugh that lasted until tears came to his eyes.

Then he cried, rivers of tears running down his cheeks, down his beard-stubbled neck, to stain the light blue collared shirt he wore. Crying was the natural progression of killing for him, the cleansing act that reset everything again.

After he finished, Frank wiped the tears off his face, grunted at the dead man lying near his feet, then lumbered off into the shadows of the mild October night to find somewhere to sleep in Kellum's barn. The axe never left his hand.

* * *

It took little time for the town of Dover to find out a serial killer had escaped from the nearby Elysian Fields Sanitarium. By the next morning, word of mouth had spread like a hooker at a college frat party, and everyone was on high alert. The local authorities attempted to calm everyone, but after they found Henry Kellum's body, and someone revealed details of the body's condition, there was no use. Words would not do it.

Several families, especially those with small children, left town, at least temporarily. Nobody gave them grief. You had to look out for your own, and protect those who couldn't defend themselves.

Those who stayed behind wanted to think they were ready.

But for what, they didn't know.

* * *

Benjamin Wetstone's nose was for news, and he was also friends with Jedediah Cafferty, an orderly at Elysian Fields, who, after some coaxing, told Ben who had escaped from the sanitarium.

Armed with a name—Frank Sanborn—Wetstone then connected to the Internet and within an hour, had a substantial amount of information.

Frank Sanborn had spent most of his younger years in and out of foster homes after the deaths of his parents in a car accident. The foster parents would keep him for a short time, then give him up. Statements in several articles said that he was just a bad little kid. Rotten as rotten could be.

As a teenager, Sanborn engaged in petty theft, and his list of crimes grew by the year, so that by sixteen, he had a lengthy juvenile record. At seventeen, he raped a fourteen-year-old girl, and he would have ended up in prison, tried as an adult, had an inept prosecuting attorney not botched the case and got it thrown out of court.

At twenty-two, he served two years for grand theft auto, and during that time, a prison therapist determined Sanborn suffered from severe anxiety issues. Upon release, he got a job working on a crew that cleaned state parks. One day while picking up litter, Sanborn saw someone flick a cigarette butt into the path he had just cleaned. Sanborn approached the man and, without hesitation, hit him repeatedly with a rake handle, hospitalizing him. Sanborn went back to jail for aggravated assault. He told the police officers he'd do it again if he caught another litterer flicking butts on the ground. They believed him.

Psychiatric evaluation determined Sanborn was a danger to society and required incarceration for an undetermined time period. Severe anxiety had graduated to narcissistic sociopathic tendencies.

Two years later, a prison assault left Sanborn beaten so badly that his IQ dropped by half. Still dangerous, and perhaps even more unpredictable than before, they mistakenly shipped him from state prison to Elysian Fields. Prone to random violent outbursts, Sanborn regularly hurt either himself or someone else. They isolated and medicated him.

That was the last information Ben Wetstone found online, dated three years before, a year after Sanborn became an Elysian Fields resident.

What wouldn't come out until after the entire ordeal was over was how Frank Sanborn escaped from the sanitarium.

* * *

A mistake in the pharmacy at Elysian Fields started it all. Someone who had perhaps been sampling some of the more potent meds themselves mixed up the dosages for the patients' evening nightcap. These were the meds that calmed them down and got them to sleep.

Undosed, eighteen men and three women went off the rails that night, the worst of them all being Frank Sanborn. He had apparently been building up a case of homicidal rage during his stay. When the orderly came in to do the lights out call, Frank turned his head the opposite way on his neck. While he had lost a lot of his faculties in the prison beating years before, Frank remained smart enough to grab the orderly's keys, then opened the doors to every locked room on the floor. Twenty-one lunatics—as Jed Cafferty would tell Ben Wetstone later— out of control and on the loose. Of them all, only Frank Sanborn actually escaped. He had made his way to the kitchen, one of the few places in the entire facility where there was an outside entrance not heavily guarded. Mark Reilly, head cook, was still there doing food orders for the week when Frank burst into the kitchen. He killed Mark by bashing him in the head and face with a cast iron frying pan. The last thing Mark Reilly heard beforehand was Frank complaining about the taste of Wednesday's goulash.

Frank Sanborn was out the door at the kitchen loading dock, over the high barb-wire fence and into the thick woods beyond before any- one knew he was gone. The chaos inside the sanitarium lasted for nearly an hour before someone took a head count. By then, Frank Sanborn had found the axe in the shed outside the roadside gas station, and was only a short time away from ending Henry Kellum's life with it.

* * *

Frank woke up with a start. He had been having a nightmare, and it scared him. In it, he was being hunted by an enormous wolf, twice the size of a man, with large flesh-ripping teeth. He had looked into its savage eyes and saw the primal fury existing there, unaware his own eyes held that same frightening madness.

Sweat beaded up on his forehead and began streaming down his face. He sat up against the tree he had been sleeping under and curled his left hand around the axe's long wooden handle. The coolness in his hand caused him to shiver, but he still clutched the axe like a lover. The axe was his friend; it had gotten him out of a lot of trouble since he'd taken it from the gas station shed a few miles from the institution. The axe made him feel strong, unstoppable.

Strong. That was it, the thing the axe represented most for him, that strength. The axe was power in his hand, and he liked that. He felt naked without it, and deprived of it, he would be powerless.

He rolled the axe handle in his hand. If that wolf from the nightmare came, he would

(kill)

use the axe to make sure it never bothered him again. He pictured the shadowed lupine creature in his mind and clutched the wooden handle harder, harder.

(eyes, savage eyes)

"Kill!" He screamed, standing up and waving the axe in the air. "Kill kill kill kill kill kill!"

Frank stumbled off into the woods, inadvertently headed toward the small town of Dover. All the while, he saw the face of the wolf, saw its savage eyes, and he uttered the word repeatedly: "Kill."

* * *

The townspeople of Dover never suspected the killer to attack in broad daylight. Everyone was going about their business as usual when Chuck Hentley's beat up Dodge pickup rumbled into town, tires screeching as he turned the corner of main street. He pulled up in front of the Jim Stutesman's barber shop, almost rolling onto the sidewalk. Chuck stepped from behind the wheel, his eyes wide and visibly shaken, crossing half the distance from his pickup to the barbershop door before he started shouting.

"It's him! That crazy man escaped from the nuthouse! He's at my farm and he's—he's killed my boy. He took my Jesse! And he came after me!" He collapsed on the sidewalk. Jim Stutesman grabbed his arm and pulled him back up easily. Jim was a hulk of a man in his fifties.

"Chuck, is he still there?" Jim asked, gripping his friend by the shoulders.

"Y-yeah. He's got an axe, Jim. He's crazy! The look in his eyes…"

"It's gonna be all right, Chuck." Jim Stutesman looked around him at several of the onlookers until he saw Sam Marloe. "Sam, get down to the bar and round up Greg Shelly and whoever else wants to go."

"What about the cops?" Sam said.

"We don't have time to deal with politics," Jim said. "We can end this now."

* * *

Fifteen minutes later, Chuck Hentley's Dodge rolled up to his farmhouse three miles from town. Six men had come; three had ridden up front in the cab, and three sat in the back. Each of them carried a weapon. They left the truck parked a good distance from the house and barn so they could see everything as they approached. This was one man with an axe, and with six of them all on lookout, it was unlikely the crazy man would get the drop on them. Still, he was a killer, loose from a mental institution. Best not to underestimate him.

"We need to stay together, watch each other's six," Sam Marloe said, and everyone silently agreed.

"Now let's get this bastard," Greg Shelly murmured. His bravado stirred the same in the rest of the group, giving them the sense of courage they needed to confront Frank Sanborn.

At least they hoped it did.

Hearts pounding like hammers in their chests, the group advanced through the small stand of shade trees in front of the house, moving toward the barn where Chuck had last seen Sanborn. Each of them felt the tangible presence of death around them, but none of them realized they were being watched.

Watched with savage eyes.

* * *

"Kill," Frank Sanborn whispered from his hiding place in the barn loft. He looked through the cracks in the wooden walls and saw them coming. What he saw, though, was a pack of six voracious wolves lumbering forward, teeth glaring, eyes filled with a reddened madness.

The wind squeezing through the cracks in the walls was cool, and it chilled Frank Sanborn, put him on edge. He stared out at the approaching

(wolves)

men and gripped the axe handle in his left hand. He wanted them to just go away and leave him alone, but deep down inside, he knew the only way to escape them for good was to kill them.

*Kill kill kill kill kill kill kill,* the thought ran through his head over and over, and his lips curled into a twisted Cheshire grin filled with fear and excitement. He stepped to the edge of the loft and waited.

Waited for the wolves.

Waited to kill.

Waited.

* * *

The five men walked along the barn, looking left and right for any sign of the killer. When the group walked in front of the barn door, Jeff Malcolmson was the first to see. And what he saw made him sick.

Jesse Hentley's body hung by the neck from a ten-foot length of heavy rope, strung up like so many whitetail deer had been in that barn over the years. Jesse's heavily lacerated head turned his once-handsome face into a jigsaw puzzle. His remaining hair matted to his scalp with blood. The killer had nearly removed one of his legs at the knee, and the muscle and sinew that held it to the rest of his body looked close to tearing loose. His other leg was missing the foot, a knob of shining bone protruding from the ankle. Jesse's torn shirt revealed three crisscrossing gashes in his chest, deep jagged cuts that had bled him out onto the ground nearby.

Then, Jeff Malcolmson looked up and noticed Frank Sanborn crouched in the loft like a buzzard, his axe held tight in his right hand.

Too astonished by the look on Sanborn's face, Malcolmson wasn't even able to utter a sound before Sanborn was on him.

Sanborn leapt from his perch in the loft, swinging the axe high above his head, the blood-crusted blade making a crescent swoop and landing deep into Malcolmson's shoulder, shattering his collarbone and sending a shower of blood onto Sam Marloe's new pair of steel-toed work boots.

"Ohmigod! Jeff!" Sam shouted. Everyone's reaction was the same response of incredible realization as they found themselves face-to-face with the killer. Unable to move, able only to watch as Frank Sanborn pulled the axe from Jeff Malcolmson's dying body with a thick sucking sound. The blade sliced through the air again and through Jim Stutesman's right hand, knocking his 30.06 rifle to the ground and taking 3 of his fingers with it.

More blood. More agony. Another swing of the axe, another scream. Jim Stutesman was dead, with his entrails littering the ground. Blood pulsed and pooled among the loose hay on the barn floor.

"Kill kill kill kill kill kill kill kill kill kill kill kill kill" Frank Sanborn muttered as he moved wildly around, his eyes darting back and forth at the men before him.

The remaining three men recovered from the shock and took a stand. Greg Shelly leveled his shotgun to Sanborn's head, but the axe flashed quicker than Shelley's shaky finger could squeeze the trigger, knocking the weapon from his grasp. It landed at Jack Shreifer's feet.

As Sanborn bore down on the defenseless Shelley, preparing to deliver a message of hate and pain to his fragile flesh, Jack Shreifer's reflexes took over and his 30.06 fired. Frank Sanborn felt the flesh of his left shoulder erupt in pain and blood spurted from the open wound just above his shoulder blade. Despite the spreading fire in his arm, he reeled around and whirled the blade in a backhanded swipe that connected with and completely severed Greg Shelley's head.

Shreifer's rifle bucked again and more pain shot through Frank Sanborn's body, this time just above the right knee. He looked down to see a patch of his blood growing on his pant leg and found he could no longer stand.

"Kill!" he shouted, his pain paling before the resurgent fury in his heart. He lunged forward, swinging his precious axe in a wide circle, forcing Sam Marloe and Jack Shreifer to step backwards. The pull of the swing caused Frank Sanborn to topple over into the mixing pool of his own blood and that of his victims. As his free hand instinctively reached out to brace his fall, he lost his grip on the axe handle and it banged against the wall, landing just out of his reach.

As Sanborn reached out for his killing instrument, Sam Marloe's left heel ground hard onto the back of his hand. He looked up with eyes filled with madness.

"Kill...." Sanborn whispered to the axe, as if he could will it to do his work for him. But it did not respond, only lay motionless inches away from his hand.

(He felt powerless without the axe)

Sanborn watched the barrel of Marloe's ten gauge lower into his face, the black hole at the end of it whispering a prayer for the poor soul that dared stare into it.

(powerless)

Sanborn again looked out at his axe, hoping it could save him, that it would make the wolves go away. But as before, it lay motionless, just past his reach.

Then he cried. The tears ran down his face, smearing with the dirt, blood, and saliva there. He stared up at the cold, dark gun barrel again, then looked into Sam Marloe's face. It was devoid of any pity for him. The face staring back was ruthless, and it terrified Frank Sanborn more than anything ever had before.

(eyes, savage eyes)

(powerless)

Then Sam Marloe's finger rested on the gun trigger, and Frank Sanborn saw the smile appear on Sam's face.

No mercy. None. So familiar.

In the distance, the sound of sirens grew.

"Kill?" Frank Sanborn asked. His voice sounded like a frightened child.

"Kill," Sam said, and he squeezed the trigger.

## AUTHOR NOTES - KILL

I wrote this story in 1988, during my junior year of high school. It was just one of those whack-job, no-nonsense slasher movie stories with not a lot of deep-seated psychology behind it. Frank Sanborn feels afraid, and his way of dealing with that is to chop people into pieces with an axe. Upon revisiting this one recently, I added a bit more depth to the character, some back story, something that gave even a slight motivation for his behavior. However, the simple motivation is that sometimes psychotic is just psychotic.

# FAMILIAL OBLIGATIONS

Funerals should not be joyful occasions, but on the early November day when Harold Grantham's body was laid to rest in Eastman Cemetery, his family sighed in collective relief. The old man was finally gone.

Only half a dozen attended the graveside service: Ada, the widow; Jarod and Michael, sons; Andrew and Lisa, grandchildren and progeny of Michael; Karen, daughter-in-law, wife of Michael. Family only, no friends. The sun was bright amid the fluff of clouds in the sky, the air crisp and clean as the pastor read scripture and the first shovelfuls of dirt fell onto the casket lid.

Harold, by his family's own testimony, had been a mean old bastard. His wife was scorned, his sons reviled. The sheer audacity of one of those sons to marry and produce offspring of his own fueled Harold's genealogical loathing ever the more. He had taken every opportunity to let them all know just how deep his discontent ran. No love lost there.

As the family turned away from the gravesite and the gravediggers went about filling in the departed's ultimate resting place, an older man approached from nearby, dressed for business in a black suit and overcoat. He appeared to be in his mid-to-late sixties, sporting a full head of stark white hair.

"Hello, Mrs. Grantham. My condolences on your loss," the man said. "I am Malcolm Chesterfield, your late husband's attorney."

"Condolences aren't necessary, Mr. Chesterfield," Ada responded. "Save your pity for Harold while he burns in hell, if you must."

Without acknowledging, the lawyer continued. "As executor of Harold's will, there are several things I need to discuss with all of you."

Ada's eyes widened. Her son, Jarod, gripped her arm firmly. "Mr. Chesterfield, I cannot imagine anything Harold left behind that would be of significance to any of us."

"Ma'am," Chesterfield said, peering over his glasses at Ada. "Your late husband left you and your sons just over forty million dollars."

* * *

While Ada sat on the davenport in the living room of her home, listening to Malcolm Chesterfield's legal speak, her mind peeled back the decades and she realized her husband had been a more secretive man than she had known.

The house Harold Grantham spent most of his eighty-three years—and his last days—in was a modest two-story dwelling, built by his own hands in the late 1950s, shortly after the Korean War. It had three bedrooms upstairs and one down, a kitchen, dining room, living room and a single bathroom on the first floor, and a basement. In the earliest days of his marriage to Ada, they had run a small farm to provide for the family: a sizable garden for vegetables, two cows for milking, a dozen chickens for meat and eggs, and a hog for slaughter. Meanwhile, Harold had trained with a local locksmith and developed quite an aptitude for it. This eventually earned him a position as a security expert for big industry, and he patented the design of several advanced security devices. Harold brought in an above average paycheck, and he was always a penny pincher. Being friends with a local accountant, Ada was aware, had put Harold on to some decent investment opportunities early in his career. She knew their joint bank account held somewhere upwards of twenty thousand dollars, but Harold had never divulged many numbers to her; he was king of their finances. She knew he was worth a substantial amount, however. Just not the numbers this Malcolm Chesterfield was tossing around now.

They were late parents, with Harold being forty when the first of the two sons was born, and after that he changed. No one could meet his exacting standards, and Ada repeatedly confounded him with her own wants and needs. She couldn't have things of her own. A new pair of underwear was an unnecessary luxury as long as the old ones were still wearable. She was allowed minimal input into household decisions, and if he disagreed with her opinions, he invalidated them. And if she had dared to talk back, well, Harold Grantham was of the mind that sometimes a woman needed a firm hand to keep her in line. That happened more often as the years passed, as she tried to be a buffer between Harold and the boys, to spare them his growing wrath.

Harold shunned the boys for their failures. Grades less than perfect marks resulted in a beating and a reminder that prominent men showed ambition and determination, patience and perseverence. "Children should be seen but not heard," was the mantra. And if they didn't even have to be seen, all the better. When Harold would hold parties for his friends, he allowed Ada in the room only to bring food and drink and empty ashtrays. The boys kept to their rooms, never allowed downstairs during their father's engagements. To Ada and the boys, it seemed they were an embarrassment to him, something he was ashamed of.

Nothing could, or would, make the old man happy, it seemed. And as the years went by, his anger and resentment only grew. Ada became a repressed, bitter wife, harboring a secret, growing hatred for her husband. Michael and Jarod stayed in touch with their mother as they went their own ways in life, but rarely asked about their father. Ada would have left herself, but years of dependency on Harold left her fearful of the future. Michael had his own family, and she was sure Jarod had been dealing with enough of his own problems. She would burden neither of them.

When Harold's health took a severe downturn, Ada hired a full-time hospice nurse to tend to his medical needs, to make him comfortable until the end. Even through the last bedridden days, Ada could only remember the constant moans of pain that morphine seemed not to touch, the smell of piss and shit and the looming sour stench of impending death. Ada felt no remorse, though. When he finally passed, she didn't even come into the room to say goodbye.

* * *

"Besides one-hundred thousand in life insurance," Chesterfield continued, speaking directly to Ada. "Harold deposited a portion of his investment returns into a high yield savings account over the years, with the rest kept in a basement vault at a cabin he owned upstate."

"The cottage in the U.P.?" Jarod asked, referring to a small lakeside cabin on 20 acres his father had bought when he and Michael were barely out of diapers.

"Yes." Chesterfield rifled through his papers. "There is approximately fifty-thousand dollars and change in the bank savings account. The rest is in a safety vault at the upstate cabin."

Jarod and Michael looked at one another with mild surprise. Ada folded her hands on her lap and looked at Chesterfield. "Is there anything else he kept hidden from us?" she asked with a hint of bitterness.

"Nothing he divulged to me, Mrs. Grantham. I'm sorry this has upset you."

"That's of no concern to you, Mr. Chesterfield. My husband was a cruel man for most of his years. I can presume on my own that he harbored secrets even you weren't privy to."

Malcolm Chesterfield departed shortly afterward, leaving a bewildered family behind. Ada had provided signatures to whatever documents required it to turn her late husband's accounts over to her. Chesterfield had given her the name and number of Harold's financial advisor and assured her he would contact her within a few days. He also gave Ada a sealed envelope. Overall, the Grantham family felt Malcolm Chesterfield was relieved when the visit was over.

"So," Michael said when they had all gathered in the kitchen. "Now, what do we do?" His wife stood by his side. Andrew and Lisa sat in the family room, eyes glued to their cell phones.

"I don't know what to think," Jarod said. He had a cigarette in his hand and was fidgety. Ada wouldn't allow smoking in the house, so he'd have to go outside, and soon. "I just feel like this is all going to turn out to be some kind of joke. Like, why would he leave us that much money? He hated us."

Throughout this exchange, Ada said nothing. She sat at the table with a cooling cup of tea on a saucer, staring down at the envelope on the table. Why indeed would her husband do such a thing?

Harold had bought the upstate cabin as a private getaway. Neither Ada nor the boys had ever set foot on the property, or even knew its exact location prior to today. He spent the two weeks of rifle deer hunting season there every year except the last, when his health had deteriorated to the point he was incapable of making the two-hundred mile trip. Ada had often wondered if he had possibly had a mistress in the area over the years, but no proof ever surfaced of that. Nor did it matter. Their intimate relations had ceased back when an actor had been president.

She took a letter opener and ran the sharp edge across the top of the envelope. Inside was a ring of strangely shaped keys, stamped numbers one through six, a folded piece of paper with the address of Harold's hideaway, and detailed instructions on where to find the secret cache of money. Both were, Ada noticed, printed in Harold's perfect block text.

* * *

The following weekend, Ada and her sons made the trip north in Jarod's Cadillac to put this final bit of business to rest, to be rid of this last hold over them. And each of them, though they said nothing to each other, wanted verification that this cash windfall was truly real.

Ten minutes into the drive, Jarod's anxiety kicked in, and he tried to light a cigarette.

"Smoke your damned cigarettes outside, if you must," Ada said. "I'll not have you polluting my lungs with your foul habit."

So Jarod stopped at every rest stop before reaching Mackinaw City. And hoped it pissed his mother off just a little.

The ditches alongside the highway showed signs of early snowfalls as they crossed the Mackinac Bridge, and Jarod cursed both his mother and the bitter cold of Michigan's Upper Peninsula as he exhaled into the night, standing next to the car in St. Ignace. He would take no more smoke breaks until they reached the cabin.

The dash-mounted GPS showed Harold's refuge to be just a few miles south of Paradise, a small town near the coast of Whitefish Bay. Highway 123 led off Interstate 75 just out of St. Ignace, and they traveled that road without interruption, each lost in their own thoughts.

*   *   *

Michael sat in the back seat, sending text messages back and forth with his children for the first leg of the journey, but cell reception became spotty the further north beyond the Mackinac Bridge they traveled, so he eventually gave up with frustration. Andrew and Lisa would have to spend the evening with their mother instead.

With nothing else to occupy his time—and he was certainly not in the mood to talk to his brother or mother—Michael thought back to his father's ire, to the discontent with everything he had ever done.

As a child, he remembered Harold spending little time with him, unless to administer punishment for some youthful wrong he'd committed. Otherwise, his father ignored him, and left the boy under the charge of his mother. Michael learned to depend on himself and keep to himself. It was safest that way. No punishment if you stayed quiet and out of sight. Or so he'd thought.

Michael learned to read at a young age, interested particularly in superhero comic books, and though his mother had been proud he had taken such fascination with the written word, Harold offered no such congratulations. Instead, he condemned the reading material for being juvenile, though Michael himself was a little over five years old. When he was ten, he had amassed a considerable collection of comics, all bought with the allowance he earned doing chores around the home. One night, in a likely drunken rage, Harold had taken his books and tossed them mercilessly into the fire, stating it was time to grow up and stop wasting his time and money on childish things. Michael had saved one, a prized issue of Amazing Spider-Man, but his father soon discovered that, so it and destroyed it, as well. Michael received a beating with his father's belt for disobedience. Harold made Michael's younger brother watch. Maybe he'd learn by example.

Michael graduated as salutatorian from high school, replete with a full-ride four-year university scholarship. Once again, instead of congratulations, Harold gave him a lecture, this time on how Michael would likely still amount to nothing. In some attempt to appease his father, Michael studied business administration in college, but during those early months, being away from home for the first time, Michael also met Karen Wakefield. With his attentions divided, his grades suffered temporarily, and, of course, more righteous indignation from Harold Grantham ensued. During his second year of college, Michael announced his engagement to Karen, and Harold chided him for choosing a woman over a career, for "letting his cock do his thinking for him" were the exact words. Michael and Karen married on the courthouse steps, with only his mother and brother in attendance.

When Harold's first grandchild was born three years afterward, the old man told his son that a child was another mouth to feed, and reminded him he still hadn't finished college. Michael had graduated the year before with his Bachelor's Degree, but decided his employment opportunities would significantly increase with a Master's Degree. So, student loans piled up to help pay for the additional college, with the extra money not used for classes being allocated to pay bills and to keep their Chevy Malibu on the road so Karen could get Andrew to day care and herself to work, while Michael biked back and forth to his classes, and also to his job as a copy editor for the university newspaper. The years of reading had given Michael a good grasp of words, and over time, he found he enjoyed them far more than the business management career he saw at the end of his college courses.

Michael wanted to write a book. He felt he had a novel or two in him, and wouldn't that be a great way to spend his days? He continued on with his business courses, however. With only a year left to finish, he felt it prudent to finish that. A Master's Degree would hopefully allow him to support his family well, and he could always write that book in his spare time.

Then Karen became pregnant with Lisa. Michael barely finished college before Karen delivered, and they were immediately in financial trouble. Despite having his Master's in Business Administration, Michael could not find work. He continued writing his book, a mystery thriller which Karen thought was very good, but until such time that it bore financial fruit, it meant little beyond being a dream.

Things took a turn for the worse when Michael had to go to his father for a three thousand dollar loan after their car's motor seized up. Harold refused the loan, instead offering some words of wisdom: "A wife and children will only drag you down. You'd have done better by not having either in your life. Imagine where you'd be now," Harold had said, and it was then that Michael felt the first creeping tendrils of hatred for his father.

Michael never asked his father for anything again and cut off all communication with Harold. He spoke with his mother frequently, and had become concerned for her as well. She was tough—had to be to live with Harold for decades—but Michael was concerned for her well-being. To his knowledge, Harold hadn't laid a hand on her in anger for years, but he was verbally abusive and mentally manipulative.

Michael and Karen Grantham persevered, despite Harold's assessment of their wasted life together. A growing industrial firm that designed and sold automotive parts hired Michael for a management position. He also finished and sold his first book for a modest sum, and while it never cracked the New York Times Bestseller List, he had become a published author. He was happy. Still struggling, but happy.

The kids grew, and while they saw their grandmother as frequently as possible, they rarely saw Harold Grantham, and when they did, he afforded them little attention beyond a grunt. Michael's hatred for his pater continued to rise.

When his father had fallen ill, there was little sympathy.

And now he was gone. And good riddance.

Michael's reverie jolted back to reality when Jarod pulled the Cadillac off the road onto a dirt two-track.

* * *

Jarod wanted a smoke. And a drink would be nice, too, he thought. Just a shot or two to take the edge off. Lord knows he needed that after the last few days. After the last few months, to be more truthful.

But they weren't far off from their destination now, and his mother had given him the stink eye ten minutes back when he'd suggested stopping for him to have one last cigarette before they reached their destination. Blasted old hag.

She'd always been harder on him than Michael. He supposed that was because Michael was the first, and while his mother said she had no favorite between them, he knew—felt in his bones, really—that Michael was the favored one.

And his father—oh, that glorious bastard—couldn't be bothered to even teach his son how to ride a bicycle, much less take interest in anything else he did. Michael had taught him how to ride a bike when he was four, and Uncle Darren, his father's younger brother, had taught them both how to fish the following summer while visiting.

Jarod had grown up in his brother's shadow, envious of Michael's superiority in nearly everything. Michael was reading by the time he was five. Jarod struggled with words and was nearly seven when he finally could read unassisted. He loved his brother's comic books, though. They had pictures to show what was going on, and the words were mostly just people speaking. He remembered his father burning Michael's sizable collection when his older brother was ten. While their loss saddened him, part of him—some deep down selfishness—was glad his brother had lost something.

Jarod took the brunt of most of his father's ire, however. Perhaps it was because he wasn't as smart as Michael. Perhaps it was just because he felt his father hadn't wanted one son, let alone two. Harold beat Jarod for the most minor transgressions, and he guessed that afforded him one advantage over his brother: he was stronger.

At fourteen, Jarod started down the road to alcoholism, beginning with occasional stolen nips of alcohol from his father's liquor cabinet, but that became worrisome. The old man was sharp, and he'd likely notice an inch of brandy missing from the decanter. So Jarod came up with another plan. They kept the liquor behind the counter at the nearby convenience store; you couldn't get that unless you asked. But, beer and wine were just there for the taking. And so he took. And because his baby face features made him look younger than he actually was, nobody really paid attention to him.

Smoking came next at sixteen, and he quickly made friends with a senior in high school who would buy smokes for him in exchange for Jarod's talents as an alcohol thief.

While Michael graduated high school as a salutatorian, Jarod barely made grades enough to graduate at all. When the school principal called to tell his parents Jarod would not make the cut if he didn't bring up his grades in three classes, Harold took that personally. His father noticed, it seemed, only when it was his sterling reputation at stake.

Jarod at seventeen wasn't the Jarod of seven, or even fifteen, and his father was getting older. The physical confrontations had stopped over the past two years, likely because of his father's realization that Jarod could—and probably would—fight back, but his father used words like swords, and when he brought them out on anyone, he didn't hesitate to cut deep.

The day after graduation, Jarod left home. He honestly surprised himself for staying at the homestead as long as he had, but thinking of his mother, left alone with that man, worried him. Even as he took his last walk down the steps of the place he'd grown up in, he worried. While he thought his father was slightly afraid to hit him anymore, he didn't think Harold had reservations about laying hands on his mother. And without him there to protect her, what then?

He and Michael had both talked to her about leaving, but Ada refused. Her reasons, Jarod supposed, were her own. And as years went by, Jarod learned that the abused sometimes have difficulty leaving their abusers, sad a fact as it was. That his mother survived decades with the man was a statistical anomaly.

Jarod worked a succession of manual labor jobs over the next two years, starting out in a factory making plastic injection mold parts, but when too many drinks at lunch time nearly left him missing three fingers on his writing hand, his boss fired him on the spot. Instead of using that moment as a turning point to help himself, Jarod simply spiraled further downward.

At twenty-one, Jarod was an alcoholic, a drug addict, and unemployed. After a serious mixture of cocaine, cheap whiskey, and a handful of pills he couldn't identify, he overdosed. Clinically dead for two minutes, it was the grace of God and an emergency room nurse named Carol Finnegan that saved him.

That started a three-year relationship between Jarod and Carol, where Jarod sobered up, got off the drugs, and took on work as an apprentice electrician. Even though the relationship ended when he fell back to drinking, Jarod stayed off the drugs, despite an urgent desire to use them again. Despite his proclivities for drink, Jarod eventually became a licensed electrician, and started his own business, JG Electrical. It was one of those surreal moments when he realized he had surpassed his older brother, the smarter one, the determined one. Michael was struggling with his marriage and family, while he had risen above his childhood. A small part of him took great pleasure in that.

And while he'd stayed off the drugs, the drinking became worse. At first, he drank after work, then it was a drink during lunch to help steady his hands for delicate work, then he started keeping a flask in his work apron. But he was in control, he told himself. The drinking was just to help him cope with life and its pressures. Lord knows he'd had enough of those.

Then, his mother had called for the boys to come home. And within days, their father was gone. Jarod shed no tears. Nor, he expected, did any of the others. There were no fond memories to recall, no stories of picnics or birthday celebrations that included him. His mother had been both parents to him and his brother. She was the sole person responsible for any happy childhood memories.

Jarod's GPS brought him back to the present when it told him to turn left at the next road, less than a thousand feet ahead. They were nearly there.

* * *

Dusk encroached on the western sky when the car pulled off onto a two-track road. Jarod uttered a visceral grunt and cursed as his Caddy bounced up and down thru ruts and over bumps, the underside scraping the ground several times. The dirt road was two miles long, though Jarod felt certain it was twenty. Ten minutes later, the road ended, and the car entered a gravel clearing.

Snow had dusted the ground in front of the car's headlamps, and small spits of white darted in front of the spearing beams of light. The car radio had warned of a storm coming off Lake Superior, and for area residents to expect high winds and two to four inches of snow.

All three Granthams exited the car into the chilling veil of growing dark. There was business they meant to see finished.

The log cabin sat nestled among tall pines some thirty feet up a minor slope from the car. Dim solar lights flanked a wood framed gravel walkway leading up to the covered porch. Jarod pulled a small flashlight from the center console and twisted the end to shine a beam at the cabin. Wind gusts wound through the trees, tossing their hair and reddening their cheeks as they approached the cabin, gravel crunching beneath their feet. On the porch, Jarod turned his light onto the solid, windowless door. Michael pulled the ring of odd-shaped keys from his jacket pocket and pushed the key with the number "1" stamped on it into the front door lock, as the note from his father instructed. He turned it a quarter turn to the right, then the key sank in half an inch further and he could turn it another quarter turn. The wind concealed the faint clicking sounds within the locking mechanism as pins and gears aligned and released. Michael twisted the key back one-eighty, pulled it out, and then turned the doorknob. The heavy door swung in with a whisper, and automatic lights triggered, bathing the main living area of the cabin in soft luminescence. They shuffled inside, and Jarod closed the door behind them.

The room had vaulted ceilings done in lightly stained knotty pine. A mixture of traditional and modern furnishings combined to create an atmosphere of decorated sophistication. The living area floor was polished dark hardwood, with a large oval rug in the center, upon which sat a soft suede-covered couch facing a 50-inch LED television mounted to the wall. A cut stone fireplace and chimney dominated most of another wall; horns of a long-ago slain whitetail buck hung centered on a varnished mount. Next to the chimney stood a locked gun case, its window revealing several rifles and a shotgun. A mammoth antique oak dining table rested with aged majesty just off the kitchen, an ornate lace tablecloth draped across the top and over its sides. The kitchen boasted new polished steel appliances that appeared unused. The cabin was silent, the growing howls of wind outside completely soundless to them.

"Huh," Jarod said, astonished. "Who'd think the old man had good taste?" Just inside the door, a heavy oaken liquor cabinet revealed several partly consumed bottles. Jarod opened the glass door, took out a fifth of Jack Daniels and a clean tumbler. He poured himself a hefty shot and raised the glass to the room. "Here's to you, Daddy-O."

* * *

"Let's get this over with," Ada said, as Jarod downed his shot. Though the wind kept at bay outside, there was no heat on, and the still air was chilling. Ada wrapped her scarf tighter. "Where is the cellar?"

Michael had the note from his father. "Just off the living room, at this end of the hallway," he said, pointing. Jarod quickly poured himself another shot, and the three Granthams crossed the room. Michael produced the key ring again and selected the key stamped with a "2". He inserted it into the odd-shaped lock all the way to its hilt, and then turned it counterclockwise, per his father's note. There was a highly audible clunk as the door unlocked. Michael grabbed the knob and pulled the door open. It was heavy, a deceiving oak veneer on the outside but solid steel plate beneath. As with the main entrance, once the door opened, four soft lights within came on automatically, one after another, descending the stairs, the last illuminating a rectangular landing at the bottom, and another door.

The Granthams crowded into the doorway. Fourteen steps led downward to the sub-level and the door, this one not disguised beneath a mask of wood; it was solid, dark steel. There was a moment of hesitation, then Michael led the way down, followed by Ada, and lastly by Jarod, who drained a last swallow of whiskey and set the tumbler on a step.

"Maybe I should wait upstairs," Jarod said. Not fond of cramped spaces on a normal day, he was less fond of them now. Damn, but he wanted another drink. And maybe another after that, even.

"No, Jarod," Ada said. She turned halfway around with stern contempt in her eyes. "Your father's note insisted all three of us needed to be here."

"Great. Should've brought the whole damn bottle down with me."

The rectangular platform before the door was large enough for the three of them to stand together. Michael took the key stamped "3" and inserted it into the lock on the door at the bottom of the stairs. This door, like its predecessor, uttered a muffled clunk as the mechanisms within whirled, clicked, and released. Michael pushed the door inward.

The air within the room beyond felt and smelled impeccably clean, noticeably devoid of the damp mustiness normally associated with underground areas. Like before, the opening door triggered caged bulbs in the ceiling, and the room revealed itself in soft white light.

The area was approximately twelve feet square, the floor and all walls save one were smooth, seamless concrete. The far wall was a polished marble sheet, the only ornamentation being three brass keyholes equally spaced across the width. Stamped into the brass of each was a number, starting from the left: 4, 5, 6.

Michael, Jarod, and Ada knew what happened next. The instructions Michael held in his hand stated explicitly that all three keys had to be turned at the same time to access the vault behind it. There is where

Harold Grantham, husband and father to those assembled, had hidden his private fortune.

The three said nothing as they moved forward in unison. Michael separated the last unused keys from the ring and handed them out. "Put them in, then we'll turn on three," he said. Each of the Granthams pushed their key into the vertical slot until it went no further.

"Here we go," Jarod said, hitching in his breath.

Ada said nothing, made no acknowledgment at all.

"One, two," Michael said, then paused a split-second before finishing. "Three." They turned the keys simultaneously to the right.

A succession of sounds reached their ears. Gears, tumblers, and electronic servos activated behind the marble panel, followed by the sound of the door behind them closing.

They all moved toward the door, but it was too late. The door at the bottom of the stairs was now re-locked. And there was no opening it from this side.

"What the hell—?" Jarod said, finding no handle on the inside. It would not have done him any good either way, he remembered. When they had come through that same door, he remembered noting it was at least six inches thick. He cursed.

The three of them stood, staring at the door, then at each other. They knew they were now trapped in the cabin's cellar, on a remote plot of acreage in the northern Upper Peninsula.

"Hello, Ada. Michael. Jarod." The voice came from behind them. They recognized its baritone instantly and turned in horror.

Harold Wilson Grantham peered coldly out at them from a video screen, dressed in a dark charcoal suit, contrasted by his stark white shirt and red tie: the same clothing he requested for his burial. Harold smiled.

* * *

"Oh my word," Ada said. She wavered slightly, but Michael caught her arm and steadied her.

"It's safe to assume you know you're trapped," Harold said. "That should also mean I've got your full attention. If not, perhaps this will work:" Beneath the video monitor a panel slid aside to reveal several shelves behind clear glass, on which sat dozens of neatly bound stacks of cash. "That's nearly forty million dollars—cash money—but you won't spend a penny without earning it.

"I'll save you the whole, 'if you're watching this, that must mean I'm dead' speech, because I'm sure you were all there for the interment, and I bet you all danced a damn jig before leaving the cemetery. I hope you enjoyed it."

"What the hell's going on?" Jarod asked, his face wrinkled in confusion and rising terror. His gaze jerked back and forth between his mother and brother, neither with an answer beyond the obvious. He reached into his pocket for his cell phone and discovered he was receiving no signal. Probably the 8-inch thick walls, Jarod thought. Michael checked his phone as well, to a similar result.

"I recorded this video several months after the doctors made the diagnosis," Harold's digital image continued. "Motor neuron disease, they said, but this was a new and extremely rare offshoot of Lou Gehrig's disease, almost unheard of, and very untreatable. A medical scientist from some backward country in Africa figured out a person contracted this peculiar strain of ALS by ingesting a very particular plant root. Here's the clincher: that they can only find the plant root in his country, but I bet you knew that already, didn't you?"

The three living Granthams' eyes opened in horror. No glances at each other were necessary. The truth was coming out.

"Oh yes, I realized too late that you had poisoned me, Ada. It happened slowly—your intention, I'm sure—the poison building up in me little by little over months. By the time it was noticeable, the toxins in my body had done irreparable damage, and the disease was chugging along faster than you'd expected. However, while my body rebelled against me, my mind stayed sharp, focused. Malcolm Chesterfield, whom you've no doubt met by now, has been my most trusted confidant for most of my life. He assisted me in uncovering your ruse, Ada. I know you administered the plant root to me in minute doses with every meal for several months until the symptoms started. I know your plan was for me to die so you could have my wealth. Well, here we are, and there it is. And it's more than you ever realized.

"But I will not make it easy for you. You likely pulled my sons into your deceptions, and that's why they're here with you. None of you are going anywhere, at least not yet."

Jarod was coming unraveled. His fear of confined spaces brought his anxieties to the surface. His palms were wet with perspiration, fists clenching and unclenching, as he slowly moved back away from the others, closer to the corner of the room. All the while, his dead father's voice continued to reveal an intricate plan.

"I applaud your scheming. A surprise, really. Otherwise, the three of you have always been disappointing. A wife with no backbone of her own, two sons with no true ambition in life, all afraid to take the chances, endure the risks, and make the sacrifices necessary to truly excel in this world. Sometimes, a person must make the hard choices to get what they want. You finally did that. Apparently, I finally pushed you all to the breaking point, and you have my congratulations and a modicum of respect. If only you'd taken this kind of initiative in the past, perhaps you would have been a family to be proud of."

Michael's face wrinkled in rising anger. Jarod continued to sweat, nearly oblivious to his father, as his anxiety rose beyond control. Ada stood motionless and silent.

"But you didn't. The three of you hated me, and truth be told, I hated you all, too. So much so that when I discovered my wife was having an affair with my brother, I didn't even care."

Michael gasped. "Uncle Darren?" He looked at his mother. Her eyes were stony cold. "How?"

"Please, Michael," she said. "Not now."

"Now then, to the matter at hand," Harold droned on. "The money behind the glass is real. Don't bother trying to break the panels, though. The glass is like that used on the windshields of spacecraft. Your meager efforts wouldn't even leave a scratch."

The three Granthams on this side of the mortal coil stood still, almost hypnotized, as the dead man continued.

A smile broadened Harold's lips, almost as if he could see them across the veil of time. "I've lined the floor beneath you with pressure-sensitive measuring plates. The instant each of you stepped onto them, it registered your weight individually and combined. That's important, so we'll come back to it momentarily."

There was a slight whisper as another long panel slid open beneath the glass case, revealing a single recessed drawer with no handle.

"Within that drawer is the instrument of your survival," Harold's visage continued, and an internal latch released, popping the drawer open. Inside was a single handgun—a Glock 9mm—for the moment unreachable beneath a shield of space-age glass.

"One of you is going to take that handgun and kill the other two." Harold said matter-of-factly. There was no remorse, no regret in his voice. The color drained from his family's faces. They knew he meant every word. "Once that is done, place the gun back in the drawer and press the button within. Doing so opens a chute in the wall to deposit two bodies into. If that is not done within five minutes, the entire internal system here will shut down and whoever remains will die a slow and arguably cruel death of starvation. There can be no fooling the system. Remember, the pressure plates have your weight measurements. The system will calculate the remaining weight afterward, and then we will continue." The glass slid away from the drawer silently.

* * *

"This is bullshit," Jarod said. "We're not jumping through hoops for you, old man!" He shouted at his father's face. Harold, of course, paid no mind. The Harold from several months past remained calm. Jarod, however, was fast approaching breakdown, and his mother saw that.

She moved closer and held out her hand, but Jarod sat down on the floor, pulled his knees to his chest, and wrapped his arms around them. Ada knelt down beside him, put her hand on his head. It was wet with sweat.

"I can't do this, momma," Jarod said, his voice almost childlike.

"It will be alright, dear," she said, stroking his hair, but she knew otherwise. Her vengeance-driven husband had seen to every eventuality, it appeared.

There was a loud crack, and Jarod's face exploded in a spray of blood, flesh, and bone. Michael held the Glock at arm's length, hands shaking. Ada's expression of horror matched his own, and Jarod's ruined face bore no expression at all as blood poured down the front of his shirt in a crimson waterfall.

"I'm sorry, momma," Michael said. There were tears on his cheeks. "But I don't have a choice. I love you." The Glock barked sharply twice more, putting two 9mm bullets into Ada's chest, and she slumped backward against the body of her youngest son, crimson pools spreading across the front of her blouse like flowers.

Michael's hands still shook as he placed the gun back into the drawer. Next to the pistol was a raised red button. He pressed it down, and the drawer retreated into the wall, while a three-foot square panel on the opposite wall moved. Behind it was open blackness, and a rush of cool, earthy air.

"You have five minutes to dispose of the bodies," Harold resumed speaking. "Once that is done, we can continue."

Michael stood for a moment, staring at his father's stoic face on the monitor. In the image, the elder Grantham had steepled his fingers in front of his face, peering over them at his firstborn son, with the slightest hint of a smile tugging at the corners of his mouth. Of course, there was no way Harold could have known who would stand before the monitor, but Michael felt his father staring directly into his soul.

He turned away, toward the bodies of his mother and brother. Tears still ran in small trickles down his cheeks. He leaned over and kissed his mother on the forehead, then grabbed both of her arms and began dragging her across the room toward the black hole in the wall, surprised at the weight of her. In life, she barely broke one-hundred five pounds, but in death she seemed to weigh much more. Michael laid her gently in front of the opening. He could see the inside of the hole sloped sharply downward at a forty-five degree angle. Michael pulled his mother to the edge and draped her arms into the hole, then grabbed her legs and hoisted her into the opening, where she slid away into the dark. Michael didn't hear an impact. How far did that hole go? He gave it no more thought as he turned around for his brother, wiping the last tears from his face. There would be no more.

Jarod was more difficult to move. His bulk was considerable, and the sight of his ruined face made Michael uneasy, and he barely held back from vomiting. Before pushing his brother's body into the chute, Michael removed his brother's car keys. Thank God he'd thought of that, otherwise he'd have no way to get out of this soon-to-be snowed in retreat. And being stuck here with his dead family near, wherever they were down that pitch black hole, appealed to him not at all.

Michael finished the task with a minute and forty seconds to spare, and once Jarod began his trip down the rabbit hole, Harold began speaking again.

"Congratulations. It's all yours," He said. The glass panel slid aside, exposing the stacks of money that had caused everything. "You'll also find a satchel large enough to carry it."

He did.

As Michael was stuffing the money into the duffel bag, Harold Grantham expressed one final thought. "I hope this was all worth it." Then the screen went black. The door that had closed behind them automatically now opened again. It seemed like days had passed, but as Michael loped up the stairs, his watch told him it had been a little over an hour since they'd arrived. He passed the empty tumbler Jarod had left on the step during their descent, and a quick feeling of guilt washed over him, then faded as he felt the weight of the money bag over his left shoulder. At the top of the stairs, he stopped, set the bag down, and stretched.

"I didn't figure it would be you," the voice to Michael's left said. As Michael's head jerked to the left, Malcolm Chesterfield stepped into the light.

* * *

"Dad's hotshot lawyer?" Michael was puzzled. "What are you doing here?"

"I'm here to congratulate you, Michael." Chesterfield said. He was standing in the living room, his overcoat hanging on one arm. "I honestly thought your younger brother would be the only one with enough selfish motivation to do the deed."

"Desperation makes or breaks you, Mr. Chesterfield. But I can't imagine congratulations are your only reason for being here."

"Would you care for a drink?" Chesterfield asked, reaching inside the liquor cabinet to pull out the bottle of Jack Jarod had poured his drink from earlier.

Though wary, Michael accepted. His nerves needed some calming. Chesterfield handed him a rocks glass and Michael downed it in one large gulp. He asked for another, and Chesterfield generously refilled.

"You didn't answer my question, though," Michael said, and took another drink. "Why are you here?"

"For the money, of course," Chesterfield said. "Don't be a fool, Michael. Do you think your father would let any of you live after what you did to him?"

"What we did to him? Do you have any idea how he treated me? How he treated all of us? He was a monster, and, terrible as it sounds, he got what he deserved."

"I'm sorry to hear you say that."

"Someone once told me you spend your entire life gathering guests for your funeral. You were there last week, Mr. Chesterfield. Who else was there in the cemetery besides us? Nobody. Almost everyone disliked my father. So, just who are *you*, Mr. Chesterfield?"

"I've been your father's attorney and confidant for forty years, and we grew very close over that time. He meant a great deal to me, so when he came to me with his suspicions about the three of you, I was quite concerned. After we confirmed the ALS to be true and irreversible, we put together this little scenario of retribution. You murdered your father, Michael, simple as that. And that can't go unpunished."

"That was all my mother's doing," Michael said. "I just found out about that today."

Chesterfield drew the gun from his coat, and Michael slowly set his shot glass on the counter, his face ashen with fear. "Hey, there's enough to go around. It's almost forty million dollars, man. Even a fifty/fifty split would leave us both set for the rest of our lives and nobody would have to find out."

"Thanks, but no," Chesterfield said, and pulled the hammer back on the .38. He waved Michael back toward the cellar door with the gun. "That's not how your father wanted it to end. You deserve nothing, least of all that satchel of money. In fact, your father insisted on that detail."

Michael's mind whirled. His father had been ruthless, but this was so cold and calculated.

"As I said, I'm quite surprised it was you, Michael. You never seemed like the killer type."

Michael stood in the doorway leading to the sub-level and turned, his face now hardened. "Jarod was a waste. He had no life other than dealing with his pathetic existential crisis during the hours between the waking hangover and his next drink. No significant loss. And my mother? She was old and on her way out, anyway. Consider it a mercy killing for both of them. I have my family to support, and debts to pay. Hell, I have over a hundred thousand just in student loans. That's why I did it. Simple greed. I'm tired of my family having to struggle. It's our turn to come out on top."

Malcolm Chesterfield's face drew taught. "Avarice is always a powerful motivator. Perhaps the most powerful. I never expected it to be you, but that just proves how depraved all of you were. Now, down the stairs." He waved with the gun again. Michael stepped down into the stairwell, and at the bottom of the stairs, Chesterfield directed him to the hole in the wall. "Kneel in front of it."

Michael knelt down and turned back one last time. He was no longer afraid. "You're a monster, just like my father."

"We're all monsters here, aren't we?" Chesterfield said, then shot Michael in the back three times and watched the body slump forward. He put his foot against Michael's buttocks and pushed him headfirst into the darkened hole. The body slid out of sight with a whisper and was gone.

Ten minutes later, Malcolm Chesterfield stood in the living room again, having another drink. Once finished, he pulled on his coat, grabbed the duffel full of money, and walked out into the frigid evening air.

## AUTHOR NOTES - FAMILIAL OBLIGATIONS

On its surface, this is a story of domestic violence, and what may seem like justified vengeance against the abuser. But, beneath that, we see the motivations for various other characters to commit their own despicable acts. Harold Grantham was a wicked man. But what about his family? When I wrote the first rough draft, I didn't have a solid idea of how to end the story. I tossed around several scenarios, and then the story sat for over a year before I wrote the final few pages in a single day. It's not a happy ending, perhaps even anticlimactic, but I believe it really suited the story. More recently, I pulled this story out of the dusty confines of my computer's "Short Stories" folder, and added some extended backgrounds on the main characters to help flesh them out a bit more, and provide more descriptive motivation for why these characters felt justified in committing the sins they did.

Oh, and trivia fans: I plucked the last name Grantham from George Romero and Stephen King's 1982 movie *Creepshow*, particularly from the segment called "Father's Day." The elder Grantham in that story was a mean old bastard, too, played impeccably by Jon Lormer.

# LAKE LIFE

I love the water.

And the beach, and the sun. It's all connected, you see. Digging my toes into the sand at the edge of the water, then laying back in my zero-gravity chair with my eyes closed as the sun kisses my skin, and listening to the eternal waves rolling into the shoreline, all those elements combine into the best experience there is.

If you're an astrology-minded individual, I was born under a water sign. Take from that what you will. All I know is that being near the water soothes my soul; it's where I find my peace. Always have. Always will. Your mileage may vary.

I spend my time on the beach alone now. But, for a long, long while —over thirty years—my husband was with me. He loved the water, too, though if I'm being honest, he didn't embrace it as much as I do. He would agree, I'm sure.

Rich loved being *on* the water, though. He enjoyed boats—owned a couple of small ones, even—but he especially loved kayaking. We'd do it together often, and I loved it, too, paddling around the lake, the warm sun and light breeze on your skin, tuning in to the birdsongs in the trees along the shoreline. That was almost as satisfying to me as laying on the beach. Sometimes we'd stop paddling and just drift in whatever direction the lake wanted.

We retired to his father's cabin on this small lake in northern Michigan ten years ago. Perhaps I'm biased, but it's one of the most magnificent places on the Earth, and while I don't remain there year round anymore, I always return every spring, to dig my toes into the sand, lean back in my chair, and let the sun kiss my skin while the waves come ashore.

And to be with my husband.

* * *

Rich died on the lake, on an early July morning four years ago, kayaking by himself in that sweet spot of time before the rising sun burns the previous night's fog off the lake. The medical examiner's report said he had a sudden, massive heart attack and likely died with no suffering. If I had to apply any poetic license to the entire thing, he died in one of his favorite places. I'm quite grateful for that.

Rich enjoyed just sitting at the water's edge with me, though he wasn't as much of a sun person as I am; I absorb it like a sponge. He would sit next to me for a brief time, often holding my hand, then retreat to the shade, where he'd read a book, drink a beer or two, maybe grab a nap. Sometimes he'd do all three in an afternoon.

Lake life, it's hard to beat.

* * *

I travel during winter now. I've never enjoyed cold weather, even as a child, but as the years stretch on, my body rebels against it more and more. Age and arthritis both work against me in winter. So, I find somewhere warm to be in the months between November and April. And I always turn up on a beach, whether it be on the ocean or a lake, or even a river. Moving water is my reset button. It's how I keep on keeping on.

Wherever I am, I begin most mornings and end most nights at the water's edge. I like to sleep in, so I rarely watch the sunrises, but I enjoy almost every sunset nature allows, and there aren't many sunsets as beautiful as those seen over the water.

No matter where I spend my winters, though, I can't wait to get back to the cabin and the lake come springtime. Soon after I make my comeback, we see the return of the lake's other annual visitors, usually beginning with Canadian geese in all their honking glory. Out-of-towners own most of the property on the lake, and use their cabins as a retreat from life in the cities, I suppose. They arrive for lengthy stays after the school season ends in early June, but they keep mostly to themselves, and that's fine with me. I'm not much of a social person. I prefer my peace and quiet.

Sound, however, travels well on the water, and during the warmer parts of the day, I'll hear children playing, splashing on their own beaches, diving off docks and rafts, and enjoying the water in their own ways. I'm okay with that, too, as long as it doesn't continue all night. Fishermen troll the waters, and you'll barely hear them casting, then the soft plunk as their lines hit the water. They like their peace and quiet, too. At night, you'll catch the occasional cry of a loon as it echoes across the stillness, both haunting and beautiful.

* * *

A year after Rich's death, something appeared on the water for the first and only time that brought a tear to my eye, but also made me smile.

It had been a beautiful day, bright sun, near-cloudless sky, and the slightest of breezes to keep the gnats and other flying insects away. As perfect as it could get. When the sun had reached its apex in the sky, I had already been on the beach for three hours. It was just blissful, with little noise beside nature itself. I read for a while, drank some iced tea and nibbled on sandwiches I had brought in the hand-held cooler, all while dangling my toes in shallow water so warm it was practically like a bath. Late-July summer in Michigan is arguably the best time anywhere.

I busied myself with housework in the late afternoon, then ate my supper on the deck, looking out at the lake a hundred yards away. Two fishermen floated by further out, almost soundless. A pair of ducks flew in and came to rest in the small inlet nearest the house. Squirrels bounced across the yard in search of tasty acorns. A fox trotted down the hill, stopping two dozen feet from me, watching as I watched it, then it darted off into the underbrush.

After doing dinner dishes, I poured myself a glass of wine and walked down to the beach to enjoy the sunset. The boat dock jutted fifty feet out into the lake, and at the end is where I sat, feet in the water, following the myriad colors of the clouds blend and change on the western horizon, while a low-hanging fog drew itself across the water. As the last light shrank behind the trees, the surface calmed to glass, and the fog hung there, wisp-like, unmoving.

That's when I saw the kayak, as red as can be, floating toward me through the haze on the opposite side of the lake.

I knew who it was.

Richard was watching over me.

Waiting for me.

And letting me know he was okay.

## AUTHOR NOTES - LAKE LIFE

I read in bed almost every night. Sometimes it's only for a few minutes, sometimes it's for hours. I love that quiet time, laying next to my wife as she plays games on her phone, or listening to her breathing after she falls asleep. One thing reading often does is inspire me in my writing (as it should). So it was the other night, after I finished reading a couple of short stories. I lay in that black silence just before falling asleep, and ideas started forming in my head. Knowing I'd never remember the exact details in the morning, I grabbed my phone and jotted notes into the memo pad. I won't lie and say there wasn't a tear in my eye as I did.

Two days later, when I sat down to write the story, I made some changes. I wrote it in the first person, and I gender swapped the narrator to a female, talking about her deceased husband. I write most of my fiction about men, so I wanted to try it from a fresh perspective. The story's plot changed a bit from my initial notes, and I think it was all for the better.

# SHIFTED

Mrs. Kamen was a kind old lady, that sort of petite grandmotherly woman we all remember with fondness from TV shows, or—if we're lucky enough—from our own families. Though she was well into her late eighties, every week she came into the Family Grocer store, where I worked as a stockman. She came on the same day, and almost always at the same time. We would exchange a 'hello' and engage in small talk about the weather or items on sale in the store, and she would always update me on her great-grandkids (Jared was studying to be a doctor, while Greta was on her third marriage and fourth child). She would always ask how I was doing and wondered when I was going to put in for a promotion.

As I said, a kind old lady. Always a smile on her face, and a pleasant conversation for everyone she came in contact with. I liked her.

That was before my accident.

Six months ago, on one of those late fall/early winter nights where precipitation could quickly change from rain to freezing rain to snow within a brief span of hours, I had worked the closing shift at the store. I was tired when I got into my Ford Fusion. It had started a cold rain several hours before, but the temp didn't appear to have dropped enough to turn to snow. I started for home, kinda zoned out with the radio on and my body ready for sleep. I hit a curve going a little faster than the posted speed limit, and caught a slippery patch. The back end of the car slid around, sending me into a tailspin and I left the road, my tires digging ruts in the embankment beyond. My journey ended when my mid-size car met with a hundred-and two-year-old oak tree some twenty feet off the road. My memory deserts me there, though I vaguely recall a paramedic speaking to me at some point. He sounded warbled, like he was underwater, and I couldn't tell you exactly what he said. When I finally regained consciousness to the smell of antiseptic and the beeps and bloops of hospital monitoring equipment, a balding orthopedic surgeon informed me I had sustained several displaced fractures in my left leg, which necessitated surgically implanting multiple plates and screws to position the bones for healing. Basically, I'd be setting off airport metal detectors for the rest of my life. Though I also had what they considered a fairly severe concussion, an MRI showed no signs of long-term brain damage. I had gotten lucky, and everything seemed on the mend by the time I went home with my cast and crutches.

Once the cast came off, I started physical therapy, some of the most agonizing pain I've ever felt, but if I wanted to walk again, that was my one and only option. After two months of PT (also known as Pain and Torture), I could walk with a pronounced limp and was itching to get back to my job. Sitting around the house hopped up on Vicodin wasn't my idea of fun, so as soon as I was able, I returned to work. Though earlier than Dr. Markwell would have liked, I knew my body better than she did, and for me, it was time to get back on the horse.

The first few days were tough, though they scheduled me for fairly simple tasks that required little heavy movement. The damaged leg often talked to me in angry tones, but over the course of probably two weeks, it fell back to only an irritating whisper. At home, I might pop a Vicodin if it started talking too much, but otherwise, going back to work was exactly the therapy I needed. I missed the work. More importantly, I missed the people.

* * *

So it was that one of my favorites, Mrs. Kamen, came into the store at 2:00 in the afternoon on the first Sunday I was back, just as she always had. Church services got out at 12:30, then she and some of her church group went out for a light lunch, then it was to the store for the week's shopping.

"Routine is the name of the game, when you're as old as I am," she had said more than once. Considering how close she was to her ninth decade, I had no reason to not believe her. She got around pretty good for her age.

I was stocking in the soup aisle when I noticed her that day. She had her back to me, but I recognized that tiny slouched over posture as she opened an egg carton to check for cracks.

"Hello, Mrs. Kamen," I said, approaching her.

As she turned, the surrounding air seemed to shimmer, to shift, and then I could see both the person standing before me and beneath that, something else. There was a dark, twisted thing behind that veil, like I was seeing her in layers, as though the kindly old lady face was only a mask. Rows of needle-like teeth grinned at me from behind black, slippery lips. Bulbous yellow alien eyes, dotted with flecks of orange and split with long slitted irises, peered out from the mottled slate-grayish skin of her face. Then she spoke, in a voice that was not gentle as I'd always heard before, but deep and raspy, like sandpaper.

"Oh, Douglas!" she squelched. "It's so good to see you back to work. How are you feeling?"

I hesitated for a moment, trying to process this thing I was seeing, to understand the distinction of her voice. Hearing her kind words in that horrid, scratchy tone rattled me.

"I'm doing better, Mrs. Kamen," I said. "Taking it one day at a time, as they say."

"That's good to hear," she said. Those needle teeth mesmerized me. "I was so worried when I heard about your accident. We prayed for you every Sunday at church, and I prayed myself every night before bed."

"Thank you," I said. "It's much appreciated. Please tell everyone I said thank you." I struggled to not let my expression match my feelings. I was terrified and horrified. It was hard to look at her, to contact those inhuman eyes, with their slitted irises expanding and contracting over and over. Finally, I turned my head away.

"Are you okay, Douglas? You're looking a bit pale."

"Still have some bouts of pain, I'm afraid," I told her. "I get off work in half an hour, then I'll go home and take a pain reliever. God bless the pharmaceutical companies, right?" I tried to laugh, but it came out weak and unconvincing. She didn't seem to notice.

"Well, I will let you alone, then," she said. "I hope you feel better, and I'll see you soon." She shuffled off, pushing her grocery cart slowly toward the dairy section.

I saw her again ten minutes later when I went past the paper goods aisle to return to the stockroom. She was chatting with Anna Broadhurst, another clockwork regular. She was talking to Mrs. Kamen today like nothing was out of the ordinary, her hands accompanying her conversation in wild sweeping motions. Did Anna not see Mrs. Kamen's other face? If she did, like me, she was trying to hide it.

* * *

I went home and took a pain reliever. My leg really was hurting, but not so badly I *needed* a painkiller. I just wanted to forget that face, those eyes, those teeth, that leathery gray skin; she was like a mummy crossed with a reptile. I popped a Vico and went to sleep. Thank God I didn't dream of anything. At least, not that I can remember.

When I woke up, I thought maybe my medication dosage was too high. I saw nothing else like this throughout the entire next week. My leg felt better, too, so I could cut back on the times I had to take a pill for the pain. I was glad about that. Never enjoyed taking medication, and I was sure that had somehow made me hallucinate Mrs. Kamen as a monster. Either that, or I was suffering from some sort of strange PTSD.

* * *

The following Sunday, I was on a stepladder, building an end-cap display, when I saw her again. I didn't notice her until she approached me, and I heard the dry scratch of the voice she now used. When I turned, the gray mummy-like face was there again, shifted slightly behind a transparent shimmering mask that was the face she pretended to wear, the face that everyone else saw but me. I almost cried out when she approached, but I held myself together.

"I hope you're still on the mend, Douglas," she said. She had a small litter of groceries in her cart.

"Yes, ma'am," I replied. "Feeling better every day."

"That's good," she smiled her needle-toothed smile. "I imagine you'll likely have a terrible bout of arthritis in that leg when you're older, though."

"The doctors have told me the same thing, Mrs. Kamen."

"Sorry to bother you, Douglas, but I'm cursed with a lack of height, just like my Grandma Betty." She laughed—an inhuman sound—and my arms broke out in gooseflesh. "Could you be so kind as to get a bottle of lemon juice off the top shelf for me?"

"Sure thing," I said, hoping that she didn't get her looks from Grandma Betty, too.

I got the lemon juice off the top shelf for her, then excused myself. As I turned to walk away, she grabbed my arm. I looked down at what wasn't a hand at all, but a curved, dark, clawed thing with cracked yellowed nails extending from the long sleeve of her blouse.

"Are you certain you're okay?" she asked. "You seem out of sorts when I've talked to you lately, Douglas. I hope I've done nothing to offend."

I held my composure, but the feel of that skin and her grip, tight with strength beyond that of an almost ninety-year-old woman, nearly made me lose it.

"I'm fine, Mrs. Kamen. Honest. Just have a lot going on right now, and my mind is elsewhere." She relaxed her grip, and I pulled my arm free of her. Then I saw the facade that concealed her actual face shift back into view, shimmering in the light. I could still see the dark, leathery skin underneath as well, and that almost made it worse. What was it I was seeing?

"You take care of yourself, Douglas. You're getting bags under your eyes."

That I did not doubt.

* * *

While in the hospital, my doctors told me that my concussion hadn't been serious, and the MRI showed nothing to be concerned with, but something had changed. I'd seen Mrs. Kamen dozens of times before the accident and had witnessed nothing out of the ordinary. Something must have gotten knocked loose in my head during the car accident that made me able to see her as she really was. That had to be it. I had seen no one else look this way. If I was going mad, it would stand to reason I'd see this everywhere. Everyone would look like a leathery mummy with toothpicks for teeth and yellow-nailed claws for hands. To verify this, I went to the mall and sat in the food court dining area, watching everyone as they came and went, and nobody, none of the thousands of men, women, and children I observed, looked anything other than human.

So, what exactly was Mrs. Kamen? Was she an alien? A demon? I like to think I'm fairly open-minded regarding people, but this was something I couldn't even fathom. She didn't seem malicious. Despite her appearance, which was frightening, she didn't seem intent on harming me or anyone else. She acted exactly like any other old lady in a quick sprint to ninety.

* * *

Monday, before my work shift, I went into the store office and got onto the employee computer, a dusty relic likely ten years out of date. While we mostly used it for store associates to look at or print out pay stubs, and to request time off, it also had access to the store's customer database. Customers could sign up for a loyalty rewards card which gave them extra savings throughout the store. The database stored their names and addresses to mail or e-mail additional rewards items as the customer chose. After logging into the database, I searched for Margaret Kamen and found her home address. I really enjoyed my job, and this was most definitely against company policy. I'd likely be fired on the spot if it ever came out. Regardless, I was going to pay Mrs. Kamen a visit.

* * *

Margaret Kamen lived in an apartment complex six blocks from the supermarket. I walked there and stopped in front of the building, unsure I should continue. I stood in front of the intercom for several minutes before finally marshaling my courage and pushing the buzzer for M. Kamen 402. At first there was no response, only agonizing silence, then after nearly 30 seconds, a voice came over the intercom.

"Hello? Can I help you?" I had been expecting the voice that would make a 3-pack a day smoker jealous, but it was merely the voice of an elderly woman. I was surprised. Maybe whatever I could see and hear required me to actually be in her presence.

"Hi, Mrs. Kamen. It's, um, it's Douglas. Douglas Weatherly. From the Family Grocer store."

"Douglas!" she exclaimed. "To what do I owe the pleasure?" She sounded so regal.

"I'd just like to talk to you if you have a minute."

"Of course," she said. "Let me get the door."

Then I heard the mechanical buzz, and the front door clicked. I pulled it open and slipped inside, found the elevator, and rode it to the fourth floor. My palms were wet with sweat and my heart beat faster with each ascending floor. When I stepped off the elevator, I hesitated, unsure I could go through with it. Not sure I could stand to see that face again. By the same token, I couldn't stand to see that face and not know how or why she was what she was. Her apartment was second on the floor, just past the elevator. I stood in front of it for a moment before knocking. The door immediately opened.

The Margaret Kamen that met me at the door looked like the doting old lady who I'd seen come to the Family Grocer once a week in the years prior to my accident, and nothing more. Her skin was a pallid white, her fingers long and bony, with fingernails that were prim and neatly manicured. Her teeth were almost too perfectly straight and normal, most likely dentures.

"Come in," she said. "It's so very nice to see you." She stepped aside and closed the door behind me.

"It's nice to see you, too," I said, and I wasn't lying. I doubted myself now. Had I imagined all this? Was she nothing more than an elderly woman? And that, of course, made the reason for my visit questionable.

"Would you like something to drink?" she asked. "I just made some tea. Or there's Coke if you'd prefer. I don't drink the stuff, but I keep it here for Greta's kids when they visit."

"A Coke would be fine, Mrs. Kamen. Thank you."

"Make yourself to home, Douglas," she said, and disappeared into the kitchen. I sat down on the couch in her modest living room and felt almost guilty for being there. What would I say? How do I accuse this woman who has always been kind to me of being a horrific monster? Maybe it was something my mind had made up for whatever reason. The PTSD angle I had considered before seemed more plausible.

When Mrs. Kamen returned, she had a serving tray with a cup of tea and a Coca-Cola can. She set them down on the coffee table, then settled into her recliner.

"How has your leg been feeling?" she asked. "With the rain lately, I've been worried you'd be feeling something unpleasant."

"It's been mostly fine. I still have my moments, but it's a little less each time. And today, I feel great."

"Good. Very good," she said, and smiled. "Now, what brings you by?"

And here was the moment of truth. What would I say? Do I just come out with it? How do I even do that? I'll sound like a complete lunatic. I guess I must have had an expression of dismay on my face, because Mrs. Kamen leaned forward and spoke.

"Are you alright, Douglas? You seem to have something on your mind."

"I—" I started, but didn't have the words I wanted. After a few more seconds, I finished. "Do you have Internet access here, Mrs. Kamen?"

"Yes, I do," she responded. Her face looked puzzled.

"Family Grocer will soon offer home delivery of your grocery orders, and I wanted to stop by and introduce you to the program. As a valued Family Grocer customer, you can order your groceries online from our website, and we'll deliver them to your door within an hour."

Mrs. Kamen looked at me for a moment, then smiled. "Thank you, but I like to come down to the store on my own. It gets me out of the house. Though I might take you up on that offer come winter time. These old bones don't like the cold much anymore." She gave me a wink, and I smiled.

We talked for a few minutes longer, and I finished the Coke she'd brought me. I kept looking at her, expecting to see that shift from her perfectly pleasant face to something ancient and monstrous, but it never changed. I ended our conversation and left her apartment feeling guilty and bewildered.

*  *  *

The next morning, I phoned Dr. Markwell for an appointment. If I was hallucinating, and it seemed likely related to the trauma of my car accident, I needed help. Luckily, the office had a cancellation that morning and could get me in at 10:30. I arrived fifteen minutes early, filled out the requisite paperwork, and waited less than five minutes before I was called back. The antiseptic smell took me back to my hospital stay months before. I shuddered slightly.

"How has the leg been feeling?" Dr. Markwell asked once we were alone in the exam room.

"Pretty decent," I said. "But it's something probably related that brought me here today."

Then, I described the hallucinations following my return to work after the accident, going into as much detail as I could, explaining how I saw Mrs. Kamen's face almost floating above something that looked ancient, alien, and sinister.

I expected her response to be in disbelief. She surprised me.

"30% to 40% of PTSD patients report auditory or visual hallucinations," she said. "So, it's not as uncommon as you'd think."

"What do I do about it?" I asked.

"I'm going to prescribe you a month's worth of Zoloft for your anxiety," she said. "And schedule you an appointment with a therapist."

I wasn't particularly excited about taking more medications, but considering the circumstance, I wouldn't argue.

I met with the therapist twice that week, and thus started what I hopefully considered the last lap in my recovery from the accident. Seemed that physical therapy wasn't the only help I needed.

* * *

I had the following Sunday off work, so I didn't see Mrs. Kamen at the store. I took the afternoon and went to the park on the river at the edge of town. Late spring weather is often unpredictable, but this day was sunny with a light breeze. I sat on a bench and watched the water flow past. The Zoloft was working, taking the edge off my anxiety, and Dr. Samson, the therapist, seemed confident we could get me back on track quickly.

The next day, when I clocked in at Family Grocer, store director Cory Nederland called me into his office. He was a thin, middle-aged man with equally thin hair. He'd be bald in the next few years, I'd willingly bet. His normally cheerful face looked solemn.

"I'm not sure if you've heard the bad news yet," he said.

"What bad news?"

"Margaret Kamen passed away over the weekend. Died in her sleep, they say. She was eighty-nine."

"I hadn't heard," I said. My heart sank.

"Anyway, she's been a Family Grocer customer for ages, and everyone on the staff loved her, so we're sending a flower arrangement to the funeral, and we'd like you to be our representative. She always seemed to like you the best and spoke so highly of you to the other associates."

"Of course I'll go," I said. "She was such a sweet old woman."

* * *

The funeral was the following Wednesday, at 11:00 AM, with a viewing half an hour prior. It was drizzling, and my leg bothered me some that morning, just like Mrs. Kamen had warned it would. I arrived at Lashford Funeral home at 10:35 to pay my respects before the service. Ned Lashford, mortician and funeral director, ushered me into the building, which was full to brimming with friends and family.

I recognized Jared Kamen (soon to be Dr. Kamen) and Greta Kamen with her four children from photographs Mrs. Kamen had shown me during several of her store visits. I walked over to them.

"Hello, I'm Douglas Weatherly," I said.

"The guy from the grocery store!" Jared said and smiled, shaking my hand. "Great grandma spoke of you often."

I looked down at the hand that held mine, and it shifted, becoming a dark-skinned claw with long yellow and brittling nails. I looked up to see the faces of both Jared and Greta change, shimmering and shifting to something behind that veil, something dark and mottled, with thin blackened lips stretched over now too familiar needle-like teeth.

"She really loved coming to your store," Greta said, and the wash of her breath smelled of decay. Then her four children ran up to her, and I saw their faces slide away to reveal the horror underneath as well. I tried not to gasp, but let go of Jared's hand and stepped back.

"You okay, boss?" Jared asked. His yellow alien eyes blinked.

I could not answer. As I looked around the room, I'm sure my expression was unmistakably terrified. Throughout the crowd of mourners, interspersed among the friends, I watched the faces of Margaret Kamen's blood relatives shift and change into something else.

## AUTHOR NOTES - SHIFTED

I wrote the beginning sequence to where the main character first sees the true Mrs. Kamen, then the story sat for about a year. While on vacation in 2019, sitting on the beach, I brought my laptop so I could write while looking out over the water. I wrote the rest of the first draft in about 4 hours. At the time of the writing, I was in management at a local grocery store, and there was this tiny, kindly old woman I would see about once a week. I took that basic premise and twisted it around into something macabre. Lots of fun to write.

# THE IMAGO SATANAS

"**C**'mon, let's go inside," Cheryl said, grabbing my arm and pulling me toward the door. The large two story brick building that housed The Antiques Mall had once been the thriving Vaughn's Department Store on 2nd Avenue. Now it was home to over two dozen antique vendors. An indoor flea market, if you will.

Cheryl's infectious curiosity always won out, and we stepped through the heavy, aged door into a world full of every corner of history.

At first glance, you might call it junk, and there was a fair amount of that interspersed throughout, but if you took the time to hunt, to dig through the shelves and sort through the boxes, you could find some interesting things. It honestly took little to convince me to come in. I was a collector of a few different things, and places like this often had that one item you'd been searching for, that hidden gem needed to complete a collection.

And you always meet some interesting people. Cheryl had gone off toward old dishes, china, and other assorted glassware. I stopped and chatted with a portly gentleman who displayed a massive collection of classic vinyl rock and roll records, going back to the genre's beginnings. Most of them weren't what a collector would call "mint condition" as the sleeves were worn, but the discs themselves were quite playable, despite a scratch or worn label. I flipped through a box and pulled out a slightly worn copy of Elvis Presley's debut album.

"My good man," the vendor said, chewing on a toothpick. "Do you know how many weeks that there album spent at number one in the year of our Lord, 1956?"

"Ten weeks," I said. The vendor nodded his head and grinned around his toothpick.

"Not worth a bunch," he continued. "Every kid with an allowance back then snatched them up, but it's a solid debut album from his majesty, The King."

"Absolutely," I responded. "I also know that if you can find a mono copy, it might be worth upwards of a thousand bucks if it's in great shape."

"Oh, ho-ho." The vendor's eyes lit up. "You know your stuff."

"Big Elvis fan," I said, and put the self-titled album back into the box. I continued flipping, and found a decent copy of Hendrix's Electric Ladyland, but I already had a near-mint one in my collection at home. Cheryl had gotten it for me on my birthday two years ago. She was damn good at gifts.

The vendor and I talked albums for a few more minutes, then I drifted off when the conversation got stale. I found a dealer with a massive collection of old comic books, but they were mostly unbagged and in such poor condition that I browsed for less than five minutes.

Bookcases twelve feet high dominated a large area in the center of the building, their shelves filled with not only books, but every sort of knickknack you could imagine. I found a shelf of assorted old Hardy Boy mystery hardcovers. Man, I'd devoured those as a kid. I remember checking them out of the school library, three and four on a Friday, and bringing them back read and enjoyed on Monday. Those were the good old days, for sure, when your thoughts weren't on paying the mortgage, but on how many books you could cram in over a weekend sitting under a tree in the backyard.

I caught Cheryl on the opposite side of the bookcases. She came toward me with a smile.

"Find anything?" I asked.

"A decent carafe and tumbler set that would go nice on the patio this summer, but that's about it."

"You going to get it?"

"Maybe, but I don't want to lug the box around while we're window shopping. I'll go back and get it before we leave."

"Sounds good. What now?"

"Let's go upstairs." Cheryl said.

A massive split staircase centered on the back wall of the ground floor. The wide bottom section went up halfway between floors to a generous-sized landing, then two narrower flights of stairs rose on either side of the landing, ending at the second floor. In its day, that staircase was likely a wonder to behold. Now, the risers were worn, the banisters scarred and weathered from more than a century of heavy use. On the landing between staircases, more small displays sat in disarray.

On our way up, I stopped mid-stride on the landing. A small unremarkable table there held a single item, a toy monkey, its brownish fur matted and missing in places. Yellow teeth grinned at me with a menace unexpected from a child's toy. It held brass cymbals in its paws, poised roughly a foot apart, and just thinking of the sound they would make banged together—Jang! Jang! Jang!—had the hairs on my neck at attention. If Cheryl noticed me move a little faster to get off the landing, she didn't say so.

We took the left-hand set of stairs off the landing. The top floor was mostly junk—real junk—and we made the rounds in quick fashion, coming back down the right-hand stairs. I tried not to look at the monkey on the way back down, but that fucking thing drew my eyes to it, anyway. I swear, I almost bought that monkey just to keep some little kid from having to possess it. If I had, I would have chopped it into pieces and burned it. It was that terrifying. At that moment, I hoped I would never see something like it again.

Unfortunately, in less than five minutes, I'd see something that chilled me even more than that goddamn monkey. And, Lord help me, we took it home.

The ground floor of The Antiques Mall was expansive, and you could get lost in the maze of displays if you weren't careful. We continued around the shelves and boxes and curio cabinets. At the far right of the ground floor, we turned and saw a set of stairs leading down into darkness. As overused as the split staircase looked, these basement steps looked positively dilapidated. At the top end of the stairs, the male and female ends of an electrical cord hung, with a sign on the wall next to them: "More Items Downstairs! Plug in to turn on basement lights." I looked at Cheryl and she shrugged. I grabbed the two cords and married them, then a dim bulb lit above the stairs themselves while other lights came on in the basement beyond.

We descended the stairs, listening to each one groan under our weight. I thought for a moment one would give out and we'd tumble down into something under the building, but the boards held and we touched down on a cracked and uneven concrete floor.

The basement was large, but half the size of the first floor, full of rows of tables, each covered with odds and ends, mechanical devices that looked like ancient, strange pieces of equipment, ceramics and sculptures. We walked up and down the rows together, studying the myriad pieces there with piqued curiosity.

"My God, Michael," Cheryl said. "What is this stuff?"

"A lot of the machinery looks like it was part of the industrial revolution." I laughed, but my assessment may not have been far off. "The rest of it? Who knows?"

We split up then, each of us taking a row and gawking with astonishment at the unique things we saw. I was inspecting some sort of archaic engine device when Cheryl called to me.

"Michael, come here!"

She was directly across from me, a row away, when I turned. I shuffled between two tables, careful not to knock anything over. The "you break it, you buy it" policy on this stuff had to be steep. When I got to where she was, I looked at her smiling face, and then at where she was pointing.

The mask seemed so out of place among the other things down there in the basement when I saw it for the first time. It was wooden, carved into an intricate face that, while it didn't have horns or any standard Hollywood accouterments you'd associate with demons, beneath the surface, if you saw it just so, it looked like almost like a devil. Someone, a child perhaps, had painted it with garish white and red and yellow colors. To hide the menacing facade beneath, I'd imagine.

"Interesting piece, isn't it?" the voice came from behind, and startled us both. We turned, and he stood there, only five and a half feet tall, a man looking older than time itself. Long, deep wrinkles on his face reminded me of the Iron Maiden mascot, Eddie. He wore jeans and a long-sleeved collared shirt, buttoned all the way to the neck. He sported a red bandana on his head and a thick handlebar mustache. An aged biker, perhaps. Either way, he just seemed odd to me.

"Yes, yes it is," Cheryl replied. I had turned back to the mask. Like the monkey earlier, I couldn't not look at it. And I cursed myself for being so weak. But I could see beneath the vibrant colors, and I could see something there beyond that facade that touched the dark part of my soul.

"That mask has been around since before the founding of this country," the old man said. "Came from somewhere in Eastern Europe. Carved by a gypsy so old she dated Judas, I'm told."

"Fascinating," Cheryl said. I was having trouble listening, my focus split between the mask and the old man.

"Where are my manners?" the old man said. "My name is Walter. Walter Scoggins. All this you see down here is mine." He swept his arms out as if proud of his collection.

Cheryl introduced herself and mentioned my name, and I remember shaking hands with Walter Scoggins, but my mind was a thousand miles away, hooked into that stupid mask.

"You interested in buying it?" Walter asked.

"I might be," Cheryl said, and I couldn't have disagreed with her if I'd tried. "How much?"

"It's been a slow week, Cheryl," Walter said. "I'd be willing to let it go for fifty dollars cash. Now, that's a steal, let me tell you. A piece like this could easily go for several hundred."

"We'll take it!" Cheryl said, pulling her pocketbook from her purse and handing Walter a crisp fifty.

"You got yourself a conversation piece here, missy," Walter said as he wrapped the mask in an old newspaper and put it in a plastic bag.

"I'm sure it will be," Cheryl said. I remained unusually quiet.

Walter led us back to the stairs, and Cheryl thanked him. He thanked us in return, and I glanced at him as we mounted the stairs. He had an unnerving, wide smile full of crooked, yellowing teeth. Almost like a certain monkey up above. I shuddered. To make matters worse, I swore Walter winked at me as we passed out of sight.

That's how we came into possession of the mask. Cheryl also stopped by to get the carafe and tumbler set she'd found earlier. I believe they are still in the box, untouched. The mask, however, that had her full attention from the get-go.

* * *

"You're back!" Lucy yelled, and ran across the driveway as we exited the car. She had just turned eleven this year, and her eyes were as big as her dreams. People talk of the perfect child, and while I won't be so bold as to say Lucy is perfect, she's perfect for us.

Cheryl had a hard time giving birth, and I almost lost them both, so to say they're my miracles would be apt. It made me approach life differently afterward, and you can say it's a cliche, but every time I looked at the two of them together, the sky seemed a little brighter.

Lucy collided with me halfway, wrapping her arms around my middle. Kelly, the babysitter, sat on the front porch step, and said: "She missed you guys."

"I see that," I said. "How was she?"

"Same as always," Kelly said with a smile. Lucy was a bright kid, full of hope and not a mean bone in her body. She kept to herself a lot; she loved to read and draw, and those things were a babysitter's dream. Lucy practically watched herself, and it wouldn't be long before she wouldn't need a sitter. I thought Lucy was more advanced, and could probably stay home on her own for short periods now, but Cheryl was still mother-hen, and we deferred to her instincts on it. If I'd had to guess at that moment, Lucy would have been running the house soon, and I'm only partly joking.

"How was your date day, daddy?" Lucy asked.

"It was fine, honey," I replied. The Antique Mall was only part of our day out. The rest was more browsing throughout downtown shops, followed by a late lunch at Applebee's. We try to get out alone once a month. Not that Lucy's an issue, but adult time is adult time.

"Did you get me anything?" Lucy said and gave me the doe eyes.

"Check with your mother."

Lucy released me and shot across to Cheryl, her eyes wide with excitement.

"Dad said you got me something!" She beamed.

"Maybe," Cheryl said with a wry smile, and handed Lucy a small plastic bag. She opened it and gasped.

"A new journal and pen set!" She looked up from the bag, at her mother, then at me. Her smile was as wide as smiles get. "Oh, thank you!" Lucy took up journaling the past year, something school teachers are encouraging younger and younger. It's been a great thing for Lucy, and her vocabulary has grown. She loves it. Each night over the past eight months, for half an hour before bed, she's been writing in a composition book. Her journals are for her private thoughts, but she's read things to us occasionally. She's got a lot of intelligence in her writing, and I'd like to see her do something with it. Sometimes it's difficult to remember that she's only eleven.

We bought the journal at a hole-in-the-wall bookstore a couple of blocks from the antique shop. It was of those stores crammed floor to ceiling with books and all related things. They had an entire corner area devoted to journals and writing, and that's where Cheryl found the perfect journal for Lucy. It had a deep reddish-brown leather cover with an ornate brass clasp to hold the front flap closed. The paper was thick, off white, with a roughened texture.

The shop owner, a silvery tuft-haired gentleman with wrinkly jowls and round spectacles (the kind John Lennon wore), helped us pick out a writing pen set to go along with it, and even gave us a discount when we told him who it was for.

Lucy ran into the house with her gifts, no doubt to write the date she received it at the top of the first page. Whenever we buy her a book, I write Lucy's name and the date we bought it on the inside of the cover page. My mom did the same for me when I was a kid, and it became a sort of time capsule of my reading life as I got older. Once mom passed, I never kept up with it on my own, so that became a kind of cap on the time capsule. I still pull the last book she bought me down off the shelf sometimes and look at my name and the date on that inside cover, written in my mother's looping cursive handwriting with a blue ballpoint pen.

Cheryl took Kelly home and picked up pizza for dinner. We sat around eating and playing old board games and laughing until it was time for Lucy to go to bed at 9:00. She no doubt spent her half hour of writing time with her new journal, her innocence laid out on the page. I wonder how she felt when she first touched that pristine pen tip to the paper and felt it glide along, so smooth, leaving its indelible impressions.

I'm sure it was a glorious feeling.

After Lucy was asleep, I made love to my wife for the last time.

* * *

The next morning, I made pancakes and bacon for breakfast. Cheryl and I like our bacon crispy, while Lucy likes her's a little more rubbery. Where she got that gene from is beyond us.

Afterward, Cheryl brought out the mask, in all its blue, white, and yellow wooden glory, to show Lucy.

"Where'd you find that?" she asked and picked it up.

"In an old antique store," Cheryl said. "We'll have to take you there sometime. I think you'd really like it."

"Sounds neat," Lucy said, and then her interest went off to the next thing, which today turned out to be reading in the backyard hammock.

"Honey, do we have any paint stripper?" Cheryl asked me.

"There might be some with the paint supplies in the garage. If not, I can pick some up when I run to the hardware store. I need to get a new garden hose, since I'm pretty sure our old one has finally shit the bed." The hose had so many holes it was more like a sprinkler.

"Okay, thanks."

"What do you need paint stripper for?"

"I think I'm going to refinish the mask. The paint job looks like something a toddler would have done. The woodwork underneath on this thing is amazing when you really look close at it." She was inspecting the details, holding it very close to her face. I had no desire to get that close.

"Carved by Judas' gypsy whore, don't forget," I said with a smirk.

"Michael Roberts! Stop!" Cheryl gave me a jab.

There wasn't any paint stripper in the garage, so I picked up a spray bottle of some gel-like stuff that literally liquified paint, but somehow wouldn't harm wood. Chemistry at its finest.

I also got my new garden hose so I could water the flower beds without watering the entire lawn while doing it. It was a spectacular sunny day, with just a hint of a breeze to keep the summer gnats away, so I spent a couple hours doing various chores, while Lucy read in the backyard, suspended between two trees, and Cheryl stripped paint from the mask in the garage.

I had been washing our cars in the driveway when Cheryl called me into the garage. She had the mask in her hand and was holding it up to her face.

"Don't do that," I said, my tone very terse.

"Calm down, mood-killer," Cheryl joked, but I didn't feel like laughing.

Without paint to make it look clown-like, the face was quite terrifying, long and thin, with sharp jawlines that angled to a pointed chin. It was very intricate line work, with finely detailed strands of hair carved with astonishing skill. The inside had perfect, smooth contours. Impressive as it was, it still gave me a shudder.

Cheryl took the mask away from her face and looked at me.

"You don't like it, do you?"

I hesitated one moment too long.

"Well, you don't have to like it. It's mine." She laid it on the table where she'd been working and put her hands on her hips. I knew she wasn't joking.

"I'm sorry," I said. "It just creeps me out a little."

"And that's what I like about it."

Cheryl had a sense of the macabre, and normally that never bothered me, but something about that mask did not sit well. I didn't like it in the house.

One time, I should have trusted my instincts.

And it cost me so much.

* * *

We had cold leftover pizza for a late lunch and sat together on the back deck while the sun bathed us in tender warmth. I cracked open a beer, Cheryl drank a wine cooler, and Lucy had a glass of sun tea. She'd put the gallon jar of cold water and tea bags out in the sun late morning, and by 2:00 it had brewed a dark golden brown.

Cheryl hung the mask in the den. If it had to stay in the house, that was a good place for it, since I rarely went in there. I'd still rather it wasn't in the house at all, but I had little say on that one, I knew.

* * *

I jolted awake in bed that night. I don't remember having a dream, but something startled me enough to bring me out of what had been a deep sleep. My phone said it was 2:43 in the morning. Cheryl was on her side, facing away from me, and I could hear her steady, rhythmic breathing. My body told me I needed to piss, so I got out of bed, slipped on my robe, and shuffled down the hall.

Slightly more awake on the way back, I noticed Lucy's door open. I peeked in and her bed was empty. I walked down the hall into the living room. She wasn't there, either. The kitchen stood empty and dark except for the light over the stove.

I found her in the den, sitting cross-legged on the floor, with her hands laying limp in her lap.

Looking at that mask on the wall.

That damned mask.

"Lucy?" I whispered.

No response. No movement.

"Lucy." I said, louder.

Still no response.

I felt a heaviness in the air then, an electricity that made the hair on my arms stand straight. I didn't like it. And I didn't like that Lucy wasn't responding.

"Lucy, honey," I said, touching her shoulder. She didn't move. "What are you doing?"

"Listening," she said. Her voice was flat, emotionless.

"Listening to what?"

"To him," she said, and dragged her left arm up to point at the mask. "I'm listening to him."

I grabbed her shoulders then and turned her toward me. Her eyes stared, empty and lifeless, at nothing. "Lucy, wake up!" I shouted.

Her eyes then opened wide and filled with awakening realization.

"Daddy? What—?"

"It's okay, honey," I whispered, and pulled her close. She hugged me tight, and I heard footsteps thumping down the hall. Cheryl appeared in the den, her face frightened.

"I heard a shout. What's going on?"

"That thing," I said, pointing at the mask. "It's got to go."

Cheryl's eyes were incredulous. "What are you talking about?"

"I found Lucy sitting here in front of it. She said she was listening to it."

"Honey, what happened?" Cheryl asked Lucy, ignoring me.

"I don't know. I got up to get a drink. When I was in the kitchen, I heard something in the den, then—I can't remember anything until Dad just woke me up."

"Is she sleepwalking again?" Cheryl asked. It had been years since the last incident, but Lucy had been prone to sleepwalking between the ages of five and eight. It happened regularly enough that after a few times, we took her to a doctor, who wanted to prescribe medication. We were against that, so Cheryl taught her some meditation techniques and began giving her melatonin before bed. That seemed to lessen the sleepwalking, and after the age of eight, she hadn't sleepwalked again until tonight. If that's what this was, and it did not convince me of that.

We put Lucy back to bed, sat with her until she went to sleep, then Cheryl and I had a talk.

"That mask has to go," I said.

"Don't be ridiculous, Michael."

"Didn't you see what it did to her?"

"What did it do? Seriously?"

"She came out to get a drink and then can't remember anything after. When I found her, she was sitting on the floor in front of that thing."

"She was sleepwalking, Mike. That's all."

"She said she was listening to the mask, Cheryl."

"And she was asleep. Don't try making something bigger out of this than it is. We're not in a horror movie, for God's sake."

"I've had a bad feeling about that mask since we first saw it in the antique store."

"So you don't like it. I get it. But don't project that into a ridiculous scenario. Jesus, you're so damned odd like that sometimes."

I grabbed my pillow and went to the spare room for the rest of that night. I slept little, though. All I could think of were the words Lucy had said:

"I'm listening to him."

* * *

I left work early on Monday to drive back to The Antiques Mall. After the incident with Lucy, I needed answers. The person I thought could provide them was the one we'd bought that blasted mask from.

Cheryl had been cold that morning. While I understood her disbelief, I couldn't agree with her just blowing it off. It wasn't just sleepwalking, and I believed that, one-hundred percent. I'm not necessarily a superstitious man, but my grandmother once told me something when I had gotten scared as a kid that left an impression on me. She told me that there are bad things out there, evil things, things we might not understand. But there were always good things that acted as a counterpoint, things that would protect us and save us.

We'd found the evil thing. Now I needed to understand it so I could find the good thing to act against it. Maybe even *be* the good thing, if that's what it came to.

It was quiet in the mall when I arrived, understandable since it was a weekday. I went in the main door and twisted through the vendors, heading for the basement. I plugged in the light and took the steps down into the coolness beneath the building.

The tables were there, still roughly organized into rows, but outside of a few block-like mechanical pieces littered throughout, most of the things Cheryl and I had seen when we'd been here before were gone. I looked around the area and saw no Walter Scoggins among the sea of flat tabletops, either.

I looked from one end of the room to the other, hoping there was some adjoining area that served as an office or some such, but found nothing.

I took the stairs two at a time going back up, and when I hit the ground floor, I found the nearest vendor, my old friend the record collector.

"The guy who has the basement setup, is he here today?" I asked.

The vendor scratched his scruffy beard and looked around.

"Nobody been down there in a while, man," he said.

"I was just here a couple weeks ago with my wife, and we met an older man down there, sold us an old mask. His name was Walter Scoggins."

"Sorry, friend, name doesn't ring a bell. Like I said, nobody's been down there selling in a long while. The basement gets used mostly for storing junk parts or stuff that won't sell."

"Who owns the store?" I was becoming irritated.

"Jacob Rickard. If he's not on the floor, you can find him in his office, over by the musical instruments."

"Thanks," I said, and set off in that direction. I was lucky, and found Jacob Rickard in his office, at an old wooden desk, its expansive surface strewn with tall stacks of paperwork.

"Can I help you?" Rickard said, looking over heavy-rimmed glasses. He was a thin man, almost too thin, with equally thin hair receding from his forehead.

"I hope so. My wife and I were here a couple weeks ago and bought an item from a vendor—"

"All sales are final. No refunds," Rickard said, his tone even and uncaring.

"I don't need a refund," I replied. "I just need to speak with the vendor. His name is Walter Scoggins. He was selling items in the basement when we were here."

"Hate to break it to you, but nobody sells anything from the basement, and I don't have a Walter—Scoggins, was it?—vending here."

"But he was down there. My wife bought an antique mask—"

"And I'm telling you, nobody sells from down there."

I leaned over his desk. "And I'm telling you, my wife paid fifty dollars for an antique mask from Walter Scoggins in your basement two weeks ago."

"Do you have a receipt?" Rickard asked, looking over the top of his glasses again.

"I—no," I said. "But that doesn't matter—"

"It matters very much. Now, you're becoming belligerent, and I will not tolerate it in my place of business. I'm asking you to leave."

My lips tightened, but I kept my mouth shut. There really wasn't much I could do. I couldn't force him to tell me how to find Scoggins.

"Fine," I said, and turned to leave.

"Please don't come back. Ever. Next time, I will call the police."

As I banged out of the main entrance to the street, I wondered if maybe old Walter Scoggins hadn't taken us for a ride. Maybe Rickard was being honest, and Scoggins wasn't a vendor there at all. Maybe he'd just sold us something from the basement that wasn't his, pocketed fifty bucks, then went on his way.

After the past couple of weeks, though, I knew Walter Coggins was real. I just wasn't sure who—or what—he actually was. And I wasn't sure I wanted to know.

* * *

The second incident with Lucy and the mask happened a week later.

In between, there had been nothing overly strange, at least not that I was aware of. I got up every night to check on her, though. Paranoid? Perhaps, but this was my daughter, and no matter what Cheryl said, there was definitely something wrong with the mask.

I hadn't yet told Cheryl about my return visit to the antique store. There really seemed no point right then. She was still mad at me, which I considered odd enough that I continued sleeping in the spare room just to avoid her. We hadn't spoken to each other much beyond a cursory greeting during the entire week.

Lucy seemed fine, but she was a quiet kid, so it's hard to tell. I asked her about that night once, a couple of days later, but she recalled little of anything, and seemed no worse for it.

I was, however, concerned. Which is why I checked on Lucy every night. I checked on Cheryl, too, though she never knew that. There's no such thing as being overprotective in being a husband and father.

Even now, I believe I should have done more, though. Maybe things wouldn't have turned out the way they had if I'd been more assertive right from the beginning. But that's irrelevant now. You can drown yourself in "what ifs" and "should haves" and neither will make a lick of difference.

This time, I found Lucy in her room on my nightly check. She was sitting on the floor, cross-legged again. The mask was in front of her, and I froze in mortal terror.

"Quo modo serve," Lucy said in perfect Latin, which I learned during later research meant: "How can I serve?"

My mouth dropped open, but no sound came out. I tried to move, but stood rooted to the spot instead.

"Ego thuribulum. Carpe corpus," which meant, "I am your vessel. Take my body."

There was silence for a few moments after that, then I heard a low, almost thrumming sound, followed by a voice not Lucy's that said: "Dimittere est anima mea," which translated to "release my soul."

My body found its thrust again, and I leaped forward.

"Lucy!" I screamed as I scooped up the mask and threw it across the room. She jolted out of whatever trance she had been in, her eyes full of rising fear and welling tears.

"Daddy!" she cried, and I took her into my arms. She was trembling. "I could hear myself saying the words, and I knew what they meant, but I couldn't stop myself."

"It's alright honey. You're okay now." I held her head against my shoulder and she sobbed.

I looked at the mask laying face down on the floor just feet away, and I wanted that fucking thing gone. Cheryl could be as mad as she wanted, but I'd had enough.

I heard Cheryl pounding down the hall, and she appeared in the doorway, pulling her robe over her shoulders.

"What happened this time?" She questioned, and I very much disliked the tone of her voice.

"Take that thing out of here," I told her, and pointed at the mask. She leaned over and picked it up. "There's something very wrong with it. I want it gone."

"Christ, Michael. Dramatic much?" was her reply.

"Our daughter was just speaking Latin to that thing, Cheryl. And Lucy doesn't speak Latin."

I could tell she wasn't believing it.

"And—and I heard something speak back."

Cheryl sighed and left the doorway.

I held onto Lucy for a long time, and afterward, when I'd gotten her to go back to sleep, I went to the den and took that damned mask off the wall.

It was past time for some answers.

* * *

I flipped open the lid to my laptop and sat there, silent, wondering what the hell I was even looking for. The screen's dull glow illuminated my dark office and cast my shadow behind me.

The mask, frightening as it was, sat on the edge of my desk. I didn't want anyone else near it right now. Not until I knew what it was we were dealing with.

First, I translated the Latin Lucy had spoken. That raised the hairs on my neck. Then, I entered a search for "Demon Mask" and got dozens of images of plastic and latex Halloween masks. That was of no help. I changed my search to "Carved Demon Mask" and that got me into something more approximating what I was looking for. The popular results at the top of the page were still novelty items, but the further down the page I scrolled, the more serious the links became.

I was three pages into the search when I found a link to a long article on the Imago Satanas, or Mask of Satan. When I saw the image at the beginning of the article, my breath stopped, and I felt that peculiar hair-raising electricity again.

While it wasn't exact, the rendered drawing was a very close approximation of the mask that had been hanging in my den. Too close for coincidence. Far too close for comfort. I sat back in my chair and bit my fist to keep from screaming.

According to the legends, a gypsy woman of over three hundred years carved and enchanted the Imago Satanas out of wood taken from a tree in the Garden of Gethsemane during the time of Jesus Christ himself. Crafted at the request of a still unknown individual, its purpose was to reveal, exorcise, and trap demonic souls. Rumors of the time were that it was created to drive the demonic entity from Judas Iscariot that led him to betray Jesus (Luke 22:3 suggests the possessing entity was Satan himself, hence the name Mask of Satan). Accounts vary whether they ever used it for its intended purpose, but the most popular opinion is that it was a successful endeavor, and once freed of the demon's influence, Judas, overcome by remorse, committed suicide by hanging himself.

In the centuries since, occult texts noted the mask turning up multiple times, most often in times of global crisis. It was instrumental in many battles of The Crusades. One unsubstantiated account had it bought by the British government on the order of Winston Churchill in early 1945 to be used against Adolf Hitler to exorcise the demon they believed had possessed him. Like Judas, it's rumored that upon being freed from the demon's influence, Hitler committed suicide. I saw an explicit pattern forming.

How it ended up in the basement of an antique shop is baffling, as it seemed to be an instrument of good, its purpose ultimately noble. So, why then did it make me feel so uneasy?

Over the next two hours, I joined several forums claiming to have information on the Satan Mask, and most were full of conjecture, but not all. Just as I was about to end my excursion into the bowels of the Internet, I got a private message from a user named JCParanormal on one forum where I had asked questions. The message was simple: "If you want to know more about the Imago Satanas, check this link." Followed by a web address. JCParanormal also included a phone number to text or call if I needed anything else.

I'm not normally one to click on unknown links, as everyone's probably gotten a virus from doing so at one time or another, but I clicked on this one without hesitation, and what I read turned by blood to ice.

In 1969, the Imago Satanas was in the hands of a Catholic Priest who attempted to stop the possession of cult leader Charles Manson, whose "Manson Family" followers committed a string of murders in the summer of that year. However, Manson's possession proved unorthodox, and he was, through unknown means, able to reverse the enchantment on the mask with inexplicable results. Instead of exorcising and trapping demonic souls, it was now releasing those it had once ensnared.

By 1971, the mask's whereabouts were unknown. Underground sources say it was being safeguarded by a deeply connected network of occult experts, researchers, and investigators, though no proof of that exists.

A related artifact, known as the Os Daemonium, or Demon Mask, was reported discovered in a Mayan temple on the Yucatan Peninsula in the early 20th century, its whereabouts also shrouded in mystery.

I don't know where the mask had been since 1971, but I knew where the Imago Satanas was right now.

It was sitting on my desk, its sightless eyes watching me. Prior to that, it had been hanging on the wall in the den, drawing my daughter's attention. Before that, it had been in the basement of an antique store, waiting for a buyer.

As I closed the laptop lid and sat in my darkened office, silent and thinking, I wondered what happened to the demon who possessed Manson when his physical body finally died in 2017.

And then, in an instant of realization, I pictured the old man in the antique store basement and I knew. It was him.

I felt like I was losing my mind.

And I believe the mask knew it.

"We need to talk," Cheryl said then, from the doorway behind me, and my heart nearly stopped.

* * *

"I know you don't believe me," I said. "But that mask is evil."

We were sitting at the dining room table, each of us with a cup of coffee. She sipped hers and peered at me over the cup as she did. I didn't recognize her anymore.

"Oh, I believe you, Michael," she said, her tone haughty, bordering on arrogant.

"You're not Cheryl anymore, are you?"

"No."

"When?"

"The day she stripped and cleaned the mask," the thing in Cheryl's body said. "She was already curious. All she had to do was wear the mask for a moment, and I took her."

"And you are?"

"My name is Alrac," it said, and my wife smiled. "That mask has been my prison for six hundred years."

I remained calm, almost a kind of numb feeling.

"So, Alrac, what do you want?"

"Want? To live, of course."

"There has to be more to it than that," I said. I was really stalling, trying to come to terms with my wife being possessed and trying to figure out how I was going to get her back and then get my daughter safely away. I was a mess inside.

"I want to bring my brothers and sisters back from the brink of oblivion."

"And to do that, someone has to put on the mask?"

"Correct. The transference of souls is instantaneous. And painless, in case you were wondering."

"I was, thanks," I said.

"Once we have your daughter, then we'll move on to your neighbors, and to their neighbors, so on and so forth. I already got Becky Smith down the street when she stopped over to gossip the other day."

"How many of you are there?" I got up to pour more coffee. I brought the carafe over to fill Cheryl's cup.

"Thousands since the time of Christ," Alrac said from my wife's lips. "During biblical times, our kind thrived on this planet. It's a true shame to see what you've left us to come back to."

"Yeah, it's a bit of a shithole. Sorry."

Alrac laughed Cheryl's laugh and I shuddered. "I like you Michael. You'd make a magnificent vessel. My associate, Regor, he is the perfect soul for you."

"Yeah, I'm gonna pass," I said. I was still holding my shit together, but barely.

"That's a pity," Alrac said. "It's easier if you go willingly."

"Yeah, that's usually how rape works," I said, and this time I smiled. "Tell me, is my wife still in there?" I pointed to her head.

"Nah, we swapped places. She's in the mask now."

"Good, then she won't feel this," I said, and swung the coffee pot at her head. It collided and shattered, spilling hot coffee across her face, down the front of her, shards of glass cutting her scalp and slicing her cheeks. The thing that had taken my wife's body screamed as I kicked the chair out from underneath her. She hit the floor hard as I ran down the hall toward Lucy's room.

"You fucker!" I heard her scream as I reached Lucy's doorway.

She wasn't there.

"Lucy!" I yelled, and I could hear Alrac scrambling to get to her feet. "Lucy, where are you?"

Then there was ten feet of hall between myself and my demon-possessed wife, and that distance was closing fast. Alrac rushed at me, and I ducked into Lucy's room and slammed the door on Alrac's reaching arm. I heard bones crunch and an anguished howl outside the door. I swung it open and kicked out, catching her in the middle of the knee with my heel and dropping her to the ground with a grunt.

"That hurts like Hell, doesn't it?" I said, breathing hard. I rushed past her before she could regain footing and flung open the bathroom door.

Lucy was standing there with the mask in her hands.

"Lucy?" I said and held my arms out.

"Not anymore," the thing in my daughter's body said, and my heart sank. But I didn't have time to react before Alrac had my arms and was holding me fast.

"Get the mask on him," she said, and whoever had taken over Lucy came toward me, a smile spreading wide across her face as she held the mask up.

I kicked out then, and caught Lucy in the chest, pushing her back into the bathroom where she crashed into the sink. I twisted and pulled my arms free from Alrac's grip and shoved her backward. She'd planted herself well this time, and didn't go far. She swung at me and caught me with the flat of her hand against the side of my head. I saw stars for a moment, then tackled her midsection and slammed her against the hall wall. She pounded on my back and I shoved her aside.

Then I was running down the hall, my heart a hammer in my chest. I grabbed my phone off the dining room table where I'd left it, and bolted out the front door into the driveway. There was no time to take a car, and the keys were inside the house where I was no longer welcome, anyway. I padded down the street in my slippers and pajamas, running until my lungs felt like they were on fire. I wanted to throw up, but I pushed myself a little farther.

I finally stopped at a gas station at the end of our subdivision. After I caught my breath, I sent a text to JCParanormal, then hid out behind the station near the garbage dumpster, where the shadows were long and I felt safe for the moment.

I'm wasn't sure if Cheryl and Lucy would come looking for me right away, or at all. They'd probably want to bolster their numbers first, either way. So, I'm sure they visited the Gruenwald home and the Mackies next door, probably then down the street to the Byrne residence. Good luck there, demons. That guy is a tough old bastard.

* * *

JCParanormal turned out to be Jeremy Cochran, though he prefers to go by JC. He's part of a group of paranormal investigators, people who seek the weird things that happen. The fella who came with him to pick me up was a real quiet guy named Thad. Jeremy doesn't talk much about him, but from what I've gleaned from listening over the past week, there's some major tension between them going back to when they were kids, but I guess that's a story for another day. Oh, and Thad is a telekinetic. That means he can move things with his mind. I'm an engineer. My wife is an accountant. Our daughter is in middle school. Weeks ago, I thought the world was normal. Now, I wonder just how much of it truly is.

Demons. Telekinesis. Damn.

They got me clothes and some food, and I told them everything that had happened over bad coffee at a roadside diner off the interstate, while people milled about outside the windows, smoking cigarettes or walking their dogs before continuing on their journeys to who knows where. Just people acting like it's a normal day, and I suppose for them it still is. But not for much longer.

JC confirmed that what Cheryl bought from the Manson-Demon was indeed the Imago Satanas, and getting it out of the hands of a cluster of demons who'd been cooped up inside it for hundreds of years was his team's top priority.

My top priority is getting my wife and daughter back. A member of JC's group named Apostle John has spent some time scouring texts, determining that it is indeed possible to save them, and we'll do everything we can to pull them from the mask and swap them back into their bodies. But JC also told me the hard truth: if that's not workable, I needed to be prepared to put them down.

That's been a hard pill to swallow.

It's been a few days since I ran out my front door. Supernatural activity has spiked to an all-time high since then, the experts with us are saying. It's likely tied to that damn mask and all leading to something big, but nobody is certain what it is. That there's a growing army of subversive hell-spawn out there being led by my wife and daughter undoubtedly ties into it all. They'll stop at nothing to spread themselves to every corner of the Earth, like a virus. That means they're busy, and I'm likely forgotten by now.

I haven't forgotten about them, though, and I'm coming to save my family.

But they don't know that I'm not alone anymore.

And that gives me hope.

## AUTHOR NOTES - THE IMAGO SATANAS

I'll admit, this is my favorite story from this volume. It just wrote itself in a whirlwind, and that first scene with Lucy in the den with the mask raised every hair on the back of my neck as I wrote it.

In 2009, my wife Carla and I went to an antique mall that was originally an enormous department store in the town of Alpena, Michigan. They filled this place wall-to-wall, floor-to-ceiling with every variety of stuff imaginable. We loved it, and as we browsed, my wife found a strange painted mask sitting on a table. That sparked a story idea, and later that night I jotted down some quick notes, so I'd remember. Good thing, because I was more than a decade older when I wrote this story.

The basement, as described in the story, existed. You had to plug in the lights to go down there, as I recall. The monkey on the landing to the second floor did not exist, however. That's a nod to The Monkey, one of my favorite Stephen King short stories I'd just re-read when I started writing this, and an antique store seemed like the perfect place for an homage.

The real antique store closed down in 2019, I discovered when I researched the place as I began writing the story. It saddens me that places like that are disappearing, because I always found them fascinating, like time capsules of odds and ends.

When I started forming the origins and history of the mask, I thought I was the cleverest sonofabitch on the planet, being able to tie Judas, Hitler, and Manson together. Now, I don't think I'm the cleverest, but I might be in the top five. (I kid. Seriously.)

Jeremy Cochran and Thad Matthews have appeared in a couple other of the other short stories in this volume, REACTION and MONSTERS. This is more of their tale, though both were really only behind the scenes here.

Oh, and the demon Alrac is just my wife's name written backwards. And no, I don't think she's a demon.

# VOICES

At seventy-six years of age, there were few days when Elias Witherton didn't wake with some part of him in pain, but the headache at 5:55 AM today wasn't normal. It seemed to radiate out from the center of his brain in pulsing waves, each one growing stronger than the last. These headaches had been coming and going for most of a week now, and this one eked into migraine territory.

Elias shuffled to the bathroom and relieved his bladder, then washed up, brushed his teeth, shaved off three days of whiskers with his brand new Norelco electric razor, and finally put his glasses on. He opened the medicine chest, thumbed open the Excedrin bottle, and shook three tablets into his palm. He swallowed them with cool tap water, thankful he wasn't a pill-popper like crazy Natalie Goodman down at the senior center. That woman took fifteen pills a day and even carried them around in a big plastic organizer to remember what she took and when she took it.

Back in his bedroom, Elias dressed with arthritic slowness, laboring to even button his shirt. The past summer had been dry. As a result, he'd had a noticeable decrease in joint pain, but now it was October, and since early September it had rained seven days out of ten, it seemed, and something about that change kicked the old arthritis into high gear. One of these days, he'd have to consider moving to Arizona, like his old chum Lester McLeod had done a few years before. Lester mailed a handwritten letter every few months, most often boasting about how the dry heat of the American Southwest had pushed his arthritis symptoms back a decade. He felt better than he had in years, and writing the notes by hand was a testament to that fact. But Lester had worked thirty-five years for the United States Postal Service, and his pension left him in good financial shape. Elias, however, had spent his working years as a machinist for a local job shop, and his meager pension afforded him few luxuries, least of which was uprooting his homestead to move to the Grand Canyon state.

"Fuckin' joints," he muttered as he finished the last of his shirt buttons and stooped over to tie his boots. His fingers were loosening up some. When he stood up, he was ready to face the day.

His days were ones of ritual. That, he figured, kept him alive. Monday thru Friday he had breakfast at Charlotte's Restaurant with several of his gentlemanly peers (a group that had once included the esteemed Lester McLeod before his exodus to the southwest). They would sit and drink coffee, share sections of the paper, and spend two to three hours discussing the fate of the world and whichever Detroit sports team was currently playing. Weekends, he would stay home and make scrambled eggs and bacon for himself. The restaurant was too busy on Saturday and Sunday—filled to the brim with out-of-towners, referred to as flatlanders by the locals. October was bow-hunting season, with firearm season just less than a month away. The influx of unfamiliar faces had grown, and would only get worse until the end of the year. And, damn it, he loathed those invaders.

At 6:25, Elias closed up his house, stepped slowly off the porch and started down the sidewalk toward the center of town. The three blocks he walked every morning gave him the opportunity to work off the final stiffness of sleep with some measure of certainty. Half a block before Charlotte's, he could smell the aroma of baked goods. Charlotte's also included a decent-sized bakery, which meant some poor soul came in at 3:30 every morning to have bread and donuts ready and on display before the doors opened to the public at 6:00.

Elias claimed Lansford, Michigan as his hometown, and Charlotte's Restaurant had been there almost as long as he. Its namesake, Charlotte Whitaker, had run it until she passed in the mid-1980s of a brain aneurysm. Family had kept it for a dozen years before selling it off to current owner Pamela Goldberg, whom Elias thought was doing a commendable job. It was his favorite place in town, somewhere he felt comfortable.

* * *

Elias stepped through the restaurant door, and a small bell hanging from a string above it jangled to announce his arrival. Certainly old fashioned. The Lansford Cafe, on the outskirts of town, had an electronic sensor than did the same, but the one time Elias had gone there, he was equally unimpressed with that as he was with the food.

"Good morning, Eli," a middle-aged waitress said as she swept lithely by with a platter of plates bound for the dishwasher.

"Mornin', Rosemarie," Elias returned with a nod and a smile. Rosemarie Swenson was the only living person in Lansford he allowed to call him Eli. His late wife Betty had called him that since they'd been barely out of their teens, but she had been the only one until now. Rosemarie was a sweetheart, and a widower herself, so Elias guessed that made it okay for her to call him Eli, as well. He was twenty years her senior, and he was sure there were no romantic sparks to fly, but she still made him feel good with her warm smile and friendly conversations.

Charlotte's regulars, Chet Brinkley and George Mason, sat at a large round table just off the kitchen. Chet was working on a Boston Crème filled donut, and George was reading the Detroit Free Press and sipping an Earl Grey. Elias gave them both a cursory nod as he approached the table and pulled out a chair.

"What's the good word for today, Elias?" Chet asked. A gob of Boston crème had squeezed out the end of his donut and onto his fingers. He licked it off his hand and reached for a napkin.

"Too early for a good word, Chet," Elias said with a grin. His head still ached, just a dull pulse at the base of his skull now, and he felt he would soon be on the mend from that ailment.

Rosemarie emerged through the metal swinging kitchen doors and grabbed a pot of coffee and a cup before heading toward the table. "You look under the weather today, hon," she said to Elias as she poured deep amber liquid into the cup. She set it down in front of him and the steam rose, fragrant and wisp-like.

"Got a bit of a headache this mornin'," Elias said. "Probably just need a good jolt of caffeine to work out the kinks." He took a deep breath over his coffee cup and smiled at her.

*Maybe you're going to have a stroke and do us the good favor of dying, you withered old bastard.*

Elias's eyes widened. He was still looking up at Rosemarie, but the voice he'd faintly heard had been George Mason's. "What was that, George?" Elias asked.

"I didn't say anything," George replied over the top of his paper, but his face looked slightly surprised.

"I swore I heard you say something."

"Nope," Chet added. "He didn't say a word."

Elias's face wrinkled.

*Maybe the old coot's finally losing his mind.* The voice was Chet's, but Elias had not seen the man's lips move. The voice had been inside his head.

"What'll it be today, Eli?" Rosemarie asked, taking a pad and pen out of her apron.

"French Toast, link sausage, and hash browns," Elias said, more out of habit than actual thought. Four days out of five, he had that same breakfast when he came to the restaurant.

"Onions in with the hash browns?" Rosemarie added, but she knew the answer.

"Yuh," he stammered.

"You sure you're okay, Eli?" Rosemarie asked.

Elias was having trouble gathering his thoughts. Everything suddenly seemed jumbled, his brain incapable of filtering and deciphering input. He was trying not to show any emotion on his face, trying not to let on that he felt like he really was losing his mind.

"I'm fine," he said, not convincingly. He picked up a container of non-dairy creamer and tore open the top, but his hands shook so badly the liquid sloshed over the sides and onto the table. A rivulet ran off the edge and onto his slacks.

*Jesus, please don't let him die on my shift,* Rosemarie's voice said in Elias's head. He watched her pull a towel from her apron belt and mop the imitation creamer off the table. Elias grabbed the napkin that came with his silverware and dabbed at his trouser leg. He looked up at Rosemarie, then over at Chet and George. His face was turning pink with embarrassment.

"Fuck," Eli muttered under his breath. "Damned hands don't want to cooperate." His smile was weak. Chet nodded in an equally unconvincing agreement, and George simply went back to reading the sports section of the Free Press. Elias excused himself.

"Gotta hit the head," he said, and pushed his chair away from the table. Behind him, Rosemarie Swenson let out an inner sigh of relief that only Elias Witherton heard.

* * *

In the restroom, Elias took off his glasses and splashed cold water on his face. The mirror reflected a man much older than the one who'd started back at him when he'd brushed his teeth that morning. Dark circles surrounded his eyes, and his silver hair seemed whiter.

*Jesus H Christ, how long does it take to get a goddamn omelet these days?* A man's voice exploded in Elias's head.

*If Harry knew I was cheating on him.* A woman's voice this time.

*Fuckin Lions ain't gonna do worth a shit this year.* Elias recognized George Mason's baritone.

*I am so tired of cooking this slop every goddamn day. Hope whoever gets this omelet chokes on it.* The morning shift cook.

*If I don't find a job soon, I'm going to lose the house. Then what'll we do? But there's no work here anymore.* Robert Densmore.

*If Bob doesn't find a job soon, I'm going to leave him. Just take the kids and leave.* Jennifer Densmore.

Elias felt the surge of voices in his head building in pulses. The reflection in the mirror showed so much fear, and a small, slow trickle of blood had run from his left nostril. "Oh God, what's happening to me?" he whispered, cupping his hands over his ears, trying to drown out the sudden onslaught of voices in his mind that had joined his own. "Please make it stop."

But it did not. It was as though some long-standing barrier had broken down in his brain, allowing an unholy bond to be forged between him and the minds of others. Elias felt as though the overload might well kill him.

He cranked the handle on the towel dispenser and pulled a sheet from the spool. He ran it under the cold water and held it to his nose, soaking up the trail of blood resting now on his upper lip.

*Man, those are some nice legs*, the voice came unbidden. Fresh blood oozed from Elias's other nostril.

*—if she only knew how much I—of them going to the Super Bowl—wearing any panties—coffee tastes like crap—that job in Illinois—where's the ketchup?—gotta get to work—if the old man's dead in the crapper or not—these heels are killing me—*

Elias fell against the wall, trying to get to the door. He had to get out of the restaurant, go somewhere there weren't any people, get these voices out of his head. He wrenched open the restroom door and limped sideways back into the dining room. Chet and George both stood up out of their chairs, and Rosemarie dropped the pot of decaf she had just taken off the warmer and it shattered against the worn yellow tile. Elias ran headlong into a small table outside the bathroom, knocking it over, spilling the salt and pepper shakers and napkin holder onto the floor. Blood spurted heavily from both his nostrils, like he had red streamers hanging from his nose.

*—holy Mary, mother of God—bleeding—stroking out?—goddamn aneurysm—now what?—geezer's kickin' the bucket—oh Lord, the blood—bet it's a thong—holy fuck, what's he doing?—*

Elias staggered across the room toward the door, his hands curled in knots, clawing at the sides of his head. Customers at three tables shifted aside to let him pass, the looks of growing horror on their faces lost on him. The only thought in his head belonging solely to him was of making the voices stop. He crashed into the entrance door, flinging it wide, and he stumbled onto the sidewalk, the bell-on-a-string jangling behind him.

*—Oh God—body call 911—he's having a fit—lots of blood—gonna be sick—sale at the market—*

The truck had no time to stop as Elias hurtled into the street, arms flailing wildly. There was a screeching of tires locking up, and Elias bounced off the truck's grill, spinning forward through the air like a crazed ballerina before smacking face down on the pavement. He did not move.

Chet Brinkley and George Mason followed Rosemarie Swenson through the door, and she rushed over to Elias's still unmoving form.

"Somebody call 911!" George Mason bellowed.

"Oh my—Jesus!" Wendell Redford, the truck drive, shouted. His face was pale white and his eyes terrified. "I didn't even see him come into the street! Oh my God! Is he dead?"

Chet grabbed the truck driver by the shoulders and moved him back. Rosemarie knelt beside Elias, and she heard a groan. He was trying to roll over, but having no success because his hip and one of his legs were broken. Rosemarie helped him, and he lay on his side, gasping. Blood still coursed from his nose, running into the cracks of the asphalt, and now there were two wide gashes along the left side of his forehead bleeding as well. His body was limp, and his eyes were glassy and unfocused when Rosemarie looked into them.

*Oh God, he's going to die! I just know it!*

"Yuh, I am. Sorry to die on your shift, sweetheart—" he whispered. Rosemarie scooted back, her face suddenly drained of color and her eyes went wide.

"It's going to be all right," George Mason squatted down next to Elias to check his pulse. It was very erratic. "You're going to be fine. Ambulance is on its way."

*He's not gonna make it.*

"You're right, George," Elias said weakly. "I'm not gonna make it. Looks like I'll be doing you that favor after all, you rotten sonofabitch." He coughed, and blood sprayed from between his lips.

George Mason's face changed to a shocked realization as Elias Witherton gave a weak smile and closed his eyes. George helped Rosemarie to her feet, and they both stood silent and stunned as the ambulance siren drew closer.

* * *

Barry Wells and Kimberly Templeton, the EMT and paramedic who arrived at the scene, were fresh on their shift as of 7am. They were out of the ambulance and on Elias quickly. Barry immediately began working a cervical collar onto Elias' to keep his head from moving.

"Anybody know who this man is?" he asked, scanning the growing crowd. Kimberly had brought a stretcher and a backboard.

"Elias Witherton," Chet Brinkley stepped forward and said. "He was having breakfast with us. Next thing we know, he comes out of the bathroom with blood squirting from his nose and ran right out into the street! Truck driver never even had a chance to stop."

Barry finished with the collar, and Kimberly knelt down by Elias as they rolled him onto his side. "Mister Witherton? Elias? Can you hear me?"

There was no response. No eye movement. Breathing shallow, labored, raspy. Likely a collapsed lung.

They got the backboard under Elias' body and rolled him gently onto his back. Barry motioned to Chet Brinkley. "We need your help to lift him onto the stretcher."

Chet moved into position on one side of the backboard. In unison, they lifted the backboard onto the stretcher. Barry immediately began buckling it down.

"Mister Witherton, are you still with us?" Kimberly leaned in close and asked.

Elias' eyes finally fluttered open, the pupils dilated to near pinpoints. "Wha—?" he said.

"Mister Witherton, are you still with us?"

"Wither—? But, I'm not—that's..." and he trailed off, his eyes rolled back and closed again.

"He's losing consciousness. We need to move him now!" Kim said as they wheeled the stretcher to the back of the ambulance.

* * *

Elias felt something at the moment his body failed, a reaching sensation, and he could hear more of George Mason's thoughts, not just what he was thinking, but what the man remembered. He wasn't just reading thoughts now; he had gotten inside George's mind. But those memories were fleeting, there then gone, as if they were merely passing by his own.

Conversely, George Mason felt a tugging in his own mind, as if something was pulling on his consciousness, prying it open like the pages of a well-read book. A sharp nimbus of light appeared at the center of his inner eye a moment later, followed by a score of white tendrils snaking out like the arms of an octopus, flailing and spreading across the expanse of George's mind.

There was a loud sound in his head, like a rubber band snapping, then George saw darkness and heard nothing for long torturous moments. Then, there were muffled voices, like he was underwater, but swimming slowly upward.

"—are you still with us?" the voice said, still muffled, but discernible. George opened his eyes, but whoever was talking to him was only an amorphous shape.

"Wha—?" George said, but the voice he heard saying his words was wrong, tenor to the baritone he knew was his.

"Mister Witherton, are you still with us?"

"Wither—? But, I'm not—that's..." and his voice trailed off, while the voices became more muffled again.

"He's lost consciousness! We need to move him now!" the amorphous shape shouted. And that was the last thing George Mason remembered.

* * *

George Mason put his hand on Rosemarie's shoulder as the ambulance pulled away. She was crying.

"Do you think he's dead?" she asked, turning to look at him. Tears had smeared her makeup, and lines of eyeliner streamed down her cheeks.

"Hard to tell," George said. "But I think maybe so."

Inside George Mason's head, Elias Witherton thought: *I sure hope so.*

The street cleared now that the spectacle was gone, though Elias still heard murmurs as the gathered crowd separated.

Some of them he heard inside his head.

*—leg was all fucked up—poor bastard didn't even see the truck coming —blood gushing—feel sorry for him—paramedic chick was hot—lost my appetite—wait'll I tell them at work—*

Thankfully, George Mason's nose hadn't started bleeding, but the voices were maddening. He had to shut them out, somehow.

*—didn't like him, but I didn't want him to die—*

Elias recognized Rosemarie Swenson's voice.

*Well, you high-heeled bitch,* Elias thought. *Go fuck yourself.* His anger swelled, but he kept his arm around Rosemarie's shoulder, and tried not to squeeze too tightly, though for an instant, he wanted to put his hands on her throat and choke the life out of her.

The voices kept pouring in, though, and that had to stop if he was going to survive. He closed his eyes, and he could see the voices, each of them, flashing as a tiny pinpoint of light. He concentrated on them, herding them together until they formed a small ball of light. Then he envisioned a door in his mind, and pushed that pulsing light through it, then shut the door tight.

The voices stopped. A wave of relief washed over Elias. His thoughts were his own—only his—and that was a relief. He could finally take stock of his situation.

George Mason was seventy-two to Elias' seventy-six, but Mason had been a carpenter for most of his life, so the body beneath his flannel shirt reflected a still decently muscled physique. Elias had endured nothing but physical issues for most of the last twenty years and watched his musculature melt away. Elias didn't feel any pain at all in George Mason's skin, and that, well, that felt goddamn good.

Rosemarie slipped out from under George's arm and wiped her face with a hand towel she pulled from her apron pocket. George followed her back into the restaurant. The bell over the door jangled, and a small smile creased George Mason's face. The last time he'd heard that sound, an arthritic old man ran into the street and died.

Chet Brinkley had resumed his position at the coffee table, and Elias slid into the seat George had been in when Elias had arrived.

"Ain't that some shit?" Chet said.

"Yeah," Elias said. It was still strange to hear his words coming from George fucking Mason's mouth. "It sure was."

The restaurant was mostly empty now. Apparently, death on the street out front was bad for business.

Rosemarie didn't come back, replaced instead with a younger version that Elias noted would probably be Rosemarie in another twenty years if she kept on with this job.

"Crazy stuff, huh?" she said. Her nametag announced her as Heather. "Can I get you two anything?"

Chet held up his coffee cup for a refill, and she poured from the carafe she had brought along. "Thanks," he said.

Elias looked up at the pretty redhead and said, "I'll have French toast, link sausage and hash browns. With onions."

"Got it," Heather said with a smile. "I'll be back with your food in a few minutes." George's eyes watched the pronounced sway of her hips as she disappeared into the kitchen.

"Since when do you have French toast for breakfast?" Chet quizzed, his brow wrinkled. "Isn't that what Witherton ordered?"

"I dunno," Elias said, and George Mason's lips curled into a smile. "Just sounded good."

## AUTHOR NOTES - VOICES

Originally intended to be an epilogue of an unpublished novel, this one never got past the character's first name and the power of telepathy that I jotted down in 1993. In 2009, I picked up that tiny thread and wrote the entire story in a morning. It's not a long one, but I feel it captures the frailty of the human mind when it's overwhelmed with something it can't understand. Do you ever wonder what others are thinking? What they're thinking of you? The restaurant table scene came to me from watching and listening to a group of men at a local eatery one morning when my wife and I went for breakfast.

Originally, the story ended with Elias' death, but I always felt there should have been something else. More recently, an idea popped up, and I added two scenes at the end that revealed that Elias had swapped minds with George Mason. By adding those scenes, Elias went from being a sympathetic character to an outright villain.

# MURDER BY THE NUMBERS

"**I** killed them all," Raymond said nonchalantly, then smiled.

"Yes, you've mentioned that several times today," Dr. Kellerman replied.

"But you don't believe me, do ya, doc?" Raymond's widened smile unnerved the doctor a bit more than it should have. Kevin Wellington, the attendant orderly, stood close and kept his composure for the moment.

Raymond sat on the edge of the small mattress, in an uncluttered room of the Elysian Fields Sanitarium. The walls were bare, there was no window, and the only light came from a recessed fluorescent in the center of the ceiling. A stainless steel toilet sat next to a wall-mounted sink in the far corner. There was a chair against the wall opposite Raymond's bed, and that was all.

"I can only look at the evidence in front of me, Ray," Kellerman said, noting something on his clipboard. "The killer committed those four murders over the last month—one each week—and you've been here, in this very room, that entire time."

Raymond laughed then, an unholy sound, wholly indicative of his madness. Winston Kellerman had been a practicing psychiatric physician for twenty years and had heard a lot of things from a lot of disturbed people during that time. He had looked past the majority as the ravings of the lunatic mind, but couldn't dismiss Raymond Schalk's laughter.

"Doc," Raymond said, breathing harder now. Redness rimmed his milky eyes. "Just because my body was here doesn't mean my mind was." He tapped his temple with a long forefinger, then his laughter cut the air like a blade again. Kellerman barely noticed his orderly take a step back. While Raymond looked like a caricature with his long, thin, wiry hair, and pronounced, pointed nose, he was dangerous, and everyone knew that.

"I think we're done for today, Raymond. I'm going to have the nurse up your Thorazine dosage."

"Do what you gotta do," Raymond said, settling back on his bed. Then he whistled, low and droning, an unrecognizable song. Unnerving, regardless.

Dr. Kellerman exited the room and Kevin locked the door behind them. Kellerman peered through the small window at Raymond, who was now sitting Indian style on the bed. Raymond shot him with a set of finger guns and gave a sly wink. Kellerman shuddered and turned away.

* * *

Dr. Kellerman opened the door to his office and flipped on the light. His desk sat toward the back of the space, and his expensive executive chair called to him. He was exhausted. It had been a long day.

He had barely settled in into the chair, and leaned back when head nurse Janine Crowder appeared in the doorway.

"Got a minute?" she asked. Janine was a thick woman, curvaceous but solid, with a take-no-shit demeanor, and here and now, she looked serious.

"Sure," Kellerman sighed and sloped forward, resting his elbows on the desk. He looked anything but sure, yet here he was.

"Raymond Schalk. I see you upped his meds again."

"He's off the rails, Janine. Claims over and over, he committed the four "numbers" murders from the last month. If anything's an indicator for a med bump, that would be it."

"How would he even know about the murders?"

"Huh?" Kellerman's brown wrinkled.

"How would he know anything about those four murders? They've had locked him in that room for better than two months. He doesn't get rec room time, at least not since the incident last fall." Crowder was referring to Schalk trying to stuff a handful of puzzle pieces down the throat of another resident who had put a piece in the wrong spot.

"Maybe he talked to an orderly?"

"Not likely. Everyone knows not to talk about anything outside these walls with the residents. And especially not to talk about something like murder. My people aren't imbeciles, Winston." She sounded hurt.

"So, how do *you* think he knew, then?" Kellerman's eyes narrowed.

"Maybe you need to ask him."

"Tomorrow. I'll talk to him tomorrow. I've had more than enough for today."

"Suit yourself." Nurse Crowder walked out and Kellerman could finally lean back and relax for a minute. He fished a hard candy out of the jar on his desk and popped it into his mouth. He spun his chair around and looked out the window. Beyond the grassy yard and the ten-foot razor wire-topped chain-link fence, the oaks and maple trees stood tall. It was a very serene view, and one he enjoyed, especially when he needed to think.

How did that kid know about the murders? He hadn't meant to put Crowder on the spot, and her people knew their jobs. So how, then?

Maybe he wouldn't wait until tomorrow to quiz Raymond Schalk.

He sighed, sucked on the hard candy, and got up from his desk.

Lord, he was tired.

* * *

"Back so soon?" Raymond said, smiling again. Kellerman wondered if he had stopped smiling in the last twenty minutes. Something made him think not.

"Got some questions for you, Ray," Kellerman said. He sounded more confident. Wellington was with him again, a mountainous black man whose arms stretched his scrubs to their limit. Kellerman felt better with him there.

"Shoot, doc." Raymond did the finger guns again. Kellerman didn't acknowledge.

"How did you find out about those four murders?"

Raymond sighed. "Already told you. I killed them."

"Raymond, you know that's impossible. You were here 24/7 the past month. Most of the past year, even."

"Impossible for you, maybe," Raymond said, his voice lowered. "But I got ways you ain't never considered." His eyes widened, still milky and red-lined.

"That's not really answering the question, Ray," Kellerman said.

"Okay, how about this then: the first one, the very first, was Stella Markham. Met her at Dillon's Saloon, over on Broadhurst. Talked the talk and got her hooked, fed her a couple of drinks. She was pretty, blonde, worked for an accountant, made a decent living. She had a cute freckle on her nose. We ended up outside in the alleyway behind the bar. She was short and petite, but man, she was feisty. A shiny straight razor to the throat shut her up good, though. Then I ripped open her blouse and carved a big #1 onto her chest. Left her propped against the bar's garbage dumpster, like the trash she was."

Kellerman's face pinched. "I think we're done here, Raymond," He said, frustrated. "I won't encourage your delusions any longer."

"Suit yourself, doc," Ray said, and gave a nod. "Be seein' ya."

* * *

Kellerman went home to his modest apartment after that, took a long, hot shower, filled a tumbler with whiskey, and tried to let go of the day. However, Raymond Schalk was right there, at the fringes of his mind. He'd dug in a good hook, and wasn't letting go.

It had often crossed Winston's mind that it was this continuous devotion to his profession, the inability to leave work at work, that had brought on the divorce a year ago. Certainly, Regina hadn't ever been truly supportive of his chosen field, but she liked the money it brought and saw no need to take on a job of her own. After fourteen years of marriage, he assumed she understood he loved his work, but in the months leading to the divorce papers being filed, she had let her bitter disdain be known in full force. And he resented her for it every day since.

Irreconcilable differences led to Regina keeping their slightly upscale home in the suburbs, while he moved to a two-bedroom apartment in town. The alimony payments kept him financially submerged in debt. Thank God they'd never had children.

Kellerman went to bed after finishing his drink, but only stared at the ceiling, and floating there, feet above him, was Raymond Schalk, like an apparition haunting him. He wasn't really there, Kellerman understood that, but he almost felt a presence alongside his own.

Unable to sleep, he slogged down the hall to his home office, where he kept duplicate files on any of his active patients, and thumbed through his file cabinet to find the details on Raymond Schalk. Though he knew everything in the file already, he reviewed it again.

Raymond Schalk, twenty-seven years old, had murdered both his girlfriend and his roommate when he discovered them having an affair. Walked in on them having sex, more precisely. He forced them to finish the deed before he slit both their throats and painted their mingled blood on the walls. Schalk was arrested, tried for murder, deemed insane, and therefore remanded to Elysian Fields Sanitarium for treatment and rehabilitation.

Kellerman himself thought Schalk was the perfect candidate for clinical trials of an experimental psychosis-suppressing drug that a major pharmaceutical company had contracted Elysian Fields to test. Schalk was fast-tracked into the program two weeks after arrival. However, during the experiments, something went horribly wrong. Kellerman assumed a bad dose of the drug, but that remained unsubstantiated. Schalk had a massive psychotic break, and became even more violent, exhibiting almost superhuman strength, resulting in one dead clinician and three severely injured fellow patients. The sponsoring company immediately shut down the clinical trials and scrubbed all evidence from the official record. No experimental drug trials ever happened at Elysian Fields.

Schalk remained under Kellerman's care, but the following several months showed little progress. Every time it would appear the slightest headway was being made, Schalk would exhibit more psychotic behaviors and end up back in confinement. Six months ago, they finally denied Raymond Schalk all social privileges after the puzzle incident. Now, he claimed to have murdered four women.

Kellerman set the file down on his desk and sighed. Something about that kid just sat wrong.

* * *

Kellerman got to the sanitarium early the next morning, despite having not slept at all. His body was exhausted, but his mind hadn't stopped working. In his office, he brewed a pot of coffee and picked a hard candy from the dish while he waited for the brew to finish. Butterscotch, his favorite.

He laid his cell phone on his desk and looked at it for several moments before picking it back up and dialing a number. Glenn Wallace worked at the coroner's office, and was a friend he might ask some questions of and get some answers. Off the books, of course. Kellerman's curiosity had gotten the better of him, and he had to scratch this itch.

The phone rang twice before being answered.

"Winston," Glenn Wallace said. "To what do I owe the pleasure?"

"Hello, Glenn," Kellerman said. "Hoping you can help me out with some information."

"If I can, I will," Glenn said. "What'cha got?"

"The recent murder cases, the four 'numbers' victims, what can you tell me about the first one?"

"You gotta promise me this goes no further than us. It's an ongoing investigation, so they've released very little to the public."

"You have my word, Glenn. No further than us."

"Her name was Stella Markham, twenty-three years of age. They found her in the alleyway behind Dillon's Saloon with her throat slit wide open. She had a '#1' cut into her chest. We assumed it was the beginnings of a serial killer spree, and that was right on the money."

"Did she have any distinguishing markings? On her face, maybe?"

"Yes, a large freckle on her nose."

Kellerman was silent for several moments. "Thanks, Glenn. That's all I needed."

"What's this about?"

"Hopefully nothing, but I'll let you know as soon as I figure it out."

"Alright. Just remember, keep it under your hat, okay?"

"Of course."

"Oh, hey, you gonna be at poker this Wednesday? You've missed a few."

"I'm hoping to. Just been so backed up with patient workloads lately, I haven't felt much like being social, y'know?"

"Oh, I get it. I work in a morgue, and still don't feel like talking to people. Hopefully, we'll see you Wednesday, buddy."

Kellerman hung up the phone and sat behind his desk for several minutes. Then, he poured himself a cup of coffee and sat it on a coaster. As he watched the steam rising from the mug, he ran his fingers through his salt and pepper hair. Forty-seven years, a messy divorce, and nothing had made him feel older than the possibility he was considering today.

Details hadn't been released yet. So how in the hell did Raymond Schalk know any of it? And it was almost word for word what Glenn Wallace had told him. That made no sense at all.

Unless, of course, you believed what Raymond had said.

*Just because my body was here doesn't mean my mind was.*

Jesus Christ, that couldn't be true, could it? Impossible. But maybe there was one way to find out.

Kellerman grabbed his notepad off the edge of his desk and was out the door, leaving his steaming coffee to go cold.

* * *

"Tell me about the other three murders, Ray," Kellerman asked from the chair opposite Raymond's bed. He didn't have an orderly with him this time. He didn't want to involve anyone else in this conversation if he could avoid it.

"Oh, so you believe me now, doc?" Raymond asked, raising an eyebrow. He had slicked his wiry hair back to his skull and the expanse of his forehead made him look more like a caricature than before.

"Let's just say I'm curious, is all."

"Curiosity killed the cat, y'know? Killed that fucker dead. Woohoo!" Raymond seemed extra energetic today, and Kellerman wondered if coming without an orderly was a good idea after all.

"Can you just tell me about the murders?"

"Sure, I can. Sure, sure, sure," Raymond said. "Buuuuut what's in it for me?"

"I'll get you outdoor privileges for the next week, though not during normal hours. I can't trust you around other people."

"Outdoor privileges?" Raymond blew a raspberry. "Tell you what, you just get me an extra chocolate pudding with lunch for the next week, I'll tell you all you ever wanted to know. Deal?"

Kellerman studied his patient for several seconds. "Sure, deal," he finally said. He was growing more wary of Raymond by the moment.

"First, tell *me* something, doc," Raymond said, tilting his head. "You feeling okay? You're looking kinda out of sorts."

"I'm fine, just haven't been sleeping well lately." Kellerman realized the mistake of engaging his patient in small talk. He knew better and righted his course fast. "But we're not here to talk about me."

"Alrighty then, doc. Whatever you want."

"Get on with it, Raymond."

"Marge Stegbauer, she was a bona fide MILF. You know what a MILF is, doc?"

"I'm familiar with the term, yes."

"Yeah, she was a hottie. I think they call 'em cougars nowadays, too. She was definitely that. Long legs, brown hair—though I bet she dyed it; she just seemed the type, y'know? Anyway, met her at the laundromat, got some details while washing my tidy whiteys. She seemed to dig me, if you know what I mean. So I followed her out to her car to help her load her laundry. She had a Mercedes. Imagine that, a lady with a Mercedes, who washes her lace panties at a coin laundry. Strange fuckin' world, am I right?"

"Go on," Kellerman grunted.

"I followed her home. She had a nice little apartment on the west side. I forced my way in, and she tried to scream, but I silenced her the fast way. I had wanted it to last longer, but screaming is a no-no. When I was done, I carved a #2 into her chest and left her propped up on the couch like she was watching TV. Even put the remote in her hand and got her a glass of wine before I left. She drinks the cheap shit just to let you know."

Kellerman was taking notes as fast as he could write. He intended to call Glenn Wallace again to see if Raymond's "first-hand" accounts matched up. If they did, he wasn't sure what he was going to do. He hoped the first one was a coincidence, but the line between logical and illogical was blurring fast.

"Next one was Erica Lawson. Redhead. Tall, thin, almost anorexic. I'm not attracted to that sort. I mean, I like a bit of meat on the bones, some cushion for the pushin', right? What about you, doc?" Raymond paused for a moment, and Kellerman said nothing. Raymond waved him off. "Nevermind. Anyway, I snagged her at an interstate rest stop in the middle of the night before she could get back into her car. She kicked and screamed for a few moments, but it didn't matter. I put the blade into the side of her neck and that ended that. Afterward—you guessed it—I put the big "#3" between her a-cups, and left her on the bench outside the restrooms, like she was taking a nap with her shirt pulled wide open. You know, kinda like Clark Kent when he's running off to change into Superman."

Kellerman had stopped writing. He just stared, unbelieving, with his hands and the notepad settled in his lap. Raymond, however, seemed to enjoy regaling his audience with his tales.

"Number four, Patty Greenberger, was an older one—mid to late fifties, I'd guess—but a lot more buxom than Erica. Nabbed her coming out from work at the Family Grocer supermarket. They really should make it policy for employees to walk out together at the end of the night. But hey, makes my job easier, right? She put up a fight, but I wrestled her into the backseat of her car and stuck her. I watched the life drain out of her eyes, then gave her the incremental number treatment, right between the saggy ol' double-Ds. Left one was bigger, in case you wanna jot that down."

Raymond remained silent after that. Kellerman took a deep breath, gripped his notepad, and stood up.

"I'll see to it you get your extra pudding," he said, turned, and left.

On the bed, Raymond Schalk's smile spread almost as wide as a circus clown's.

* * *

Behind his locked office door, Kellerman's coffee had long gone cold, but he replaced it with a shot of bourbon from the bottle in his lower desk drawer. He felt almost feverish after hearing Raymond's confessions, though he still ultimately doubted how what he said could be true.

He dialed Glenn Wallace again and got him before the second ring this time.

"Two calls on the same day," Wallace said. "Must be important stuff."

"It is. Describe the other three victims to me, Glenn. Don't spare any details."

"Can you tell me what this is all about?"

"I will, I promise. And soon. For now, just the details, okay?"

"Sure, Win, sure. Let me get my reports."

Kellerman listened as Glenn Wallace read off the victim's descriptions for the next three murders, and the details matched perfectly with what Raymond had just told him. Glenn didn't even finish before he thumbed the "End Call" button on his phone screen.

He drained the tumbler of bourbon and fished the bottle out of his desk drawer for a refill. Two more shots left him feeling no better than before. He sat in silence, staring out the window at the clusters of trees beyond the yard fence. Like the bourbon, they helped not at all.

* * *

"I'm going to ask you one last time, Raymond. How do you know about these murders?"

"Same answer as before, doc. I killed them all."

"Unacceptable. There has to be another explanation."

"There isn't. Now, let me ask you a question, doc." That sly smile was back.

Kellerman squinted, then nodded. "Okay."

"Where have you been these last four Wednesdays?"

"Wednesday night is my poker night."

"But you haven't gone in four weeks, have you?"

"I—" Kellerman said, then thought about it. "No."

"So, where ya been going?" Raymond raised his eyebrows.

"I—I don't know." Kellerman's puzzled look got Raymond excited.

"I do," Raymond said, grinning. "I know where you've been spending every Wednesday night this past month, doc. And let me tell ya, it's gonna blow your mind!" Raymond cackled then, a noise beyond chilling, and leaned forward off the bed. Winston Kellerman cringed back, his mind reeling.

"No," He stammered. "No, you're wrong. That can't be right. How could that be right?"

"How indeed, doc? How indeed?"

"You're lying!"

"I'm a lot of things, doc, but a liar ain't one of 'em. Always been a straight-shooter, but you know that."

"Then what are you saying, Raymond?" Kellerman had shrunk back and sat in the chair by the door.

That horrific smile lit up Raymond's face again. "What I'm saying, doc, is we—you and me—committed those murders together."

The color drained from Kellerman's face.

"I can see by the ghostly expression on your mug that you know I'm telling the truth. But you're needing some explanation anyway, aren't ya, doc?"

Kellerman made no acknowledgment, just stared forward, entranced.

"Well, here goes: After that botched clinical trial last year, something in my head changed. I felt more aware, but in a splintered, disjointed way, like I was peering through a pinhole into someone else's mind. I started poking at that pinhole, making it bigger, and soon it was like I was seeing through two sets of eyes at once. It took me a while to realize that's exactly what I was doing: I could reach out and see the world through other people's eyes. It took a few weeks, but I realized I could also influence whoever I was looking through. Like working a muscle, I kept pushing at people until I could suggest just about anything, and the person would do it. Imagine my complete exhilaration when I found my way into your head."

"Oh my God," Kellerman said. His eyes were wide and his mouth had involuntarily dropped open.

"I'm pretty sure God had nothing to do with this, doc. I'm certain this power came from somewhere south of the border, if you get my meaning." He winked an eye at Kellerman, who shrank back from it.

"This can't be real," Kellerman said, looking away, his own sanity now on the downslide.

"But it is," Raymond said, and hopped off the bed. "I got inside your head and pulled the strings, and like a good puppet, you did exactly what I wanted you to." He poked Kellerman's forehead with his thin bony finger. "But, let's be real here, doc. You liked it. After that disaster of a divorce, your contempt for females was in the stratosphere. I could feel that anger, all that hatred, eating away like cancer inside you, poisoning your thoughts, twisting your perceptions. You were so very easy to manipulate after going through all that."

"No," Kellerman said, monotone. All the fight had left him.

"Oh, yes. You were the one who picked up Stella and her daddy issues and ended up in the alleyway. While feeding quarters into a washing machine filled with your Fruit of the Looms, you struck up a conversation with Marge. You were driving the interstate trying to forget all your problems, and were the only other traveler at the rest stop with Erica Lawson. You were late night insomnia shopping at the

Family Grocer when Patty Greenberger caught your eye. It was you and me, buddy. I was just riding the sidecar in your head and pushing you to do what you wanted to do, anyway."

"I couldn't have—" Kellerman stammered in a last effort of defiance.

"Tell you what, doc. You go to your office and check your bottom left desk drawer. Behind the files. You'll find a sandwich baggie with four driver's licenses in it. Guess who they belong to? Go ahead, guess."

Tears ran down Winston Kellerman's face, but his expression had gone emotionless. Raymond leaned in close.

"So, the new question is: what do we do now that you know?"

They both sat silent for a few moments after that. Kellerman's face was pallid and lifeless, chin fallen against his sunken chest. Then he lifted his head, and a smile twisted itself onto his lips.

"Regina," he said, almost in a whisper. His face and eyes appeared quite childlike. "Can we go kill Regina?"

"Can we kill your ex-wife? Oh ho ho, I think we most certainly can."

"Please? Can we—can we do it now?" Kellerman pleaded.

"You're speaking my language now, doc."

"Number five," Kellerman said flatly, and stood.

"And why stop there, doc? Why. Stop. There?"

## AUTHOR NOTES - MURDER BY THE NUMBERS

I wrote this story pretty quickly over the course of a few days in the spring of 2020, but I don't remember the exact spark that started it. In retrospect, it bears a slight resemblance to a Stephen King story I'd read a few years prior, but wasn't consciously thinking of it while writing. Subconsciously? Sure, most likely. Who knows what goes on in there?

The minds of serial killers have always fascinated me, and I found this was a suitable vehicle for exploring that just a little.

# THE THING IN
# UNIT 57

Ross Clifton started his shift by checking the security gate as he did every night without exception. Jeff Albright was supposed to be on the 8pm-8am Wednesday shift, but had called in sick with the flu.

"Got it coming out both ends, boss," was Jeff's exact wording. Flu season was always a bitch, and by mid-October, it was well into making its rounds. Kids seemed to breed the flu after going back to school in the fall, and Jeff had three of the little snot-gobblers at home, so it stood to reason he'd get the bug. But Jeff was a good guy overall, so Ross didn't give him much hassle, and besides, it was a Wednesday night, and likely to be dead quiet.

After verifying the gate's magnetic lock, Ross walked back into the gatehouse and sat down at his desk. Four computer screens revealed 16 camera views of the facility. He quickly scanned them all, verified no one was still inside, then leaned back, kicked his feet up on the corner of the desk, and pulled out his phone.

By 10:30, Ross was halfway through his sixth game of Texas HoldEm Poker (and losing in spectacular fashion) when a white panel van pulled up to the gate. He set his phone down on the edge of the desk, adjusted himself in his seat, and pushed the button for the intercom.

"Evening," Ross said. The van driver gave a cursory nod and inserted a keycard into what largely resembled an ATM. When Ross first started at Seagram Storage eight years before, he didn't have to deal with this keycard business, but it was a sign of the times, he supposed. During his early days, there were no cameras either. He and another guard walked the perimeter of the storage grounds every 2 hours and logged visitors by hand in a ledger. Increases in vandalism and break-ins over the intervening years required changes, so three years back, real estate mogul and site owner Everett Seagram hired a security company to outfit them with the latest in high-tech surveillance and security systems. They installed sixteen remote-controlled cameras across the grounds and linked a keycard verification system to the entrance. From that point onward, the gate operated on an encrypted magnetic lock, so if it did not approve your keycard, that gate wasn't opening.

A small screen lit up on Ross' office desk, verifying the inserted card as belonging to one Vernon K. Rutledge, the account was in good standing, and that Rutledge had rented one of the large 10x20 units near the rear of the facility, specifically Unit 57. A camera inside the card reader scanned the driver's face and used facial recognition software to match it with an approved list of card users.

With the keycard and driver verified, Ross pressed a large green button on the screen. The magnetic lock disengaged, and the front gate slid open. They could do this automatically via the keycard system, but Ross argued it was still a good idea to have a person allow opening the gate, and Everett Seagram approved. A marriage of old school and high-tech.

"Have a good night," Ross said, but got no response as the driver pulled through the gate, both he and his equally stoic passenger looking ahead as if Ross wasn't there. Ross released the intercom button and finished with, "Asshole." That made him smile a little.

Ross grabbed a turkey and Swiss sandwich and a Coke from the mini fridge, and once again leaned back in his chair and kicked his feet up onto the desk. Five minutes later, Ross grabbed his phone and prepared to resume his unlucky streak at Texas HoldEm Poker. He glanced at the security cameras and noticed camera #12 showed the white panel van backed up close to the door of Unit 57. A simple joystick device allowed control of all cameras. Ross selected the camera by touching it on the screen and then used the joystick to zoom in and rotate. The van, however, blocked anything happening inside the unit.

Therefore disinterested, Ross resumed his poker game (and lost). Ten minutes later, a soft buzzing pulled him from his reverie.. Motion sensors had detected a vehicle approaching from the inside, and Ross fingered the button on the screen to open the gate. The white panel van motored by his checkpoint and onto the street.

"Toodle-oo, a-holes," Ross mumbled.

* * *

Jeff called in again on Thursday, leaving Ross to cover another extra shift. Lots of overtime hours this week meant lots of lost sleep, and he was feeling it. Not even Texas HoldEm Poker was keeping him from feeling drowsy. He traded the Coke for a peach tea Monster energy drink, and even that wasn't helping much. It was going to be a long night.

He wanted a cigarette. That would keep him awake. Having quit nearly a year before, he had mostly suppressed the urges, but sometimes, especially on nights like this, a Marlboro sounded like heaven wrapped in a paper tube.

Didn't matter, though. He had no smokes on him, and nobody to relieve him at the gatehouse so he could drive to the nearest gas station to get some.

At 10:30, the soft buzzing of the motion camera alarm brought Ross out of the early stages of REM sleep. His head snapped up, and he looked at the cameras, then out the window of his security booth. The white panel van from the night before was approaching the gate.

The driver inserted his keycard, and Ross noticed the timestamp on the entry was almost the same as the previous night. While that didn't seem odd overall, Ross made a mental note of it, anyway. Once approved, the van passed the opened gate and into the corrugated metal expanse of the storage grounds.

Ross turned to the cameras and followed the van as it headed inward. He zoomed in with Camera 12 as the van pulled past and then backed up to the unit. The driver got out and used the keycard to unlock the unit door. Once again, the camera angle would not allow him to see inside.

The passenger got out, and the two opened the back of the van, then unloaded a large crate. He could see some lettering on the side, but the camera couldn't zoom close enough for him to make it out.

Like the night before, the two men were inside the unit for approximately ten minutes, then closed up their van, dropped the door on the unit, and drove back toward the gate. Ross passed them through and watched as the van moved back onto the street.

Tired as he was, Ross sat in his chair for minutes afterward, curiosity tickling the back of his brain. He considered taking the security cart down and checking the unit out for himself. He had an override card allowing him access to all units in the facility, but the fine print of the client contracts only allowed that with suspected illegal activities. As yet, nothing unlawful had gone on, just strange visitors at the same time two nights in a row in a windowless white panel van. Not suspicious at all.

Wishful thinking, perhaps? Seagram Storage's most exciting moment since implementing the new security protocols came the previous year when two teenage ne'er-do-wells jumped the fence to spray graffiti on the outside of the units. Ross apprehended them before they got too far, but that was the extent of notable incidents. Old man Seagram also added razor wire to the fencing and that put an effective end to fence-hoppers. Seagram had many high-profile clients who stored everything from classic cars to top-shelf fishing boats on the premises.

Ross settled back into his chair and dozed off for most of the rest of his shift. Thankfully, Charlie Wellman relieved him at the gate at 8am, and Ross went home and slept hard, except for one point when he dreamt of the men in the white panel van. The driver and passenger were monsters, their faces twisted into sullen alien grotesqueries, wet slithering tentacles for hair and yellowish globe-like eyes with slits that darted back and forth. It sat Ross straight up in his bed, heart hammering in his chest, and caught his breath. Even six hours later, when he officially woke up for the day, the lingering image of those faces stayed with him.

* * *

Back on the clock at 8pm, a worse for wear Jeff Albright greeted Ross. Friday and Saturday nights, Seagram doubled security. Ross wasn't really sure why, as it wasn't busier than any other day.

"You look like death, man," Ross said.

"I feel worse than that," Jeff replied. "But I haven't puked or shit myself since yesterday afternoon. And I couldn't afford to take off another day."

"Just keep that crud away from me, okay?" Ross formed a cross with his two index fingers and pointed it at Jeff, then pushed the plunger of the sanitizer bottle on his desk and rubbed his hands together. He figured he'd be doing that a lot tonight.

Despite Jeff's contaminated presence, Ross soon fell into his routine. He played three losing games of Texas HoldEm Poker before a 1995 Ford F-150 pulled up to the gate at 8:45 with a load of mismatched furniture in the back. Ross pressed the intercom switch and greeted the man behind the wheel, who then tearfully recounted how his wife kicked him out for cheating on her, but it wasn't his fault, and now he had nowhere to live. Ross and Jeff exchanged simultaneous eye rolls. Some people were just a little too open with their private lives.

After the homeless soon-to-be-divorcee left, Ross told Jeff about the men in the white panel van and their routine with Unit 57 the past two nights.

"Did you look him up?" Jeff asked.

"Who?"

"The dude who rented the unit? Google that shit, man."

Ross pulled up his phone's web browser and typed Vernon Rutledge into the search bar. According to his Wikipedia entry, Rutledge was a 67-year-old biochemical engineer originally from California, graduated Stanford University with dual doctorates in biochemistry and biology, and was now a top government contractor in mutagenic R&D. Rutledge started his career at CrossTech Genetic Research, a secluded government facility in the forests of Oregon, helping to pioneer gene-splicing programs that produced many breakthroughs in the agricultural sector. Rutledge eventually became head of GeneCorp, another government funded genetics think tank. Most recently, Rutledge spent an extended period in Brazil on the Amazon River, studying the genetics of various species there.

"Whoa. Didn't expect that," Jeff said after Ross read him the text.

Ross' face wrinkled. "What the hell is a biochemist from California renting a storage unit in Podunk, Michigan for?"

Before Jeff could answer, the proximity sensors detected an arrival. Ross looked out the window and saw the white panel van approaching the gate. *Early tonight*, Ross thought, double-checking the wall clock. It was only 9:50.

Ross and Jeff observed the cameras. As per the previous two nights, the van backed up to Unit 57 and the two men spent nearly 15 minutes inside before closing up and leaving. After the van passed through the gate, Ross again considered checking out the unit, contractual obligation be damned. However, thoughts of the alien faces in his dream made him decide against it.

By 11:45pm, Ross had played more poker games, eaten half his lunch, drank two Cokes, and chatted on Facebook with his brother, Sam, who lived in Oklahoma. He and Jeff also exchanged small talk, though they had little in common. Ross was a 45-year-old lifelong bachelor who enjoyed hours spent playing card games on his phone while Jeff was a thirty-two-year-old married man with three kids, who only carried a cell phone out of necessity.

Looking away from his phone for a moment to the monitor station, Ross noticed one of the sixteen screens was black.

"Holy shit, check this out," Ross said, and Jeff rolled his chair over.

"That's not possible, is it?" Jeff asked, looking from the screen to his partner.

"Shouldn't be. Cameras are all night-vision ready, so even if the lights go out, the cameras automatically kick over to compensate."

"Maybe they lost power?"

"Doubtful. Lights and cameras are on totally different circuits. The odds are super slim both would go down at the same time. And just in that spot? Nope."

"That's fuckin' weird, man."

"Even weirder," Ross said, stabbing a finger at the display readout. "Look which camera."

It was Camera 12. Where Unit 57 was.

"Oh, fuck me," Jeff exhaled. Then he sneezed into the crook of his left arm.

Ross activated Camera 11 and used the joystick to pan it as far as possible toward Camera 12, but it still came up short. The area around Unit 57 was almost totally dark. He tried Camera 13 with the same outcome. Unfortunately, there was also a new moon that week, so no ambient light source to help him.

"Damn it," Ross said. "I'm going to have to do a drive by, and then we'll call maintenance. Henry Kellum will not like coming out in the middle of the night, but old man Seagram pays him extra for emergency stuff."

"Couldn't maintenance just wait 'til morning?" Jeff asked.

"I'd say yes, but Seagram is kind of a prick about that sort of thing. I'd rather not have him climb up my ass because I didn't call Hank."

Ross checked his belt to make sure his flashlight was there, then double-checked his .44. Locked and loaded. He hadn't needed to pull his weapon in quite some time, but he kept it in prime working condition just the same.

"Keep an eye on me, would ya?" Ross said, stepping out of the booth. The door closed and auto-locked behind him as Jeff sat down at the monitor station. Next to the booth, two golf-cart styled security vehicles sat, plugged into charging outlets on the side of the building. Ross disconnected the cable to one, and it spooled back into its recess on the cart.

Ross topped out the cart's 15mph limit as he sped off toward Camera 12 and Unit 57. Was it vandals that somehow hopped the fence he would deal with tonight? Was it possibly just a coincidence that both the lights and camera went down at the same time? He doubted it. Ross knew down deep in his gut that it would not be that easy.

"Got you on visual. Over," Jeff said thru his walkie. Ross heard him sneeze again.

"Copy that," Ross replied.

He was 50 feet from the shrouded Unit 57 when the security cart slowed, then coasted to a stop. No power. The cart had been plugged in and charging since he'd gone on shift four hours before, so it had a full charge. Ross' gut once again told him something wasn't kosher.

He exited the cart twenty feet from the envelope of darkness. He pulled his flashlight and began walking. The flashlight beam weakened with every step forward until it flickered and went out altogether.

"What in the Hell?" Ross muttered. He shook the flashlight; it flickered for a moment then died.

"Jeff, you read me? Over."

What came back was largely static, with Jeff's voice faint and fading. "Barely. What's going on? Over."

"I'm losing signal. Over." At this point, all he got back was crackling static. A few seconds later, not even that.

"Fuck," Ross exhaled. He stopped and let his eyes adjust to the gloom ahead of him. When he could see enough to walk, he started toward Unit 57, less than a hundred feet away.

As he approached, his eyes swept left to right repeatedly, looking for some perpetrator. Nothing. No movement, save his own, and no sound beyond his own heartbeat.

Whatever was happening seemed centered on Unit 57, and Ross felt that meant he was justified in opening it up. The keycard locking system on the unit doors used a battery backup during power outages, but Ross noted that like all other electrical devices currently nearby, it wasn't working. However, there was also a manual override option for just such occasions. Ross felt along the side of the card reader for the manual override lock, then inserted his master key. When he turned it, he heard the locking mechanism disengage with a metal-on-metal sound.

"I'm going into Unit 57. Over," Ross spoke into his walkie. But his handheld was completely dead. No surprise.

Ross took a deep breath and exhaled slowly as he grabbed the door handle. He wasn't sure what to expect on the other side.

* * *

"Ross, do you copy? Over," Jeff Albright spoke into his walkie, but all he got back was silence. Standing in front of the monitor system, he'd watched the security cart come to a stop just outside the circle of darkness. He saw Ross heading forward, saw his flashlight go dead, and heard Ross over the walkie, but the signal had gotten so weak it was as if Ross was out of range.

After Ross disappeared into the darkness surrounding Unit 57, Jeff sat down in the chair and watched the monitors. He wasn't even getting static back on the walkie now, and that concerned him. If Ross was dealing with a B&E, near-total darkness was not helpful. He considered calling the police, but decided he would give it just a few more minutes.

* * *

Ross lifted the door slowly, holding his breath. The area inside the unit yielded no visual point of reference, only total unending darkness. He stood in the doorway, wondering what his next move should be.

Then something within Unit 57 moved.

Ross drew his .44 and pointed it into the deep ebony maw before him. The shuffling sound stopped.

"This is site security. Come out of the unit now with your hands in front of you," Ross said, and felt his heartbeat move into his throat.

No response. No movement.

"I repeat: this is site security. Please come out of the unit with your hands in front of you."

It began low, the sound of breathing, ragged gasps for air that turned into a slow growl far back in the unit. Ross felt the hairs on his neck stand up. To him, it sounded like a big animal, but why would there be an animal in Unit 57?

Ross took a step backward and reached for the door handle. Whatever was in there, he couldn't see it and wasn't interested in engaging it. Best to just shut it back in and call County Animal Control. Let the Beastmaster deal with it.

Then the lights came back on. Startled, Ross lost his grip on the door handle and stumbled backward, landing on his ass in the gravel outside the unit with a grunt. The overhead light shone just enough inside for him to make out vague shapes in Unit 57, electronic equipment with blinking lights and monochrome monitors. He could hear pumps and mechanisms cycling back on. With his pistol still directed forward, he pulled his flashlight off his belt and directed it into the unit.

What he saw turned his blood cold.

* * *

Jeff Albright watched Camera 12 come back online along with the lights and saw Ross on the ground in front of the open Unit 57 with his gun pointed to the inside. Jeff's heart jumped 20 beats per minute as he fumbled for the joystick, then zoomed in with the camera, and grabbed his walkie.

"Ross, what's going on?" He said, and released the button, waiting for a response.

* * *

Ross didn't hear Jeff over the walkie. He was oblivious, transfixed by what his flashlight's beam revealed to him.

The thing in Unit 57 was humanoid, but not human, its grayish-black skin slick and wet, almost oozing. Its large opened mouth showed no teeth inside. Round, bluish eyes the size of nickels darted back and forth as it recoiled from the light. Ross could hear its labored breathing. It was scared. He knew how it felt.

Ross scanned the interior of the unit and saw medical equipment, computer systems, all hooked into a series of high-output generators. Near the back of the unit, where the creature stood, he saw a long cylindrical tank on a wheeled table, and from the broken glass, and a viscous liquid dripped out and pooled on the floor. Whatever this creature was, it had been in that tank until recently.

Despite the light, the creature shuffled forward a few small steps, making Ross uneasy. He got to his feet, keeping both light and pistol trained on the thing in Unit 57.

"Ross, do you copy?" He heard over his walkie. Jeff sounded frantic. Unfortunately, with his light in one hand and gun in the other, he had no way to respond. He really wished they had put in a requisition for headsets.

Ross backed away and returned his light to his belt. He'd rather have his gun at the ready in case that thing came out after him. He thumbed the button on his walkie.

"Yeah, I'm here. Call the cops, Jeff," he said. "There—there's something in the unit."

"What is it?" Jeff said.

"I—I don't know. I—can't—"

Then the lights and the camera were gone again, and Ross heard a humming sound, like a high voltage electrical line. He didn't even finish his sentence, as he knew the walkie was down as well. He took a few more steps back, hoping to gain enough distance in the gloom that he could make out the creature if it came forward.

The humming sound got louder, and then Ross felt it push against him. The jolt sent him reeling backward where he slammed into the unit opposite 57, collapsed to the ground, and his gun spilled from his hand. As Ross scrambled in the darkness, the lights flickered back on for a few moments, giving him just enough time to find his weapon. Shaking, he pulled the pistol up in front of him as he saw the creature emerge from the unit. He fired the gun once, twice. The creature jerked backward with each impact and howled in savage terror. Ross felt more than heard the humming this time, and as it built in intensity, he scrambled to his feet.

The second blast hit him square in the chest, pushing him back against the door as the lights pulsed, then went dark again. His head felt like it was going to explode, and as the humming subsided, he could hear his heart beating hard and fast.

It felt like the creature was giving him an electric shock. It wasn't quite up to police issue taser voltage yet, but the second shock was worse than the first. He was sure he didn't want a third.

Ross raised the gun and fired two more shots that found their target. The creature twisted backward, howling louder, its square toothless mouth gnashing as runners of spittle flew. Despite the recoil, and despite the pain, it kept advancing.

*  *  *

Jeff was in the middle of the 911 call when he heard the gunshots and his heart skipped a beat. When he hung up, he was out of the booth and on the second security cart, moving toward Unit 57 as fast as the cart would allow, his pistol already drawn. He knew he was abandoning his post, but gunshots meant things had escalated, and with radio communication down, Jeff did not know what was going on out there, or what he was heading toward. Ross had said some*thing* was in the unit, not some*one*. Dog perhaps? But how a dog could have gotten into the unit made him wonder even more.

The lights flickered off and on across the entire complex. It couldn't be good that the outage was spreading. Jeff's security cart slowed, then sped up, slowed, then sped up. Jeff finally jumped out and ran.

He rounded the corner at the back of the facility in time to see his partner backed against a unit door, and he saw the thing that had him there.

It was pulsing, its body almost incandescent. With each surge, the lights dimmed, then brightened, accompanied by an increasing electrical hum. Ross had his gun out in front of him, but had not let off another shot. He seemed paralyzed.

Jeff centered his weapon and fired, hitting the creature in the shoulder. It whirled toward him, the corona of its electrical pulse visibly widening. Jeff saw the lights dim and go out, but the creature gave off enough light of its own to illuminate the area. The electricity spiked as

Jeff fired again, and he watched the bullet disintegrate before it could hit, and the out-rushing surge knocked him off his feet.

The creature looked back and forth between Jeff and Ross, then lunged toward Ross, the surrounding electricity flaring in lightning bolt patterns. It grabbed Ross with long humanoid fingers, digging deep into the flesh of his shoulders. Jeff got back to his feet just in time to see the pulse and had to shield his eyes.

Over the humming, he could hear Ross Clifton's screams.

The electricity poured into Ross' body, an unfathomable voltage, and his arms and legs stiffened. Then he fried. His flesh reddened as blood boiled to the surface, browned and peeled off in flakes, while his clothing first smoldered, then burst into flame. The screaming grew as his body cooked from the inside out, organs and muscle turned to charred meat and then ash. The screaming stopped in an instant, and Ross Clifton was more than dead.

Jeff had to choke back his own vomit as he watched the thing toss the smoking corpse of his partner to the ground. It turned its attention away from the husk toward him, and Jeff noticed it looked unsteady. *Using that much energy must've weakened you, huh?* He thought, and leveled the pistol, firing two more shots toward its head. The first tore into the creature's jaw, splitting the flesh and splintering bone as it went, but the second missed. The creature howled as a slick liquid drained from its broken jaw, yet it continued forward, building up another charge with each step, and Jeff began backing away.

He emptied half his remaining clip into the creature, the first three bullets hitting it in the chest, the last falling apart a foot away.

Jeff fell backward, hit the ground hard, and the thing was on him. He felt hands holding him down, and the electricity intensified.

He thought of his family. He would not see them again, never get to take his son hunting for the first time, or lecture his girls on dealing with boys, or hold his wife's hand and kiss her.

Then he sneezed.

The thing recoiled backward and let go of Jeff. It staggered, disoriented, and the electrical pulse weakened. Jeff steadied the pistol and let off his remaining rounds into the thing's face, which exploded in a spray of grayish sludge and fragmented bone. It hit the ground and writhed for a few moments, then ceased.

Jeff lay on his back and heard the vehicles approaching. *The fucking cops finally show up*, he thought, laying his head back. He closed his eyes and sighed. He wanted to sleep for a week.

* * *

Breaking News Story, October 21st:

"In the early morning hours of October 21st, two security guards died during a break-in at the ultra-secure Seagram Storage facility in Northern Michigan. Department of Homeland Security and Centers for Disease Control agents have quarantined the scene, and while full details of the incident are currently being withheld as investigations continue, CDC spokesman Joel Devers stated that their presence is only a precaution and there is no immediate danger to the community. Nearby resident speculation is that a potential biological contaminant was being stored at the facility, but local authorities have made no official statements.

The identities of the two security personnel who lost their lives remain classified, and we could not reach site owner Everett Seagram for comment. More details as they become available."

## AUTHOR NOTES - THE THING IN UNIT 57

First off, Unit 57 is the number of a storage unit I once used, though the site isn't ultra-secure like in the story. While visiting the unit once upon a time, a random thought came to me: "What if there is something inside here when I open the door?"

That was enough to plot a story. Initially, it was just the monster in the unit, just one of those random horrors with no explanation. As I began working out details, I had this vision of some X-Files-ish containment center and that provided some reason for the monster to be there. It's an overused plot device, but who doesn't love some governmental experiments gone awry, right?

The monster itself had no form when I started. Monsters will often define themselves as the story evolves, and this case was no different. As I made notes on the plot, the blackout around Unit 57 changed from being caused by the monster's actions to being caused by the monster itself, generating an electrical impulse that shorted out the lights and cameras. The first thing in nature that came to mind that naturally generates voltage was the electric eel, so after doing some minor research, the monster became the humanoid equivalent of an electric eel.

Vernon Rutledge is a character who makes no appearance in the story itself, but is integral to the plot. Originally, he was just a name I plucked out of the ether to drop into the story. In my head, though, I started fleshing out his background, and it occurred to me he could tie nicely into another story I had started years ago about a genetic experiment gone wrong. As noted elsewhere, I'm a big fan on interconnected fictional universes and characters crossing over from one story to another, so Vernon got easily shoehorned into that old story by name-dropping CrossTech Genetic Research and that helped expand the backstory that Ross looks up on Wikipedia.

As the first draft rolled along, I originally ended the story on a brief scene with Rutledge, where he explains the creature, why it was in a storage unit, and how they covered it up. At first I thought this tied up the plot and created a harbinger of future events, but, after some discussion, that ending seemed out of place and a bit too on the nose. Outside of the scene with Ross' dream, the entire story takes place at the storage facility. To shift the narrative to an office in Washington DC for a page and a half seemed harsh, and the scene didn't really allow time to get into Rutledge's character, so it got chopped (for now). I could have expanded the scene, but I also liked the idea of leaving some mystery to the ending, and not having the story tied up with a neat little bow. You can, however, turn the page and read the Rutledge excerpt in all its first draft glory!

Initially, Ross Clifton was the only character to encounter the creature. But as I wrote into the confrontation between Ross and the Thing in Unit 57, I wanted an emotional gut punch, and it really seemed that Ross would die. So, I rewrote much of the story to include parts for Jeff, and I think it worked out rather well.

The big question is, of course, what *happened* to Jeff Albright?

Maybe we'll both find out someday.

## BONUS! CUT END SCENE FROM THE THING IN UNIT 57

Vernon Rutledge switched off the TV, then turned and faced the two men in the room with him.

"That was a quick and dirty cover up, but unfortunately necessary," Rutledge said. "You did well, Kellum."

"It should keep the masses at bay for now. We'll push for focus on the 'local heroes' angle as long as we can," Jared Kellum responded.

"Just what the hell happened out there, Vernon?" General John Joseph McAllister asked. He didn't sound happy with the preceding events.

"After that PETA individual spent months infiltrating my research team, I felt I couldn't trust anyone. I moved the prime research out of GeneCorp to my private home facility.

"Not disclosing that important information isn't sitting well with some people, myself included. *You* work for *us*, Vernon, not the other way around."

"They gave me complete autonomy to continue this project any way I saw fit after the unfortunate death of my predecessor. The massive failure of that integral leg of the project was largely because of incompetent interference from the military sector. Science works at its own pace, General, so don't patronize me."

"I've read the reports that were filed, but I want to hear it from you. What exactly happened to the subject in the storage unit?"

"Unfortunately, bonding DNA traits from an electric eel with that of a human subject produced a hybrid organism with a complete lack of an immune system. Despite that, we were very close to success, and there was so much to be learned from that creature. Instead of disposal, I placed it in a hibernation tank and housed it at an ultra-secure storage facility. Being in a small, out of the way location, it seemed the perfect place to store our failures while continuing research on the other subjects."

"How did it get out?"

"Even in hibernation, it began giving off pulses of electricity. These eventually built up enough intensity to cause a low-level EMP which temporarily killed the generators and also shut down the failsafe monitors. It woke up and got out of the tank. It might have actually escaped, but one of the security guards was carrying two strains of influenza. Even if the dolt hadn't shot it in the head several times, the flu bug would have killed it nearly as fast."

"How much will that set back the project? People I answer to are getting anxious," General McAllister said.

"Tell them not to worry. Things are proceeding according to schedule. They'll have their biological weapon well within the current timetable."

"They've heard that before, Vernon. Just a warning that they're going to be keeping a closer eye on you from here on out."

"I expected as much," Rutledge said. "You can see yourself out." General McAllister turned and left the office without another word. Rutledge stood at the window, looking out at a sunny October afternoon, and smiled.

"Why did you lie to them, Dr. Rutledge?" Kellum asked.

Vernon K. Rutledge turned to his assistant, still smiling. "Remember the adage 'knowledge is power', dear boy. They don't need to know that we've already successfully completed the project."

* * *

# OUT OF PLACE

The snow blowing at the front of my car looked like the jump to light speed in Star Wars, except this was no George Lucas special effect. Both high and low beams were useless against the onslaught of heavy wet snowflakes, so I focused on what I could see of the yellow center line, but that was disappearing fast under the accumulation.

Upon first getting my driver's license, lo, those many years ago, my father had warned me about driving in blizzard conditions. "Don't pay attention to the snow," he'd said. "Pay attention to the lines on the road. Otherwise, you'll lose your sense of direction and end up off into the ditch." Sage advice from the old man, God rest his soul, and I heed it every time I get behind the wheel in a snowstorm.

Thankfully, my car handled the roads fairly well. I had just replaced all four tires last fall with brand new all-season radials, so I wasn't really worried about sliding off the pavement. Caution was still a priority, though, because the last thing I wanted was to be stranded out there on a desolate stretch of road. I hadn't seen another car in a long time, but that stood to reason. It was 8:30 at night, and all day and the day before the weather bulletins had warned of this damn storm coming in from Wisconsin. When storms cross Lake Michigan, they either dissipate, or grow into even worse storms. Most people—sane people, perhaps—had done whatever business they had to do long before the storm made landfall. And once it did, and proved to be the worst storm of the season, everyone got in where it was safe, with their cases of bottled water and generators full of gas, because power outages were inevitable when the snow got wet and heavy. If you were an adult Michigander, this wasn't your first rodeo. Get inside and be prepared to stay there.

But not me. Oh no.

I am a lead sales manager for Simpson Fluid Systems, one of Michigan's largest automotive supply companies, specializing in tube and hose assemblies. Think brake and transmission lines mostly, and you'd have our major contributions to the automotive industry. I had an important business meeting sixty miles away from home on the shores of Lake Huron, in the town of Alpena. Williams Innovations, one of our major component manufacturers, called Alpena home, and our company was negotiating a buyout of this smaller business. Simpson tasked me with meeting their sales team to discuss how we would continue to work together after the buyout. For what it's worth, the meeting went well. Williams has a great team with an excellent work ethic. That's why we started working with them. I have no intention of dismantling that group. I'll fight for that, if I have to.

Now, here I was, driving home, after dark, in a blizzard, because the meeting ran way longer than we expected. That happens a lot. I probably could have canceled my attendance at the meeting in the first place, but it was an important meeting, and I was sure the storm would break down over the big lake and all the ruckus would be for nothing.

I was wrong.

Still thirty miles from home, I was crawling down the highway at barely twenty miles per hour, and the weather didn't look to be getting better. The roads themselves weren't really that slick, but the wind blowing snow in all directions cut my visibility from slim to almost none. The yellow line was coming and going, and there were stretches of road when I couldn't see it at all. I wondered what Dad's words of wisdom were when you couldn't see anything.

"Get off the damned road, dummy," was probably the advice he would have offered.

But that wasn't an option now. I had considered getting a hotel room in Alpena, but convinced myself I could make it home before the storm got terrible.

Again, I was wrong. I was seeing a pattern forming.

I couldn't see over ten feet in front of the car. There could have been a brick wall in the middle of the road and I wouldn't have seen it until I hit it.

That's why I almost didn't see the hitchhiker that night. Probably would have driven right past him if he hadn't nearly stepped out in front of my car. Now, looking back, I almost wish I had driven past. Truth being, I wish I had either taken an alternate route, or stayed in Alpena like I had considered.

My headlights spotted him just ahead, standing at the edge of the road, his arm out and a thumb jutted into the air. I didn't realize how close to the edge of the pavement my car was until I saw him, and I had to swerve slightly to the left to avoid plowing him over. The roads were slicker than I thought, and the back ass of my car fishtailed a bit. I pumped the brakes lightly and brought the car under control, pulling off the road about fifteen or twenty feet ahead. I would have impressed dad.

Mom, however, would have been less than happy with me stopping.

"Never pick up hitchhikers," she'd drilled into my head thirty years ago. I'm sure everybody's mother had similar maternal advice for their young first-time drivers. I'd listened to that advice until that night.

I wouldn't have left my worst enemy out in this blizzard, so I doubt my conscience would have let me pass this guy by. It wasn't nice out there, for anything or anyone. My heater was working overtime just to keep the car's interior warm, and I could only imagine that the wind cut like daggers on someone standing outside.

When the passenger door opened, a gust of snowy wind swirled in ahead of the hitchhiker himself. And it might sound cliched, but it chilled me to the bone.

"Thanks," he said as he settled into the passenger seat. He had a thick growth of beard covered with ice that melted immediately, and he wiped his hands through it to clear the moisture.

"You're welcome," I replied. "Nasty night be out."

"I was thinking nobody would ever come along."

"There haven't been many cars on the road," I said as I pulled back onto the highway. The snow was really accumulating now.

"I went in the ditch a half mile or so back. Hard to tell how far now. I feel like I've been walking for an hour."

I had seen no cars for the past several miles, ditch or otherwise, but I wasn't counting on what I could or couldn't see at this point. "I hate to say, but I don't think you would have made it much longer."

"No doubt. It's the worst storm I've seen in years."

"Yeah, same here," I said, and suddenly felt rude. "Sorry, I'm Robert Sanberg."

"Jim Oakfield," he said, rubbing his hands together over the dashboard heater vent. "Nice to meet you."

"Wish it was under better circumstances."

"For sure."

"Where you headed?"

"Curran."

"I can get you there. I live in Lansford, so you're just a mile or so past my turn."

"Thanks. I can call my wife when we get there. She'll come out to get me."

"Oh, I can get you home, no problem."

"Probably not. We live on a two-track a couple of miles back in the woods. No offense, but this car won't make it twenty yards. My wife has the four-wheel drive, so she can come out."

"Definitely the better option," I laughed. He smiled and continued rubbing his hands over the vent. I turned up the heat a notch.

"Thanks. Can't seem to get the chill off."

"That wind is a biter, that's for sure."

We drove in silence for the next few minutes as I concentrated on navigating the road. Three to four inches of snow covered the pavement now, and I hadn't seen a plow truck yet. This was only going to get worse.

The car fishtailed a bit, but I corrected the wheel and brought it back under control. The spots where the wind was arcing across the road left it slick. I'd push snow for a hundred yards and then hit one of those windswept spots and she'd slide. Thankfully, three decades and change living in northern Michigan made me a pretty well-seasoned winter driver.

I wasn't cocky, however, and kept my speed at twenty-five or less. If we ditched now, who knew how long it would be until someone came along? Plow trucks would eventually be out, but there were much more populated areas of roadway that got plowed first.

Jim finally broke the silence. "Things like this make you realize what's important, though." He sounded somber. "I have two toddlers at home with my wife, and I get stranded on the road. After I started walking, the storm got so bad I couldn't see anything around me. It just seemed like the entire world ceased to exist for a while. And let me tell you, if there's a more hopeless feeling, you'd struggle to find it."

"Hear that," I said, but I really couldn't relate much. I had no kids, and my divorce from Melanie had been final for almost a year. If I died out on this road, there wouldn't be anyone to miss me. Both my parents are dead, and I speak to my sister on Christmas. Honestly, I feel that's more out of familial obligation than actually wanting to talk to me. I'm fine with that. She was a rotten older sister anyway, so the feeling was mutual.

We came to the intersection where I needed to turn for the last leg of my journey home. Curran was only a mile further straight. I noticed the light at the intersection was out. You never really pay attention to it—it's only a caution light—but when it's not there, the absence of it is immediately noticeable.

"Power must be down," Jim said. Apparently, he'd noticed too. "Good thing I bought a generator a couple of years back."

"Same here," I said. Two summers before, we'd had one hell of a thunderstorm that took down trees across several counties. We lost power for three days, and some areas of the state were without juice for upwards of a week. I bought a generator from Home Depot a few days later. Haven't regretted it.

We rolled into Curran, and the old saying "blink twice and you'll miss it" totally applies there. Town limits comprised a bar, post office, gas station, and a small church. Desolate would describe it even if it wasn't the middle of a blizzard.

"Pull in at the station," Jim said. "I'll call from there."

I pulled the car off the road into the parking lot and parked by one of the gas pumps. The store was long closed.

"I can wait for your wife to get here," I said, genuinely concerned. There was nobody here in town. Everything was closed, even the bar.

"That's okay, man," Jim said. "You've got a bit of a trip left yourself, and you'd be smart to keep on moving."

"Are you sure? Waiting's not a problem."

"Yeah, I'll be fine. Marissa will be here five minutes after I call her."

"Okay," I said, still not feeling totally comfortable. "It was nice meeting you, Jim. Hope next time we talk, it'll be over a beer at the Buck Stop."

"It's a deal," Jim said, and opened the door. Another swirl of snowy air coiled into my car like a snake as he exited. He turned back and leaned his head inside. "Thanks again." Then he was gone, swallowed by a swoop of windblown snow that had come over the top of the gas station building.

I put my car in drive and pulled out from the parking lot back onto the highway. I looked out my window one last time and saw his brief silhouette contrasted against the building.

I never saw Jim Oakfield again.

The road from Curran to Lansford would normally be a twenty-minute drive at most during the summer, but tonight it took me well over an hour. I was exhausted by the time I pulled the car into my garage. Luckily, the power was still on, otherwise even getting into the house would have been more of a chore than I wanted to handle.

I stayed up long enough to have a beer before I went to bed and thought about Jim Oakfield. I hoped he made it home safely. When my head hit the pillow, I slept through the night and the rest of the storm.

The next day, most everything was closed. I worked from home. My muscles were beyond sore, and I ate pain relievers like candy most of the day. Four hours of white-knuckling the steering wheel had taken their toll on me.

I was just glad the storm was over.

* * *

I admittedly forgot about the hitchhiker over the next few days. Work got very intense with the buyout looming ever closer. Lots of stressful meetings and terms being offered, rejected, and revised. I thought my company was being a little overbearing with their conditions, but that's just me. I had no pull on that; ultimately I'm just another cog in the wheel.

I used to stay up on weeknights for the 11:00 news. It was just one of those holdovers from my younger days when I really followed the news of the world. I'm older and require more sleep now, but I still like hearing about the local stuff, so I DVR the late news every night and watch it in the morning while I'm having my coffee and getting ready for work. I could just as easily watch the morning news, but I like the 11:00 news anchor.

Last night's top story got my attention. I've watched it half a dozen times now, and I'm just sitting in my chair, trying to wrap my head around it, while my coffee is going cold.

"Earlier this week, two hunters discovered the body of a man in the woods near Curran, Michigan, later identified through dental records as James Stewart Oakfield. Oakfield has been on the state Missing Persons list since January 1987, when police found his abandoned car on a long stretch of M-65 ten miles north of Curran, but did not find him. Michigan State Police are currently investigating, and we'll have more on this story as information becomes available.

So, I sat there in my chair for a while, kind of numb. It was too early for a beer, but Lord knows I wanted one. Instead, I reheated my coffee while I watched the newscast one more time. Then I called into work and took a sick day. I had some investigating of my own to do.

I sat down at the desk in my home office and flipped open my trusty, but aging, laptop. I searched for information on the James Oakfield missing persons case and found quite a bit of archived information. The case baffled investigators in 1987, with one State Police officer stating, "It's like he just disappeared off the face of the Earth." Maybe that was closer to the truth than he'd known.

Deeper searching got me more details on Oakfield himself. He had been a journeyman carpenter, owned his own company, Oakfield Construction, and had married Marissa Wilkins in 1983. They had two children, David and Connie, who were three and two years old, respectively, when their father went missing.

Out of curiosity, I searched for Oakfield Construction. The company closed in 1988, several months after founder James Oakfield went missing, but reinstated ten years ago. I found an article titled: "David James Oakfield, 26, reopens construction business once owned by father." Photos accompanying the article showed a memorial sign in front of the construction dedicated to James. There was brief information about the missing persons case, all of which I had already read elsewhere.

Connie Oakfield is a child psychologist in Baltimore, Maryland. She's married and has two kids of her own. She named one of them after her father.

I sat there in the chair at my desk, silently staring at the screen. My coffee had gone cold again. And I still wanted a beer.

I'm a rational man mostly, even though some weird, unexplainable things have happened in and around this town. But it all comes down to the things he said, and the things I've seen today.

I remember James Oakfield, sitting in the passenger seat of my car, telling me about his toddler children. They were toddlers in 1987, but today, they're full-grown adults.

I also remember something else he had told me, that while he was walking, the storm had gotten so bad he couldn't see anything, that it seemed like the entire world had ceased to exist for a while.

Perhaps it had. Maybe the entire world got lost in that storm. Maybe Jim Oakfield existed outside the world for a few minutes in the middle of the storm. And maybe when things finally snapped back into place, Jim Oakfield was in a different time, decades ahead of when he'd been.

Maybe?

## AUTHOR NOTES - OUT OF PLACE

I originally wrote this story in 1987, during my junior year of high school, after driving home from a friend's house one night in what became a severe blizzard. It stuck with me for a long time, that night, and eventually, as with most things that stick with me, I pulled a story out of it. I remember not recognizing the roadway because of the intensity of the blowing snow. It was a simple extrapolation (for me, anyway) to get to the question: What if the world folded in on itself during a moment of severe weather and took someone from one place and moved him a few hundred miles away to another? From that, I wrote the story about a young man picking up a hitchhiker who had gotten lost in a severe snowstorm, with the big reveal of this hitchhiker being transported from Minnesota to Michigan in the blink of an eye.

I thought it was an okay story, and I'd tried to revise it over the years—quite a few times, in fact—but some parts of the narrative never felt quite right. The conversation between Robert and James Oakfield always appeared forced, and Jim's motivations for being out in a raging snowstorm seemed convoluted. So, I shuffled the story off to a computer folder where my "not-quite-finished" stories go. Luckily, almost every story that has ended up there has also made it back out.

So it was, when I finally sat back down to give this short another pass a couple of years ago, I started almost completely from scratch. I kept the original version nearby for reference, and while the plot in the most general sense is the same, the writing is almost completely new. Robert Sanberg went from teenager to his forties. Maybe that's because in the time from the first writing to the last, I went from teenager to my forties as well. One other big change I made is instead of Jim Oakfield shifting sideways through space from one state to another, I turned him into a time traveler, coming from 1987 to now. For what I was trying to do, it made more sense. And, well, I love time travel stories.

# BENEATH THE SURFACE

"Time is three-forty-seven PM. State your full name for the record, please," Detective Brent Kellum said.

"Dwight Alan Stedman."

"Mr. Stedman, please acknowledge that you are fully aware we are recording this conversation."

"I'm aware."

"Why are you here today?"

"I'm here to confess to the killing of eight children between August, 1968 and April, 1973."

Kellum had a jaw so square it would make Superman jealous, and I watched it tighten at Stedman's words. Brent was a father to three kids at home. I was ready to step in front of him if he made a move, and right now, I wouldn't blame him if he did.

"If you're the killer, why come forward and confess to it almost fifty years later? You got away with it. So, why now?"

"Because they're after me," Stedman said, and despite being over six feet, he suddenly looked tiny.

"Who is after you?"

"The kids." Stedman looked up, his sunken, red-rimmed eyes full of fear.

"What kids?"

"The—the ones I killed."

"Oh, for fuck's sake, get this idiot out of here," Kellum yelled. "I can't believe I came all the way down here for this shit."

"I say we hear him out," I said, and the sound of my voice surprised me.

"Jenkins," Brent said between gritted teeth, and his jaw was getting more square by the second. "This guy needs a psych eval, not an interrogation."

"Would you like me to take over?" I offered.

"Be my guest," Brent said, and tossed the clipboard at me. Brent receded to a chair at the back of the interrogation room, folded his arms across his chest, and stared off to the corner like a child who'd had his favorite toy taken away.

There were five of us there that day, when Dwight Alan Stedman confessed to the murder of eight kids nearly five decades ago. Besides Brent Kellum and myself, my partner Jack Banner and Franklin Hopgood rounded out the law enforcement side. Cecil Gladwell, defense attorney, was in the office when Stedman came in, and thereafter appointed himself Dwight's attorney, and was now along for the ride to make sure we did nothing too stupid. Or maybe to make sure we did.

"Dwight," Cecil reminded. "You don't have to say anything."

"Yes, I do," Dwight said, and I thought he looked older than seventy-four in that moment, as if the mere thought of talking about it aged him. His brow was wet with sweat. When his eyes caught mine, I swore I saw genuine remorse in them.

"Saying you killed those kids doesn't just automatically make it true, you realize?" Jack Banner said.

"Oh, I know," Dwight said. "But I think you'll believe me soon enough."

"Let's start with the obvious question: why do you think these kids are after you?"

"Because I see them everywhere."

You could almost hear the eye rolls.

"Are any of them here now?"

"No," he said, and lowered his head. "I know how it sounds. I realize you all think I'm crazy. But I killed those kids back then, and now they're back to make me pay."

"That's not possible, Dwight," I said, but the way he looked at me, I wanted to believe him.

"I know it's impossible, but the line between possibility and impossibility stretches pretty thin sometimes. There was a time when I believed little, but since then, I've seen a lot. Learned a lot. And it changes your perception of what's real and what isn't."

People are capable of amazing things, and people are also capable of horrible things. In this line of work, I've seen a lot of both. I wasn't sure what I was seeing here, but he'd sure as hell gotten my attention.

*  *  *

"I was born in November 1946. My father had been in Europe during World War II, and according to what my mother said to me in hushed whispers years later, he had seen horrific things there, things that changed him. He had gone into that war a young man of eighteen, barely needing to shave, and had come back with something inside of him he never talked about.

"I can't tell you if it was what he held back that created me, or if it was the father he was after I was born that made me think the bad thoughts. I honestly don't know. But my father was not a whole man the entire time I knew him."

Dwight hardly looked us in the eye while he told his story, preferring to stare at a coffee stain on the table.

"He beat me a lot. Beat on my mom regularly, too. A lot of the times she took the beating because she was trying to keep him from me. I suppose that's the lengths mothers—good mothers—will go for their children.

"Anyway, dad would beat on me for whatever reason, if I left a toy out, or didn't rinse out my milk glass after dinner. The reason didn't matter, because I think they were just excuses for him to take out his frustrations on someone who couldn't fight back. As I got older, I got the belt for any grade in school less than top marks. That went on until the end.

My father died when I was fifteen, they say of a brain aneurysm. I think more than likely it was his anger that killed him, but I'm not a doctor. Either way, things should have gotten better for mother and me after that, but they didn't. Mom worked as a waitress in a small diner for a few years, but that wasn't enough income to sustain. I did odd jobs for cash, lawn mowing, raking leaves, cleaning out gutters for old people who couldn't push the mower or climb the ladder anymore. Did that until I started working at Greenbaum's Garage after school as a shop assistant when I was seventeen, cleaning up, organizing tools, picking up parts, basically whatever menial jobs needed done. I always had an aptitude for mechanical things, so I started watching over the shoulders of mechanics, in particular a hulking black man named Ulysses, who would show me how to do things and loved to talk about it. Within a few months, they let me wrench on cars, and within a year I was up to my elbows in grease and engine repair every day.

"I graduated high school in May, 1965, two months short of my nineteenth birthday. We were ass-deep in the middle of the Vietnam conflict by that time, but I didn't get drafted, by some stroke of luck. Instead, I kept working at Greenbaum's, and it was there that I had my first murderous thoughts.

"Vic Greenbaum, the shop's owner, had a boy named Bradley, who was—and I mince no words—a little peckerhead. Vic let him run around the shop unsupervised after school until closing time, and he annoyed the piss out of everyone. He'd take your tools away and not give them back, he'd taunt us all to the point of rage, and if you said anything to him, he'd mention that his father owned the place, and stick his damned tongue out at you. So you didn't dare say a word. Paul Tremont, who'd been working at the shop for over ten years and could tell you what was wrong with an engine by just listening to it, got fired for asking Vic to keep Bradley off the shop floor. Nevermind the dangers of a kid running around under a car hoist, you know? So, after Paul got the axe, we all learned to keep our mouths shut, and shut good.

"Maybe it was keeping my mouth shut that put the first terrible thoughts into my head. I don't know for certain. All I know is that I imagined 'accidents' befalling the kid. I'm sure we all did. Lucky for him, his dad stopped letting him hang around in the shop about a year later, after Bradley slipped on a creeper and knocked his head against one of the rolling tool boxes each mechanic kept with them. Bradley got eighteen stitches, and that was the last we saw of him for a good long time. Nobody missed the little shit.

"But the seed that planted in my head, it grew. I'd imagined some horrific fates for Bradley, everything from running him up a chain fall by the neck to roasting his balls with an acetylene torch. But they were just thoughts, not actions."

"Not yet," Brent said. I gave him a look.

He licked his lips and looked up. "Could I get some water, please?"

Banner nodded to Hopgood, who stepped out to the break room next door and came back thirty seconds later with a plastic bottle of water. Nobody spoke during that thirty seconds.

Stedman took a long drink from the bottle and set it on the table. Beads of perspiration had already started forming on the sides of the plastic. It was warm in the room. We do that purposely to make perps feel uncomfortable.

There were beads of perspiration on Stedman's forehead, too, when he started back up.

* * *

"It was the summer of 1968, and I drove the same route home every day after work, taking the back streets to avoid the traffic from all the summer folk that had been trickling into town since the schools let out. I get they help the economy here, but that doesn't mean we have to like how they overrun the town from the end of May until early September."

We all silently understood that. Summer is party season, and the population of the town nearly triples for most of four months. Lots more action for law enforcement.

"Partway down Beaufort Street was an old fenced-in basketball court in front of a rundown building. Tall grass had grown up through the cracked cement and around the chain link, and the painted lines on the court had long faded. I believe at one time it was a youth rec center, but I can't be certain. I drove by it every day, and shortly after school let out, there was a young boy there, playing basketball almost every evening. By himself mostly, but sometimes there would be another young boy or two there, and they'd be playing HORSE or one-on-one.

One day, I drove by. It was in the upper-eighties, humid as all get out, with no wind coming off the lakes that day. I rolled down the car's windows, and I was drinking a cold Coke I'd gotten from the machine at the garage before I'd left. Idling down the road, it was hot enough to see the heat coming off the pavement in little waves. As I got up to the basketball court, the kid was walking out the gate with his basketball under his arm.

"'Need a ride?'" I asked him, and he stopped. I hit the brake.

"'No thanks, mister,' he said. 'I'm not supposed to take rides from strangers.' Smart kid."

"'What's your name?' I asked him."

"'Charlie Wellman,' he said.

"'Well, Charlie Wellman, I'm Dwight Stedman,' I replied with a smile. 'There, now we know each other.'"

"'I'm still not supposed to get rides from anyone but my mom or dad.'"

"'Fair enough,' I said, and didn't push it further. 'I come by here almost every day, so if you see me and want a ride, just ask.'"

"'Thanks,' he said. I was idling alongside him as he walked down the edge of the pavement, with my arm hanging out the window, when he turned to me. You're already not believing that I killed those kids, so this might push you right to calling for the straightjacket. I don't even like speaking of it."

"Take your time," I said. By this point, I was beyond intrigued by his story, as horrific as I knew it would turn.

Dwight took another long drink from the bottle, and sweat dripped off it onto the table.

"When Charlie Wellman turned to me, something changed. The air around his face seemed to shimmer, to shift might be the better word. And what I saw then, God as my witness, it wasn't human. The kid's face was still there, but it was like a thin veil you could see through. Behind it was something else, wrinkled gray skin, and large, bulging yellow eyes with vertical slits like a cat. And a wide mouth, covered with wet black lips, and filled with hundreds of razor-pointed teeth."

"Fucking Christ," Kellum said. He had already been skeptical, and I knew what we'd just heard would put him over the edge. "I hope nobody's believing this shit."

I had to admit it was the most outrageous thing I'd heard in all my years upholding the law, and believe me, I'd heard a lot of things that would make you wonder about the world. Still, something seemed genuine about him, and I'd interrogated many.

Dwight paid no heed to Kellum. As hesitant as he was to talk about it in the beginning, now that he'd opened that floodgate, I think he wanted to rid himself of it. He had been holding it in for fifty years, if you were prone to believe him.

"'You okay, mister—Dwight,' the kid said, and as horrific as he looked, it was his voice that chilled me the most. It still sounded like a kid, but it was rough, like the sound of heavy grit sandpaper." Those enormous eyes blinked, and the irises opened wide, then slitted again. I thought I was losing my mind.

"'Um, yeah,' I said, then turned away. I couldn't stand to look anymore. 'I'm fine. And I supposed I should let you get on your way.'"

"'It was nice to meet you,' the thing beneath Charlie Wellman's face said, and I actually shuddered.

"'You too,' I said, and sped off. My heart was beating like a hammer until I turned the corner and he was out of sight. I pulled over a couple blocks further up the road and vomited my Coke into the gutter."

"Is that why you killed him?" Hopgood asked. "You thought he was a monster, so you murdered him?"

Dwight remained silent for a few seconds, then whispered: "Yes."

"You sonofabitch," Hopgood said.

"But I didn't believe what I'd seen at first. I couldn't look at him again for a while—I was that terrified of what I'd seen—but eventually I offered a wave as I drove by when he was there. It was a couple weeks later that I finally stopped and talked to him again, and just like that first time, I saw the thing that Charlie really was: a monster.

"I stopped again a few days later, and found it was getting easier to look at him, to hear that guttural gravel sound when he spoke, and not act like I was terrified. And somewhere inside me, fear quickly gave way to growing and panicked anger.

"And before you ask, no, I didn't see anyone else that way. Nobody at the garage, or any customers I spoke with there. Nobody at the grocery store or at the restaurant. It was just him. Just a third-grade kid named Charlie Wellman, who was a monster pretending to be human.

"So, you believed a nine-year-old kid was a monster and killed him?" Kellum was back at it again.

"It sounds outlandish, but—"

"Outlandish? Is that what it sounds? Jesus H. Christ, it doesn't sound outlandish. It sounds downright batshit insane!"

"Brent," I said. "Maybe you need to take a few minutes. Step outside, get some air."

Brent Kellum grunted and flung the door open hard enough that it banged against the doorstop and rebounded closed.

"He's not wrong," Stedman said, and drained the rest of the water bottle. "I've wrestled with it for years. Even got it through my head that it wasn't real, any of it. But I know now it's true. I know it all happened. And I know it's coming back around again, and this time, it's my turn.

"After seeing this thing Charlie was hiding beneath his childlike face several times, I decided I needed to stop him, to save us from the monster, or alien, or whatever he was. I decided to kill him.

"It wasn't a simple decision, and you can take whatever opinion you want of me for making it, but there was something sinister behind that facade. He wasn't a kid, not to me. He might have looked like one, and maybe that was part of the plan, to look like something innocent, to deceive everyone who might discover him.

"I didn't have an actual plan. I wasn't even sure I could do it. But in early August 1968, Charlie was playing basketball by himself as I drove by after work. I almost drove past, then before I even thought about what I was doing, I stopped and backed my car up. I got out and approached the basketball court.

"'Hey there, Charlie,' I said. When he turned, his face shimmered and changed and there it was, a horrible yellow-eyed thing with toothpicks for teeth, staring at me and smiling.

"'Hey, Dwight,' he said in that raspy voice that caused my neck hairs to stand up. 'Wanna play HORSE?'"

"I didn't hesitate then. I just grabbed him. The thought of him just going on with this ruse, pretending to be a kid, it panicked me. What if he had killed the kid and took his place? What was its plan?

"I never found out. When I grabbed him, he felt my grip and tried to twist out of it, but I had both his arms. I pulled him off the ball court to the blind side of the old rec center fast. There were no cars to be seen, and the road rarely traveled, but I wasn't taking any chances.

"As I wrestled him to the ground, I watched him change. Gone was the veil that had covered him for however long, replaced with the full face of that thing. Its jaw opened, and a sound issued from it like a tin can being dragged across cement, a terrible grating sound. And its hands curled into claws that worked to free it, but I held on. I could feel my heart hammering in my chest, thumping in my ears. I was barely twenty-two years old, and I thought I was going to have a heart attack.

"Charlie clawed at me and got a good dig into my left arm. I still have a scar from it," he said, and rolled up his shirt sleeve. There was a long strip of whitish flesh on the inside of his forearm that stood in contrast to his otherwise tanned arm. "When anyone asked, I said I got it at work. It took a long time to heal, and it burned something fierce for days, like someone had poured straight alcohol on it.

"I was choking him, and I could feel the leathery slipperiness of his neck in my fingers, and knew I would not hold him for much longer. He was fighting back, and was far stronger than a nine-year-old kid. I panicked.

"On the back side of the building, someone—kids probably—had built a makeshift fire pit with heavy rocks. I let go of Charlie for a moment and reached for one of the bigger rocks. Charlie pulled away from me and was scrambling to his feet when I brought the stone down on the back of his head. It made a dull, heavy thud as it connected and Charlie's body sprawled forward, the back of his malformed head dented from the blow. He was convulsing, like he was having a seizure, and I had to fight back my urge to just run away. He turned over, and I met those cat-like eyes as I stepped forward and brought the rock down on him again. This time it made a wet thump, combined with the cracking sound of bone breaking.

"Charlie Wellman was dead. And as that moment of fear-induced rage subsided, all my strength drained out of me and I collapsed to the ground, dropping the rock covered with Charlie's blood and bits of brain matter into the grass. Then, I cried. I couldn't tell you if it was from remorse or relief, because I remember little for a while after that. I was in a fugue state as I dragged his body further behind the building, into the tall brush. There was a shovel in my trunk—I learned long ago to always carry one—and I used that to dig a hole in the ground and put Charlie's deformed body down. I was sweating something terrible and my arm was on fire where he'd clawed me by the time I finished. I covered the burial site with loose brush, and that was the end of the thing that had looked like Charlie Wellman.

"So, they did not find the body?" I asked.

"Not that I know of. I spent the next couple of weeks in mortal fear, wondering when the cops would show up, but by some miracle, they didn't. I hadn't planned this out, so I was sure I'd slipped up, left something behind that would lead them to me. But nothing ever came of it.

"I followed the newspaper articles and heard about the search for Charlie from pretty much anyone and everyone over the next few weeks. It was after Labor Day when the searches were called off, though I heard Charlie's parents still kept looking for a while after that. I assume any parent would, and I wondered if they knew what their child really was, or if they were the same thing he was. I had a million questions.

"It was determined that someone abducted Charlie, and had taken him elsewhere, but the case remained unsolved. I calmed down a little after that.

"I saw the Wellmans once, at the Family Grocer, just shortly after the searches were called off. I had never seen them before, but they were ahead of me at the checkout and the cashier was saying how sorry she was about Charlie. A heavy knot grew in my stomach, and I was sure I was going to either vomit or pass out, but I made it back to my car, where I collapsed into the seat and wiped a line of sweat off my forehead.

"One thing that came from that encounter, though," Dwight said, and his eyes met mine. "They didn't look like Charlie did beneath that veil. I didn't see another one like him until late January 1969."

* * *

I suggested we take a quick break after that. It was five-thirty at night and I needed some air that wasn't in that room, if just for a few minutes. I motioned to Jack Banner, and then to the door.

"We'll be back in a few minutes, Dwight," I said. "Would you like another water?"

"Yes, please," he said.

We stepped out into the hall and closed the door.

"Jack," I said. "Can you get somebody to look up files related to the Charlie Wellman missing person's case? I just want some more details on whatever the department thought and did back then."

"Sure, I'll get Glen Rhoads on it. He loves digging into the archives." Jack headed down the hall, and I stepped into the break room. I grabbed two bottles of water, unscrewed the top of one, and took a long drink.

It was refreshing, but I wanted something much stronger than water right then.

If Dwight Alan Stedman was indeed a child killer from nearly fifty years ago, he had the advantage of time on his side. Forensic science didn't become a thing until the mid-1980s, and nowadays, they could track the particulate matter of a wet fart and have your ass in jail before dinnertime. Those science geeks made it almost impossible to get away with murder.

Jack came into the break room and grabbed a Gatorade from the fridge.

"Glen's on it. He'll gather what he can and get with us ASAP."

"Thanks," I said. "So what's your take on Stedman?"

"What he says sounds absolutely insane," Jack said, taking a swig from his bottle. "But, as someone who's seen some weird, even unexplainable shit over the years, I don't want to fully discount him, either."

"Same," I said. "I'll be interested to see what Glen comes up with that might give us even a little guidance. Dwight said he buried the Wellman kids' body behind the old building on Beaufort Street, and he didn't think anyone had ever discovered it. That we can follow up on."

* * *

Back in the room, Dwight took his second water, drank long, and then surveyed the room.

"I can't expect anyone to believe what I've told you so far, but I have no reason to lie about it. I'm not trying to go for an insanity defense."

"Why don't you give us details from the other murders," Jack said.

Dwight leaned forward, put his elbows on the table, and started talking again. He still looked aged, but there seemed to be something rejuvenating him with telling his tale.

"February 1969, we had a decent snowfall and record cold temperatures. Over those months, I'd made peace with what I'd done. A monster using a child's face, what an awful thing. So, when I saw the second one, using the face of Darcy McCollum, I didn't waste time in removing her from the world.

"She was ice-skating at the public rink. I was there, strangely enough, to pick up Bradley Greenbaum from skating practice. Vic was hip-deep in an engine overhaul, and asked me to grab the little bastard and bring him back to the garage. I was standing at the edge of the rink with my hands in my pockets. I hadn't dressed for being outdoors that day, so I zipped my jacket tight and pulled the lapels up around my neck.

"Despite being a peckerhead, Bradley was actually an excellent skater. I guess being a rotten little prick didn't exclude you from excelling at other things. So, I was actually paying attention as the kids finished up their last laps and came off the rink. Darcy came to a stop just feet away from where I was standing.

"In an instant, I saw that same shimmering I'd seen with Charlie, and even though she had her face bundled up with a scarf across her mouth, I saw those yellow eyes looking at me, blinking, and the dark sunken pits where her nose should be."

"'Hello,' she said, and the voice sounded like running a serrated knife across a cheese grater. I returned her greeting and then looked past her for Bradley, who executed a final spin, then glided to a stop next to Darcy. His face wrinkled when he realized it was me, but I wasn't concerned with him now. I had seen another monster, and suddenly I wondered just how many of them there could be out there. And why was I the only one who could see them? That's something I've pondered for the past five decades.

"I had Bradley to contend with, so I couldn't take care of Darcy then, but as we left, I noticed she was walking alone. I hoped that would be the case after the next practice.

"And it was. Two days later, I parked my car a block away from the rink, and caught her walking alone again. I grabbed her fast, knocked her in the head, and tossed her into my trunk. So simple, but she fought a lot harder than Charlie did at the end, and the growls and howls that came from her wide, tooth-rimmed mouth chilled me as I brought the axe down on her. On it.

"What did you do with the body?" Jack asked.

"It was too cold, and the ground frozen too deep to bury her then, so I dismembered her and dragged the parts out to an ice-fishing shanty on Greenscore Lake in a burlap sack. I chucked the pieces down the hole and that was the end of Darcy McCollum.

"There was another missing person's case, of course. That same sense of dread I had with Charlie hit me, afraid I'd be caught, unable to explain the reasons I'd done what appeared to be an unspeakable act. But, as before, the case went nowhere. Nobody had seen me take Darcy, so once again, I'd gotten away with murder. I seemed fated to carry out this string of monster killings, unimpeded. Eventually, that's how I looked at it."

"You said there were eight total," I said. "That's a lot of killing."

"After Darcy, I didn't see another one until late fall of 1970. Fred Dunning was his name, an eleven-year-old boy I discovered when I was in Black Rapids for a doctor's visit. The next spring there was Leroy Crawford, a young black boy who went to the church my mother attended. Christie Robinson and Jimmy Alhoff were teenagers, and together. That was a difficult one, but I caught them off guard and got lucky. The last two, Fabian Newell and Melanie Bamford, happened within days of each other, though towns apart."

"And that was the last of them?" I asked.

"I haven't seen another one since 1973, though I went on looking everywhere I went. I couldn't fathom why I'd been given this hellish ability, but I decided it was my burden to bear. After the summer of 1973, though, I never saw another one of those things.

"Until now."

* * *

"Now, you say they're back?" I asked.

"Two days ago, I was at Woodwind Mall looking for a new pair of shoes. They have a good shoe store there, and my feet bother me something fierce these days, likely from all my years standing on concrete wrenching on cars. I walked out of the shoe store with my purchase, looked up, and stopped.

"Charlie Wellman and Darcy McCollum stood there together, holding hands. Staring right at me. I've etched those kids' faces in my mind, so there was no doubt it was them. They dressed like kids today would, and hairstyles were a little different, but it was them. Darcy would have been a couple of years older than Charlie, and she stood a few inches taller than him here. I met their human eyes, then saw the real eyes behind them, and the mottled gray flesh of their faces.

"I turned away and walked across the hall to the food court, thinking I had probably just imagined it. I hadn't thought about them in some time, but my heart beat pretty hard in my chest just the same.

"I got a two-item plate from the Teriyaki Grill and sat down at a table to eat. As I forked pieces of chicken into my mouth, I saw them again. On one side of the food court there was a large carousel for the kids. There were lots of games and simple child entertainment there to suck up their parents' money. Charlie and Darcy were on the carousel, going round and round on those large fake painted horses, their inhuman eyes following me.

"I finished my food fast, not even enjoying it, convinced I was probably going mad. After getting up, I grabbed my shoe bag and headed for the main entrance. I looked back as I pushed through the entrance, and Charlie and Darcy stepped off the carousel and came after me.

"I crossed the parking lot fast and glanced back to see them pacing me several yards behind. My hands were shaking when I pulled the keys from my pocket and I dropped them. I stooped over to pick them up, and then there they were. Five feet away, standing together. Holding hands again. Looking at me.

"I pushed the key fob and unlocked my car. They just stood there, looking at me, not advancing.

"'Stay away from me,' I said, and slid into the driver's seat. They didn't move. I started the car and backed out of the spot. They still didn't move.

"As I drove away, I looked in the rearview and saw them step out of the parking space and watch me leave."

"Sounds like a hallucination," Jack said.

"I considered it, even though it seemed so real. But yesterday, seeing Melanie Bamford convinced me something was wrong."

"So, you saw another?"

"Yes. I went out to get the mail shortly after lunch, and she was standing at the end of my driveway, still looking thirteen years old. Like Charlie and Darcy, her clothes and hair were modern, but it was definitely her. I never forgot their faces, the real ones or the masks, and it was her, without a doubt. I stopped short, and she just looked at me. She said nothing. None of them did. Just stood there, emotionless and staring. But I could see the real them behind the human faces.

"I didn't get the mail. I turned and went back to the house. She just stood there for probably ten minutes, looking at the house. Then she turned and walked down the street. I watched until she disappeared past the corner, where the trees were thick and blocked my view.

"I woke up around six-forty this morning after a restless sleep, did my morning business, then got dressed and came downstairs. I looked out the window next to the door to see if they had delivered the paper, and as the morning sun spread across my front lawn, there they were. All eight of them this time, holding hands side-by-side in the dew-covered grass, looking toward my house through lifeless eyes."

"So, you believe these kids came back to life and are stalking you?" I said.

"I don't know what to believe. I killed the things that looked like these kids decades ago. How could it be them, and why are they here now?"

"Maybe it's psychological. These shapeshifting aliens are trying to spook you by looking like the kids you killed."

"You believe me?" Dwight said.

"I'm not sure where I stand on this right now," I said. "We've got some serious investigating to do before anything."

* * *

The door opened, and Glen Rhoads popped his balding head into the interrogation room.

"Petra, can I see you and Jack for a minute?"

We stepped out of the room and closed the door. I gave Glen a look of puzzlement. "What's up?"

"I didn't want to just leave this info on your desk, Petra. Something odd's going on."

"Such as?"

"So, police officers discovered a body behind the old rec center on Beaufort during their searches for Charlie Wellman in 1968. But— and here's the weird part—someone mostly redacted the file. There's confirmation that the body is not Charlie Wellman, then nothing, no identification, no follow up. However, I did a little more research, and a local newspaper page three article stated the FBI was in town a day after that, for reasons unknown."

"Redacted file and a visit by the FBI? That doesn't sound suspicious at all."

"Not at all." Jack Banner rolled his eyes.

"Any of the police officers on that job still with us?" I asked.

"Thought you might ask," Glen said, and handed me a printout. "Whitman Vickers was in his second year on the force in 1968, but he's still alive and kicking and living out his golden years on the family farm a few miles east of town."

"Thanks, Glen. I think we can work with that."

* * *

Jack and I stood on the porch of the Vickers farmhouse, an expansive single-story ranch style complemented by a newly repainted barn and a pole building. It was seven-fifteen, and the sun had turned into a deep orange peach dropping low in the west.

Whit Vickers answered the door and gave us both a piercing Clint Eastwood stare. He was seventy-four years old (same age as Dwight Stedman), but looked to be in excellent shape. My grandfather was stooped over with a hunchback by the time he was seventy. Whit Vickers looked like he could still whip some ass and not be out of breath.

"You're the law," he said matter-of-factly. A good cop never loses his intuition. "What brings you way out here?"

"Mr. Vickers, my name is Petra Jenkins, and this is my partner, Jack Banner. We're here to ask some questions about an investigation you were part of back in 1968."

"Good Lord," Whit said, and laughed. "You expect me to remember something from over fifty years ago?"

"I'm hoping so, sir," I said. "Do you recall the Charlie Wellman missing persons case?"

"Oh, *that* case. Yeah, I remember that one. Everyone probably does, who's still above ground, anyway. Have a seat here on the porch and I'll grab a pitcher of sun tea and we'll talk."

Whit disappeared back into the house, and we found a couple of wicker chairs at the far side of the porch. The smell of freshly cut grass hit my nose. God, what a wonderful scent. I don't have time to leave the city much, and I sure missed it right then.

Whit came out with a carafe of tea he said he put out on the east deck that morning to brew. He set three glasses down on the table and filled them. He sat down on a bench, took a good long drink, and looked at us.

"So, the Wellman case, eh?" he said, and took another drink. Ice clinked in the glass, and sweat ran down the side and I thought of the water bottle Dwight had been drinking in the interrogation room. I took a drink from my glass, and it was some mighty fine tea.

"Yeah, I was hoping you could walk us through what you remember? In particular, finding a body behind the old rec center on Beaufort."

"I figured that was the thrust of your visit," Whit said, and gave a sly wink. He grabbed a small carved cedar box off the table, opened it and pulled out a cherry-wood pipe. "Do you mind?"

"Not at all," I said, and turned to Jack, who gave a thumbs up. My grandfather, the one with the hunchback, smoked a pipe when I was a kid, and I loved the sweet smell of it. I don't even remember what brand of tobacco he used, but the smell of any pipe smoke makes me seven years old and sitting on grandpa's knee again. Whit puffed out a cloud of pipe smoke as he lit, and I caught the scent. It was a good one.

"When Charlie Wellman's folks came in saying their boy was missing, we took it seriously," Whit started. "Kids going missing wasn't a big thing back then, so when it happened, we didn't waste time. But we were getting nowhere. Charlie had become a loner kid, for whatever reason. When I talked to his parents, they said he was going through some things. At nine, you shouldn't be going through things, I thought. You should be a kid, doing kid things, riding bikes, playing baseball, reading comic books, hanging out with your friends. But the Wellmans said Charlie really didn't have friends, that he'd shut even them out over the previous few months and become reclusive."

I shot a quick glance at Jack, who returned a look. My mind went back to what Stedman had said about thinking Charlie the monster wasn't the original Charlie. That the thing he killed had replaced little Charlie Wellman at some point, for whatever purpose. Not a one-hundred percent justification for strange behavior, but noteworthy.

Whit Vickers was still sharp, possessed of the detective's eternal skill in observation, so he knew we had thoughts of our own, and took a drink and puffed on the pipe twice before he continued. "We thought maybe he'd run away, but if it was of his own idea, he planned poorly. He literally had nothing with him other than the clothes on his back."

"The eventually filed the case as unsolved," Jack added.

"Yeah," Whit said, leaning back in his chair. "So, we continued searches, looking for clues, with the prevailing opinion being someone had abducted Charlie. I wasn't so sure, however. I did a little more digging, tracked down and talked to his school teachers. They said he had always been a very social child, but became withdrawn about six months before his disappearance, which jibed with what his parents had said. I looked at the Wellmans with a bit more scrutiny, too, and they came back clean. Good parents, no record of violence, nothing between the two of them that could cause a kid distress. I covered my bases and felt no closer to answers than before.

"Then, me and my partner, Virgil Williams, we stumbled across a recently dug and hidden grave behind the old rec center on Beaufort while searching for the boy. You can't imagine how we felt seeing that mound of dirt, almost sure we'd find Charlie's body."

"But it wasn't Charlie, was it?" I asked.

"No, it wasn't. But I'm sure you already know that, and that's why you're here."

I nodded and looked at Jack again. He was leaning forward with his hands on his knees.

"I'm not sure what was in that grave when we dug it up, but it—" he paused and took a deep breath. "—it wasn't human." He paused again and let us absorb that bit of information.

"It wasn't animal either, was it?"

"Not any kind of animal I'd ever seen. And when I say what I think it was, well, you can take of that what you will."

"We're becoming more open-minded by the minute, Mr. Vickers," Jack said.

"It was an alien. If it wasn't from outer space, it was some sort of mutant. That still qualifies as alien to me."

"Can you describe it?" I asked.

"It's still as clear in my mind as the day we unearthed it," Whit said, puffed on his pipe a couple times, then described in perfect detail the creature that Dwight Stedman had told us about: Needle teeth, bulging yellow eyes with cat-like slits, leathery skin, taloned fingers, all of it.

We sat there for a few moments in silence, then I told Whit Vickers about Dwight Stedman. That's not usually protocol, but Whit had been an officer of the law longer than I've been alive, and I thought he deserved to know, after all these years. I'm not sure if it ultimately brought him any measure of peace.

"Holy Mary, mother of God," he said, and set his glass down. "I need something stronger than iced tea for this." He went inside and returned with a bottle of Jameson and three rocks glasses. "I realize you're on the job, but I think all three of us could use a belt of this."

We didn't disagree. The shot burned all the way down, and as it warmed my belly, I considered I might become an alcoholic after all this was over.

"So, what happened to the body?" I asked.

"There were only a handful of us that actually saw it, and we kept it under wraps as best we could. Obviously—at the time anyway—we concluded it wasn't Charlie Wellman, but it was way out of our wheelhouse. The Feds showed up soon after and took it away. They scrubbed our files, redacted as needed, and that was it for us. We wrote the Charlie Wellman case off as unsolved, but presumed to be child abduction."

"Nothing after that?" Jack asked.

"A few weeks later, after the Charlie Wellman case had wound down, those of us who discovered that deformed carcass behind the Beaufort Street rec center started whispering to each other about talking to the press. Just idle chitchat, but I tell you, it wasn't two days later my phone rang in the middle of the night, and when I answered it, I was told in no uncertain terms to zip my lip or my wife might have an unfortunate accident. I never uttered another word about it until today. My guess is everyone else got a similar late-night kiss-kiss from our friend, the government."

"So, why talk now?" I asked.

"I've got nothing left to lose. I'm seventy-four years old, I've lived what most would consider a good life, and Gloria left me six years ago via the Big C. If my own life ends today, I'm okay with it." He tipped back another shot and offered us a refill. We both politely refused.

"You realize what we've got here, right?" Jack asked both of us. "We've uncovered the existence of aliens, or monsters, or something. That's a whole new ballgame."

"I've never discounted the existence of life outside ours," Whit said. "But to have it confirmed like this sure makes my balls tighten up."

That was an understatement.

I gave Vickers my card, and asked that he call me if anything else came to him he thought might be important.

"If you need me to come down and make a statement, I'm more than willing," he said.

"I'm sure we'll need that eventually," I replied, and we stirred up a little dust behind us as we idled down the drive.

There was a lot to discuss.

* * *

It was a little after eight and we hadn't even gotten back to the pavement when my phone rang. It was Hopgood.

"Rhoads is dead."

I put the phone on speaker. "Say again."

"Rhoads is dead," Hopgood repeated. "His wife just made the call. Came home and found him strangled in the living room, I guess."

"Text me the address. We're on our way," I said, and Jack pushed the accelerator down.

"It can't be a coincidence that just a couple hours ago, Glen fed us some very important information," Jack said.

"I don't believe in coincidences," I replied and looked out the window as corn fields passed by with increasing speed.

Rhoads lived in a little cul-de-sac on the north end of town. It took us less than ten minutes to get there. Three patrol cars and a couple sedans were already on site, the CSU already doing their jobs. As we approached the house, I saw Nancy Rhoads sitting on the steps with a female officer who was both consoling her and getting information. We left them alone for the moment.

I didn't know Glen Rhoads that well. He'd been with us less than five years, but he loved information gathering, and became our go-to guy when we needed a deep dive into the archives. Glen was good at finding the needles in the haystacks. I had a feeling finding the one he did today cost him his life.

A civilian would say that's part of the job, and while that may be true, you never like to see one of your own taken down.

Inside the house, we found CSU working the murder scene. Jack and I strapped on some rubber gloves and approached lead CSI Mark Ward.

"What we got?" I asked.

"TOD looks to be about an hour ago, roughly seven-thirty. Ligature marks indicate strangulation with a braided wire." Ward held up an evidence bag. I took it and looked at the contents. The wire had loops crimped at each end, specifically for handholds. So, the murder weapon wasn't a spur-of-the-moment pick. Whoever killed Glen planned it.

I handed the bag back and looked at Glen, propped in his recliner. His head bent oddly to the right, purplish bruises surrounded his neck, spreading out from the where the wire had cut into the skin.. Glen's eyes bulged out, and he wore an expression of complete shock.

"There were no signs of a prolonged struggle," Ward said. "Whoever did this, Glen wasn't afraid of them beforehand."

I looked at Jack, and he raised his eyebrows at me. It was someone he knew.

I turned and went back outside where Nancy Rhoads was still sitting with the female officer.

"Mrs. Rhoads," I said, sitting down next to her. "I didn't notice any-thing inside just now, but do you have security cameras installed here?"

"Oh, yes. Glen insisted on installing his own, and not going with one of those security companies that charge too much. He didn't buy the bulky ones that stick out like a sore thumb, either. His hide in the wall and ceiling vents."

"How are they monitored?"

"He has an app on his phone, but there's also a computer upstairs in his office that he uses, too."

"Do you know the password?"

"Yes," she said, and chuckled through her tears. "It's 'IAmThe-Law01' with each word capitalized. He's such a goofball." Was such a goofball. I felt a lump in my throat.

"Thank you," I said, nodded at the officer, and turned back to the house. Jack was standing just inside, and I motioned him toward the stairs. We took them two at a time and found Glen's office at the second door, past the landing. His computer was on the desk, hooked to two monitors. I woke it up and entered the password.

The screen brightened to life, and I found the desktop icon for the security system. The dual monitors filled with four cameras on each screen. I located the living room camera and clicked the button labeled "Recorded" and a separate window popped up with the living room camera only and a time slider underneath. I moved it back to shortly after seven o'clock and pushed the "Play" button.

Glen was sitting in his recliner, and another man was standing with him, his back to the camera. The two men talked, but nothing heated. There was no sound to corroborate that, but body language showed Glen didn't believe he was in danger. The other man moved behind the chair, pulled the braided wire from his pocket, and turned. The camera caught enough of his face that Jack and I both sucked in our breath.

"Jesus," I exhaled. The camera continued playing as Brent Kellum looped the wire around Glen Rhoads' neck and strangled him to death.

* * *

I sent two officers from the scene to Whit Vickers house, told them that Brent Kellum was wanted for Glen Rhoads' murder.

"Dispatch isn't picking up," I said with my phone against my ear. At this time of night, there would only be the dispatch officer there, and maybe one or two deputies at most. The rest were on patrol, or on site at the Rhoads' home.

Brent Kellum would know all that, and with dispatch not responding, that meant the worst. Brent was going to kill Dwight Stedman.

"Why?" Jack asked.

"I have two ideas," I said. "The government covered up what Vickers found, because it was proof of extraterrestrial life or something. Kellum is either working for the government and tying up loose ends—"

"Or he's a monster himself," Jack finished.

I looked at him in agreement. "Or that."

"Jesus Christ, I didn't think this was how today was going to go when I rolled out of bed this morning."

"Tell me about it," I said, and tried the station again. There was still no pick up. Daisy Menard was on dispatch tonight. Sweet girl in her early twenties, had her eye set on a career in law enforcement since she was in grade school. I prayed that career hadn't just been cut short, but something inside me knew the answer already.

Jack floored the car, and we made it to the station in five minutes. Two other officers were right behind us, also concerned about the unresponsive dispatcher.

Brent's car was outside the building, parked in his usual spot like it was any other day. Jack filled in the patrol officers while I opened the trunk and got out Kevlar vests and my shotgun. I was loading up the shotty when Jack grabbed my arm.

"Um, Petra," he said, his voice flat. "Look."

I turned and saw them standing there. Eight children, standing in line, holding hands on the recently mowed lawn in front of the station, staring at us with expressionless faces. I knew who they had to be.

It was, honestly, the damn creepiest thing I'd ever seen in my law enforcement career. Hell, in my entire life. In a single instant, I understood why Dwight Stedman turned himself in after seeing this octet of kids in his front yard.

I moved away from the car, toward them, and stopped 10 yards away. "We won't hurt you," I said, but I wasn't sure of that now. I had my left hand out in a gesture to show I meant no harm, but my right hand was gripping the shotgun tight. Jack hadn't drawn his weapon yet, and the patrol officers had their hands on their holsters. The moment was tense.

Then they let go of each other's hands and turned away. One girl looked back over her shoulder, and I saw a swimming water look around her head, and for the briefest second, I saw alien eyes looking at me and bared, needle-like teeth behind black, slithering lips. Then the veil was back up, and eight children walked away, down onto the street and out of sight.

"I could have gone my entire life without seeing that," Jack said, and leaned over, resting his palms on his knees. "Whoo-boy!"

"Ma'am," one of the patrol officers said to me. "What was that?"

"Son, I don't have time to explain this minute, and I'm honestly not sure how I will two days from now, either. Right now, though, we have to get inside."

* * *

We entered the building in formation, myself and Jack taking the front main entrance, while the two other officers came in the back, where we moved prisoners in and out of the building. Our station was small enough that we only handled prisoners for short periods. If you did something in our town that required a longer stay, we shipped you to the next county over, where they had more long-term facilities.

We found Daisy Menard at her post, but no longer able to perform that function. She was dead, her neck broken, her eyes staring wide and lifeless at the ceiling. I bit my lip as I closed them for her, but kept my composure. There would be time to mourn later.

We swept two other rooms before we heard the shouts from the back of the station, followed by gunshots. By the time we got there, Brent Kellum had taken the two young officers down, and was standing over their bodies.

"Drop the weapon, Brent!" I shouted.

Without hesitation, Brent pulled up, shot in my direction and caught me square in the chest, knocking me backward and to the floor. Jack returned fire an instant later and hit Brent in the shoulder, spinning him sideways. He grunted and leaned against the wall, bleeding.

"Don't make me shoot again, Brent," Jack yelled. "Put the gun down!"

I had the wind knocked from me and I felt like an elephant was standing on my chest, but I sat up and tried to regain my footing. Brent was on one knee, still holding his gun, and it was then I saw his face change, to shift from human to something else. The surrounding air shimmered, as if a mask was being lifted. The face staring back afterward was just as I'd pictured the thing Dwight Stedman and Whit Vickers described.

Brent's bulging yellow eyes locked onto me and he pulled up to take another shot, but I triggered my shotgun a millisecond sooner, and watched his head explode into a splattered mass of bone, slick leathery flesh and spongy brain matter. His body fell back against the wall and slid into a sitting position, leaving streaks of blood as he went down. What remained of his head fell forward onto his chest, unmoving. His now claw-like hands opened and his pistol clattered to the floor.

Jack slid over to me, helping me up.

"Jesus H. Christ," he said. "You okay?"

"Yeah," I huffed. "Good thing he didn't go for the head."

I like to think that Brent didn't go for the head because, despite whatever it was he turned into, he had been a fellow officer, one that I'd had drinks and burgers with at a backyard cookout. I'll never know the answer to that, but that's my rationale, at least, for why he didn't outright kill me.

I was going to have a nasty bruise, and it would be a while before I could take a deep breath without wincing, but I was alive. I stared at the thing against the wall. He—that—however, was dead.

"Stedman?" I gasped, and man, did that hurt.

Jack got me to my feet, and we rushed to the holding cells. Dwight Stedman was on the floor of his cell. A dark red flower of blood had spread on the chest of his light blue shirt, and at the center of it was a darkened bullet hole.

"Shit," Jack said. "Shit, shit, shit."

* * *

Jack Banner and I are both lifelong loners, which made our next steps that much easier. Without family to consider, we were both able to pick up and disappear literally overnight. The alternative was to stay and face whatever the government had in mind, and my faith in the system went south the moment I saw Brent Kellum's actual face.

I contacted Whit Vickers shortly after we left, told him what was likely coming, and he said he'd weather it like any other storm. A couple days later, I heard he died in a farming accident, something to do with a combine. I'm sure it wasn't an accident, but after the past few days, I'm skeptical of everything.

I'm not sure how the FBI is going to cover up this whole thing, considering Brent Kellum's body was on display in its true form when the rest of the officers arrived, but I'd be shocked if they didn't have some Men in Black mind-wipe options available. Hopefully, it's something that simple. The alternatives are messy.

As for Jack and me, we're in the wind. Jack Banner was an excellent partner, and I'll miss him. We worked well together and had a like-minded approach to solving cases that makes you look forward to your job every day. It would have been nice to have a kindred spirit in all this, but we both agreed it's easier to hide alone, for now.

And there's still work to do.

I'd like to have a normal life again, but when I put on this badge and took the oath to protect and serve, I meant it. The world still needs protecting, more now than I ever realized, and as I'm finding out, there are many people out here who understand that not everything in the world is what it seems. They might not be official officers of the law, but they're helping to protect the world from threats most people can't even imagine.

Thinking about Dwight Stedman again puts the entire thing in perspective. Our own government has been covering up the existence of these things for decades, so what does that tell us? Who can we trust? Is your neighbor one of them? Your boss? Your spouse? I can't even imagine how this could unravel society if word got out.

Once I uploaded pictures of Brent Kellum to the dark web, it became abundantly clear just how deep this conspiracy goes. Dozens of people came forth with stories and photographs of their own, information far too similar to what I know for them to be discounted as crackpots.

Theories range from extraterrestrial replacement, to human/alien hybridization, to demonic possession. Whatever they are, their goals are unknown. World domination? Maybe they just want to hide? In the late 60s and early 70s, they possibly killed and replaced children, so their motives can't be pure. They must have some malicious intent, otherwise Brent wouldn't have murdered to cover up the revelation of their existence.

It all keeps going back to Brent. He was a good cop. He'd had my back on a lot of cases over the years, and I'd returned the favor as many times. How long had he been one of them, or had he always been? He had a wife who hung on his every word, and three kids under the age of ten who thought he literally was Superman, jaw and all. What about them? Were the kids even human? So many questions, and I can't go back to get the answers now. All I can do is move forward.

Rumor has it there's a guy out there who can see beneath the surface and identify these things hiding behind human skin. I don't think I have to tell you how valuable a guy like that is. I've made it my job to find him and protect him, because if the good guys know about him, most likely the bad guys do, too.

So, I'll track him down. Keep him safe. And then we'll take the monsters out, one at a time.

## AUTHOR NOTES - BENEATH THE SURFACE

This story started out as a straight-up serial killer tale with a slightly supernatural twist, and the opening scene was just an absolute joy to write. My original intent was to have the kids Dwight Alan Stedman killed come back from the grave to exact revenge. However, as things moved along, I suddenly had the urge to carry over a plot thread from another story in this volume, and pulled the monsters from SHIFTED into this story, because we never really figured out what they're up to.

I like Petra Jenkins and Jack Banner. I also liked Brent Kellum, despite his rough around the edges demeanor early on. However, he seemed the most likely candidate to be a monster, and the story flew along at a rapid pace after that. I love it when plot threads converge and become something more than I expected.

Petra and Jack will be back. I've got some big plans for them. Brent Kellum might be back, too. You just never know...

# IMMORTALIS

"Six to eight weeks at the most," Dr. Garotte said flatly, so monotone it sounded like the words were coming from some place far away.

Edgar Holt sat in stunned silence, staring at the floor. Beside him, his daughter Lucy reached out and touched his hand, but he did not feel it, or see her eyes rimmed with welling tears.

"Oh, dad," Lucy whispered.

Edgar's head lifted, met the doctor's eyes. His lips opened and at first, there was nothing, then: "You're sure?"

"Unfortunately, there isn't any way to be one-hundred percent positive. Metastatic pancreatic cancer is very aggressive. We can begin chemotherapy immediately, but at the rate it appears to be spreading, chances are slim there would be any success."

"I won't do chemo," Edgar said sternly. He turned to Lucy, and his own eyes were becoming wet. "I've seen what that can do to a person. Lamont Wallace—you remember him?—when he had the prostate cancer five years ago, he did the chemo, and I'd lay odds that made him far worse than the cancer did."

"So, there's nothing more you can do?" Lucy asked the doctor. The tears had streamed rivers down her face. Garotte's face offered no solace, only a blank, expressionless forward stare.

"I'm sorry," he said.

The rest of the doctor's visit was a blur of emotions for Edgar and Lucy, and pleading by Dr. Garotte to at least try the chemo. Edgar steadfastly refused, and while Lucy wanted to convince her father to do it, she agreed to his wishes for the moment.

When Edgar and Lucy left the oncologist's office, thick gray clouds swelled in the late morning sky. It was going to rain soon. A perfect symbolism for the day.

"Just try the chemo, dad," Lucy begged. "Please."

"I can't," he replied. His lips were tight. "I won't be pumped full of chemicals. I won't end like Lamont did."

Edgar had watched his friend of thirty years wither away, and while the cancer did the most damage, he remembered Lamont's own words: "If I'd known how this was going to feel, I'd have just had the nurse pump me full of morphine and end it weeks ago." Edgar had seen the sadness in the old man's eyes, the sullenness of looming death. But he'd also seen the hopelessness there, and that look was what he'd remembered most of all.

They crossed the parking lot slowly. Edgar was shuffling, unsure of his footing, but he was still upright, by God.

He needed Lucy's help to get into the car, but once seated, he put on the seatbelt by himself, then leaned back and took a deep breath. He wondered then just how many more breaths he would take before the end. How many more sunrises? Sunsets. How many more 6am Sunday morning farm reports he'd watch on cable? How many more ribeye steaks he'd get to eat? He had a bottle of Jameson Irish whiskey, and he wondered if he'd see the bottom of it. He had one tumbler after dinner every night. Maybe if he bumped it up to two, he'd polish off the bottle before the reaper came calling. And when she did, Edgar would spit right in that skull-faced bitch's dead eye socket. That made him smile.

"What's so funny?" Lucy quizzed as she buckled her own belt and started the car.

"Nothing much, just making an agreement with lady death."

"Geez, dad. Morbid much?" Lucy attempted a smile herself, but her father saw through that facade with practiced ease. Lucy had never been a good liar, and he was adept at noticing the odd tick or two that signaled she was being untruthful.

Lucy pulled the car out onto the highway, merged into a noonday traffic jam, and cursed. "Shit!"

"It's just lunchtime traffic, Luce. Nothing we can do about that." Edgar settled back into his seat and watched the clouds overhead moving swiftly west to east. If he started now, how far east or west would he get before the cancer took him? If he hopped on a plane today, maybe he could spend his last days on the beach in Hawaii, or looking out over the nighttime sky in Paris. Or—

"Move, dammit!" Lucy shouted at the car that had worked its way into her lane and then slowed down to a crawl.

"Honey, calm down," Edgar said, and put his aging hand on her forearm. "It's okay."

"No, dad," she said, and the tears started again. "It's not. It's not okay, and it's not fair."

"No, it certainly isn't fair," Edgar admitted. "But God has everything under control."

"How can you say that? You just found out you're dying."

"Sweetheart, that's part of living. You take the bad with the good. And I've had a healthy share of good."

"But I'm not ready to lose you."

"I understand that, and I'm not certain I'm ready to be lost, but that die is cast, and nothing—chemo or prayers or voodoo—is going to change that I'm going to close my eyes forever one day soon."

"That sounds melodramatic, dad," Lucy said, and half-smiled. The tears were still rolling down her cheeks and her eyes had become puffy. "Can we talk about something else?"

"Absolutely, kiddo," Edgar said. "Say, I'd like to stop at the flea market on the way home, if that's okay?"

"You sure? Are you up for it?"

"Not to bring up a poor subject again, but when you find out you're dying, it's best to do the things you love while you still can."

"Then we can stop at the flea market."

Edgar leaned back in the seat and rested his eyes while the traffic finally moved forward.

* * *

Edgar Holt had always loved the flea market. He still remembered with sharp clarity the first time his father had taken him to the local market near his hometown. Edgar had been eight years old and astonished at the sheer number of interesting things to be found under the tents and makeshift buildings. That day, he and his father were going to see a vendor who dealt in gardening equipment. Everyone knew the Holt family for their green thumbs, and Chet Holt needed some replacement tools. The local hardware sold what they needed, but Chet was a dealing man, and while the prices at the hardware were unchangeable, you could always try to talk a flea market vendor down from the asking price. Sometimes it was only a few pennies, sometimes it was a fifty-cent piece, and on rare occasions a whole dollar. As Edgar grew older, he realized that his father probably saved little in the long run, but that he just enjoyed the art of the deal.

Edgar shared that enjoyment, and even as he'd gotten older and left home, if he passed a flea market while traveling through some nondescript town, he would stop.

The flea market Edgar had frequented over the past two decades had begun as a small 24x48 pole barn where half a dozen peddlers of various wares had set up their stands. Within a year, the building expanded to twice its size, and tents of many sizes had sprung up around the perimeter. It ran from early May to mid-October every year, then, like a traveling circus, the tents would disappear and the building would empty. Edgar always lamented those few months when the building stood silent alongside the road, and he was one of the first there on opening day each spring to see which vendors had come back, which had moved on, and which were new.

It was half-past one in the afternoon when Lucy pulled her car off the pavement and into the dusty parking lot. Edgar smiled.

"Are you sure you're okay to go in alone?" Lucy asked.

"I'm certain," Edgar replied. "You said you had to check in at work, so you go ahead and do that. I won't be long, I promise. I can still walk. Just can't sprint like I did when I was a grasshopper."

Lucy smiled, and Edgar opened the door. "You have your cell phone on you, right? In case you need me."

"Yup," Edgar said, and patted his breast pocket. "You'll be the first one I call if Greg Simms tries to swindle me out of a ten spot."

"Have fun, dad," Lucy said, and he thankfully closed the car door before she started to cry again.

* * *

Edgar shuffled up the walkway to the pole barn, passing several small tents with ornate woodwork, cheap stained glass ornaments, and various knick-knacks for the hoarder in everyone. That wasn't his thing, but Edgar didn't begrudge them their spot at the market; they were mostly older folks—his age and sometimes older—just trying to make a few extra coins to supplement the pittance of Social Security they received the first of every month.

Edgar passed them by slowly, because he was already tired. Several of the vendors he knew, some because they were townsfolk he'd grown up with, and some because he'd stopped to talk to them occasionally. The flea market wasn't there just to buy things. It was also social hour for Edgar, and by the age range of the clientele, he assumed it was the same for many.

Inside the pole barn, which was completely open on one end, was what they affectionately knew as "The Alley", a 10 foot wide walkway with vendors on either side and lit overhead by long fluorescent fixtures. There were sword and knife vendors, someone selling ATVs, two or three food vendors offering hot dogs, chips, and a Coke for a nominal fee. A salty former Army Ranger sold used vinyl records, DVDs, and even some old VHS cassette tapes. There was a man and his wife who had been selling gardening tools and decorations for the past half dozen summers, and Edgar had, of course, felt almost obligated to get to know them. He'd even bought an implement or two, though he was not nearly the gardener his father had been. While he had the green thumb, he did not get nearly the satisfaction from it that his pater had. Edgar planted flowers around the perimeter of his house, and grew a few vegetables in a modest plot in the backyard, but that was all.

He exchanged nods with a few vendors and spoke briefly with a few others. Suddenly, he didn't feel much like conversation. His original intent was to take his mind off his predicament—six to eight weeks at most, the doctor had said—but even here, he couldn't shake the weight of the situation. And he was growing increasingly tired.

He shuffled down "The Alley" to the end of the main building, which then veered off to the right into the new addition. Four years ago, whoever owned the flea market property added a second pole barn to accommodate more vendors, and it filled within the first two years. The vendors in the main building were the dedicated long-timers, the ones who'd been here since the beginning. The secondary building was mostly for newcomers, or those one-and-done vendors who come and go each year, of which there are several.

As if to illustrate that point, Edgar noticed a small vendor setup in the back corner of building number two, a modest table arranged with small antiques, what looked like essential oils, and other unique items. Never one to shy away from something new, Edgar shuffled closer.

"Hello, my friend," the short, grizzled vendor said. "Feel free to take a look around. I have all manner of trinkets, baubles, and accouterments for the discerning collector. You might say I always have something for everyone."

He was no more than five and a half feet tall, stocky, with deep wrinkles in his face that suggested a long and storied life. As he grinned through a thick and graying handlebar mustache, Edgar saw teeth yellowed from decades of smoking, likely more than just cigarettes. He wore jeans and a long-sleeved denim shirt buttoned all the way to the neck. The man leaned forward and put his hands on the table in front of him, each thick, stubby finger decorated with an ornately designed ring. A silver skull and crossbones topped his right index finger, Edgar noticed. How appropriate.

"Haven't seen you around here before," Edgar said, looking over the table's items with keen interest.

"Just passing through," the man said. "Walter Scoggins, traveling purveyor of rare and exotic artifacts, at your service." He extended his hand and Edgar obligingly shook it, once again noting the skull ring as the hand pulled away.

A symbol of death. And he, Edgar Holt, sixty-four years old and riddled through with cancer, was chugging along at breakneck speed to meet the reaper. Not happenstance, he supposed, that he'd see the reaper's visage at the small town flea market he loved.

"You seem deep in thought, my friend," Walter said.

Edgar gave a sideways smile. "Yeah, got a lot on my mind."

"Ah, say no more," Walter said with a wide grin. "I have just the thing to melt your worries away." He knelt down below the tabletop, which was draped with a deep red satin cloth, and came back up with a small apothecary jar filled with an orange powder. "A pinch of this in your tea will ease your mind—"

"Got anything to cure stage four cancer?" Edgar half joked, but when he saw Walter Scoggins' expression change, he felt it was no laughing matter to the short man.

"I no longer feel it was happenstance that I stopped in this small town to set up my table of wares for a day. I feel something brought the two of us together."

"What do you mean?"

"I mean, I may just have a potable with me that could ease that concern forever."

Edgar looked into the old man's eyes for long seconds, gaging his intent. He was a flea market vendor, which more often than not makes him a swindler of unparalleled skill. This man, Edgar determined, was likely no different.

"Even if I believe this potion exists," Edgar said. "How could I afford such a thing? It would be priceless."

"Psh," Walter said. "Priceless, indeed. I could no more take your money that I would cut off my own hand."

"Then it's free?" Edgar scoffed. Preposterous.

"I said I wouldn't take your money. I didn't say there wasn't a cost."

"And that cost would be?"

"Let's call it an exchange. In exchange for the elixir, you'll owe me a favor one day. When I call that favor due, our deal will come full circle."

"What if the cancer kills me before then?"

"I assure you it will not."

"I'm still unconvinced. They have literally given me weeks to live."

"Western medicine is as useless as tits on a hog. The very Earth we stand on provides us with everything we need to survive and thrive, to heal all maladies of the mind and body, completely and utterly. But we've found ourselves overwhelmed by artificial supplements, additives and preservatives. Let me offer you this: If you follow my instructions, and you're not 100% convinced this potion works, you come back to me and I'll make it right with you."

"That seems too good to be true."

"Another western fallacy. Your skepticism betrays what your mind knows to be fact. What I offer you is a cure for your illness, complete eradication of the disease that consumes your body from within."

Edgar said nothing for long moments, his hands trembling almost imperceptibly. Finally, he said: "I'll take it."

"Perfect," Walter Scoggins said, and his grin was enormous, like a sideshow clown. "Edgar, my boy, you won't be disappointed." He squatted behind his stand again and came back up with a long test-tube vial filled with greenish liquid, capped with a wooden cork.

"What's the worst that could happen?" Edgar said with a hint of sarcasm.

"Right on, brother," Scoggins said. "Worst case, you're already dead. Anything is better than that, am I right?"

"That really puts it in perspective."

"Indeed." Walter put the vial into a leather drawstring pouch and handed it across the table to Edgar. The leather was soft, almost warm.

"You said there were instructions?"

"Yes," Walter said, and put both of his hands palm down on the tabletop. "Tonight, before you go to bed, take a hot bath. Relax. It works better if your body is at rest. Drink half the vial, then go to sleep. You'll wake feeling better than you have in a long while. Drink the second half of the vial before breakfast, and by the end of the day, you'll be right as rain."

"No side effects?" Edgar asked.

"Only if feeling better than you've ever felt in your life is a side effect, my friend. You have nothing to fear from what I've given you. It will work just as I've said, and you'll know that for certain soon enough." Walter's smile was there again, filled with the yellowed teeth. A Cheshire Cat who smoked two packs a day.

"Thank you," Edgar said. His tone was soft. "Thank you so much."

"Think nothing of it. Just remember, one day I'll call on you for a favor."

Edgar turned to leave. "I won't forget. If this works like you've said, I'll do anything you want."

"That's what I'm counting on, Edgar." Walter Scoggins said as he watched Edgar Holt shuffle away.

* * *

Lucy had just finished up her phone call when Edgar emerged from the large pole barn. The clouds had dispersed and the afternoon sun felt warm on his skin.

"How was it?" Lucy asked as Edgar settled into the passenger seat.

"Good. It was good."

"Buy anything?"

Edgar thought of the three-inch vial of green liquid in his breast pocket, next to his phone, but decided not to mention it just then. She'd tell him he was crazy to drink some potion from a flea market vendor, and when he recited the words in his head, he wondered the same. So, for now, he'd keep the acquisition to himself. "No," he said, and felt an instant pang of guilt for lying. Hell, he wasn't even sure he'd go through with taking it. Walter Scoggins seemed well-meaning enough, but there was something off, something slightly creepy about him that Edgar couldn't quite pin down. He'd take the rest of the day to think it over. If he decided by bedtime he couldn't do it, he'd pour the vial down the bathroom sink and be done with it. And nobody would need to know.

Except him. Him and Walter Scoggins. They'd know about it.

"I have to go into work for a while, dad," Lucy said, wiping the visage of Walter Scoggins from her father's mind. "Apparently, they're having a crisis only I can fix." She gave an eye roll, and Edgar chuckled. "Will you be okay if I drop you off and go?"

"Of course. I'm feeling tired after all this, so I think a good nap on the back deck in this blessed sun might do me a world of good."

"Okay," Lucy said, and they pulled back out onto the road. Home was only two miles away.

* * *

Edgar did nap on the back deck that afternoon. The sun warmed him for nearly two hours before it ducked behind the tall maples in the backyard of the Holt homestead. It wasn't the lack of sun that woke him, though. It was the sudden onset of stomach pain that brought him back awake with a start.

God damned cancer, working its hot, evil fingers into him, spreading out and taking more bits of his body with each moment. He could almost feel it now, if he stayed silent and concentrated inward. The pain radiated from his stomach to his lower back, extending into a dull throb that was irritating more than anything at this point. But no regular pain reliever would touch this pain. This wasn't a normal ache. This was his body eating itself, and you'd need something far more powerful than that to ease that pain.

He wasn't ready for the potent drugs yet. He knew those also put you in a near mindless stupor, and while he'd done his share of mind-altering drugs during his youth, he wasn't willing to put himself under for the sake of pain management.

Edgar got up off the deck chair, slowly pushing himself into an upright position. The pain was throbbing now as he headed into the house.

He hadn't eaten since breakfast, but he had no appetite.

* * *

By eight-thirty that night, Edgar was exhausted. His body's fight against the thing eating him alive taxed him more by the minute. He stood in the downstairs bathroom and stripped off his clothes. Edgar turned on the tub faucet and regulated the water temperature. As the tub filled, he poured in a cup of Epsom salts. A nice hot soak would do him some good.

He leaned toward the mirror, noting the increased wrinkles on his face. His once rounded jawline had become gaunt. He stood back, looking at his chest and arms. Once full and muscular (for a sixty-four-year-old), they now sagged in defeat against the assassin wreaking havoc inside him.

After the tub filled, he turned off the faucet and slowly lowered himself into the water. The smell of eucalyptus caught his nose, and he leaned back and smiled. The pain had lessened but was still there. When he relaxed, he could almost feel it moving inside him. That probably wasn't actually happening, but he felt it anyway.

His eyes closed, and Edgar's mind reflected on his life. A cliche, perhaps, but his life had been a good one, mostly.

Edgar Holt was the second (and last) child born to Ned and Esther Holt, in the very house he himself now lived. Ned Holt had been a skilled carpenter, plying his trade in their growing suburban town since the early 1950s. He'd built their homestead and several other homes when the land was only a field. Esther had been a homemaker, taking care of the boys and the homestead. Edgar grew up a typical male child of his time, reading comic books and playing baseball with his friends. Edgar's brother Teddy, seven years older, died in the Vietnam conflict, and Edgar felt his parents were never quite the same again. Teddy was supposed to become a partner with his father in the construction busi-ness once he'd finished his enlistment in the Army. As Edgar got older, he began helping his father on jobs and while he often wondered if it disappointed his father that it wasn't Ted alongside him, Ned Holt never showed it.

The business did well, and Edgar learned the role of businessman. His father always said that any profession you get into should require a basic business course, especially if you're going into self-employment. He'd seen too many people lose their asses because they didn't know how to do their taxes. So, while Ned taught Edgar everything he needed to know about construction, he also imparted his business wisdom, and Edgar took an entry-level business management course in community college.

One fated summer day in 1983, while the sun burned hot in the cloudless sky, Ned Holt had a massive heart attack while carrying a stack of shingles up a ladder. He fell fifteen feet to the ground and was dead before he got there. Edgar witnessed the whole incident in what felt like slow motion and relived it that way often for several years afterward. Holt & Son Construction became a sole proprietorship. Edgar kept the name, even though he had no male children to pass it onto.

Three years later, he met Clara Belmont at the wedding of his best friend, Stuart Halliday. Six months later, Edgar and Clara were married, and a little over a year after that, Lucy Holt was born.

Family life turned out to not be what Clara Holt wanted for herself, so when Lucy was four, her mother dropped her off at the babysitter, then disappeared, while Edgar was remodeling a living room on the opposite side of town.

Edgar spoke to Clara exactly two times after that. The first was when he'd tracked her down to a small suburb of Chicago and had traveled to confront her. She turned him away, told him their marriage was a mis-take, and that she didn't want the burden of motherhood. The second time he spoke to her was at the divorce proceedings. After that, there was no need.

Edgar raised Lucy on his own, and thankfully, some of Clara's family helped. Clara's sister Margaret was a homemaker who took on daycare duties.

Edgar never faltered as a father, and Lucy grew up to be a confident, successful young woman. Edgar couldn't have been more proud.

Lucy left home for college, then began her career, then she entered a marriage which also ended in divorce. It was always the two of them, though. Three of them once Samson came along.

He wouldn't have had it any other way.

* * *

Edgar opened the drain and stepped out of the tub, toweled off slowly, and thought about what happened next.

Laying on the edge of the sink was the glass vial of green liquid. The elixir of life, Walter Scoggins had more or less promised. What if the grisly old man had lied? What if it was poison and killed him?

What if it did? He was already dying, wasn't he? Stage four cancer isn't something you come back from. At least not with current medicine. So maybe something else could work. Would work.

The veins stood out on the back of his hand as he grasped the vial with his bony fingers.

"What's the harm?" Edgar whispered and popped the cork with his thumb. The ichor within sloshed a little, bubbled, then settled back. He looked at it for several seconds.

"Bottom's up," he said and tipped the vial to his lips. The taste was sweet, with a hint of bitterness somewhere in the mix. It felt warm going down, like a shot of whiskey, but the burn quickly subsided.

Edgar stood silent and motionless in front of the bathroom mirror for several minutes. How soon would he feel something? Walter Scoggins had said to drink half the vial, then go to bed, then drink the rest in the morning before breakfast.

Not wanting to deviate from the instructions he'd received, Edgar grabbed the cork and pushed it back into the half-empty test tube. He laid the vial on the back of the sink and grabbed his toothbrush, did the requisite two minutes of brushing, rinsed his mouth, then shuffled to the bedroom.

He sat on the edge of the bed for a few moments, pondering the future, however short or long it may be.

Tomorrow would be a new day, regardless.

* * *

Lucy woke the next morning at eight-thirty to the smell of bacon cooking. She could hear rustling in the kitchen and light music playing. She threw on her robe and as she made her way down the stairs; she heard her father singing along to the tune, out of key, as she always remembered.

"Good morning!" Edgar said as she turned into the kitchen. He was making scrambled eggs. There were two plates on the table.

"Dad, what are you doing?"

"Making breakfast, little girl."

"How are you feeling?" Most days of late, her father slept until nearly ten and was very uninterested in breakfast beyond a cup of coffee. This was new.

"I'm feeling great, Lucy. Absolutely great." He scooped eggs onto the two plates and set the pan back on the stove. "You want toast?"

"Sure," she said, sitting down. "Are you sure you're okay?"

"Yes, dear," Edgar said, buttering a slice of toast. "I'm feeling fine."

She believed him. He even looked better than yesterday. His skin had taken on the yellowish tint of jaundice over the past weeks, but now that was gone, as if it had never been.

Edgar had gotten sick fast, out of nowhere. Lucy's son, Sam, was with his father, Dillon, for one entire month of the summer, so she felt it was a good idea to monitor Edgar and moved back into the house she'd grown up in. Sam would come back soon, and she had said nothing to him about his grandfather, though she'd mentioned to Dillon that her father was sick and she was worried.

Thankfully, Lucy and Dillon had kept an amicable post-marital relationship. Their marriage hadn't collapsed because of infidelity or abuse; the two had just drifted apart. Dillon was a figurehead in corporate management, always gone, always late, always on the phone. In short, his job was more important than his family.

Sam was eleven years old, and Dillon had spent more time with him of late. Maybe it was because he regretted missing out on the boy's early childhood. Or maybe it was just because Sam was beyond the "needy" stage of youth. Lucy didn't know and didn't care. She felt it important that a boy spend time with his father, and Dillon, despite his faults, was a good man and could be a positive influence on the boy. Especially with Sam's teenage years looming close.

"Take it easy, dad," she said, sitting down at the table.

"I'm not pushing it, kiddo," Edgar said. "I'm just hungry for the first time in days. Thought I'd take advantage of that."

"Well, I'd be a fool to complain about someone making me breakfast. Thank you."

"You're welcome."

They ate in silence, but Lucy watched her father closely. He looked better, sounded better, and based on the way he was shoving forkfuls of scrambled eggs into his mouth, he felt better.

She hated to get her hopes up. Stage four cancer isn't something you just shake off and everything's okay. You don't just wake up the morning after your diagnosis and the cancer has just disappeared.

Of course, that's exactly what happened.

* * *

While Edgar sat across from his daughter, he reflected on the past day and the miraculous concoction that appeared to have saved his life.

After drinking half the solution before bed, he'd felt restless, and assumed he would have trouble sleeping. That was not the case, however, and he was fast asleep minutes after climbing into bed.

He didn't set an alarm. Unless he had a doctor's appointment or was expecting someone, he had given up on that routine. Today, he woke at seven o'clock, more rested than he could put to recent memory.

Back in the bathroom, he held the vial for a full minute before popping the cork again and downing the last of the liquid in one swallow. There had been the syrupy heat flowing down his throat, then it was gone.

He realized then he was hungry. That was a miracle, as food had lost its taste and therefore he'd lost his appetite. But today, food sounded wonderful. And he knew what he wanted.

And it tasted like heaven.

* * *

At ten o'clock that night, Edgar stood in front of the bathroom mirror again. Already he'd noticed a change in his face, as if the hands of time were reversing. He looked better. Bags under his eyes had receded, his features had filled out slightly again. He still looked like a sixty-something man, but a healthier sixty-something man.

Though he could not have described it, he still felt the cancer inside him, maybe even more than before, certainly more than he had earlier in the day. But it wasn't pain he felt, not exactly. It was a movement, as if his body was working the poison out of his system.

And with that, his stomach lurched, and he vomited into the sink. When he wiped his eyes afterward and looked down, what he saw in the basin wasn't his half-digested dinner, but a black, tarry liquid, speckled with flecks of brightest green.

"Bye bye, cancer," Edgar said, and washed it down the drain.

* * *

"It's a miracle!" Dr. Garotte said, pushing his thick hair back on his head while he looked at the test results. He was sitting on a rolling stool three feet away, and his face was a display of astonishment. "The cancer is gone, Edgar. Gone, as if it'd never been."

"And I feel great," Edgar said with a smile. "Better than I have in years."

"I bet you do," Garotte said. "We'll need to do a more thorough blood panel and some other non-invasive tests, but from what I can tell, you're cancer free. I don't know what you've done, but it worked."

"Lots of prayer, doc. Lots of prayer." This, of course, was a lie, but there would be much praying in the future, for all the good it would do.

Half an hour later, after a blood draw and some x-rays, Edgar left the oncologist's office with a spring in his step. He'd driven himself to the doctor, his first time behind the wheel in over six months. It astonished him how rapidly his miracle cure worked. It had been only four days since he'd ingested the elixir, and every day he felt better.

* * *

TWO YEARS LATER

Edgar's cell phone rang at 2:43 AM on March 24th, jolting him awake with its klaxon-like ring tone. Edgar sat up and swiped the phone from the nightstand.

UNKNOWN CALLER displayed brightly in the center of the screen. Edgar fingered the red IGNORE button and put the phone back on the stand, then settled back into bed and closed his eyes. *Who the hell calls at damn near three in the morning?* he thought.

Edgar felt sleep tugging at the edge of his consciousness, about to pull him back under, when the phone went off a second time. Edgar shot up, grabbed it, and this time touched the pulsing green ANSWER button.

"Who is this?" Edgar barked.

"Edgar, Edgar, Edgar," a flat, monotone voice came from the other side. "Is that any way to greet an associate?"

"Who is this?" Edgar repeated.

"I'm hurt you don't remember me," the voice said. "It's Walter Scoggins. We made a gentleman's agreement a couple of years ago. I'm sure you remember that."

Edgar's balls tightened, and hairs stood straight on the back of his neck and forearms.

"Walter," he said faintly. "Yes, I remember."

"Then I'm sure you also remember that I'd call on you for a favor one day."

"Yes." Edgar's mouth was suddenly dry.

"That day has come, Edgar. Time to pay the piper, as they say." Edgar could almost hear the smile spreading across the flea market vendor's face.

"How did you get my number?" Edgar asked sharply.

"Peddling wares at flea markets and street fairs is only one of my many talents, Edgar."

"I'm sure," Edgar replied. "What do you want from me, Walter?"

Walter Scoggins told him then, and Edgar's face turned ashen white as he listened.

* * *

"I won't do it," Edgar said.

There was a long pause before Walter replied: "A deal's a deal, Edgar, my friend. You got what you wanted. Now it's time for you to pay up."

"I can't do what you ask."

"Oh, you can, and you will. If I recall correctly—and my memory is razor sharp—your exact words were, 'If this works like you've said, I'll do anything you want.' Am I correct?"

A long pause, then: "Yes."

"And your cancer is gone, is it not?"

"Yes."

"And not just in remission, Edgar. That little vial of green juice eradicated genetic markers for cancer from your DNA. You'll never have to worry about cancer of any kind ever again."

"I—I understand."

"So, considering what I've done for you, I don't think I'm requesting too much in return, am I?"

"But what you're asking me to do is...unconscionable."

"Listen to me closely, Edgar Holt. If you think this is a game and I am just fucking around with you, perhaps you need to step back and look at the big picture again. You'd be two years in the ground if not for me. Not cheering from the stands at your grandson's little league baseball games. You wouldn't be reading the Sunday paper every week on your deck with a coffee and raspberry scone. And you wouldn't be thinking about putting the high hard one to that silver-haired banshee you've been chatting with at the senior center."

"How do you know—?"

"Don't interrupt me, Edgar. I really don't enjoy being interrupted when I'm in the middle of a fucking monologue!"

Edgar heard the rising anger in Walter's voice and realized he was dealing with a madman. A madman who had asked him to do something unfathomable.

"If not for me, you'd be rotting away in the cemetery, riddled with worms and grubs. But I'm going to forgive this minor hiccup in our conversation. Just so long as, going forward, you fucking do what I tell you to fucking do and don't dare question me again! Is that understood?"

Edgar said nothing, just sat on the edge of his bed, holding the phone to his ear in the gloom of the small hours.

"I said, is that understood?" Walter's voice sounded angry, and the person behind the voice, Edgard decided, was very petulant, which also made Walter a very dangerous man.

"Understood," Edgar replied. His tone was flat now, too.

"Good," Walter said. "And don't think of going back on our deal. I can fuck you up five ways from Sunday, Edgar, and you'd better bet I can follow through on my promises. Do you believe me?"

"Yes."

"Also good. Because if you screw me over, I'll make you wish the cancer had eaten you down to your miserable decrepit bones."

"Are we done?" Edgar asked. He was becoming bold himself.

"For now. And Edgar, I'm not sure I like your tone, but I'll let this one pass, too. I am asking something big of you, after all."

The line went silent after that, and Edgar just sat on the edge of the bed for several minutes and stared at the floor.

* * *

Two days later, Edgar Holt looked in on his daughter and grandson, both of them sleeping with no idea of the atrocity he was about to commit.

He dressed in black jeans and a long-sleeved black hooded shirt. He was sixty-four years old, but his years in construction had left him more muscular than the average person his age. And with Walter Scoggins' magic elixir inside him, he felt twenty years younger. Maybe more.

There was that, if nothing else. But at what cost? He was about to do something terrible as payment for this new lease on life. And once he committed this heinous act, there would be no going back, not like had been done with his cancer. That had disappeared as if it had never been, like smoke in the wind. A miracle, some might say.

And now, after two years, that miracle's price was due. With interest.

Edgar slipped down the stairs, avoiding the creaky step three from the bottom. The back door opened with a whisper and he was out into the night air and headed for the shed in the backyard. There was something there he would need.

A half moon cast shadows down from the trees as Edgar left the yard through the side gate and got into his car in the driveway. The engine purred to life, and he backed out, turned the car east, and motored off. Behind him, his suburban home remained tranquil.

As he neared his destination, things fell into place. Walter Scoggins hadn't come to his little town by happenstance. He'd known the item he was looking for was here, though Edgar wasn't sure why he couldn't get it himself. That was a question he was going to be sure to ask when this was over. One of many questions.

Edgar drove slowly down the street, checking house numbers until he came to the nondescript ranch style home with the number 866 on the mailbox. He pulled a block past the drive, parked under a burned out street light, and sat behind the wheel.

Walter Scoggins had described Jeffrey Tremont as a collector of peculiar artifacts, of which he had a particular one Walter needed. Walter had given a precise description of the item and specific instructions on what to do to get it.

Edgar let out a heavy sigh and exited his car.

What happened next was a blur.

Edgar pulled the hood up over his head, then mounted the steps and rang the doorbell. If the owner had any security cameras, he'd want to keep his face hidden. At first there was only silence, then the thumping of footsteps, and finally the door opened with a jerk and Edgar saw Jeffrey Tremont standing before him in blue and white striped pajamas and nightshirt.

"Who the hell are you, and what do you want? It's midnight, for Christ's sake." Tremont said, visibly agitated.

Edgar said nothing, only stood there for agonizing moments, frozen in fear. Thoughts of his daughter and grandson flashed in his mind, then he thrust his right arm forward and stabbed Tremont in the throat with a gardening trowel. Blood instantly filled the end of the trowel and as Edgar removed it, that blood gushed down the front of Tremont's striped nightshirt in a wave.

Tremont uttered a "Huuuukk" as his knees buckled and he fell forward, face down. A pool of blood spread out from his head. He gasped one last time, and then all was silent.

Edgar felt his stomach knot. He'd just killed a man. He closed his eyes tightly and drove the thought out of his mind. His family was all that mattered, and Walter Scoggins had backed him into a corner with no other recourse.

Fuck, he thought, then stepped over Jeffrey Tremont and further into the house. It took him five minutes to locate what he had come for, then leave the house and its dead owner behind.

* * *

Edgar found himself a seat near the back of the bar where Walter had said they would meet. It was a place that made your skin crawl just by being there. Overhead lights were low, and a country band probably twenty-years out of popularity played from the backlit Wi-Fi jukebox on the wall. Old school meets modern tech.

The waitress came by and he ordered a Jack and Coke. While he waited, Edgar scanned the room. There were ten people other than himself there. Three sat at the bar with drinks, watching the big screen, one at a table eating greasy chicken wings and polishing off a Bud Light, and the other six fixated on playing darts. Probably normal for a Tuesday evening in a hole-in-the-wall saloon.

The waitress came back with Edgar's drink. He slid a ten-dollar bill to her with fingers that only shook a little, and she went to make change.

He felt sweaty, but hot and cold at the same time. Nervous? Certainly. Afraid? Absolutely. But he was also angry. What he'd done— what Walter had forced him to do—left him with a clawing internal fury he'd never felt before.

And he knew things weren't finished yet.

"Edgar Holt," the voice came from his left side, and he turned. Walter Scoggins, dressed in the same jeans and shirt from the day he and Edgar had met, slid into the chair across from him. "I have to say, you look magnificent."

Edgar managed a grunt and sipped on his drink. The heat flowed down to his belly and gained him a bit of calm.

Walter waved a meaty hand toward the waitress, and she approached. "Double shot of Fireball, if you could, madame," he said, and admired the sway of her buttocks as she left. He gave Edgar a wink. "Good birthing hips there, Edgar old chum."

"Let's cut the shit, 'old chum', and get this over with," Edgar said.

"No need to be so brusque, Edgar," Walter said and smiled. "We've got time. And if things go well, you'll have all the time you could ever want."

The waitress returned with Walter's drink, set it down in front of him, and he paid with exact change. Of course he would. Ever efficient was Walter Scoggins.

"I don't think I can follow through on our bargain," Edgar said. There was no waver in his voice. He was dead serious. "I'm going to the police to confess."

Walter took a sip from his glass, his eyes pinched, and he leaned across the table between them.

"Now, listen here, you Paleozoic era cocksucker. If you think I'm just toying with you, playing a game for kicks, you'd better think again."

"Why do you even need me? You could have easily done this yourself."

"Oh, and therein lies the rub, old boy. I can't do it myself. It's against. The. Rules. Can you believe that shit?"

Edgar shifted in his seat. "The rules? So it *is* a game?"

"Not so much a game, Edgar, as an imposed limitation that's persevered across the ages."

"The ages, eh? Just how old are you, anyway?" Edgar was curious now and wanted whatever information he could get. Edgar felt Walter would be quite talkative once he got started, and the more Edgar knew, the more leverage he might gain.

Walter took another sip. "Let's just say I watched Judas Iscariot swing from the redbud tree."

"Hmm, okay."

"Don't believe me?"

"A two-thousand year old flea market vendor is hard to swallow, so let's say I'm skeptical. But you are a tricky bastard, so we'll roll with it for now. Judas it is."

"I have to say, I'm not sure I like this new, cocky, self-assured Ed Holt."

"Tough shit. You made me this way," Edgar said, and sipped his drink. His eyes had met Walter's, and they never left. There was something sinister inside Walter, of that he was sure. "So, who are you? Really?"

"I have been living in Walter Scoggins skin for decades, free roaming this fine world of yours, making deals with people of all ages, colors, shapes, and sizes. And before Walter, there were others. I haven't gone by my true name in centuries."

"Let's take it a step further, then. *What* are you?"

"Oh, now there's the million dollar bonus question! Ha!" Walter's smile widened, and Edgar remembered that clown-like grin from his first meeting. But then, Edgar saw something else behind the leathery, weather-worn skin. Something just off from human. And with that, Edgar Holt felt his newfound bravado waver just the slightest.

"I'm a demon, Edgar. One of the first, one of the original breed. And we're nasty fuckers, let me tell you. With a millennium or two worth of pent up rage and our sanity just on the edge of gone."

Edgar drained his Jack and Coke and set the tumbler down with visibly shaking fingers. He wiped the back of his hand across his mouth, wishing he was anywhere but there. Wishing he'd never made a deal for his life.

The waitress came by and grabbed the glass. "Need another?" She asked, and Edgar felt she was a million miles away. He nodded his head.

"I'll take another Fireball double, as well," Walter said and winked at Edgar. "My treat." He watched the waitress sashay away again, then turned his attention back to Edgar. "I figure a free drink is the least I can do for the bombshell I just dropped on you, right?"

Edgar regained his composure. Or most of it. At least his hands had stopped shaking, but he still felt his heart thumping along at a good clip above normal. "So, what're these rules?"

"Ah, yes," Walter said, and leaned back in his chair. He stroked the wiry bristles of his mustache with his left thumb and forefinger and smiled again. "That's a fun story, Ed. One I'd be glad to tell, if you're up for it."

"Like you said earlier, we've got time."

"Indeed we do."

The waitress returned with their drinks, and Walter paid with exact change again. Once the lady with the good birthing hips retreated outside of earshot, Walter took a drink, then said: "First, show it to me."

Edgar reached down next to his chair for the shoulder bag he'd brought in with him. Then he showed Walter Scoggins what was inside.

* * *

"It's called the Infernus Umbra," Walter said, looking at the dark-covered tome Edgar had laid on the table. "In English, that means 'Hell-fire's Shadow'. Catchy name, am I right? Those Latin fuckers always had a good name for everything."

"What's in it?"

"It's magic, my friend. This is a book of ancient sorcery. Some of the oldest, darkest stuff, culled from the beginning days of evil, spells written by the first known practitioners of magic, in blood, on pages of human flesh."

"That sounds cliched," Edgar said.

"It really does, doesn't it? Nevertheless—"

"And why did you need me to get it for you?" Edgar broke in. He could see Walter's face tighten in irritation, and that felt good. "Couldn't you have gone to Tremont's house and killed him yourself?"

"Oh, if only it were that simple."

"Why isn't it?"

"The Primum Daemon—literally the 'First Demon'—created the book for our kind and penned the initial entries, leaving it for others to use and add to as time went on. The pages of the tome grew, and the knowledge within expanded exponentially. But at a point centuries ago, some prissy do-gooder twiddled his fingers and cast a cloak and locking spell on the book that made it so no demon of any class could read its words or even touch it lest he burn and turn to stone."

"But humans?"

"Humans? Oh, they could touch it all day long. They could rub their dirty bits all over the fleshy pages and not a damned thing would happen to them."

"But you're in a human body," Edgar noted.

"Doesn't matter," Walter said, leaning over the table. "It knows."

Walter reached out with his hand, and inches above the darkened leather cover, his fingers sizzled. Edgar could smell burning flesh and saw the hairs on Walter's knuckles curl. Walter pulled his hand away and blew smoke from his fingertips.

"And that's where you came in," Walter said, and turned to Edgar with a sideways smile.

"And you've got your book, so we're square."

"Ohhhh, not quite. Whoever possesses the Infernus Umbra is bound to it, and only with that person's death can the bond be severed. But it must always be bound to someone, lest its magics be lost forever. I couldn't kill Tremont myself because I can't take possession of the book."

"But that means—"

"Yes. You are now bound to the book."

"You said I owed you one favor—"

"I said I'd call on you for repayment one day, yes. And you fulfilled the first part—somewhat unwillingly, I might add—but you stepped up nicely in the end. Now, we're going to the next level."

"Why didn't you just have Tremont do all this for you?"

"Because Jeffrey Tremont was a boil on the world's ass. He had no family, no friends, not even a girlfriend, besides the ones he rented for an hour at a time. In short, he had nothing to lose, Edgar. He'd have killed himself in less than a week, and I don't even want to get into what would happen to the book if that happened.

"Instead, I found you—or rather, we found each other—and all became right with the world. You and I desperately needed something that the other could provide."

"I won't do anything more for you." Edgar said through gritted teeth, but Walter paid him no heed.

"You're going to be my little magic intern, Edgar. You'll be working out the spells in the book for me."

"I won't do anything of the sort."

"But think of the possibilities…"

"To Hell with you."

"Oh, don't tease me, Edgar." Walter smiled again. "You'll do what I ask, or you'll watch me devour your grandson like a midnight snack." His grin enlarged, his face contorted, and in the darkened backroom of a seedy roadside saloon, thirty-two teeth became ninety-six, long and pointed, like toothpicks. "And, Edgar, I've got an appetite for young boys."

"Don't you dare," Edgar said. He'd recoiled from Walter, from what he thought was likely Walter's true face, but he still held his ground.

"And Lucy. Lucy Lucy Lucy with the juicy juicy pu—"

"Stop." Edgar said, defeated, and after a pause: "Leave them alone and I'll do what you want."

"That's what I like to hear," Walter said, and his face returned to its normal weathered but human appearance.

"Just leave them alone."

"I'm a man of my word. As long as you do what I ask, they'll be just fine. But, if you don't—if you don't, Edgar—I'll be giving it to your daughter in ways you've never even heard of."

"Touch them, demon, and I'll kill you myself."

Walter laughed. "Such bravado. But I'm in the driver's seat here, Ed. Just do what I fucking tell you."

*Maybe, maybe not,* Edgar thought. *I'm going to live for a good long while now, thanks to your little magic potion. So, I've got time. And in time, maybe I'll find something in this book that will rid me of you.*

"What are you smiling about?" Walter said.

"Nothing," Edgar replied. "Nothing at all."

## AUTHOR NOTES - IMMORTALIS

This was another story that started with a note jotted down years ago. I have tons of them, and if I'm stuck for an idea, I'll draw from this wellspring. When I finally started the story, I wrote the meeting between Edgar and the flea market vendor first, as that had been in my mind for a while. That vendor quickly evolved into Walter Scoggins, who first appeared in THE IMAGO SATANAS, and here we finally see that ol' Walt is much more than he seems.

While revising and editing the stories in this volume, I saw recurring characters and places in several of them. A larger narrative started forming in my head, and I decided a few of these tales, with some tweaking, could fit into that bigger story.

*The Gathering of Nine* (tentative title) is already coming together as I finish this collection, weaving together people, places, and things from those short stories, and incorporating characters and plot elements from my very first unpublished novel, a 300+ page work I wrote between the ages of seventeen and twenty-three called *Stryke Out*. So far, it's fun to write, which hopefully translates into something fun to read. The stories with ties to *The Gathering of Nine* are:

Reaction
The Cornfield Blues
I Can't Die Dead Enough
Monsters
Shifted
The Imago Satanas
Voices
Beneath the Surface
Immortalis

Many thanks for reading! More to come!

—Rog, December 27th, 2022

# ACKNOWLEDGEMENTS

The stories in this volume would not have made it to your hands without the advice, encouragement, and knowledge of the following people: Carla, my wife and number one beta reader, for being honest about when it works and when it doesn't. Vera Sperry and Mary Lou Green both helped young me become a better writer through their expert teachings in high school. One of my very first beta readers, Cecelia Black, helped keep me going back when I was unsure I could do it with her absolute enthusiasm. I wish you were still here, because I think you'd really like this. Loretta Hudson, your excitement after reading some of the early drafts a decade or so ago encouraged me to continue. Dustin Pfeiffer, thanks for the lengthy Facebook chats while I asked a cascade of questions about how EMTs operate. Tracy Thorley and Nicole Morisett, thanks for reading first drafts of several of these stories back during the pandemic.

Lastly, to whoever is reading this now, your support is greatly appreciated. Thank you.

*Photo credit: Carla Ott*

Roger Ott has been writing stories since he was in grade school, honing his talents over the decades by crafting suspenseful short stories and novels. An avid comic book fan and historian, he has professionally written over two dozen character profiles and text pieces for Marvel Comics' *Official Handbook of the Marvel Universe* and related publications since 2011. Roger's first published fiction was a short story in the 2021 anthology title *FAMILY* by Terror Tract Publishing. Roger lives in beautiful small-town northern Michigan with his wife, Carla.

Follow Roger on social media:
    https://twitter.com/RogerAOtt
    https://www.facebook.com/RogerAOtt2